Uranium Daughter

There is something askew in a society
in which vast numbers of citizens can be organized to create
a horror like the Bomb without even knowing they are doing it.

JAMES AGEE

There's another kind of freedom,
the freedom where you know who you really
are and where you can live by it.

COLT FREEMAN

Uranium Daughter

The Journals of Chinle Miller

ISBN: 978-0-9655961-6-9

www.yellowcatbooks.com
Library of Congress Control Number: 2008943010

Cover and text design by Alice Sjoberg

Cover photo illustration by Jeannette Altes

This is a work of fiction. Names, characters, places, and incidents either are the product of the author's imagination or are used fictitiously. Any resemblance to actual persons, living or dead, events, or locales is entirely coincidental.

Printed in Canada.

• FOR •

Maya Christine Elizabeth Kurtz

And for Jan,
whose loving encouragement lives on.

Every person is an important link in the chain, the gift of life.

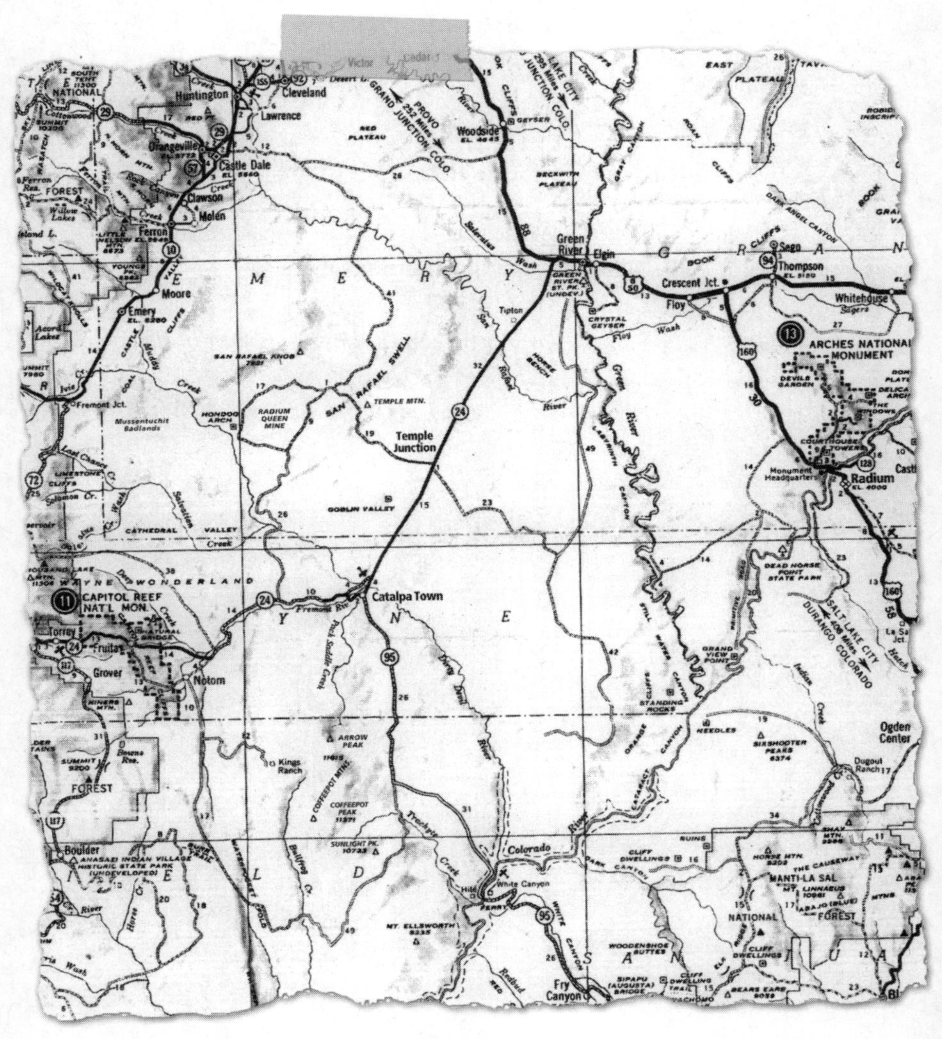

my world in 1961

CONTENTS

I dream of rocks.

Glittering fool's gold from the long ago caved-in Black Queen Mine. Purple amethyst crystals with veins of green fluorite, found only in Unaweep Canyon. Petrified wood from the Parade of Logs above Yellow Cat Flats. And the musty yellowcake uranium – always the atomic yellow uranium, from my hometown of Radium.

Colors and textures permeate the thick night. Rose sandstone cliffs tower above each dream, constant, pure, and unclimbable. Somehow those cliffs call my name without speaking.

Preface

In 1961, during the height of the Cold War, a young archaeologist set foot into the wild canyons of southeast Utah, searching for a rock-art panel that possibly held the answer to the disappearance of the Anasazi. She was accompanied by her dog, Buddy Blue, and a mysterious sometime-companion she called Mr. Yellowjacket.

Here, in her recently discovered journals, Chinle Miller records her search for the elusive Bird Panel, as well as her journey to find peace from betrayal by one of the great rascals of the era, Charlie Dundee, the Uranium King.

In one journal entry, Chinle captures the essence of her journey: "When I was young, my teacher asked me what I wanted to be when I grew up. I knew exactly what I wanted to be, an explorer, but this didn't set well with her, she said I should become a missionary, that would be the best way to see foreign lands. But she misunderstood, my quest wasn't for foreign lands, but rather, to explore the landscape of inner authenticity."

But become an explorer Chinle did. And so, here is her story of love, betrayal, and freedom, all set within the terrible wonders of the dawn of the Atomic Age, recorded in Chinle's own hand as she wanders through the desert on her perhaps impossible quest.

Dr. William Van Zandt
Department of Anthropology
Plateau University
125 College Avenue
Grand Junction, Colorado

Chinle Miller
801 Sandrocks Drive
Radium, Utah

January 22, 1961

Dear Chinle,

It is my pleasure to inform you that your request for a one-year PhD research associate stipend to study native rock art on the Colorado Plateau has been approved. The University Board was unanimous in its enthusiastic support for the project, as we're sure there is much to learn of the petroglyphs and pictographs in the canyons of southeastern Utah and their importance in understanding the ancient people who made them. Fund disbursement will be March first. Please contact Jan Gerber in this office to make the proper arrangements.

At the end of the period of your contract, you will be asked to present a final university program on your findings. We would also like to request that your forthcoming dissertation, if published, acknowledge this funding. The Board would also like to encourage you to obtain oral histories from the people you meet who best represent the essence of Utah's high desert and its heritage. We would like to include these in our Plateau University Oral History Collection. Please coordinate with Professor Rood, who can provide you with a copy of the standards we employ.

Looking forward greatly to working with you,

Dr. Van Zandt
Department Chair

1
Antonio: Cisco Desert

March, 1961

My little jeep, old Willy, drones on as I cross the border from Colorado into Utah. The cold open arms of the endless desert embrace me, chill with uncertainty. A sign says, "No services for 125 miles." I will die young.

Like a mirage, a man stands by the highway, thumb out, an Indian. He accepts the ride with quiet dignity, climbing into the jeep.

He's solid, dark, with those eyes that mark his people, eyes that hint of timelessness. Some kind of Ute, I'm guessing.

"Nice to meet you, what's your name, where you headed?" I ask.

"Antonio. That way." Thumb out, he points in the direction we're already going. A talkative guy, I can tell already.

"West?" I ask.

"West," he confirms.

"Good, 'cause that's where I'm going, too. We're going to get along fine. I'm Chinle."

No response, dark eyes look straight ahead into unmoving sagebrush horizon. Damn. I'd rather be alone with myself than alone with somebody.

I persist. "How far west? I'm going to New York. You wanna ride that far?"

Square head turns, I see an elegant silver concha on his hatband, contrasting with his black felt Stetson. Dark eyes squint ever so slightly, crow's feet at corners.

"New York's east, that way," he counters. His thumb jerks back across his shoulder.

"Well, not necessarily. You can get to any point east if you go west far enough."

Eyes stare straight ahead. "Let me off at Cisco."

Maybe he's a bit worried. Maybe he thinks I'm crazy.

"I don't know Cisco. Is it east or west of here?"

He pauses, considering the logic.

"Both. Mostly west. But east of Green River."

"How far east?"

"I'll tell you when we get there."

More silence. Unchanging blackbrush horizon, watered only by mirage clouds. Antonio takes a cigarette out of the pocket of his blue plaid shirt with mother-of-pearl buttons and places it between lips, searches for matches, then pauses and puts the cigarette back in his pocket.

"Antonio, what part of Utah are you from? You're not from Cisco. Nobody's from Cisco."

Once again, head turns, eyes squint slightly, sizing me up. It's an honest look. Maybe Antonio's like me, he just needs to get his mind off that endless sagebrush horizon. Sun setting, the light becomes cooler, hazier.

"I'm a Ute Mountain Ute. I'm a uranium miner."

Nothing more, nothing less. Silence. Eyes fixed once again on horizon, now streaked with hazy color of sunset. Sagebrush horizon fades, and we ride on in the dark together.

"Antonio, what's it like, being a miner?"

"It's OK. Hard work. I send most of my money to my family on the reservation. Sometimes, on the weekends, I hitchhike over to Colorado to see them."

The anonymity of darkness opens his mind, his soul. I can only see his square profile now against old Willy's window, backlit by desert stars.

"Don't you get lonely way out here?"

"Sometimes."

"What do you do then?"

"I walk."

"You walk? Where?"

"Into the desert. I walk the old animal trails. You got a heater in this thing?"

"Little knob there, fiddle with it."

A small meteorite streaks across the sky. We ride on for a while in silence, then I ask, "Antonio, what's it like to be Ute?"

"You ask too many questions." Silence, then finally he answers, "It's OK. The hardest part of being Ute comes when you Anglos claim you own the Sacred, then destroy it. Seeing the earth destroyed."

Now I'm quiet, taken back. Finally, I reply, "But you're helping do that, too. You're a miner."

"Maybe so. But someday the mines will play out, and all that's left will be the narrow roads. The animals will use them."

"The coyotes." I smile.

"Yes, Mister Yellowjacket, the Navajo Trickster." Antonio's voice trails off, now he's far away. Willy's engine drones on, nothing exists but jeep and highway and stars and desert and me and Antonio.

"The gray and dusty sage wears an oily armor to protect its inward small moistness." Steinbeck.

We all wear such armor.

My desert, you are my secret love. Now we're floating, high on desert wind, and far away far below yellow coyote eyes shimmer, turn to copper, fade into jeep headlights.

A very long silence. We're lost in time, lost on this dark highway in the desert, Antonio and I, lost between our two worlds. We can no longer comprehend our differences, our similarities. How can we both love the same desolation? In the black distance, burnished desert varnish melts across red cliffs bearing ancient writings.

The jeep drones on, we pass a sign, "Watch For Eagles On Highway." The desert's magic is all around us. I brake suddenly, tires squealing, for an owl on the highway. It pauses, blinded, immense wings stretched outward, lifting it into the night.

Antonio, I feel like I've known you forever, my friend, as I've known the desert.

Finally, Antonio speaks, quietly.

"The owl is an omen to the Navajo." He pauses, continues, "My people love the desert, even though it's hard for us to walk freely now."

"Antonio, to most of my people, the desert is just a place of emptiness. There's a blanket behind you."

Antonio unfolds the blanket and wraps it around his shoulders. I can see stars reflecting in its rich indigo stripes. It's a Navajo Chief's blanket, very old, a gift from a man named Charlie Dundee.

"Why are you here?" he asks, looking out the side window into the night.

Maybe he's asking himself the question, I think, but I answer anyway, "I'm studying the old pictures, the rock art."

He's quiet for a long time, then, "I had a dream once, long ago, about the lost city of ancestors, the Ancient City. One of your people called it the Ghost City. When you find it, the writings there are for you."

Suddenly, I stand in a land defined by four seasons, a land stained red by iron blood, a land free from rain shadow, a land created by many magics. The writings are clear, even though desert varnish melts across them. They are very old.

Now a small cluster of lights comes into view, a mile or so away, off to the left of the road. The desert suddenly seems lonely, with this small reminder of humankind. Must be Cisco.

Old decrepit buildings mark the block-long town. Smell of burning juniper. Antonio lives in a small shack on the edge, surrounded by tall greasewood, giving it some sense of shelter from desert's cold open arms.

Antonio opens the jeep door, gets out. He turns slowly, lighting a cigarette, says, "My wife's great-grandmother was Navajo, Nonabah Denetsosie, we called her Nona. She lived to be very old. She made this blanket, she always put the spirit line above her initials, ND. Take good care of it, it will surround you in beauty. Maybe we'll meet again, White-Girl-With-Indian-Name."

Antonio places the blanket on the seat. He turns to go, pauses, turning back.

"Some of your people understand. They love the desert, the desolation. Don't forget the City. It will take courage, but the petroglyphs there are for you. And someday, if you look clear enough to see, you will learn your real name out there."

Antonio turns and is gone.

An evening breeze stirs up a cloud of white alkali dust. To the west, far across a labyrinth of river and canyon, a similar desert breeze spins and weaves through a town teeming with tiny lights, a town set in a shrouded redrock canyon and crawling up onto the ruby mesas above.

Radium, Utah.

Loneliness envelopes me. I drive on, into the desert's cold open arms, towards my past, my future.

March 14, 1961, 7 a.m.

Boulder, Colorado

My Dearest Chinle,

I got home Sat., but yesterday fell sick. It is probably some wretched virus. I hope I am better in a few days.

Actually I hope I am better by 8 a.m. today, but that is unlikely. So far I have just tried to get my life in order. I have a number of sculpture commissions to do. Anyway, I didn't write intending to tell you about me, but rather to congratulate you on the university stipend as per your letter of Feb. 22nd. It sounds rather prestigious, and it's certainly fun to brag to my sedentary friends about my archaeologist cousin wandering about in the desert like T. E. Lawrence (though having a bit less conflict with the natives, I presume). Be sure to keep me apprised of your whereabouts and health and again, congratulations. I'm not surprised, of course.

Your loving cousin,

Sarah

El Marmol, Baja California

Dear Chin,

Fabulous banded onyx quarry here! Old school buildings made of onyx blocks. Wow! Thinkin' of you. Reminds me of Pissant Creek and the old stone buildings there. Will be exploring the west coast for a few days and will write you again from Cabo.

Love,

Charlie

march 9, 61

chinle, dose with osha' to keep the flu away and sleep a lot. that's something i always skip on (cuz i can't on much else). but i do the rip van number myself every few days. it helps. i studied basketweaving with a pomo woman out in california. coil baskets using hemp twine. that's my specialty. oh, i've always wanted to combine poems and illustrations/photos and make postcards out of them. never had the money to bankroll it though. it ought to pay for itself, but that's always a risk, as you know.

good luck in mormon country,

xxxooo art

Hi Chin,

Hope you like this postcard of the Mormon Temple. Here for a week behind the Zion Curtain at a conference called Systematic Stratigraphic Archaeological Excavation in N. America. As you know, we anarchy-ologists are a wild bunch. Met Margaret Mead, she carries a big staff some African chief gave her. She threatened to whack me on the head with it. Your new project sounds fantastic! I must admit to a bit of jealousy.

This quote is from the book about wildcatting you sent me. It reminds me of you: "Yet to each explorer at some time comes a great moment of decision, an exhilarating awareness that he must prove himself worthy of his calling."

Love and keep on living,

Bill

2
Coralee: Temple Junction

Antonio long gone, me and old Willy are flying across Antelope Desert, south of Green River, dodging sand dunes filtered across the road by spring winds. The radio crackles again and fades out for a moment. Voices come from the distance, from deep in the dark.

"Did you ever fly through an arch?"

"Well, sure, but don't tell my wife." Laughter.

"Which one?" Radio crackles, fading in and out.

"Well. Tom, I've only got one and that's enough."

More laughter.

"No, no, Bish, I mean which arch?"

"Crackle...I tried to...crackle...Corona...crackle...also flown through Wilson Arch, down there by the highway south of town, and a few others. Boy, now I'm really gonna be in trouble when I get home!" Laughter.

"Well, Bish, I bet your wife already knows, if she's like most women. They seem to know everything, no secrets around them." Chuckling. "But let's take a brief station break and you can call her and tell her to turn her radio off for a few minutes so we can talk about this arch-flying you've been doing."

"Folks, you're listening to KURA, K-Uranium, the station that talks to the people and listens to the people. From Radium, Utah, at 850 kilocycles AM. Stay with us."

The voices fade in and out. I picture sound waves floating over and down and around the buttes and canyons and hoodoos between here and there—Monitor, Standing Rocks, Dripping Spring, Horseshoe Canyon.

"And now here's a word from our sponsor, Radium Hardware, your home-town source for all your home-town needs for over 20 years. Be sure to try Radium Hardware when you need that gizmo or gadget, they're sure to have it and at a very reasonable price. Yes sir and yes m'am, Radium Hardware, everything you need for your home and also for the Bish here and his home, assuming he still has one after his wife finds out where he flies his little Piper Super Cub when she's not looking." Laughter.

"We're here talking to Bish Redd, the Flying Bishop of Radium. But let me first remind you to tune in right here at 850 AM radio to the Birthday Club each morning at 7:30. Now Bish, back to those arches, what's it like, flying through..."

The radio crackles again—I can see the outlines of the Flattops against the night sky in the east, over towards where Bish and Tom are sitting in front of that microphone way over there in the dingy little broadcasting office of KURA. Way over on the other side of the Green River—its deep muddy waters silently melting away, one grain at a time, the country between the rivers—Labyrinth Canyon, Willow Bend, Potato Bottom—flowing on down to the confluence with the Colorado, where no human voices are heard in the night.

Old Willy sings gladly along on flat straight road, bouncing on washboards. Now a gaudy light glows in the darkness ahead. Temple Junction Café and Motel. The only civilization between here and there, and not much of it.

No Vacancy. Everybody still has their hopes tied up in those dog-hole uranium mines up Muddy Creek and at Temple Mountain. They need to talk to Harold, scintillator repairman over in Grand Junction. Harold says if he could have his choice between all the money spent looking for uranium or all the money made selling uranium, he'd take the money spent looking. He ought to know. He's talked to them all—all those crazy dogholers in the glowing dust with their glowing dreams and madly ticking Geiger counters.

We stop under the flickering gold and red neon lights of the café, gravel crunching beneath Willy's tires, tread worn from thin to hazardous by time and miles. It's a cool spring night, but when I enter the café a blast of warm steamy air hits me, laden with the aroma of coffee and greasy hamburgers. They're getting a head start on the oncoming summer heat in here.

I scoot into a cracked burgundy naugahide booth and study the menu sealed under the scratched plastic tabletop. Carved into the soft plastic is the name DUKE next to a crude American flag. Contemporary rock art on contemporary manmade rock. The waitress walks over.

"Hi Hon, I'm your waitress, Coralee. Ready to order?" Coralee is all of five-foot-six with curly shoulder-length auburn hair and direct green eyes. With her smile and thick rich hair, she could easily be a model for a Lucky Strike commercial.

"Um, I'll have a grilled cheese with fries and water with ice, please."

"Sure, that's a Big Can Do. Take just a jiffy."

As I wait, I can hear the drone of radio voices in a back room with occasional laughter. Probably more of KURA's flying bishop. The only ones in this little reminder of civilization are myself, Coralee the waitress, a hypothetical cook back in the kitchen, and vacuous voices drifting over the desert. But maybe Coralee is also the cook, which would reduce our stronghold by one-third, not counting the voices.

Coralee returns with the water, smiles, and apologizes, "Gee, no ice, I always forget, we don't have ice. Sorry, Hon."

"That's OK," I smile back.

Coralee slips into the booth, opposite me.

"Mind if I sit for a minute? Hasn't been hardly anyone in all day, and I kind of miss the company."

"Sure, go ahead." I don't mind, knowing I'll be alone for days to come, wandering the wild country just out the café's torn screen door.

"What's your name, Hon? What in God's green earth brings you out here in the middle of nowhere?"

"Chinle Miller. I'm an archaeologist. I'm studying rock art."

"Really? You mean the Indian picture writing? That sounds fabulous!" Green eyes, so direct, looking at my future with envy. "You are so lucky! I'm jealous."

Taken back at her enthusiasm, I answer a bit lamely, "I'm just passing through, but you get to live out here. You're the lucky one."

"No, I'm not lucky at all. I've been out here only a few months and now I have to leave. They're closing down the café tomorrow, and I'm heading up to that darn cold Rangely country. My boyfriend, Roy, is up there. He was drilling here on Temple, but got a job driving one of them big Euclids at the Trace Elements Mill up there. I hate that dang cold country. Some of Colorado's OK, but I hate Rangely. And I outta know, I grew up there."

This story was taking a melancholy turn. "Who's this DUKE fellow here on the table?" I change the subject.

Coralee's eyes narrow. "Oh that's that crazy Duke Hughes and the Buckaroos. They played in Catalpa Town one night and practically got run out. Catalpa Town's not as Jack Mormon as those boys thought. They stopped here on their way back and got to cuttin' up." Coralee pulls a pack of Old Golds from her blouse pocket and lights up.

"But they left me a big tip, which was real nice. They're from Rangely. My ex-boyfriend got them the job down in Catalpa, but I don't think they got paid one penny. Duke plays beautiful slide guitar. Has a real pretty ivory one, a Noble. You should hear him play 'The Wig Wam Wiggle.' 'Your Cheatin' Heart' is good, too!"

Coralee pauses to savor her cigarette.

"Say, not to change the subject, but you're an archaeologist, Hon, do you know anything about Indian baskets?"

"Well, some, although rock art's more my specialty. Why, do you have some baskets?"

"Order up!" The voice confirms there are indeed three of us here.

Coralee hurries off and just as quickly returns with an overdone grilled cheese sandwich and greasy French fries. She takes a bottle of ketchup out of her back pocket, sits back down.

"About them baskets, I like to run around lookin' for Indian stuff when I'm off work. I was first clued in by old Cleo down in Catalpa Town. He runs that gas station down there and did some drilling around here. He and Roy worked together. One afternoon we were all up at his drill site under the petroglyphs up Temple Wash and got to talking. Cleo told me about some baskets under an overhang in the wash. I got curious and went and found them."

"Baskets out here are rare. How many were there?"

"Oh, four nice ones and another that had rotted out because it was where the water drips. I'm curious as to who made them. I know they're real old."

"Do you have them? Can you describe them?"

Coralee's now on her second cigarette, her slim fingers holding it at an angle so the rising smoke clouds her eyes, giving her a mysterious look.

"They're about this big, round like this, coiled, looks like they're made of some kind of reed. One was real pretty—had a green banded design around the top that looked like diamonds. It had little snakes on it, between the diamonds, and there were bird feathers in it."

"Bird feathers! What kind?"

"Well, parrots and such, the kind with lots of red and green. Real pretty."

Bird feathers. Probably Macaw. Mesoamerican influence on Fremont.

I reply,"This is Fremont country. Contemporaries of the Anasazi. Bird feathers are very rare, as are baskets. Where are they?"

Car lights shine briefly through the window, pass on. Coralee ignores my question, muses."Wonder who that was. Only a fool would be out here driving that blue highway at night. Potholes everywhere. Didn't even stop. Probably a Mormon missionary going to heathen Catalpa Town."

The glare from the neon lights outside suddenly goes out.

"Look Chinle, we're getting ready to close.You have a place to stay? The motel's full, Hon, but you could camp out back if you wanted."

"Thanks, but I'm going to go camp up in Temple Wash, under the petroglyphs.You know, the tall ghost-like fellow holding the lightning bolt, with the dog—that's where I always stay."

"That's where Cleo's drill rig used to be.They camped there for a while, too. Kind of spooky there alone, isn't it?"

"No, not if you don't think about it."

"Roy said he looked out his tent one night and saw a strange light under the rock pictures. He wouldn't camp there after that, camped by the wash down where the canyon opens up. Maybe you'd like it there better, you can see more stars." She hands me the dinner check.

"Well, maybe. But I'd better go so you can close down. Best of luck up in Rangely. Who knows, maybe you'll be down in this country again soon."

I stand and hand her the money for my dinner. She suddenly looks like she'll cry.

"Never mind that, dinner's on the house. You're our last customer, so we'll just celebrate that way. Besides, I enjoyed talking to you."

Uneasy, I say goodbye and step out into the dark. Suddenly, I see an image from the future—the café is gone, dust. All that's left is a lone Chinese elm, planted when the café was built, now stunted, trying to make a living out in the dry desert, noticed only by the more observant tourists going to nearby Goblin Valley. Now the mirage disappears as light streams from the open door and Coralee follows me out.

"Hey Chinle, I want to tell you something. Those baskets are up the wash only about a half-mile from the rock pictures, other side of the canyon. Look for some really dark desert varnish and a big dead juniper. But Chinle, if you find them, leave them there, Hon. If you don't, you'll have nothing but bad luck." She turns to go in, turns back.

"Honest. Believe me. I took one of them and sold it to a couple who wanted it real bad. I shouldn't have done that, Hon. Those baskets belong out here. Now I have to leave. I know that sounds weird, but it's true."

Coralee's gone now, back into the Temple Junction Café. Soon the inside lights go out for the last time.

I sit in the dark for a minute, then Willy and I head up the road to the petroglyph panel.

We turn off at the big sandy area where Cleo's drill cap marks another lost dream of riches. Parking old Willy on a flat spot, I lay my sleeping bag in the sand beneath the immense rock wall, red-ochre pictographs draped in white moonlight. I will sleep well here, free beneath lightning bolt and dog star, dreaming of red-green Macaw feathers, my treasure laid up in canyon riches.

Moon disappears behind an amorphous gray cloud and winds begin, whipping granular sand into airy waves, waves that bite and sting in passing.

Why are you so late?

Startled, I jump, scratching my arm on a juniper branch. I ask, *Who is it?*

A nearby sagebrush shakes.

You know me. I'm mysterious Coyote Yellowjacket. I'm elusive. You can't see me.

Yes, I know this voice.

I reply, *What nonsense. You must be seen if you wish to see.*

The voice answers, *You can't see me, even though you can see my brother, Antonio.*

I smile. *Yes, I know Antonio. But how can a human be brother to a coyote?*

You have much to learn, Little Rabbit, much.

I pull a pigeon-blood agate scraper from my pocket, one I found yesterday. *Say, I'll trade you this old Ute scraper for a look at your fuzzy yellow nose. Look, the agate has tiny spots of red all through it.*

A tawny nose pokes out of the sagebrush, sniffs.

No thanks, I'm sick of rocks. It's all those damn ravens ever talk about. Rrrockkkk! Rrrockkkk! Rrrockkkk!

A mottled flash of autumn color, then a dust devil twists away. Coyote is gone, carried upon chilly wind.

Next morning, I'm up later than usual as sun comes dawdling over the 500-foot canyon wall to my east. I sip a strong cup of coffee as the sun strikes the far wall of the canyon, turning the white Navajo sandstone buttery yellow. My water jug is filled with crystalline ice, ice that will melt when that same sun finds it.

I hear a vague sound coming down the road, a sound that turns into a voice singing an Indian-like chant, gradually getting louder.

"Hey...hey...Indian pony,

Hey...hey...Indian pony."

It's soon followed by the quixotic sight of a tall thin man on a little scraggly burro, feet nearly dragging the ground. A scruffy little terrier type dog follows, sleek salt-and-pepper coat, ears at perpetual attention. The man tips his beat-up straw hat, revealing thick red hair.

"Good morning. How are you on this fine spring day?" he asks.

"Fine," I answer, then add with surprise, "Hey Joe—Joe Hughes! Well, I'll be darned, Joe, I thought you'd left this country. Last I heard you were back on the ranch at Norwood!"

"Well, I'll be go to! Chinle! Nice to see you!" Joe jumps off the burro. "Yeah, I'm here, I just can't stay away! I'm working a claim up at Temple Mountain, the Yip Yip Mine, we call it. Had to go get this darn burro, Constantinople, Opal for short. She was heading up towards Little Spotted Wolf Canyon, lookin' for her wild buddies. Couldn't have caught her without little Duffy's help. Opal's our packer these days, about the only thing that's not broke. Anyway, how you been, Chin?"

"Fine, fine, but Joe, I'm surprised you're out here dogholin' again. You said you'd do better back on the ranch."

"I know, I know. I just gotta get it out of my system, Chin. Besides, it keeps my mind off other things, like cars and women—I'm havin' bad luck with both. My old Pontiac bit the dust the other day, whole driveshaft went out, and I'm gonna just let 'er sit up there in the wash and rust out. Might even use 'er for target practice—it'd be the only fun I've ever had with that damn pile of junk. But I gotta run, my partner's waiting for me on up the hill. He won't do a lick of work if I'm not there, just sits and plays the harmonica. Come on up later and let's catch up."

"Sounds good. I have something I need to do, but maybe I'll be up there this afternoon, if that's OK."

"OK? Chin, you know that's OK. You're still doing that archaeology stuff, huh? Well, good for you. OK, see ya then." Joe grins and swings his leg over the little burro, clicking to her. The trio continues its slow pace up the road, Joe chanting, "Hey...hey...Indian pony..."

A canyon wren joins in, its falling call echoing off the canyon walls. Secondary echoes come back, on and on, until it sounds like an entire flock fading in the distance. But like true desert rats, canyon wrens don't flock.

I fill my canteen and start walking up the wash, looking for dark desert varnish and a big dead juniper tree, the landmarks for finding the baskets Coralee told me about. After a short distance, I notice a single set of footprints coming down from the edge of the road and going up the wash ahead of me. Small footprints, almost like a child's. I study them for a moment, they're fresh, no sand sifted into them, still compacted with morning damp.

Coralee. Has she come to get the other baskets? Surely not, especially after what she said about bad luck. I wish everyone respected these ancient treasures, but then again, to live under a curse, whether imagined or not, I wouldn't wish that on anyone.

The wash turns and follows the canyon wall, and I duck under junipers and large stands of rabbitbrush and desert holly that jut out of the banks. Gradually, one bank merges with the sandstone wall of the canyon, cool and shady. Tiny frost-curls line small pools of water not yet touched by sun.

As I come around a curve in the wall, I see Coralee sitting next to a big dead juniper, head bent. She hears me, looks up, "Chinle! You're here, Hon!"

"I saw tracks, thought they might be yours," I reply, feeling like maybe I've interrupted something. "I thought you were leaving this morning, Coralee."

"No, not yet. I'm not ready to go yet."

"Did they close the café?"

"Yeah, it's closed now, Hoss left late last night for Salt Lake, and good riddance to him. He was the worst cook I've ever worked with. But Chinle, look." She holds up a perfect Fremont basket. "It looks like it was just made, doesn't it?"

Next to where she sits, time has carved an alcove into the white sandstone wall, frost and water dripping and etching sand particles away, gradually molding a perfect place for baskets. More baskets rest deep in the niche, aligned with stunning streaks of black desert varnish running down the wall above.

Quietly, sadly, Coralee says, "You should see the one I sold. It was the best one here. It was beautiful."

"Who bought it?"

"A couple came into the café and we got to talking about old Indian stuff. I told them I had a basket and they wanted to see it real bad. I came up here and got it. They were speechless. They gave me $100, Chinle. One-hundred dollars for my good luck. It seems like a lot of money, but would you sell your good luck for $100?"

"Well, maybe they'll take good care of it, if they value it that much," I reply lamely.

"Yeah, they said it was going to a museum in California. Doesn't matter, though." Her eyes drop.

"Do you remember what museum or their names?"

"His name was Clark. I can't recall hers. Nice people, very smart and I could tell they had lots of schooling. She wore the most beautiful straw hat I've ever seen, big wide brim, no juke-box taste in that gal. Said she got it in Guatemala. She offered to give it to me when she saw me admiring it, but I just couldn't take it. Jocelyn, that was her name, Jocelyn."

A sense of peace seems to blend with the sunrays reflecting off the shallow pools in the wash. "Coralee, that's Clark and Jocelyn of the Museum of Man in San Diego. I've met them at several conferences. They'll take good care of your basket."

Her brow wrinkles, intent. "I know, but it's not the same as here in this God-touched place."

Now I sit down on the bank, next to her, and begin thoughtfully poking a stick at what looks like a piece of flat wood buried in sand.

"Coralee, do you really believe a basket could bring you bad luck? Don't you think most luck is homemade? Most of my bad luck is just my making bad decisions."

"Well, maybe, but what about things that you can't affect, like someone dying, that kind of thing?"

"Well, now, that's probably not luck either way, that's just life. We all have to deal with life." I pull the piece of wood from the sand and brush it off, part of an old wooden box.

She stands and carefully places the basket back in the niche. "Yeah, you're right, Chinle. Just like I need to deal with life in Rangely."

"Why do you hate Rangely so much?"

"I dunno, maybe hate's too strong of a word. I just don't wanna go back, that's all."

"Going back is up to you, it has nothing to do with luck. Maybe you should stay here." I turn the piece of weathered wood over and see the words "Hercules Powder" below a classic helmed Roman figure. Hercules himself, way out here in this God-forsaken desert on the remnants of a powder box, left by someone trying to blow something up.

Coralee turns, looks at me with those direct green eyes, now filled with hope. "But what about a job? Where would I live?"

"Well, you wouldn't need much. I carry most everything I need in my little Willys jeep. You could travel light like that."

Coralee pauses, watching a shiny black raven float above distant rim and disappear. "Don't you miss having a real home?"

"Sure, sometimes. I have a beautiful Navajo rug collection my cousin is storing for me and I'll get back from her one of these days. I even have a few Indian baskets, though they're not old like these," I smile.

"Baskets? Well I'll be go to, you have baskets." Coralee smiles, taking a cigarette from her jacket pocket. "You lucky skunk! By the way, I kept one of the bird feathers out of that basket I sold. That's why I came out here, to put it back. You know, Chinle, these things need to stay out here, they're our only link to the early people. Maybe they loved these canyons like we do."

"You know, Coralee," I reply, "You're right, removing such things removes the history of Indian presence on the land."

I take the basket back out of the alcove and examine the long green feather in it. "It's stunning. Perfectly preserved. It's very old—800 years, maybe more." I carefully replace it. We sit together on wash bank, silent.

I finally stand and look briefly at the sun, now starting its afternoon arc. "Hey, let's go up to Temple Mountain—you might as well ride up there with me if you're not going back to Rangely. You can meet a friend of mine."

"OK, I'll go. And don't mention Rangely again, OK, Hon?" Coralee smiles.

"Sure. But what about your boyfriend in Rangely, Roy?"

No hesitation. "He can come back down here, and if he won't, it's his loss. He knows I don't wanna go back. Roy and I really haven't been together all that long anyway. He was a rebound, if you know what I mean. I was engaged to another fellow, but he got jealous when he saw me talking to Roy one day and it just irritated the hell outta me. You know what men are like, Hon."

"Well, yeah, I guess so. Let's go." I pick up my canteen and we head back downstream to where old Willy waits, sleeping lazily in the sun.

Coralee and Willy and I rattle up the road until it leaves the canyon and widens out. The chalky white ramps of Temple Mountain thrust suddenly skyward, rotten and unclimbable, resembling the pointed spires of a Mormon temple. With each fierce desert rain, the chalks fall and tumble to the washes far below, then on down Temple Wash, on down to the twisting Dirty Devil, and eventually down to the grander adventures of the Colorado River.

In contrast, a tall red plug, a volcanic blowout vent with subtle shades of carnotite yellow where the minerals were bleached by hot gas, stands below Temple's otherworldly spire, its base littered with buff rubble from the taller tower. Both melt slowly, slowly into geologic time.

Pinion jays call in the distance, far up the gentle juniper-lined slopes that underlie the chalks of the mountain, the red layer-cake Moenkopi Formation. We're completely out of the canyon now, and Temple Wash continues on, narrower and deeper as it cuts down from the uplands of the San Rafael Swell.

A small sidetrack forks off the main road and crosses the wash, winding to the flanks of the mountain, stopping immediately under a half-dozen small holes that glare like gaping black eyes with gray tailings crying, spilling out. Uranium mines. Dogholes.

Turning down the sidetrack, we cross the wash. An old rusting truck with bullet-shattered windows melts into the sand, pushed against the edge of the wash by thundering flashfloods, battered by roiling rocks, steering wheel gone. Not far from it sits Joe's Pontiac, trunk standing open. The wide wash is littered with yellow chunks of carnotite, radioactive riches bounced from the haul truck during the rough crossing.

Old Willy groans a bit as we pull up the far bank of the wash, then carries on bravely up the hill. We stop near a small old stone house with a root cellar buried so well we nearly drive over it. Willy stalls and dies before I can turn off the ignition, overheated and probably vapor locked again. Maybe another hole in the radiator. I get out and open the hood. Lucky this time, just hot.

The little burro, Opal, spies us, watches for a moment with fuzzy ears forward, then resumes grazing on scattered ricegrass clumps. High above us on the cliffside, Joe and another man are hunched over equipment at the mouth of one of the dogholes. Must be the Yip Yip Mine. Duffy barks and they turn and wave, then return their attention to the machine. Joe takes off his hat, whacks the machine with it, then scrambles down the steep hill towards us.

Coralee has been watching Opal, but now notices Joe, his thick red hair backlit by sun. Her eyes narrow. "Who's that?" she asks, then answers herself, "No way, it's Joe. I didn't know he was up here. I don't wanna talk to him."

"You know him? Why not?" I ask.

Coralee's now back in the jeep. She says, "That's my ex-boyfriend, the guy I was engaged to. Take me back to my car."

"Hey, Chinle!" Joe waves.

"You stay here and I'll go meet him, Coralee. I just want to say hi. I met him over here last fall when I got stuck up the road a ways, he helped me out. I won't take long."

"Bring him on over here so I can shoot him." Flashing eyes look dangerous.

Joe walks, half slides, down the steep grade, his little wiry dog Duffy at his heels. Now the second man is following, walking down the steep road from the mine. I walk partway to meet them. Coralee sits in the jeep, head turned away, pursed lips holding an unlit cigarette.

"Glad you made it, Chin." Joe's out of breath, hand on my shoulder, adds quietly, "I didn't know you know Cora. What's she doing out here?"

"I just met her yesterday at the café. She's looking for a job—the Temple Junction Café shut down last night," I answer.

"I'll be damned. She's been working there? I go by there almost every day. I didn't even know she was there. Thought she'd took off with Roy."

The second man saunters up, small-boned and wiry, dark hair slicked into a pompadour. He's wearing a once-white t-shirt tucked into jeans, cuffs rolled up a good six inches above his black work boots.

Joe offers, "Say, Chin, meet my partner, Sparky Marinelli, from Radium. Sparky, this is Chinle, my archaeologist friend I mentioned."

We size each other up in a friendly way, then Sparky unrolls a cigarette from the short sleeve of his t-shirt, lights up, asks quietly, "Has Coralee come back to see you, Joe?"

Joe snorts. "Not likely." He looks embarrassed. "Say, Chin, let's have some coffee, then maybe you could give me and Sparky a ride back to Temple Junction—we need to hitch a ride on up to Green River and get a part. Dang drill pump froze and busted. Got chilly down in there last night."

Sparky says wryly, "We can't even abandon all hope and start over with a new claim—dang Geiger counter quit workin' too." He grins, "We might have to go back to civilization for a while. I wouldn't mind going to see my gal in Radium, assuming she's still there."

The three of us walk to the jeep, Joe holding back a bit, collecting small pieces of firewood. I haul out a pan and a can of coffee and my hodgepodge collection of cups. Coralee sits in the front, ignoring us, but turns when Sparky leans his arm on the window. They talk, quietly, while Joe and I get a small fire going and make coffee.

Finally, Coralee gets out of the jeep and walks with Sparky to the old stone house. He goes in and comes out with a square leather box with a long handle, opens the box and removes a Geiger counter—a good one, a Lucky Strike.

Coralee takes it from him, comes over to the fire and sits on a rock, still ignoring Joe. Opening her purse, she takes out a nail file and uses it to remove the screws holding the cover in place.

She studies the device's insides for a while. "Looks like a bad resistor, Sparky," she says. "Burned out. I'm sure you don't have a spare out here. You'll have to take it over to Grand Junction."

Sparky looks disappointed, asks, "Hey, how about that old radio in Joe's Pontiac? Don't radios have resistors? Couldn't we take one out and use it?" Now Sparky's excited, like a kid hoping to get his favorite toy back. In a flash, he and Coralee disappear into the wash where the Pontiac sleeps.

Joe and I sit by the fire, savoring the strong steamy coffee. "What's up with you and Coralee, if I might ask?"

"Short story, sad ending," he grunts, staring into the fire. "A guy named Roy. I accused her of seein' him so she started seein' him. She's the independent type, could be your sister." He kicks at the coals in the fire, continues, "I met her over in Radium. She was a friend of Sparky's girl, Maureen, the two of 'em repaired Geiger counters over in Grand Junction before they moved to Radium. Sparky and I were workin' south of town for Yellow Bird Mines before we decided to go out on our own. Cora and me got engaged. That's about when Roy and my idiocy came into the picture."

Pinion jays chatter in the distance, Sparky and Coralee are coming back.

Nonchalantly, Opal, all but forgotten, wanders across the wash to the deep potholes called Mormon Tanks, drinking from the clear waters, nosing fresh wild-burro tracks as if thinking perhaps to join them.

Coralee and Sparky walk back up from the wash. "Look, Sparky, it may be the right color coding, but I can't put it where the old one went without a soldering iron. I'm sure you boys don't have one out here." Coralee shoots Joe a sarcastic look. "You boys typically don't have anything out here, not even brains. Besides, if I fix this thing, what's in it for me?"

Sparky smiles painfully, "Aw c'mon, don't be mad. You know Joe's dumb, you knew it when you met him and confirmed it when you were goin' out with him, but don't take it out on me. Let's look at it. I need this darn thing bad. I'll buy you dinner at Temple Junction if you can fix it."

Coralee runs her hands through her auburn hair, taking out a bobby pin. "The café's closed, and I wouldn't eat at that greasy spoon even if it weren't. How about a steak dinner at Smitty's in Radium?"

"Sure, you bet, if we can figure out a ride. Maybe I can see Maureen! Can you fix it?" Sparky asks anxiously.

"Radium," she replies. "We'll go to the air show tomorrow."

"Sure, sure, Radium would be great! Fix it!"

"Get the pliers!" Coralee commands.

Sparky quickly retrieves pliers from the stone cabin and hands them to Coralee, who carefully picks up the bobby pin with the pliers and pushes it into the campfire coals. She then holds the hot bobby pin against the wires on the radio's resistor, heating the solder until it melts, connecting the wires to the lugs on the Geiger counter. Sparky watches every move with intense interest.

Cover now back on, Coralee hands the device to Sparky, who walks down to the wash to test it on the spilled ore, case hanging over shoulder, probe in hand. A whoop soon echoes back up. Coralee smiles, and for a brief moment, her eyes meet Joe's.

I leave them and offhandedly wander down the wash to find Sparky, thinking about external simplicity and internal riches.

Now it's evening, and old Willy and I climb that slow steep grade up the San Rafael Swell, the Moroni Slopes fading in the misty distance. We make good progress, though Willy's doing all the work. Now up out of the canyons, we should be able to pick up a station, and I turn the radio on.

Crackle...crackle..."Hal, let's continue with our discussion of why everyone is so up in arms right now. Hal Lundstrom of Recla Mining here, and he's talking about the role of government."

"Well, Tom, we had Federal Mine Inspection come in to ostensibly do radiation help for Industrial Commission. We gave them the red carpet, and they turned around and issued a ten-page report on Recla. Ten pages of violations, if you can imagine that. Things every mine on the Plateau does. If we tried to do all the stuff they wanted, we'd go broke! Government has no place in private industry."

"What do you think the remedy for this is, Hal?"

"Well, one thing is to start paying attention at the local level. My friend Wilmer Watt, he's the super at Union Carbide over in Dove Creek, he and I spent all day last Friday traveling 468 miles with the

Grand Country Commissioners and road superintendent. We're working hard on them to keep spending in line. Taxes aren't the nation's basic problem, the problem is spending and fiscal irresponsibility! And it is each citizen's duty to take more interest in this matter and in such things as legislation on the Wilderness Bill and labor laws!!" Sound of pounding.

"Now, Hal, don't yell into the mike, it'll make people turn their radios down, and we sure don't want that. But let's stop here and take a minute to mention Morgan Electric. Bet you didn't know there was an outfit here that could rewind your motor for you, did you, Hal?"

"Well, Tom, right now I need it slowed down, not rewound! But actually, I know George Morgan real well. We do lots of business with him. He sells Fasco motors, the best there is. Also accessories, controllers, fan blades, and centrifugal blowers. They have good prices and good service. A fine example of private industry. You can tell George ain't no government man, he's too efficient." Laughter.

"Right, Hal, and I bet he doesn't put up with inspectors messing around in his place!" Laughter. "For good service, call George at AL 3-3551, Morgan Electric, 433 North Main, here in Radium. And while I'm at it, Hal, are you going to the air show tomorrow?"

"You bet, Tom. I heard there were going to be some wingwalkers, and maybe even a UFO or two!" Laughter.

Radio off and night nearly here, I'm now on the upper part of the San Rafael Swell, with a 360-degree view of fading sky silhouetting occasional pinion tree. I spot a clearing over there, a good place to camp, and turn off, headlights shining through sagebrush. Old Willy is happy enough to stop, and I wouldn't mind a cup of hot tea by a cozy fire.

As I unpack my gear from the back, something small falls to the ground. A single star reflects from it, a woman's compact, ornate copper with scrollwork, Made in France. It opens like an oyster shell, mirror on one side and cake makeup on the other. Inside is a delicate powderpuff and a small folded piece of paper.

I take the paper out and read the elegant handwriting by Willy's headlights, the same handwriting that made out my dinner check at the Temple Junction Café.

There's a sweet wild freedom here that washes through everything,
Through the falling call of the canyon wren,
Through the joyous crack of lightning on the canyon rim.

Coralee. Must've fallen from her purse onto the floor of the jeep. I look up at the Milky Way and feel like I could fall into its infinite shimmer.

The metal compact feels cold and smooth in my hand, and now I feel happy, knowing she and Joe and Sparky and Duffy are flying in her '55 Thunderbird across that empty desert this very moment, on their way to Radium, to the Promised Land, civilization, hot coffee and dinner at Smitty's Steakhouse, then tomorrow, Stearman airplanes and acrobatics and World War II dogfighters—all those cold gaping doghole mines forgotten.

I lean back against Willy's warm hood, contemplating the sky. Far to the east, what might be the light from Radium reflects off a cloud, although it's probably Grand Junction, a hundred miles further. Gilded cloud hangs there forever, suspended by cool air—tomorrow's warm air currents will take it to adventure.

I turn in a slow circle, looking up. The sky is stunning, rich with sterling points of light set in deep-blue velvet. I think of my Navajo friends to the south who wear such velvet, who walk in beauty, abundant beauty, beautifully over them moon is rising.

And tonight, like them, I stand surrounded by beauty, my treasures laid up carefully: weather-carved ripple rock, black-and-white-jacketed magpies, wind-spinning dust devils, forlorn coyote's yip, Willy's rattling gas cans.

I turn the compact over. Engraved on the back:

Cora, two hearts, one path.
Love, Joe. Christmas, 1960

Where your treasure is, there your heart will be also.

Pinion fire now warms the soles of my boots, and hot tea warms that lonely sense of distance. I think back to a time when my treasure, my heart, was over in distant Radium, my hometown.

Stars disappear into firelight, night becomes pensive, moody, and memories of Charlie Dundee return in the silence. Always Charlie—his smile, his blue eyes, his betrayal, they follow me everywhere I go.

I recall a night like this, stars hanging so close you could almost touch them, Charlie drinking whiskey while I drank hot chocolate, feet to a fire just like this, though no two fires can ever be the same.

"Chin, why are you called Chinle? It's a Navajo name, and you sure as hell ain't no Injun with that blonde hair," Charlie asked.

"Gramps called me that and it turned into my nickname. It means 'flowing from the canyons' in Navajo, though Gramps probably didn't know that."

"What's your real name?"

"Meg."

"Meg. Hmmm, that's 'gem' spelled backwards. So, Gem, Meg, Chin, what do you want to do with your life? What do you want to be when you get outta this hole called Radium?"

"Smart. Happy."

"Don't you have any goals, any plans? What do you want?"

"A barn full of deer antlers."

"Deer antlers? What the hell would you do with deer antlers?"

"I'd look at them and feel rich in deer antlers. They'd remind me of bone china, like my aunt sent my mother from Scotland on her birthday. I'd have a barn full of antlers, like some women have a hutch full of china. All naturally shed. Old gnarly antlers that look like deadfall from juniper trees. Fresh new antlers, smooth with a pinkish cast like alpenglow on distant peaks. Little one-point antlers, the first lost by young bucks. Big serious antlers, ten points, covered with smooth velvet. That would make me both rich and happy."

Charlie shook his head slowly in disbelief.

"You never cease to amaze me."

"I won't let you down," I replied wryly.

Charlie's gone, like long-fallen antlers lost on some blackbrush hill near Radium, a hill where his big house now stands. Maybe this rock art project is my attempt to find purpose, meaning, healing. I slip into my longjohns, lay out my sleeping bag under the stars, light my little

propane lantern, and retrieve my latest batch of letters from the Hercules Powder box I keep in old Willy.

Dear Chinle,

Your life seems a lot more interesting than mine at the moment. I would love to go camping with you. It must be superb. But when? I am totally bogged down in house maintenance. And now I've decided to put the South Boulder bungalow on the market. Taxes are still not finished. Oh dear, this is not what I had in mind when I retired. I don't see a light at the end of the tunnel. I don't even see the tunnel.

It was strange hearing from Linda. Don't you think that Irma would have lived a lot longer if she had had a drink now and then and gone shopping on Sunday? My good friend Terry (ha! you know the story) and I have talked about a trip. I will have to phone to get messages every day to see if I have a contract on the bungalow. Maybe I can sell it right away! Calloo, Callay!

Your loving cousin, Sarah

Hello,

Keep the letters coming, I was thinking about you this weekend. Had to go to a memorial service and it was well done, and it made me think about how much I am missing by not going to church. Millie and I try to love thy neighbor as thyself, be honest, good, etc., and we say thanksgiving at meals (how ungrateful to Grandfather Creator, if we did not), but I can't get into the exclusive we are the only way anymore. Spirits, yes, I believe in them most assuredly and much more...but I don't know if they would ever appear as a coyote, but why not?

Love and keep on living, Bill

Chin,

I'm back from Mexico and you're not here. Where the hell are you? Why the hell didn't you tell me about this research thing? I know it's best to be a moving target, but this is pushin' it a bit. You probably think all this money has gone to my head, but you know I was an egotistical SOB before I ever got a dime, and now I've changed, I'm real humble. I sure miss you, and I'd like to see you soon.

Love, Charlie

3
Johnny: San Rafael Swell

Letters tucked away, I lie in my sleeping bag, looking up into a black bowl of stars. Camped high on the San Rafael Swell, there's nothing between me and the night's mysteries. Soon sleep finds me, gently walking me into the Dreamtime.

I dream of rocks. Moss agate from Wyoming with delicate black rivulets in white marble. Glittering fool's gold from the long ago caved-in Black Queen Mine. Mysterious orange Tiger's Eye from mystic India. Purple amethyst crystals with veins of green fluorite, found only in Unaweep Canyon. Cool blue granite from Laughing Creek. Heavy smooth galena from Lead King Basin. Petrified wood from the Parade of Logs above Yellow Cat Flats.

And the musty yellowcake uranium, always the atomic yellow uranium, from my hometown of Radium.

Colors and textures permeate the thick night. Rose sandstone cliffs tower above each dream, constant, pure, and unclimbable.

Somehow those cliffs call my name without speaking.

I awaken, and the stars look different now, the Big Dipper turned half around and Orion long gone below the horizon. I guess it to be about three in the morning—the Hour of the Wolf, that time when you're most likely to die, when your breathing slows and your heart beats slower. I toss and turn, the ground seeming harder than usual.

Though now half-awake, the dreams remain, like shimmering rainbow trout just beneath the surface of a mountain stream. I close my eyes again, and milky images drift from my past, from my last year of high school, when I first began to have these dreams, dreams of rocks, of ruby-red cliffs.

Even then, back in high school, the images would linger throughout the day, and the red and buff cliff-colors would stray in and out of declined Latin phrases, into algebraic equations, through sentence diagrams, then gradually fade until night brought them back again.

And each day after school, I'd walk downtown to the rock shop. There, surrounded by shelves of lifeless minerals of all shapes and colors, I studied life, each lesson adding another layer of veneer, of desert varnish.

Charlie Dundee owned the small dusty rock shop that set at the end of the street, a few blocks down from the county courthouse, and just across the street from Sinkhole Lanes, Radium's bowling alley, which sat next to a shallow sinkhole.

I wasn't supposed to go into the Sinkhole because they served beer. I'd been in, though, with my friend Karen. It was full of grizzled old men, smoking, drinking, nobody bowling. They were all dying, dying from radioactive lung poisoning, from lung cancer. They were all that was left of the radium rush back in the early part of the century, these dying miners who mined radium. They also mined their health, their lungs. Now they were filled with elemental poisons, with radium, with elemental regret.

Radium. My college chemistry book defined radium as a metallic chemical element found in the mineral uranium. "Radium—an isotope that undergoes spontaneous atomic disintegration, changing into many more isotopes, uranium daughters, before it reaches its final state, its final resting ground, as polonium lead."

Madame Curie discovered polonium and named it after her native Poland. It was Madame Curie who wrote the words, "We must believe that we are gifted for something, and that this thing, at whatever cost, must be attained."

What my high-school book didn't tell us was that after her many discoveries, Madame Curie died a painful death from radioactive poisoning. At whatever cost.

Radium. A fitting name for a town once supported by doghole mines, surrounded by rocks and big dome-like cliffs, uninspiring, no reason anyone would want to be up there. Cliffs called the Sandrocks, rumored to hold deep caves. They echoed the spirit of Radium, hot, closed, uninviting, myopic.

Radium is where I was born. Radium is where I'd always lived until I finally found my way off to college, with Charlie's help. And Radium is where I met Charlie. In retrospect, entering his rock shop proved to be much more my undoing than anything they served at the bowling alley.

Sometimes I wish I could go back and undo all that undoing.

I haven't been to Radium since that night up at Charlie's big house above town, nearly a year ago, on break from graduate school. I haven't seen Charlie since. He writes me, but the only thing I've ever sent back was an empty envelope. I have nothing to say.

But Charlie's shop, the Rock Garden, was different from anything else in Radium. It held a world of color, glimpses of distant eons—heat, pressure, weathering, cataclysmic explosions, floods—events igneous, metamorphic, and sedimentary. Each rock, polished or not, had its own beauty, its own history, its own magnificent story.

My last year in high school, I worked after school in the shop for Charlie, doing his books, cleaning, dusting each shelf carefully, unobtrusively, eavesdropping on him and his customers, watching the sun glint on his golden curly hair through the windows of the dusty little shop.

"Did you notice this little gem?"

Charlie would take a small half-cylindrical sandstone rock from the shelf.

"It may be small, but it'll tell you quite a story! Put it on your dresser, listen to it carefully late at night when everyone's asleep. What this little Moki marble can tell you! It'll tell you about the canyon country, where it sat for a million years, lonely, high on a bluff, while the wind blew everything else away! Pretty plain looking, huh?"

Charlie's customer, maybe all of seven years old, would nod his head in agreement, eyes big, all caught up, as Charlie continued.

"Turn it over, slowly, and you'll see its real soul! Look at those beautiful concentric rings! Pure sandstone. Pure Navajo sandstone.

You're looking at what took nature forever to sculpt. That's a lot of work for only a quarter!"

Charlie's charisma held aspiring pebble pups spellbound, and he always made the sale. Ten cents, a nickel, sometimes even several dollars for a nice geode. Each customer went home and proudly displayed treasure on dresser or shelf, complete with the little card Charlie had mimeographed down at the newspaper office:

Moki Marble,
Variegated sandstone,
From a secret place in Utah,
Where nobody's ever been.
Long time in the making,
Bring your friends in for a free Wyoming moss agate.
Desert Peace from the Rock Garden, Radium, Utah.

Charlie's play on words usually didn't make sense to anyone but Charlie, but he didn't care. Charlie had a degree from some college in Colorado, a degree in geology. Sandy beard, unkempt hair, piercing blue eyes, independent, focused, a loner, Charlie lived in an old silver-metal Airstream trailer near his shop at the edge of town, surrounded by rocks. I was intrigued by his self-confidence.

Intertwining like the fibers in raw asbestos, like the icy tails of two comets passing in deep space—rocks and Charlie.

Charlie knew rocks, but since I was a child I've had my own gift. I can read the old writings, the old Indian petroglyphs and pictographs. To others, these images in stone are just scratches and strange figures. But I know their mysterious meanings.

My grandfather was the first to discover my gift while I was very young. Together, we hunted arrowheads on sagebrush hills in the desolation near Radium, wandering for hours, eyes intently fixed to ground, focusing for rocks shaped by the ancient people, rose flint and yellow chert knapped into sharp edges for killing—points, archaeologists call them. We called them arrowheads. We hunted these points made for hunting.

Long ago, on late hot summer afternoons while rattlesnakes slept under rocks, staying cool, we hunted arrowheads in thick sagebrush.

I wandered toward sandstone bluffs, intrigued, rock art mysteries waiting in cool shadow. I somehow knew the old writings were there, hidden by an old juniper against the sandstone. I stood, entranced, timeless.

Hours, days, centuries later Gramps found me, he too saw the old writings. He knew I could read them.

"What do they say, Chin? Can you really read them?"

"Yup, Gramps, they're easy to read. They were written by Walks In Sleep Without Stumbling. He was very old."

"What do they say?"

They say, "Come into the canyons and be healed."

Gramps smiled, pulling a well-melted Three Musketeers bar from his pocket. We used a flint scraper he found under a sagebrush, scraping chocolate and marshmallow from wrinkled wrapper, smiling chocolaty smiles of wisdom at each other.

Now my dreams of rocks, of Charlie, dreams of my past all slip away, as dawn finally comes to the San Rafael Swell. Instead, I dream of willow catkins floating through soft juniper night. Orange shafts of light push across the horizon.

I awake, drift back to sleep, toss and turn. Finally, Antonio floats in and out of my dreams, his dark eyes lit by the reflection of a ghost city somewhere in the depths of endless desert.

Faint scratch of cougar-claw on slickrock wakes me, and I gaze into fading memory of desert stars. I can't remember where I am, then I know, way out here in the God-forsaken desert, where daybreak sneaks up on you, catches you asleep, up on the Swell, a good hundred miles or more to the west of Radium, 30 miles or so southwest of Green River, and another distance northwest from the town named for the hundreds of graceful catalpa trees planted along its streets by early pioneers, Catalpa Town.

A few clouds float to the south, peach and gold from sun's first rays, hanging in the direction of the town of Los Alamos, several hundred miles to the southeast.

I wonder if Antonio's ever been to Los Alamos, that once-secret place where scientists found a way to separate U-238 and U-235, uranium's two isotopes, so similar, only three neutrons apart.

U-235, uranium, fodder for the Atomic Bomb, fodder for restless dreams. The uranium used for the Bomb came from a doghole mine not very far across the plateau from where I'm camped, over in Colorado, near the town of Uravan, a town named for uranium and vanadium.

"Now we're all sons of bitches," one of the physicists said when they stood at Trinity, the first atomic test site, huge cloud billowing into the New Mexico night sky, souls naked in blazing light. A military man stationed near Ground Zero, where the Bomb exploded, exclaimed, "The long-hairs have let it get away from them!"

I close my eyes. Dark cousin of Cougar Sun, this new light, born of U-235, a light that now illuminates a new madness.

When Charlie and I were still together, I asked him what he thought of the Bomb. His reply was terse. "Those damn little slant-eyed Japs were irritating us, made us mad. We were tired of doing the South Pacific hula with 'em, tired of mickeymousin' around. We had a damn good reason for building that Bomb." He paused, looked at his scuffed boots, "Even if we end up blowing the whole damn planet to kingdom-come."

The images fade with rising sun, and I stumble from my sleeping bag and start a small fire from rabbitbrush, its golden seeds flashing crimson smoke.

Coffee soon boils in the pan. Wrapped in my jacket, I think about when I was a kid, sitting around the kitchen table, drinking coffee diluted with cream and sugar while my mom and aunts talked. Their coffee was thick, black, steaming.

One particular morning is seared into my memory. As we all listened carefully, the radio announcer described two smoldering Japanese cities, cities with the strange names of Hiroshima and Nagasaki, now devastated by a terrible new weapon, the Atomic Bomb.

Years later, I read that the copilot of the Enola Gay, the plane that dropped the first Bomb, wrote in his log book, "My God, what have we done?"

My aunts and my mom all sat around the kitchen table, silent, faces ashen, and all the talk later that day was filled with hope and despair—hope that the war would soon end, despair at the terror unleashed.

My mom put her head in her hands as if to cry, but when she looked up, the anger in her eyes flashed like fire, the color of her ginger-red hair.

"Hundreds of thousands of innocent people, vaporized, just like that," she said, snapping her finger and thumb. "We're worse than Hitler. It's pure insanity. It's Armageddon."

To this my aunt Marg thoughtfully replied, "President Truman says it will save millions of our boys by ending the war, so how can you argue that? We won't have to invade Japan. You know what barbarians they are, kamikazes and all that. It saves their honor and their lives, too, they wouldn't stop till they were all dead. You shouldn't say such things, Jeanie, people will think you're unpatriotic, maybe even a Communist."

My mom shook her head in disgust, "Women and children, just like us, with no warning. I don't care, it's a disgrace, it's immoral. Why didn't we just drop a bomb somewhere uninhabited to show them what we could do to them if they didn't surrender? History will judge us harshly."

My aunt Donna, eyes downcast, slowly sipping her coffee, added, "They didn't even give the Emperor time to give up before they dropped the second bomb, according to the shortwave radio. They say we did it to scare the Russians, the Japanese were already defeated anyway."

Aunt Marg's eyes lit up, "Well, at least Sammy and Leonard will be coming home soon, thank God. And no more rationing. Chin, honey, you can have lots of those Three Musketeers candy bars you can't stay away from."

My mom tried to smile, face drawn, fingers running thoughtfully through my yellow curls. "Maybe she'll get those cowgirl boots she's been wanting."

Japan soon surrendered, unconditionally. I got a pair of bright red cowgirl boots several months later and wore them everywhere, even to Sunday School, where the pastor praised God for giving the Atomic Bomb to us instead of to an uncivilized nation. My cousin Howie got a pair of toy cowboy revolvers, complete with inlaid holsters, and he proceeded to shoot up everything when he wasn't making tiny villages out of sticks and rocks and bombing them with buckets of water.

Now I look up at the clear blue morning sky above the Swell. Time for me and Willy to move on. Time to explore this land of ancient dinosaur bone and dinosaur dreams, my own Trinity of Rock and Sand and Sky.

Where have you been?

Startled, I jump, dropping my canteen into the deep sand.

You again. Why are you hounding me?

The branches of the pinion tree shake above me.

I'm a coyote. Coyotes don't hound. Only common dogs hound. Look up! Try, but you won't see me. I blend superbly into the yellow sun.

I can see a branch outlined against the bright sky, a rather bushy-looking branch, maybe part of a bushy tail.

Look, Yellowjacket, I'll make you a deal, if you'll stop bothering me. It does take one back a bit, you know, having trees shake when there's no wind.

What kind of deal, Little Feather? I like deals, I'm a deal-making fool, and I like to gamble a bit, too, you know.

I'll tell you who you are, where you came from, then you can leave me alone.

I know who I am, thank you. I'm Mysterious Coyote Yellowjacket. A rather elegant and descriptive name, not meant to be personable or even remotely sociable.

But you don't know who gave you that name, do you?

Of course I do, I did!

No, you're a figment of my imagination. You know, kind of like an imaginary friend. I gave you that name.

What nonsense! Coyote is an old Aztec word, coyotl. The Aztecs revered my ancestors, you know, as well they should have. The real issue here is, do you know your name?

Of course, it's Chinle.

How did a white girl get a Navajo name?

My grandfather called me that because I liked to rock hound in the Chinle Formation. Lots of petrified wood, interesting stuff like that.

Well, I know you by a different name, as do these pinion trees and these jumping leaping twisting cougars. I know who I am, Little Feather, but you obviously don't have a clue who you are.

Before I can ask, Coyote is gone. A small cloud of alkali dust obscures the sun and settles onto the trail.

Pure madness, I muse, searching for coyote tracks in the sand—nothing, as I suspect.

A similar madness, uranium prospecting, seems to have taken hold of everyone—the seasoned miners who should know better and the greenhorns from back east who will find out they should know better. This madness claimed Charlie and the whole town of Radium, especially after Charlie discovered riches.

Out here in the desolation, wandering, dreaming of rocks, studying rock art, I'm wonderfully away from it all. Alone.

A twig snaps in the nearby brush.

I pack my gear into old Willy. It's getting late. Soon Cougar Sun will be high in the sky, blazing mad at my indolence.

Leaning against the jeep, I pull a folded yellowed piece of paper from my notebook and look at it for the millionth time. A rough sketch of a giant snake winds across a rock face, split tongue pointing around the corner, trailing around the edge. Another part of the sketch shows a strange bird looking askance at three ghost-like figures with bug eyes and triangular-shaped bodies, wearing robes with intricate designs.

Under the sketch reads a caption: "One small portion of the Bird Panel, found by the author in the Ghost City in the desert of southeastern Utah. This extensive panel may offer the key to the disappearance of the Anasazi and the lives of prehistoric Native Americans."

Along the top of the page runs a header: "Archaeology of the Southwest United States, Albert Davidson."

The lost Bird Panel. Nobody's ever seen it except Davidson, and what did he mean by a key to the disappearance of the Anasazi? Quite a statement from an archaeologist as prominent as Davidson.

Intriguing questions. Throughout his career, Davidson never said more than those two sentences about the Bird Panel or the Ghost City.

When asked by his colleagues, he simply deferred, said nothing. It didn't make sense to anyone.

Many question its existence. I've vowed to find it. It will be my way to honor Gramps' memory.

Willy and I take off, scooting along a sandy two-track towards dark cliffs that cradle the far edge of sagebrush flats. Soon, the climbing sun turns the low-slung cliffs into ivory—cliffs bounded by rubble, rocks climbing atop each other, scrambling for the best views.

Once, long ago as a child, exploring with Gramps, I stood on those cliffs. Gazing east—all the way past the little town of Green River, past the Cisco Desert, past the city of Grand Junction—I could see clear to the immense peaks of the San Juan Mountains, drifting like tiny white ships in a sea of sky. Peaks now from my past, way off in Colorado.

Ahead of me, several doghole mines form dark cavities in the creamy-white sandstone. The holes look old and abandoned, probably radium mines from the turn of the century, back when the madness first began. Radium was thought to be a miracle element and was widely used for medicines, in bath salts and drinks. It eventually turned on everyone, killing those seeking respite.

Those cliffs ahead are well-guarded by a rock art figure with horns and pointed tail, red on buff. My friend Bill ran across that devil a few years ago and drew a dot on the map that, if I orient it right, due north that way, looks to be straight over there, in the cliffs by the mines. Perhaps those same cliffs guard the lost Bird Panel, my holy grail.

Willy spins out a little as we hit a deep pocket of sand. The road tilts and turns, following the contours of blow sand from long-ago decayed cliffs. Soon I notice a fine dust rising ahead, a dust that soon shapes up to be a dark-brown pickup caked in grit, recklessly bouncing down the narrow two-track towards me. I quickly pull off the road.

The pickup slows, then stops next to me, and the driver nods and smiles, elbow propped on open window. He's wearing a ragged red plaid shirt with the cuffs torn off. Curly reddish-blonde hair, distant green eyes with signs of crowsfeet on suntanned skin, he looks surprised to see me. A rack across the back window holds a rifle.

"Howdy, M'am. You might not wanna go over that way for a bit. They're fixin' to do some blastin'. Might bring down some rockfall."

"Thanks," I answer.

"See that alcove to the far left way over there? That's where the mine is, kind of hard to see from here. The road dead-ends there. You lookin' for somebody, if you don't mind my askin'?" His pickup rattles and rocks, wheezing. Needs new plugs or timing, I suspect.

I reply, "No, I'm an archaeologist. I was heading for those cliffs farther over to look for some rock art." I point to the rock walls that curve north away from the alcove.

Distant eyes warm as he extends his hand through the window. "I'll be go to heck. My brother's an archaeologist, Barry Taylor, up in Alaska. Nice to meet you, my name's Johnny Taylor."

His hand is rough and course, his grasp warm and strong. He adds, "Rock writings, huh? Petroglyphs and all that?"

"Yeah, better get going, though. Thanks for the warning."

I feel uneasy. For some reason, this man reminds me of Charlie, of wandering through big canyons together, discovering dripping springs cradling red monkeyflowers.

Johnny nods, says, "Say, I didn't catch your name."

"Chinle Miller," I answer.

"Nice to meet you, Chinle," Johnny looks at me intently, smiles. The pickup rocks, and he adds, "Say, there's a big red devil over there, I'd be glad to show you exactly where. I just came over to check on the fellas and ain't really in much of a hurry to get back."

Suddenly, a blast rocks the cliffs. Overhead, a dozen or more powder-blue pinion jays turn in unison in the air, fleeing in the opposite direction. The sound echoes first from west, then north, then south, like a seismograph defining the cliff boundaries that hold these alkaline sagebrush flats.

"That should be the last powder they set off today," Johnny says, "'Cause now they've done run out. Some of my buddies, we reopened that old mine, the Radium Queen. Pretty interesting operation. But hey, this dang truck won't idle, so I have to keep one foot on the gas and one foot on the brake."

He smiles, waiting. I want to tell him no thanks, I've been wandering this damn desolate desert just fine on my own, me and Willy, but instead I answer, quietly, "Sure, let's go."

A grin breaks across a handsome face framed by reddish stubbly beard."Head for the dogholes, we can park there and walk along the cliff face. I'll introduce you to my buddies."Johnny guns the truck from its rocking stop, pushes through the road bank and turns around, leaving me in a cloud of fine sandy dust.

Old Willy bumps back onto the road, and we're soon headed towards cougar cliffs, buff-yellow Coconino sandstone, burnished by mid-morning sun, creamy and smooth like petrified butter.

I hesitate, almost turn around, some sort of intuition trying to get my attention. There's something about the vertical bluffs and twisting canyons out here, something that makes you want to be alone, go wild, feral, forget civilization and people.

But there's also something out here waiting, just on the tip of your consciousness, like a yellow-cat cougar skulking in the rocks, making you want a little company sometimes. Hardscrabble claim jumpers maybe. Or could be it's the shadow that sits unsettled on everything out here in uranium country—the shadow of Trinity.

There, standing in the horror of that first atomic test at Trinity, Oppenheimer, one of the Bomb's creators, quoted the Bhagavad-Gita,"I am become death, the destroyer of worlds."It was July 16, 1945.

The shadow of death haunts most those who fear it.

I follow Johnny to the farthest of the doghole miles at the end of the road. He parks near a big shady juniper close to a tailings pile of reddish-gray silt. Here, the junipers look frosted, they're so thick with pale-purple berries.

As I pull up beside him, Johnny leans casually against his pickup, tall and lanky, drinking from a waterbag slung over radio antenna. He wipes the cool water from his chin with what's left of his sleeve.

Johnny Taylor. I suspect he's part of the Taylor family over by Catalpa Town, old-time cattle ranchers who own half the country around there. Their ancestors were pushcart Mormons, those tenacious lunatics who let nothing get in the way of finding Zion. They found it, too, or perhaps created it.

"Come on over and meet my buddies."

Johnny yells towards the shadowy portal of the mine,"Hey, fellas!"

Unlike where Joe works at Temple Mountain, this mine's at ground level. It's surrounded by rubble, cables, and machinery in various states of rust, remnants of the good old days when radium was king, or in this case, queen.

A broad-shouldered muscular man wearing low-slung jeans, a hardhat, and no shirt emerges from the shadows, his chest black with oil and dirt.

"Hey, boys, we got company!" he shouts to whoever is still inside.

"Chinle, this is Pete Black," Johnny introduces us. "Blackie, this is Chinle Miller, an archaeologist. Hey, Leland, come on out. Where's Harris?"

The second man walks up. "Leland Marsing," he introduces himself, touching his hardhat, a short stocky fellow clothed in bib overalls caked with grime. "Harris probably won't come out, he's pretty pissed off, 'scuse my language, miss. He's recoverin' from a bad day."

Blackie turns to me, "Did Johnny tell you about what we're doin' here? Tell her what we're doin', John."

Johnny explains, "They're going straight down, got a 30 foot shaft in there right now, using a ladder they add to as they go along. That cable over there's run by that old GMC truck engine and hoists the ore bucket out. What happened to Harris?"

"He had a religious experience down in there just now," Blackie replies. "He's thinkin' about becomin' a preacher boy."

Johnny says, "Harris is our blaster. He's Blackie's brother-in-law, God bless 'em—Blackie, not Harris."

"You know much about mining?" Leland asks me. I shake my head no. He continues, "See, when you make up a stick, you crimp a blasting cap into the end of a piece of fuse, then you stick it in a hole in the dynamite, that's called the primer. This mornin' we made up a dud primer with no cap and Harris took it down, lit the fuse, and when he turned to run up the ladder, he found there weren't none."

Leland pauses, laughing. "Took 'em a while to realize he wasn't gonna blow to kingdom come. Course, we knew he had a dud, but he didn't. Sure was one mad hombre."

"He's still over there sulkin', but he'll be a little easier to get along with after this, we're tied of him bein' such a pissant," Blackie muses.

"He wouldn't go back down, so I had to do the blast. We're headin' home for a few days now to take an Easter break and resupply. But say, Johnny, tell us about your friend here."

"Chinle's an archaeologist out here lookin' for rock pictures to study, like that devil over on the cliff," Johnny answers.

"No kiddin'," says Leland. "I didn't know there was nuthin' to study about that stuff. What do you do with it once you've found it?" he grins.

"I just look at it, mostly," I answer, "then I try to sketch it and figure out who made it. I take photos of it, too." It was all starting to seem a bit academic out here, maybe even bordering on the absurd to these pragmatic guys.

"Well, I'll be go to," Leland adds. "You can figure out who made them pictures? How do ya do that? Wasn't it all made by Injuns?"

"Look fellas," Johnny interrupts, "I promised her I'd show her the devil, so we need to get going."

"Seems 'bout right, havin' Johnny show you the devil," Blackie adds amicably, winking at me and touching the brim of his hardhat. "Nice to meet you. Johnny, we're headin' back to town. There's a storm comin' this way, according to Leland's bad knee. Don't push your luck. See you in Catalpa Town."

The fellows gather their stuff, throwing it into a big army-green WWII surplus truck. Harris finally comes out of the mine, just in time to join them, ignoring me and Johnny. I watch their dust recede as they bounce down the two-track.

Johnny leans against old Willy, emptying sand from his worn cowboy boots as I gather my camera and pack. We're soon joined by three ravens, two conservative types dressed in black who watch from above on the cliffs, and another braver soul, similarly dressed, who ventures into the upper branches of the tree.

I take a letter from my jacket pocket. "My friend Bill's an archaeologist over in Colorado, and he told me about the devil over here. Drew me a map." Johnny nods, watching the ravens.

I unfold the letter, which has a map sketched on the back. It's on government stationary, written in casual yet precise script:

U.S. Geological Survey
Federal Building
Delta, Colorado

Dear Chin,

Good to hear from you. Congrats again on the research grant. On the back is a map of a rock art site I stumbled across while camping over there with Millie a few years ago. It has a devil, sort of a weird character, worth taking a look at. Probably Fremont. Did I tell you Millie's expecting this October?

I'm jealous of you getting to wander around the desert. Go lay on a rock naked on my behalf (if it's sunny enough). I never have liked clothes, but I try to keep them on most of the time so as not to shock anyone. But in the desert, that's another thing. Like to just lay on a rock like a lizard. Sounds great just now with this snow melting around here and the temp. fairly nice.

As for your question, I hear voices in the desert all the time, so another noise (B-52 or whatever) wouldn't surprise me, but I've never heard what you call the desert hum before, although I know a mountaineer who claims to have heard it at high altitudes. He says it's the sound of the world turning, like a gigantic spherical ball of machinery rotating slowly on its axis. He told me he's also heard it over in the canyon country. His name's Carl Wilcox if you ever run into him.

Do you ever see Charlie? He's sure been in the news a lot. The government is really using him to keep everyone fired up. Not to be nosy, but a lot of your friends would like to hear that story. Take care and keep in touch and be happy wherever you're at.

Love and keep on living,
Bill

I think of Bill and Millie, way over in the broad Uncompahgre River Valley, fixing up their cozy little clapboard house on a wide street with big trees, non-desert trees that need lots of water, maples and birch and linden, Bill with his stable government job and Millie running her little laundromat, Millie's Dime-O-Matic with its sign, "Head Down To Millie's With All Your Frillies."

A sweet smell wafts through the air—a smell of spring, of cliffrose in bloom, sweet creamy blossoms on big gangly brush. Thinking of Bill and Millie takes me back to civilization, which I sometimes forget about out here where you can just become part of the landscape, wandering, sun's warmth on your back.

But once in a while I catch a glimpse of my own shadow, and I remember I'm a human, that animal all the other animals out here fear. Except black raven, who sees me and always calls—rrrockkkk, rrrockkkk, rrrockkkk, welcome back, welcome home, what's for lunch, snackwagon?"

Twin black raven,
Floating above White Rim,
Calling: "Rock...Rock...Rock..."
Now apart,
One glides downward into desert shadow,
The other glissades upward.
Little desert lizard,
Poignantly waiting on slickrock,
For Kachina spirit to return.
Do you dream of distant stars?

I toss several crackers out for the birds. Wisps of white clouds dance slowly across a turquoise-blue sky. Welcome home, Chinle.

Warmth radiates from the cliffs, and canaigre, wild rhubarb, splashes ruby-pink blooms against yellow cliffbase. Now, Johnny and I follow the face of the cliff as it pushes its way through holly and an occasional curly-leaf scrub oak.

Suddenly we're in a gentle south-facing alcove with black patina, desert varnish, on yellow stone. All the makings of a rock art site.

Johnny looks up, and I follow his eyes, scanning the cliffs, high above where any human could've reached, then I see it, Bill's devil. Did the artist hang from a rope like the Utes claimed their ancestors did?

"It's big," I comment.

Johnny nods. "How the H-E-double-hockeysticks did they get up there?"

"I dunno, but look at that bighorn with the big antlers, that's Anasazi. The Navajo say the ancient ones had wings, so maybe they just hovered in mid-air while making the paintings. Kind of crazy, most people don't realize that they made wooden ladders, some of them went up hundreds of feet. Most of the wood's gone now, decayed, but I've found a few Anasazi ladders."

Johnny whistles,"Whoeee, long ways to go on a ladder. Say, what's the difference between the Fremont and Anasazi?"

"Well, mostly we think the Fremont had a more northern range than the Anasazi, although they seem to be contemporaneous. But sometimes we see panels like this with both styles, and sometimes they include Barrier, which is much older. But everybody just seems to have disappeared. Maybe a drought pushed out the Anasazi, who may be the ancestors of the Hopi. Some Utes say the Fremont were their ancestors. Lots of questions, some I hope to answer."

"Sounds interesting," Johnny nods, looking back upwards at the petroglyph.

The figure is about four feet tall, red ochre brushed directly on buff-yellow cliff. Horns curve out of a square head, and a long tail ends in a wedge. Could be straight out of Dante's Inferno.

I think of the time, the work, it must've taken the ancient ones to collect the red ochre and grind it with mano and metate, mix it with animal fat as a binder, shred and plait the yucca to make a brush, then reach that cliff from above or below, however they did it. The careful movement of arm, of wrist, guided by the creative focus, all pulled that powerful figure from the artist's mind's-eye.

"Crrrk, crrrk," ravens gently remind us they're still around, hoping for another snack. They sound a bit like ducks, not very dignified—but most beggars aren't very dignified. All three birds are on the cliff above us, heads bent down, watching, preening glistening black feathers, standing on one leg, then another, hopping around.

"We'll have dinner later," I tell them. Johnny looks amused, poking around in the sand with a stick where something brownish-red sticks out. He finally unearths it with the tip of his boot.

"Hey," he says, "Here's an old artifact for you." He holds a tin can, thin enough to fit in a shirt pocket, lid riveted on. I shake off the sand and read the words "Prince Albert." Rust rubs onto my fingers.

"Tobacco can. Maybe it's from the radium boom, back at the turn of the century," Johnny speculates. "That was the heyday of our mine, the Radium Queen. But hey, let's go visit a couple of old timers up in the cliffs a bit, I'd like to check up on 'em. And there's something I'd like to show you up there."

We're soon on a cow path, which immediately detours from the cliff face, a thick stand of desert holly blocking the way. As we brush against a small juniper, stiff straight needles fall to the ground, sickly yellow, brittle. The tree's lower branches are completely dead, the same rusted-red as the Prince Albert can.

Johnny comments, "This one's not likely to recover. A shame, after all the years it survived, but it probably won't live through this summer's heat. The pinion are dying too, drought and beetles both. It's been six years now since we had much rain."

Dead needles dust my boot-tops. Will Cougar Sun ever let the rains return? I sip from my canteen, offer it to Johnny.

A leggy jackrabbit bolts in front of me, veers off towards the stand of holly and lays low, heart beating like hail on corrugated roof. It's a beautiful spring day, perfect for hunting—but we hunt rock art, not flighty rabbits.

I'm beginning to feel like I'm in a landscape painting. Prickly-pear cactus blooms splash the overgrazed flats to my left with white, yellow, and crimson, giving the scene a creamy haze. The desert surrounds itself in beauty, even in time of drought.

"Hey, Chinle, over here."

Huge pinion trees, green and thick trunked, hug a small twisting arroyo that drains the area above. Little arroyo, water bearer, creating a break through the cliff face.

Above Johnny stands a large cairn, rocks stacked upon one another, forming that universal desert signal to come this way, drawing you hither, like the sirens of Odysseus.

Sun goes behind cloud. A small rabbitbrush trembles, and a dappled leopard lizard pushes through to sun itself next to a bunch of flowering white peppergrass.

This would be a nice place to camp, a protected spot. Johnny leans against a large rock, one side thick with pale-green lichen growing in curious circles.

"Getting hot early," he comments, accepting the offer of water from my canteen. I sit on the edge of the rock.

Silent for a while, finally he says softly, "Back there when I met you, I guessed right away who you were. You sure as hell fit the description."

I'm taken back. "What description?"

"Charlie's."

A dark cloud swiftly drifts over sun, causing breeze to stir.

"You know Charlie?" I ask hesitantly.

"Hell, yes, the sunuvagun and I went to college together. Geology. Colorado School of Mines. The company his dad worked for paid Charlie's tuition as part of a settlement after his dad was killed, but Dundee didn't have a penny to his name otherwise, and my family helped feed and house him. Charlie spent his college years sleeping on my couch and eating at my table. After we both graduated, he went to work for the oil company his dad had worked for, I think it was Mobile, then came back to Utah and looked me up. We caught uranium fever and grubstaked together over by Dove Creek for a season, ran out of money. I went home, and he moved to Radium and opened that little rock shop. I spent plenty of time with Charlie Dundee and his B.S. for a number of years."

"Guess it's a small world," I say, an old familiar feeling clutching at me.

"Don't worry, he didn't say anything bad," Johnny smiles, "and I can see why. Probably the only time in his life he didn't bullshit, 'scuse my French."

We sit in silence until he finally continues. "Look, I'll be honest. He told me all about you guys. Said you'd been together once, but you left him to go to college. Broke his heart, he said."

Johnny watches a quick flash of anger cross my eyes, then grins and adds, "Now, you and I both know nothing and nobody could break that poor rich weasel's heart, 'cause he ain't got one. After he struck it rich that was a confirmed fact on many scores."

After a moment, I reply, "Charlie told me lots of lies, but he did pay most of my way through college, even though it was from guilt. Do you ever talk to him?"

"Yeah, I go up to his house on the hill once in a while. I used to fly for him, but I got tired of his craziness, wanting me to fly him under bridges, through arches, that kind of stuff. He finally got his own license, which was probably a big mistake. He's actually helping me grubstake the Radium Queen, but he's a tight sunuvagun, counts every penny, the only change he likes is the kind you put in your pocket. But hell, me and Charlie, we go way back, and he has a lot of respect for my family, and he's a damn good geologist. There's a reason he struck it rich."

Johnny pauses, continues. "Charlie talks about you every once in a while, wonders where you are and how you're doin', worries about you. He told me to keep an eye out for you, but I didn't figure we'd ever cross paths." After a moment Johnny adds, "I'm sure glad we did."

I suddenly long to be alone, to wander, forget Charlie, forget Johnny, forget everything but rock art and finding the Bird Panel for Gramps. I watch the greening stalks of rabbitbrush, chamisa, sway in the breeze. It'll be a while, late summer, before the rabbitbrush flowers turn bright yellow. I wish it were then and I were here, immersed in rabbitbrush blooms, alone.

Johnny watches me, changes the subject. "Check out the plants—Prince's plume, vetch, locoweed—indicators. You wouldn't want to drink the water out here, providing you could ever find any. Selenium, poison, slow death. Probably contains arsenic for a kicker. Not like the gyp water over at Goblin Valley, which just makes your stomach ache till you get used to it."

I nod, not really listening to what he's saying, thinking of the postcard in my pocket.

Chin,
Feeling lonely and depressed. Please send me a nude photo of yourself.
It's damn hot here.
Yer pal (maybe?)
Charlie

It was just a few years ago, before Charlie struck it rich, that we drove his old Scout over to Grand Junction, to the Atomic Energy Commission's headquarters, those low-slung lime-green buildings down by the Gunnison River, driving all the way from Radium to get the jump on that month's AEC hotspot report, to check out the anomaly maps.

Always hoping to get an insider's tip, legal or not, prospectors made the long trip to Grand Junction once a month to get the first look at the maps, posted at noon on the 15th—hoping also for any lucky tips from the AEC boys. The building itself was classified, and you couldn't enter without a badge, so the maps were posted on a makeshift bulletin board by the front entrance.

When we arrived, Charlie and I were immediately hailed by an AEC boy answering questions in the center of a melee.

"Hey, Charlie, how's it going?" he yelled, coming our way. He was a tall skinny fellow with dark hair that stood straight up and made me wonder if they conducted secret electrical experiments inside.

"Nice to see you, Eddie," Charlie replied, shaking hands. "How do you like being on the other side of the search?"

"Must say it's been interesting. Never saw so much government B.S.—you'd hate it. I never dreamed I'd fly for the government again. But Charlie, what're you doin' over here—ain't you struck it rich yet?" Eddie grinned for a minute, motioned us aside.

In a low voice, he said, "Listen, there was a little guy who came in here last week with some cores, and he'd done pretty darn good for himself. A strike over in Slick Rock. He didn't know squat from shinola, like most of the fellows in this so-called business, from Ohio or someplace like that. He told me his secret, and I'm gonna pass it on to you."

Charlie looked skeptical, but interested. Eddie, wearing a cockeyed grin, leaned over a bit toward him and said, "Locoweed." He paused to note the effect on Charlie's face. "Yep, you heard me right, look for locoweed. If you find a place where it grows thick, check it out. Probably more valuable than these damn anomaly reports. It's true—it's called an indicator plant, and it grows right where there's carnotite. Flourishes in the stuff."

Eddie looked pleased, standing there all gangly in his khaki-brown cotton government shirt and pants. He was soon back in the middle of the melee of bedraggled souls, uranium hunters looking to convert the earth's hide to riches.

Since Charlie never owned a Geiger counter or scintillator, I've often wondered if he took Eddie to heart and looked for locoweed to find that big strike, but I doubt it. Charlie studied the geology, a rare trait among prospectors—most who think an anticline is someone's relative, Auntie Kline, not a convex upthrust in the earth.

Now Johnny stands, holds out his hand, pulls me up from the rock, nods towards the cairn above us. "Let's go visit them good old boys."

We start climbing, picking our way up through the rubble of broken rock. We're quickly up on the flat mesa. Locoweed, astragalus, is growing everywhere we can see, its purplish pea flowers in bloom, sweet looking on a palette of soft silver-gray leaves, one taste a torturous death to cattle.

I should stake a claim here. Eddie said locoweed cohabits with carnotite, toxic consorts. But I'm here to hunt rock art, not fool's gold, and all I'd probably find would be selenium or claimjumpers or trouble.

Now looking over the cliff edge for old Willy, I see only the green of junipers below, the little jeep blending in.

Now, we're next to the cairn—it's about five feet tall and took some doing, some rock hauling. Looks like it's been here a while, as there's a huge packrat nest in under the rocks.

Johnny says, "The only place anyone would build a cairn this high would be in the middle of a claim, but there aren't any corner markers around, and there's no location notice."

"What's a location notice?" I ask.

"It describes the property and claims it under your name, you stick it in a Prince Albert can and nail it to a stake in the middle of the center cairn, then you file it with the county registrar next time you're in town. You give it a name, like Charlie's Tengo Dinero."

"Tengo Dinero—that's Charlie for you," I remark.

"You bet, just like him. What the hell does it mean, anyway?"

"Spanish for I'm in the money."

"Just like that bastard, lucky SOB," Johnny replies. "He has you, then he gets rich, too. Look, here's a location marker if you wanna see what one looks like." He pulls a crumpled piece of paper from his wallet.

NOTICE OF LOCATION
Notice is hereby given:
That the undersigned, having complied with the requirements of SECTION 2324 of the REVISED STATUES of the United States, and the Local Laws, Customs and Regulations of this District, have located Fifteen hundred feet in length by 600 feet in width, on this the Uranium and Vanadium Lode, Vein, or Deposit, bearing Gold, Silver, Copper, Lead and other valuable minerals, situated approximately 3 miles down North Wash from the mouth of Hog Canyon, in the Coffeepot Mountain Mining District, Garfield County, State of Utah, the location being described and marked on the ground as follows, to-wit: beginning 10 feet east of this location (Discovery) monument, at the east and center monument, and running thence west 300 feet to S.W. corner monument No. 1; thence north 1500 feet to N.W. corner monument No. 2; thence east to North end center monument; etc.; The above described Mining Claim shall be known as the Dog Leg #3, located this 5th day of March, 1961. Names of Locators: Thomas J. Simmons, George Samuelson, Jr.

I look it over. "You found this?"

"This claim was filed on top of mine, a damn good way to make an honest man blow a cork. You just don't do that out here, not unless you wanna get shot. Kind of like stealing someone's water. I've had three claims jumped now."

"What happened?"

"I was with old Cleo. You ask him sometime, if you ever meet him, he can tell you. Has a service station down in Catalpa Town. I'll just say I never wanna get involved in that kind of deal again."

Johnny pauses, continues, "Cleo had a hired guy with him he'd just sprung from jail, and the guy went berserk and just about killed one of those claim jumpers. Cleo thought it was really something, he can be a character himself, but it taught me not to prospect without a gun on my hip." Johnny stops, adds, "Say, did I ever tell you about the first time I ever hauled ore?"

"We just met a few hours ago," I remind him.

He grins, "I was in high school and had a friend named Rusty, and Rusty was a short sunuvagun, had short legs, and he always kicked back to put his feet on the dash of whatever vehicle he happened to be ridin' in, it was more comfortable for him. Rusty and me got our first haulin' job together, was up at the Susan B Mine. I was drivin' the truck, since I had more experience, growing up on a ranch. Neither of us could've been a day over 16, and I'm not even sure we were legal.

We came through Catalpa Town our first day, our very first load, drivin' real slow, and Rusty was ridin' along with his feet on the dash. Neither of us knew it, but he put his foot on the handle that engaged the dump, and unbeknownst to us, we left a big pile of ore right in front of City Hall. We were a ways out of town, merrily goin' our way, when the county marshal caught up with us."

"What happened?"

"He said if we didn't come back and clean it up he'd send us to reform school. Took a good half-day with a loader, which was Rusty's uncle's, and his uncle wouldn't let us touch his machine, so we had to pay him to do it. That was my first try at hauling. Cost us more than we made, took us both a week of workin' to pay him off. About then the mine owner found out about the whole shenanigan and fired us. That ended our career."

I laugh, and Johnny grins, says, "This is a cowboy cairn, marking a way through the cliffs where you can push cattle down from this upper tier of the Swell. This is Taylor cattle range, I grew up herding cattle here. My uncle Lige built this cairn."

We carefully pick our way through scrub plants, prickly-pear and Mormon tea that seems to shelter occasional small holes. I ask, "What're these holes—Giant Desert Centipedes? I saw one out here a foot long once."

Johnny shrugs, "Probably, but I ain't gonna take a look to find out. Nocturnal. The worst biters out here like to strike in the dark, when you least expect it. Like people."

"Hey, over there against the cliffs," I point. Blending into the yellow Coconino sandstone leans a tumbled rock shelter, roof made of rough-cut pinion trees, bark still on, dried and wrinkled. We make out way over to it.

Johnny smiles, "Them good old boys." He steps to the door. "Anybody home?" No answer. We stick our heads partway in, it takes a minute to get used to the dark. Something small scurries, probably a kangaroo rat.

Against the far wall of cool sandstone is a small wooden cot with a green army-surplus sleeping bag. Against the other wall is another cot, this one with a pile of moth-eaten gray wool blankets. At the end of the first cot are several large wooden boxes, and I make out a familiar figure on the sides. Hercules.

"Hercules Powder," Johnny whistles low. "Them good old boys are gonna make sure nobody steals it, sleepin' with it like that. Lunatics. Probably tryin' to keep it dry. Hauled it in by burro."

A stack of canned goods with peeling labels looks like it'll collapse any minute, and next to it is a large black oil can with a harmonica resting on the lid. A wooden crate holds some sort of radio equipment, with the letters W7OXO pasted on the front in big white stickers. Two large batteries are attached with wires to the radio, and a microphone is propped in a chipped coffee cup. A small generator sits nearby.

"Whattya suppose all that is?" I ask.

"Ham gear, amateur radio equipment. One of them good old boys calls himself Cactus Rat and he's a ham, his call letters are W7OXO. The other one calls himself Yeller Cat. Don't know their real names."

The rest of the rock structure is too dark to make out much, but dangling from the ceiling are two books wrapped in wire.

"Looks like they were trying to keep the packrats away from their books," I comment. "The rats would have to walk upside-down across the ceiling, then dangle their way down that narrow wire."

"Which they've done," Johnny replies, "judging by the chewed edges. Hmmm...look at this. 'Minerals for Atomic Energy' and 'Description of Indicator Plants and Methods of Botanical Prospecting for Uranium Deposits on the Colorado Plateau.' Pretty serious fellas." He grins, "Them good old boys are real characters, must be out prospecting. Look over here, Chinle."

A rusted-out drill bit sits in a corner, serving as a flower vase of sorts, holding a dried bouquet of orange globemallow and ricegrass, simple, elegant, as beautiful as any florist could arrange. Next to the bouquet is a piece of paper with something scrawled on it:

Yeller Cat, Yeller Cat,
Where have ya bin?
Out in the dezert,
With my pad and my pin.

We go back outside, where a breeze picks up and heavy-looking black clouds float nearby, portent of oncoming storm. Tall delicate stalks of pale blue desert phlox sway near rock-hugging red Indian paintbrush.

Johnny says, "C'mon, let's go on up into the rocks over there, I wanna show you something." We climb up a rise on top of the mesa, a rock outcropping of yellow sandstone, weaving our way through large boulders until we're on a tabletop of rock surrounded by stacked rock walls, the size of a small room. I catch my breath.

"Some kind of little fort," Johnny says. "Check this out." He points to an indentation in the stacked wall filled with a dozen or more points, arrowheads made of flints and cherts of blues and greens and reds and grays, even one made from pigeon-blood agate.

"Nice work, isn't it? I found all these in this Indian fort. Been comin' up here since I was a kid, spent many hours here just thinking, playing my uncle's old guitar. It's kind of my own secret place. But here's what I really wanted to show you, check this out."

He leads me around the backside of the fort to a break in the rocks where indentations, Moki steps, are carved into the sheer wall, leading up to the capstone of the small tabletop butte. We climb, leaning into rock, carefully placing our toes into the chiseled-out hollows worn nearly smooth by a thousand years of erosion. Suddenly, the universe sweeps beneath my feet, and I can see forever.

Johnny says, "It's a lookout. The Indians could stand here and see for miles in every direction. Probably the most amazing view in this entire country."

Shading my eyes from late-afternoon sun, I can see clear to the distant skyline, across the top of Temple Mountain and way over on the far horizon to Boulder Mountain, once a denizen of fire and molten lava, volcanic ash billowing into Jurassic skies.

A bit closer stand the Coffeepot Mountains, tamer laccolithic cousins where the lava bubbled the mountains into rounded graces but never burst through. The range still wears its cap of late-winter snow.

Lower and nearer, Factory Butte, proud of its lofty place in the long stretch of flat desert, now seems small, Mancos shales banded at the top by Green River Formation. I've stood beneath Factory Butte and marveled at its height. The lofty plateau of the Swell, where we now stand, was only a blue mist in the distance.

I turn to the east, and far in the distance, over towards Radium, a long dark ribbon flows from the ramparts of the Bookcliffs—Dark Angel Canyon, place of mystery and intrigue, of foreboding and danger, where even intrepid pothunters never go.

And now I see it, what I've been feeling for some time—the storm. "Something's coming in," I note, gesturing to the distance where an immense dark shadow cloaks the entire far western horizon, thick gray clouds, wind-blown, heavy. "Looks like the leading edge of a big storm."

Johnny replies, "Looks pretty heady. These late spring storms can be the worst, can dump most of the season's snow. Drop the temperature 30 or 40 degrees in a few hours. It'll be a while before it gets here, sometime during the night."

Looking at the dark distant mass, I wonder how many U-boomers out in this country will sit it out, cramped into tents and freezing, cussing their own greedy asses. I suspect a few of them will high-tail it back to town, just like I intend to do, cussing the weather, just like I intend to do.

But now, behold! Cougar Sun catches Coffeepot Peak in sharp claws, blood-red light bathing the entire range, flowing down ragged precipices like melting scarlet butter. And now everything before us, the world at our feet, glows with light reflected from the peaks, a soft carmel that reflects and refracts forever, lighting yellow sandstone fins and white whalebacks, burgundy buttes, soft purple hills of Mancos clays, and even ashen uranium tailings. Everything is bathed in a rich shade of carmine, a purity of spectrum that makes one forget any other colors could exist.

Sun suddenly drops behind storm and all becomes hidden, blending into an ominous uniformity of grayness. In the distance, a huge lightning bolt lights the Moroni Slopes in an attempt to mock Cougar Sun.

Johnny nods towards the bolt, so distant we can't hear the thunder. He quotes, "Behold, He spreads His lightning against the dark clouds. His thunderings speak awesomely concerning Him; the cattle are told of His coming storm."

"What's that from, the Book of Mormon?" I ask.

Johnny gives me a sidelong look, "No, the Book of Job, the Bible."

"Oh," I reply, shrugging my shoulders.

"Say, Chin, you grew up in the desert, do you think you'll ever leave?"

"I dunno, why?"

"Oh, sometimes I just think there's a big world out there and I'm missin' out. But when it comes right down to it, I dunno if I'll ever really go."

"Yeah, I know, sometimes I feel something tugging at me, too," I reply.

Johnny adds, "I often wonder why I'd ever wanna have anything to do with something as destructive as the A-Bomb, it bothers me, I wanna get away."

"Well, don't do it then, I guess."

"Yeah, I guess. Well, whattya think? Amazing place, ain't it?"

"It's the Hózhóni, the Beautyway. Beauty all around us, beauty beneath us, beauty within us. All we need to be happy."

Johnny smiles. "All we need? Ya think so? What about groceries? You can't eat the scenery, so they say."

I reply, "Well, actually, you can. Prickly-pear cactus buds are good, very sweet, and the meat is great when you roast off the spines. And there's wild celery, wild onion, cattails, wild rhubarb, ricegrass—the list is endless."

"Is that what you live on out here?"

"No, actually, I prefer polenta lasagna with a nice glass of Zinfandel, stuff like that."

Johnny laughs, and we head back down, tracking our own footprints in the waning glow of day's end.

Old Willy patiently waits, now gently rocking from side to side in a chilly wind, three black ravens rocking together on his hood, waiting for that promised supper.

"Well, it's been fun," Johnny says, again emptying his boots, which I notice have holes in the soles. He holds the brim of his straw cowboy hat so the wind doesn't take it. "You headed for Temple?"

"Probably."

"I'm gonna make sure everything's buttoned up at the mine, then I'm headin' home. You're welcome to come wait this storm out, you can stay at my grandma's house. She has a real comfortable place there on the corner of Bartley and Rosetree. You could be there by dark."

"Thanks, but I'll probably just go camp over close by Temple and wait it out there, I'm thinking of coming back up on the Swell. But I appreciate the offer."

"Well, best of luck, and I hope to run into you again," he says. "If you do end up in Catalpa Town, it's the Taylor House, everybody knows where it is. Just tell my grams I sent you, her name's Callie." Johnny shakes my hand with a firm grip, gives my shoulder a squeeze.

"Hey," he adds, "I just thought of something you might be able to use. I have some information on rock art places around our ranch, a map my grandparents made. Stop by the house sometime, it might be helpful."

"Thanks, Johnny. See ya around soon, I hope."

Something rustles around the other side of Willy in the shadows. I feel irritated.

Pssst, Little Agate, it's me, your coyote pal.

I answer in a low whisper, *Go away, Johnny will think I'm nuts if he hears me talking to you.*

Oh, he's leaving now, and you are nuts. But look, I've been thinking about what you said earlier today. What if I said that about you, that you're just a figment of my imagination, that I created you from my own overactive compulsive thoughts? And how can you prove I didn't? And if I'm a figment, why are you afraid he'll hear us talking?

Look, I don't believe in the supernatural, so you must be my imagination.

Well, it's OK if you don't believe I'm real, but if you don't believe in the supernatural, then you don't believe in God, Little Agate.

Go away, I'm not in the mood, dang it.

We'll see how it goes when you're all alone out in some dark canyon with one of those spooky Barrier ghosts.

Look, Yellowjacket, I didn't say I didn't believe in God, just not in you.

Then you must be seeing apparitions, hallucinating.

Probably.

Adios, Little Agate. Gotta go see a man about a dog. Be careful, there's a storm coming in, and I'm not talking about the weather.

Johnny's gone, and I think about his offer. The wind feels cold, and suddenly I long for warmth, for people, laughter, a home, like a hobo staring through a window, wanting to go inside, but as soon as someone comes to open the door, I run. I'd rather be outside looking in, longing.

"So what's the cure?" I ask old Willy as I put my gear away.

"Don't think there is one," I answer on his behalf.

A strong gust shakes the juniper tree. "So, I'm doomed to always want something I can never have? As soon as it starts to look possible, I'm gonna run away? That's a helluva way to live, Chinle, if I don't say so. A helluva way."

Silence.

"Any suggestions?" I persist.

No answer.

I throw the ravens the rest of my crackers, and Willy and I head back down the road, or what we can see of it in the blowing sand.

Ravens fly away, chasing the wind, on their way to the edge of the world, laughing through the swirling red sand, lost in the Hózhóni, the Beautyway.

Looking around me,
At the juniper log where I sit and read the sky,
At the sandstone alcove where I pull off my boots each day,
After taking a walk down to the litle stream,

Down to wild water, flowing endless in this canyon dream.
I wonder, will this wild place miss me
After tomorrow, when I'm gone?
Or just pragmatically embrace the next,
Like a fickle wild lover.
This in a string of places,
That for me, flow like the river,
As each eddy changes to rapids,
In a riverway of never ending movement.
Looking for solace in what cannot be still,
Searching for starlight by the light of wild moon.

OK Chin,

Where the hell is Stock Tank? I heard you were there, and I actually would drop in on you in the next few weeks if I knew where the hell you were. I'm headed back to the Tengo Dinero after taking care of a few things.

May be gone until the end of next week. Then back in Radium again. I hate this place. But I will check mail. But seriously, how would I find you out there in the middle of nowhere if I don't have more clues than that?

I'll be here two more hours,

Charlie

4
Buddy Blue: Catalpa Town

Old Willy can barely top 50 miles per hour on blacktop on a good day, but with the wind blowing directly into the windshield, we're lucky to keep cranked up to 40 on the rutted dirt road dropping down off the Swell. Sand swirls around us like snow in a blizzard, and the gusts have now turned into full-blown torment.

I'm prepared to spend the night about anywhere, since nearly everything I own is in the back of the jeep—sleeping bag, tent, shovel, warm clothes, matches, propane cook stove, water, food, and my rock art notes, sketches, and letters stored in an old wooden Hercules dynamite powder box. When your home is nowhere, it really doesn't much matter where you sleep.

We drop down off the Swell, and the wind seems to let up just a little. Nearly to Temple Junction, early darkness from the storm leaves a feeling of urgency in its wake that, coupled with inertia, keeps us rolling, rolling, rolling—right on by Cleo's drill hole, past where Coralee showed me the baskets, and finally, right on past the Temple Junction Motel, no vacancy, lights dim in the tiny windows of the weekly rented rooms. As I expected, the café's still closed, and the entire place reeks of the loneliness that only decrepit buildings rattling in a desert storm can bring.

Catalpa Town now seems comforting, and I imagine the Taylor family house, windows all lit up, lawn glistening in the rain. Inside, they're having a dinner of steak and mashed potatoes with gravy, laughing and talking, and later, while everyone has homemade mulberry pie for dessert, Johnny's grandmother Callie plays the piano, singing, "When I Take My Vacation in Heaven."

I smile at my fantasy—truth is, they're probably having cold tuna sandwiches and worrying about the price of cattle.

The distant lights from Green River hang for miles in Willy's rear-view mirror, a glow reflecting off low-hung clouds. This wind is definitely driving something in, but maybe I can get to Catalpa Town before the roads get bad. Maybe Johnny will be around, and I can tell him I've changed my mind, I want to spend the night in a real house for once. This impending storm makes me feel unexpectedly sociable.

By the time the huge car-shaped specter of Cadillac Rock (complete with tail fins) is barely visible off to my right, a light rain has begun to fall. I turn on Willy's pitiful heater. It'll be only a matter of time before the rain freezes, making the road treacherous.

I top the hill by Lariat Arch as icy rain turns to driving sleet. Combined with the wind, it's becoming more difficult to stay on the road.

Two Step Hill, just out of Catalpa Town, will probably be a slippery mess by the time I get there, and with Willy's bald tires, I'm bound to have trouble. Now we drop into a little canyon where I make out the dim doors of "the Wunderground" in cliffs that bend towards the highway, the long-abandoned cave residence of an eccentric artist. I could stop here and camp, but rumor has it that the old guy actually had his deceased pets stuffed (including a donkey) and kept them in the house to ease his loneliness. I'm having enough trouble with strange dreams lately.

By the time we make the top of the hill on the other side of the Wunderground, the road's covered with a good half-inch of slush. I'm beginning to wish I were in the Robber's Roost Motel in Green River, cozy, curled up in bed reading "The Ghost Pueblos of Mesa Verde" or "Finding Treasure by Helicopter" in the latest issue of Desert Magazine.

Finally, something says it's past time to stop, and Willy does a controlled slide off the road where the shadow of a snow-covered road meets the dark highway, the way to Fins 'n Things, a huge area of giant rugged sandstone fins and domes.

The narrow sandy road begins climbing immediately, a moderate grade that will, if my memory serves me, top out immediately on a small rise, then drop into the headwaters of Lost Spring Canyon, an immense drainage system that swings for miles around and through Fins 'n Things until it spills into Pack Saddle Creek near Catalpa Town. I've given up on staying at Callie's and am now hoping to camp on the top of the rise in the pinions and junipers.

Willy's bald tires have no trouble climbing the sandy road, even though the unpacked snow is now a good inch deep. We're soon at the top, but the problem is knowing where to turn off the road in the swirling snow and darkness, where to find a camp versus finding a place to get stuck.

A break appears in the dark trees and I stop, turning the jeep so the headlights shine onto the campsite. I leave the engine running, set the brake, and get out.

Millions of snowflakes sparkle in the light of the headlamps, the circular beams quickly absorbed by clouds. After a look, I realize I'm exactly where I'd hoped. I'd camped here before with Gramps, years ago, in this large clearing with big buff-colored sandstone boulders around it, a perfect protected camp spot.

I pull old Willy in, turn around, and turn off the engine. Home for the night. The wind has died down, and the front of the storm seems to have moved on through, leaving motionless clouds clinging to the night, clouds still heavy with moisture. It could snow all night. Like Johnny said, these spring blizzards are often the worst storms of the entire year.

I shiver, take a flashlight from the glovebox, and quickly set up my little tent, tying the guy lines to Willy and a nearby tree. I then slip into a wool sweater and hat and another layer of socks, start old Willy again and let the heater saturate everything with a meagre warmth, then turn off the jeep and quickly slip deep into my sleeping bag, stretched out on a pad on the cold floor of the tent. I rarely use my tent, preferring to stretch out under the night sky, but tonight there is no night sky, just night.

In the silence, snow sizzles on the still-warm hood of old Willy, and I'm soon asleep, dreaming of lounging on a white wicker chair in the sitting room of the Taylor house in Catalpa Town, drinking a mint julep, whatever the H-E-double-hockeysticks that is.

Dreams come in the night, hanging over old Willy in the frosty air, melting through the windows like ancient ghosts, each with something important to say, comprehensible or not. Carefully I study them like I study rocks, deep asleep.

Images tumble from my childhood, memories of wandering the high desert with Gramps, rock-hounding beneath red cliffs. The weavings of my dreams hang in the snows, colors spinning through the thick night. Lightning sears through black clouds which are maybe real, maybe not.

A few years after Gramps betrayed me by dying, I began exploring with Charlie. On weekends, he and I would slip out of town at dawn in his old faded green International Scout.

Our bond was uncharted terrain, undiscovered outcroppings, nonexistent roads—and rocks. We hunted rocks like bounty hunters. Later, after I left Radium, their images haunted me in my dreams, like caged wild animals. Later, I tried to return all the rocks, all the points and scrapers, all the beautiful petrified wood, everything I'd collected, return it back to the earth, in a clumsy ritual filled with sagebrush smoke, the same kind of ritual that the Utes used. It didn't work, the dreams continued.

I continued to dream of rocks, but now I realized that these things belonged in their own place, just as everything does, people, animals, plants. And it then became clear to me that by taking the Indian artifacts, we were finishing the job begun by our white ancestors with the slaughter of the buffalo, removing all traces of a people who once walked this land in freedom.

Many days Charlie and I walked the hills near Radium, searching for what we thought was lost, eyes to ground, looking up just in time to bump into juniper branches, our pockets full of scrapers, the tips of broken arrowheads, and black obsidian from lava fields, obsidian carried hundreds of miles in buckskin pouch and traded for tightly-woven hemp rope or corn seed. Charlie said there was a big outcropping of obsidian over by Marysvale, he'd seen it himself, and another far north at Yellowstone.

We wandered, lost, looking up only at sunset when the light had faded too much to continue the search, surprised to find ourselves in places we'd been hours before, wandering in circles.

Some days we found great treasure. Other days we were simply introspect, aware of each other's presence, admiring sunlight backlit through pinion, sunlight gracing copper hatband and filtering through sandy hair.

Some days we were hard put to carry away the poundage of agate, gizzard stones from thunder lizards, and opalized pearl-white petrified wood. Other days our treasures were easy portage, small elegantly knapped points from the hand of a great artist, art with both form and function. Perhaps it was the same artist who painted the graceful bighorn fleeing the hunter on nearby cliffs, painted the shamanistic forms on blood-red patina, forms perhaps intended to trap magic and thereby make the hunter successful.

Sometimes we would find rock art, usually when sun was low, during that transition between deep reds that glow next to earth's edge and black night in the zenith. With the lonely chill of night and warmth of sun juxtaposed, I would read messages from another time, from those who are now dust, the Ancient Ones.

Messages of dreamy solitude, of lost trails. Messages of quicksand and sudden flash floods in deep rimrock canyons. Messages of creamy Sego lily blooms. Messages of death and desolation. Messages of found water. Messages of exploding nebulae.

And sometimes, messages of strange music, messages of white willow bark, and messages of a mysterious place called the Ancient City.

I awake, disturbed. Dreams fade into far illusory horizons. It's still dark, still snowing. Turning, my feet push against the cold tent wall and I hear snow sliding down the sides. I drift back to sleep.

The strong aroma of coffee spilled on my sleeping bag filters through my sleep, comforting me. Soon my dreams wander to big cliffs,

cliffs now brushed with strange figures washed in brilliant colors—red ochre, black charcoal, white gypsum, yellow limonite.

Yucca-leaf brush strokes are still visible on the ghost-like figures, snakes with huge rattles, deer with attenuated antlers. Suddenly, a wall of red water slams against the cliffs, throwing logs and tree limbs against the figures, leaving red froth on deer antlers.

Snow falls deeper around me and old Willy, and the figures melt into yet another dream, a dream of a tall Indian, a Ute chief, a man with dark eyes and great presence. Sitting at his heels like a trained dog, a large yellow coyote watches with sand-colored eyes.

Draped over one shoulder and wrapped skillfully around the man's waist, worn in the old traditional way, is a beautiful Chief's blanket in red, white, and rare indigo stripes, bearing the initials ND under the spirit line.

The Ute chief looks at me, direct. He says softly, gently, "You must become more responsible, little Flowing-from-the-Canyons, you must find your home. Nona wishes it so."

Antonio.

I feel a chill.

Sometime in the early morning I awake, cold, groggy, my mouth tasting strangely metallic. Sticking my head out of the tent, I see snow blanketing Willy's hood, covering the entire front of the old jeep.

For a moment I think we're buried, but the first diffused rays of dawn show only about three inches of powder. The juniper trees are frosted, their blueberries poking through opaque ice crystals. The air's filled with yet more crystals, each reflecting the distant sun, veiled in cold.

Stiff, I pull myself from my sleeping bag, get dressed and pull down the tent, shaking off the snow and tossing everything into the jeep. Willy's never had a key, Gramps lost it years ago, but he bypassed the starter so you can just push a button under the dash. I push the button, hoping Willy will start. Like me, the jeep is half-frozen and unenergetic, but a rumbly slow chugging soon warms to a smooth idling.

Reluctantly opening the door, I crawl back out, snow seeping under my jean cuffs and into the tops of my boots. I clear the windshield with my forearm, stumble back into the jeep, crank the heater, sit for a few minutes, then slowly ease my foot onto the gas.

Bare tires spin a second or two, slide and push their way through the snow and on down the hill. I knew when I camped on this rise that we could slide our way back down to the highway just like this if need be.

We continue on, making new tracks on the highway until finally, Willy slowly descends the long grade of Two Step Hill, then on down the long stretch into the southern end of Pack Saddle Valley, the red-sand home of Catalpa Town and Pack Saddle Creek.

Sunlight struggles through ragged clouds tinted with a hint of rose as we approach the outskirts of the wakening town. At last, light breaks through, finally pushing its way over deep spring snows on the far-away flanks of the Coffeepot Mountains. We pull into Catalpa Town just as the high rim above town glows the rich purple-crimson of dawn.

Cradled in an alcove in that same rim, hundreds of feet directly above the County Highway Shop, an ancient Anasazi burden basket dreams deeply. A thousand years of morning sunrays have gently dyed its sumac coils a rich copper color.

A thousand years the basket has waited for its maker to return, but the small Anasazi woman with the brown eyes died long long ago, many miles away in her new home near the Rio Grande River to the south, basket forgotten.

Soon the basket will be discovered by two high-school boys exploring high in the cliffs. They will carefully haul it down into town, to the amazement of the townspeople, for the basket will be one of the largest ever found, a full three feet tall.

It will eventually be displayed in the Catalpa Town Museum as one of the area's wonders, admired by all. There it will wait in its newfound shelter, pining for the open air, the brown-haired woman, and a thousand ruby sunrises.

I haven't been in Catalpa Town for years, and I've forgotten how beautiful its huge catalpa trees are, especially when the white blossoms grace the branches, scenting the town with a delicacy that can bear no name because it's like nothing known. The trees line the streets, with the magenta blooms of an occasional Eastern redbud providing an ethereal contrast in late spring. The sheltered valley has received no snow, only a light rain.

Catalpa Town was settled by an early branch of the Taylor family, who, along with several other families, wisely decided to abandon the Hole-in-the-Rock Expedition when it passed near here on its way to incredible hardships, following ill-gotten advice on a passable route to southeastern Utah. Mormon leader Brigham Young had uprooted the Saints from other missions and sent them on their way to colonize the desert at what is now Bluff, wanting a stronghold in that part of the state against possible Gentile incursion.

One branch of the Taylors continued on with the expedition, but the Catalpa Town branch knew a good thing when they saw it. Defying Young's orders, they started a new settlement in the green valley surrounded by towering red cliffs. Young excommunicated the entire rebel bunch from the church, even though he later visited Catalpa Town and liked it so much he made it his favorite stopping place when in the area.

Mormon towns are oriented to an invisible divine axis that connects, if one has the kind of faith that can leap that far, to the great Mormon Temple in Salt Lake City, the City of Saints. Center and Main, streets in every Mormon town, pin each town in place along that invisible grid so it can never stray into the Gentile world with its sins of unpredictability and free thinking.

Other streets are always named according to distance north, south, east, or west from the intersection of Main and Center, such as 200 North 300 West, which would be two blocks north of that intersection and three blocks west. Once this basic grid had been established, the Saints were free to apply more lyrical names to secondary streets, names like Pratt and Rigdon, commemorating early pioneers who were also prominent church members.

But Catalpa Town had been settled by Jack Mormons, rebels, a fact reflected in streets bearing names like Juniper and Mulberry and even the unlikely Birch.

Brigham was a serious socialist and survivalist at heart, a fact reflected in his vision for Mormon towns with wide streets and houses set back a uniform 25 feet from the street, each on its own half-acre, allowing everyone to have large garden plots. To this vision the rebels of Catalpa Town adhered, ensuring a beautiful and pastoral place, and the Taylor House takes up an oversized acre lot as beautifully kept as any English garden.

I slow Willy to a crawl, admiring the beautiful tulips along the wrought-iron fence, benches under huge catalpa trees beginning to bud. The drought has apparently skipped the Taylor House. Early purple lilacs surround the lawn in great sweeping crescents. Somebody here loves to garden.

The house itself is a deep-red cut stone that echoes the reds of the cliffs in the background in a color complimentary to the spring-green lawns. A large covered porch extends the entire length of the front of the house, where thick wisteria vines climb to the roof. The house and grounds exude everything illusionary I'd craved last night—warmth, comfort, security, home.

But then I picture the crooked rock shelter of Cactus Rat and Yeller Cat, high on the mesa with its sweeping open views, and suddenly that old familiar desire for simplicity crashes in like a flashflood, carrying on it the urge to jump ship.

I step on the gas just as someone comes out the front door of the house. I hear a loud whistle, then, "Hey, Chinleee, stop!"

Caught, just like when I was a kid stealing Gramps' Three Musketeers bars.

I pull over just as Johnny runs up along Willy, grabbing the door handle as if to stop the little jeep by sheer force. "Hey, I was hoping you'd come by."

"Hi, Johnny, I just got into town, thought I'd swing by and pick up that rock art info you mentioned."

Johnny grins, "C'mon in and have a cup of coffee before I never see you again. Man, gal, you look like you slept on top of your head." He tousles my hair, asks, "Where you headed?"

"Down to Cap Reef country for a while."

"Well, come on in and I'll get you that rock art stuff, it's actually a map. I made a copy just for you." He puts his hand on my arm. "C'mon."

I get out, follow Johnny up the steps onto the big porch just as Johnny's grandmother Callie comes out. She's small, with thick gray hair tied in a long braid down her back. A large turquoise bracelet makes her frail arm look like it should bend from the weight. Her face bears the lines of a redrock universe, and I can tell she's very old, but she stands upright and her eyes sparkle like blue ice on a high mountain couloir.

"Gramma Callie, this is Chinle Miller, she's an archaeologist, like Barry. She studies rock art for the university. Camps out all the time."

"Nice to meet you, a friend of John's is a friend of mine," she smiles. "Sounds like you're way up there on the happiness quotient."

"Tell her what that is," Johnny says.

"Oh, that's when you take the number of days you camp out and divide by the number of days in the year. A perfectly happy life is about 320 over 360, 'cause you want to account for the really bad weather and everybody needs a few days indoors drinking tea and taking baths and civilized stuff like that. Come inside, dear."

The interior of the Taylor house is nothing like I expected. Unlike the immaculate lawn outside, the inside is unpolished, casual, with worn hardwood floors covered with huge Navajo rugs and handmade juniper furniture. A red flagstone fireplace has a huge wooden mantle graced by an oil portrait of a big yellow dog.

That same dog is now at Callie's side, and I can tell from her clouded eyes that she's old, too.

"Meet Hannah. She's a Golden Lab under all that fat. Used to be a damn good cowdog in her heyday, good as any Heeler, well, almost."

"Hello, Hannah." I bend down, look into her deep eyes and gently tousle her ears.

"Do you have a dog, dear?" Callie asks.

"I love dogs, but I'm out too much, they deserve a more stable home."

Callie replies with concern, "Chinle, you shouldn't be out here in this wild country alone. A dog would love the kind of life you lead, outside all the time, wandering around. It would be the life of Riley. Well, I'm sorry, but I have to run. Nice to meet you, dear, please excuse me. John, could you come out with me and take a quick look at my tires?"

Johnny's soon back, smiling mysteriously. He takes me into a den with a big ancient roll-top oak desk, the kind with cubbyholes and secret drawers. An old but polished .22 pistol lies on the desk with "Callie" engraved into the steel-blue handle.

Johnny sees me eyeing the gun. "Maybe you should borrow that for a while, never know who you might meet out there alone."

"If I had a gun, somebody'd just end up shooting me with it. And I'm not big on shooting things, myself, thanks anyway. Besides, Willy keeps one handy under his front seat."

Johnny smiles, gently unfolds a yellowed piece of paper, creased and brittle. "This is a map made by my great-grandfather Nephi Taylor. He founded Catalpa Town. Most Mormons were farmers, but he was a rancher, didn't like farming."

"Anyway, he and my great-grandmother, Bartley, made this map as they explored the country chasin' cattle. It's pretty accurate. Actually, it's extremely accurate, from what I've ridden horseback and flown over. Most of these places don't have roads, but you're welcome to borrow one of our horses anytime you want."

The map is old, yellowed, bearing jagged lines with the names of canyons, springs, and other landmarks, marked with dots indicating rock art panels, some with annotations such as "lots of marching figures" or "big alcove full of stuff."

"I made you a copy to take with you, thought you might find something important."

I nod thanks, studying the map, intrigued by a note that says "strange bird-like things" in a canyon not too far from what says "Taylor Ranch."

"Where exactly is your ranch?" I ask.

"Ten miles west of town. Stop by sometime, that's where I'm mostly at when I'm not out at the mine. There's a sign by the highway."

I notice a note on the bottom of the map, and reading it, a chill hits me, the same chill I felt when I had the dream about Antonio with Coyote Yellowjacket sitting at his heels.

There, in a floral script that must be Bartley's: "Nephi found a lost city, wants to take a group and go explore. It's a bit southeast of the mountain."

"Johnny, do you know anything about this?" I ask.

He answers, "Yeah, they discovered what's now called Goblin Valley, though the old-timers called it Mushroom Valley. It's a weird place, a stranger tribe of sandstone hoodoos can't be found anywhere. But there's no rock art there."

I sigh. Davidson's Ghost City will stay lost a little longer.

Now outside, ready to go, Johnny hands me a paper sack.

"Fresh cinnamon rolls from Grams."

Pushing Willy's starter button, I say thanks, then hesitate. "If you're going to be out at the ranch in a couple of weeks, I may come by."

"I need to get back out to the Radium Queen in a few days, then me and our hired hand have to get over to Indian Creek and pick up a small herd of registered cows Dad just bought over there at the old Scorup place. We'll truck them back over here, then trail them on up into the high country near Coffeepot."

I reply, "OK, maybe I'll just stop by the ranch on my way back up here, whenever that is. Sounds like fun, trailing a bunch of cattle through wild country. Keep a lookout for rock art for me."

Johnny looks a bit wistful. "Be sure to take lots of water, Chinle, it's already starting to get hot, especially with this drought, in spite of this storm that just came through. When you go for gas, tell Cleo to put it on our account." He leans over and squeezes my arm. His breath smells sweet like iced cinnamon rolls.

I open the sack and taste the sweet stickiness, wave goodbye to Johnny, then me and Willy head over to get groceries and a newspaper, then to get gas at Cleo's Texaco station, under the sign of the red flying horse, where a little merle Blue Heeler cowdog chases me right up to the pumps.

I jump out and start kicking dirt towards the dog, scolding him. He runs, tail tucked, into the station, then immediately emerges at the heels of a short stocky oldtimer who must be Cleo, the dog watching me through a cagey grin.

To my surprise, the dog comes right up to me, sitting at my heels as I watch Cleo check the oil and add a quart to Willy's internal workings, the old man talking to me the entire time.

The little dog wags his tail when I look at him, though he holds it low, almost between his legs. He's starting to make me feel bad. I find out later that he has an advanced degree in psychology.

After Cleo's finished, he leans back against the pump, grinning, watching the red and white neon lights on the nearby dilapidated restaurant flash on and off in broad daylight, advertising the No Delay Café and its equally dejected partner, the Pillow Talk Motel.

"Young lady, you just missed meetin' a big-wig," he says.

"Who's that?" I ask, studying the distant ridges of Woods Mesa, wondering if I should head up there next.

"Old Stu Udall, you know, the Secretary of the Interior. He's Secretary of the Interior of the whole United States, and that's a damn big interior. He's been through here before, used to come through here once in a while when he was a senator. You just missed him."

Cleo spits to the side, continues, "He was in a government outfit, had a bunch of guys with him. Had that Babbitt, or Rabbit, or whatever the hell his name is—stopped here to get gas."

I lean against old Willy, sensing that the old guy's gearing up for a story, a talent Johnny warned me he possesses in spades.

Cleo continues, "Well, old Stu, he got out of that truck, and he was standing there, and he walked over to that big petrified log you see sitting over there by the station. I got that log over on the mesa, you can see the road climbing up way over there.

Anyway, old Stu, he asked me, 'Say, Cleo, where'd you get that tree?'

'Well, Mr. Udall,' I said, 'I grew it!'

Well, this didn't set too well, and you could see he wasn't too happy, and he said, 'We are trying to keep those petrified trees in their natural state where people can look at them.'

'Well,' I said, 'Mr. Udall,' I said, 'You and me are tryin' to do the same thing,' I said, 'I'm tryin' to put 'em in a pile here where people can look at 'em!'

Oh, that shook him up! He was mad! Well, I filled 'em up with gas, and worked their windshield and everything and checked their oil. And they started the motor on that outfit.

It had kinda vapor locked a little bit, probably not used to the heat. And anyway, they fired it up, and boy, that government driver was just a-rockin' the hell out of that motor. I mean he had his foot right in the carburetor, and it was just bouncin' up and down!

And I walked over to the window, and I said, 'Mr. Udall, will you tell your driver to please take it a little easy on that gubmint vehicle,' I says, 'I just got it half paid for with my hard-earned tax money.'

Man, you can't imagine how much fun I had! But boy, when I told Stu that I grew that wood, man, if that didn't shake him up!"

Cleo laughs, adds, "Damn politicians, outta do some honest work for a livin' like the rest of us." He pauses for a while, and his smile makes me think that maybe he's remembering the good times looking for petrified wood, rock hounding, prospecting, dodging BLM rangers.

Cleo finally looks at the little Blue Heeler, then me, and says, "That damn worthless mutt's taken a likin' to you."

He adds, "Hellsbells, why don't you just take 'em and keep me from havin' to shoot the bull-headed tire-biter before he gets runned over. He'll chase and chase, it's his nature, and it's a shame what we humans have done, breedin' such behavior into a dog's little brain just so we can exploit 'em herdin' cattle. Damn nuisance when you ain't got no cattle."

Cleo now makes himself busy washing Willy's windshield, checking the single wiper blade. "Lights workin' OK? Just take 'im. He'll turn into your best friend, besides, you should have a little protection out there all alone all the time. Name's Buddy Blue, a year old, no charge for the gas and oil, and don't bring him back. You're gonna need a new blade next time you come through. Hell, let me put it on for you right now, no charge."

Before I can say anything, Cleo opens Willy's passenger door and Buddy Blue jumps in, ears forward, panting, with that eager look working dogs have, eager to go, go anywhere, just go.

Cleo installs the wiper, then pauses, leaning against old Willy. "Hey, you know, if you ever want some Calyx cores, there's a bunch of 'em over by Temple Mountain, huge cores, and dinosaur teeth and claws. You know a guy over there named Joe Hughes? Tell him old Cleo says he ain't never paid up on that bet he lost. Damn boat never was found. How them boys at Green River could lose a steamboat is beyond me."

"You just lay down in there, Bud, you ain't gittin' out! Anyway, if you're over there at Temple, I drilled a well over there, right in front of those rock pictures, you be sure to get a look at them, for sure. The cap's still there. There's some old Indian baskets over there. We used to go look at 'em, but we always left 'em right there."

I ask, "Say, Cleo, Johnny Taylor tells me you guys got claim-jumped once. What happened?"

"Whooey, that was somethin'!" Cleo steps back grinning, shaking his head. "Johnny and I go way back, we did some prospecting along the foot of the Coffeepots, out there on Granite Wash. I had this guy workin' for me, got 'im out of jail. Now he was a tough son-of-a-gun! I don't know what he was in jail for, but he was just as rough as they come. Name was Stormy White."

"What happened?" I ask.

"Well," Cleo replies, "We was out at the claims there one day, and there was two of them old boys, claim jumpers. One of them was sitting on the monument there, where we'd staked our claim, and the other was down on the flats a little ways.

'Ha!' I told Stormy, I says, 'we work up there, and I'll take the one on the monument, you take the one on the flats, and John, you stay close behind and back us up if we need it.' So we did. We worked our way up there. I got over to the one on the monument, they was stakin' over our claims, I got up close to him and he had a gun, and I just popped him right in the teeth.

This other old boy, Stormy, he had that guy down on the flats, and he was just killin' him. Man! So I ran down there and pulled him off. We never saw those two old boys again!"

Cleo pauses, caught in the memory, as a black and white car pulls in with "Wayne County Sheriff" painted in yellow on the door.

"Howdy, Cleo, fillerup." A lanky man in blue jeans and brown shirt with yellow sheriff's emblems on the sleeves pulls himself out of the vehicle. A large revolver hangs on his narrow hip, and he wears polished black cowboy boots. "Hope nothin's goin' on 'round town, 'cause my damn two-way radio ain't workin', can't get any kind of signal."

Cleo grabs the pump, unscrews the gas cap, sticks the gas nozzle in, and answers, "Huey, you know there ain't nuthin' goin' on, there ain't never nuthin' goin' on. Why they even pay you is beyond me, you should work for free, 'cause all you ever do is drive around and the only thing you know how to shoot is the breeze."

Hugh grins, answers, "Hell, Cleo, 'till I get this radio fixed that's all I can do. Gonna have to take it all the way over to Richfield, maybe see my daughter while I'm there. You fellas are puttin' in so many oil rigs around here you're messin' up the signal, groundin' it, soakin' it right into the earth."

Cleo snorts, "Is that right? Kinda like havin' a big floodlight, the more people you have sittin' around under it, soakin' up the light, the dimmer it gets?"

Hugh smiles, touches his hat and nods towards me, acknowledging my presence, as Buddy Blue pants out the window.

Cleo winks at me. "You don't have to pay, it's taken care of. Take good care of that good-fer-nuthin' mutt. He likes beans and be sure to carry extra water. Use the hose around back anytime you want, it's good drinkin' water. Stay away from that Goblin and Muddy Creek water."

As I pull out, I hear Cleo say, "So, Huey, you just missed your chance at gettin' to meet a big-wig. He might've appointed you to his cabinet, you bein' a member of the same distinguished liar's club and all."

I smile, heading for Catalpa Town Grocery to pick up some beans and dog food. Finally, I check in at the post office, surprised to find a few letters. Sometimes I wonder how many letters sit in post offices around southeastern Utah, addressed to Chinle Miller, General Delivery, wasting away in the "Unknown Recipient" box. Or maybe the postmasters just forward them back and forth from town to town until I come along and claim them.

Just then, it suddenly occurs to me that I've been involved in a setup between Cleo, Johnny, and Callie, a setup with the name of Buddy Blue.

Catalpa Town Times
Cleo and Emma Hanks celebrated their 50th wedding anniversary this past Friday at a potluck at the Catalpa Town LDS Stake House. The event was attended by friends and family from Catalpa Town and Green River. The couple are both descendents of early pioneers and are life-long residents of Catalpa Town. When asked to what they owed their happy marriage, Cleo replied, "Whiskey," and Emma said, "Patience and poor eyesight." The couple has seven children, all residents of Catalpa Town and Green River.

well, chinle,

my sweet honey of the slickrocks. you be as elusive as the roadrunner hisself. me, i just got back from a good time in wyoming.

but would like much to hook up and talk poetry and language and naming and coffee. maybe we can meet sometime soon. are you over in the canyon country or where, you desert rat?

anyhoo, here's a poem called "the wild" that I wrote for you.

love, art

little red ant,
monkish insect
loyal to the clan
yet a wanderer far

from one's own homeland
did the purple scent
of the onion's umbel
sing to you as well

& lead you astray
on this hillside perch
where we loaf
lost among the chanterelles

uncertain & in love
with the wild?

Dear Chinle,

Nice sunset, prob. storm by morn, maybe go to GR and mail this, seems sketchy sending it to wherever you possibly might be. Clouds turning red, have a hunch you're out there watching too. Interesting how we met again after all these years. I'll never forget that brush fire we accidentally started by floating burning hay down the ditch over at Uncle Glade's. We kids had a lot of fun, didn't we? Too bad our families drifted apart. Do you ever get lonesome way out there? This moaning wind makes me unsettled. Am out in Thompson Cyn in Roger's camp trailer, 40 acres here at the foot of the Books. Weener dogs having a blast. How the heck did I end up with 3 weeners? I dunno, but I like showing them off. OK, ha ha. Drop me a line.

Your old pal,

Jim

Dear Chinle,

It has been a beautiful spring (unofficial until Sunday). My daffodils are starting to fade and the tulips are in full bloom. I got this product to keep the deer away from the tulips. The bag shows a male and female deer in bed and the name of the product is: "Not Tonight Deer."

Linda called wanting to find you, she says she needs your advice about something or other. I think she's having another "should I leave the city and move to the country" crisis. I hesitated to tell her where you are, then I realized she'd never find you anyway. I think she might be a bit better now. Brian works for the highway dept. I always thought it was so bizarre that she and I and Irma were all three married to Brians! If I have lunch with her, I will report back.

We will get together one way or the other. My air conditioning is nearly functional. (It is now 4 months they have been working on it off and on. Motto of the garage: We will not cool our clients before their time!) I am awaiting a new fan switch. We'll see. All my life, I've wanted to be way cool. See you soon.

Love,

Sarah

OK Chin...

So do you sometimes get this incredibly anxious but lonely feeling that is almost all encompassing and you keep thinking that there is one person out there who could make you feel better but there probably isn't and you pace around feeling trapped and lonely and sad and depressed but also eager to do something but you haven't the slightest idea what it is? And sometimes the only thing that works is to just walk and walk???

No, I never feel like that either.

Yeah...right. Bad day. Where are you? Come see me.

Chas.

Chinle,

Yes, the blanket looks to me to be the missing Hearst First Phase Chief blanket. Where did you ever get it? The measurements are right (62 by 49), the design and colors are right (white, red, indigo bands). See if the warp and weft are right (7/inch and 32/inch), It should also have lots of lazy lines (couldn't tell from the photo), as well as the initials ND under the spirit line.

If so, it's worth a bloody fortune, but it's also highly black market at this point. You say it was a gift, but where did it come from? Please call me collect as soon as you can. Your petroglyph venture sounds fantastic,

Larry

PS Call me collect ASAP!!!

5
Dragons: Willow Creek

Now Catalpa Town fades into a desert mirage, and I feel a hint of wistfulness. The little pragmatic cowdog, Buddy Blue, is fast asleep. After his initial excitement at leaving Cleo, he immediately curled up on Charlie's Chief's blanket. Maybe it's something about that blanket, something peaceful. I'll have to try it out, I could use some peace.

Johnny's map is in my jean-jacket pocket, neatly folded, remarkably light for the treasure it holds.

I gear old Willy down, and we slowly climb out of Pack Saddle Valley, up the winding dugway that pushes through a huge crack in the ruby rim, the same place the renegade Taylors brought their wagons into the valley below.

Finally on top, I stop to let Willy rest, radiator steaming from the climb. Looking down into the jewel of green emerald set in the red valley below, I make out the gray roof of the Taylor House.

Catalpa Town, an oasis in the desert. The Taylors knew what they were doing, they created their own Zion.

I dawdle, my mind still tucked into the comfort of the red stone house, the cool veranda, and sweet scent of fresh cinnamon rolls. Turning away, I now see the rims of several imposing mesas in the distance, mesas scratched with vertical buff cliffs of Dakota capstone—Luna Mesa, Factory Butte, Rattlesnake Turret—all many miles away, with the

Blue Hills between here and there. Though hidden, I know that behind those huge mesas lie the white and red cliffs of Capitol Reef and the little town of Torrey, my eventual destination, the southern boundary of Fremont rock art, as far as anyone knows.

But first, I've decided to explore an area on Johnny's map, a system that drains through the Blue Hills and runs near the Taylor Ranch, starting high in the Coffeepot Mountains. The Taylor map says the canyon holds several panels, a granary, and strange beaked figures.

Willy's still hot, so I decide to brew some coffee and take a break. I start my little propane stove, then play my Peruvian flute, notes low and pure with clear integrity.

Coffee ready, I kick back in the sand, leaning against Willy's front tire. Buddy Blue looks for lizards, sticking his nose into nearby stands of shadscale. The idea of having a dog finally catches up to me, and I make up a song.

Buddy went a huntin', my oh my,
Gonna get himself some rabbit pie.
Buddy saw a rabbit, rabbit run!
Buddy got lost and it weren't no fun.
Go Bud go, gonna catch a rabbit,
Go Bud go, gonna have some fun,
Go Bud go, he's got the rabbit habit,
Gonna chase them rabbits till the settin' of the sun.

Buddy gets bored and crawls under the jeep to doze. I watch as the last remnant clouds from last night's storm break into flimsy bands of gray over in the direction of Radium, far across the big hidden Colorado River.

I graduated from high school, but nothing else changed much in Radium. The town continued to decay, to disintegrate, like a radioactive element. Charlie and I spent all our time together now, always hunting, but the search for rocks became more often a search for our lost souls, for meaning, for each other. I took to writing poetry. Charlie said it was a sure sign of a troubled mind.

We disguised our real search by discussing the unique properties of anthills, by collecting tiny garnets excavated from beneath the surface by ants, by analyzing why some rattlesnakes don't have the courtesy to warn before striking. We examined long swirls in slickrock that Charlie swore were petrified snake tracks, we watched thick mammatus clouds drape the sky with curtains of water, and we discovered infinite ways to get the Scout stuck and unstuck.

Through it all, we were drawn to each other like two comets in synchronous orbits. When apart, my own light became less apparent, and I reflected on the nothingness of an empty universe.

Charlie left Radium not long after I graduated from high school. Neither of us said much when he went. He wanted to make his fortune, and the government had just announced a new incentive program for uranium mining.

Suddenly, Charlie was tired of finite rocks. He was ready for bigger stakes, for tons of crushed rocks, for the infinity of truckloads of hot uranium ore, riches of carnotite, of yellow and green radioactivity, of gray-black pitchblende.

Charlie closed his shop and moved to the Stinking Desert, land of syncline and anticline, where he lived in a cold tent and ate canned spam.

I refused to acknowledge his absence, wandering alone, the search for rocks now lost in my search for meaning. I now had Gramps' old 1947 Willys jeep to carry me to hidden places. Somehow, I believed Charlie would return. I took to climbing the unclimbed cliffs of the Sandrocks, sitting for hours, watching the dry little town below, trying desperately to forget Charlie, to forget his warm smile, his blue eyes, his self-sustenance.

Last night I climbed the tall cliffs where the eagles call.
And as I sat in oblique sunwaves,
The Pleiades opened beneath my feet.
I was there to perform a painful ritual,
To exorcise your ghost,
But I failed.
The cacophony of the crows broke the spell.

Not wanting to go, lost in rock and sky,
Lost in a universe locked in time,
Lost in a universe spinning far,
Lost in a rhythm that is not mine.

Finally, I went to college, where I could study rock art, make a career of it—a career of studying the past, unknown people's past, called archaeology. I could also contemplate my own past, called denial.

About then, Charlie struck it rich and, to his credit and my surprise, started sending me money. It was just in the nick of time, for I was broke and ready to drop out of school and return to Radium, where maybe I'd get a job at Sinkhole Lanes or maybe even reopen the Rock Garden. I had a friend, Wilma Jean, who wanted me to help her open a beauty salon, even though I'd never even been in one. She'd already decided on a name for the shop—Atomic Hair.

Charlie's monthly checks saved me. She opened it without me.

I finger the map in my pocket. Sun wanders westward as I contemplate the task before me. In order to study these rock drawings, I need to first figure out the questions, for only then can I find any answers. Circular, but that's how we archaeologists, indeed, how we humans, operate.

And though I'm a trained scientist, I feel like a hunter—these figures that I hunt haunt me in my dreams until I become the hunted.

I gently break off a bit of the sagebrush near me, and its strong aroma fills the air, pungent and sweet. The Utes use sage in their healing ceremonies, but will it help heal lost souls? I place it in my jacket pocket, where it will stay until my own healing is complete, when I forget Charlie.

Or until I wash my jacket, whichever comes first.

I hear a faint droning hum, like a B-52 warplane over the distant horizon. Maybe it's Sputnik, the Russky's new satellite, spinning and tumbling through the dreams, the fears, of every American. The hum fades into nothingness.

Now Willy, Buddy Blue, and I head back out again, and Catalpa Town fades into the past as we rattle down the road. My thoughts fade forward as I wonder which direction the mysteries of rock art will take me. I reach my hand over to pet Buddy's silky nose. An unwanted sense of emptiness hails me along the road, jumps in, seeps into everything in the jeep, and won't get back out.

Yellowjacket, how can I do this thing that seems impossible?

Little Yucca, what thing is that?

You know, Yellowjacket, find myself again, forget love, learn to take care of myself, be self-sufficient.

You must do it one day at a time, Little Chamisa, just like you swim the river one stroke at a time, like you climb the cliffs one rock at a time. You will slowly, ever so slowly, progress. You must focus on the process, and the healing power of time will find you, free you. Then one day you'll look back and see—you're across the river, you're on top of the cliffs, you're there! The view will be like nothing you could have imagined. And you'll look back to the other bank, back to the foot of the cliffs, and the place you started will be so far away you won't be able to see your tears on the ground where they fell when you first started, afraid and alone, thinking you could never make it. Take that first step, Little Yucca. I've been looking everywhere for you—you must climb the cliffs before I can find you again.

But I'm right here, Yellowjacket.

No, you're not, you're lost. You must find yourself. Start climbing, start now, Little Cliffrose.

Coyote Yellowjacket is gone once again, gone when I need him most, as usual.

I study my road map, find the words Stock Tank. Usually such words on a map mark a spot with corrugated metal tanks, more often than not rusted out and shot full of holes. But who knows, you might luck out and find enough water to fill up a radiator boiled dry or even a canteen drank dry, if you didn't mind moss and wigglers.

In some places, like down in Navajo Land, stock tanks are filled by windmills, water pumped by wind power from deep aquifers. Sometimes it's hauled in by water truck, or, more rarely, fed by "tank rains," what my Navajo friends call rain that falls so hard and stiff that it quickly fills stock tanks. A gift from the sky, but a gift sometimes accompanied by one of the desert's most powerful and dynamic forces, the flashflood.

The flashflood is the water that gives character to the land—like the creases in Cleo's face—that molds the ravines of Washerwoman Wash north of Radium, carves the fluted walls of Little Wildhorse Canyon in the San Rafael. Takes you to a swift death if you're careless enough to not notice the black clouds miles away in the distance. Even if it's not raining where you are, caution is the better part of wisdom.

Out here, in this high desert, I have yet to see a windmill, and stock tanks out here are rare, though the flashfloods aren't, coming in summer and early fall, sometimes running deeper than the arroyos want them to—when it rains that is, only when it rains.

The Stock Tank on my map is only a mile or so away, so Willy and I decide to go take a look. Might find some Indian artifacts, for springs were as important then as now.

We wind and bounce our way across red Entrada sandflats into an abyss of red and purple siltstones that spiral their way up until we top out on a small mesa. I can see forever, and down below is something shining in the sun—must be Stock Tank. Buddy Blue and I jump out, sliding our way down.

Everything is parched around the dried-up spring that some stockman once trained to go into a long corrugated metal watering tank. A series of jury-rigged pipes are wired together, rust hanging from each connection. A dried-up cottonwood skeleton speaks hoarsely of better times, scratching against the tank in the breeze, clutching for water. Makes me thirsty.

It's been years now with no rain, and it isn't much better in the mountains. There, scattered wild turkeys that once flocked together now wander, dazed, the creeks dry or meager trickles barely enough to wet grizzled feet, difficult to drink from without bending low to the ground. And in Green River, Radium, Catalpa Town, where the water still comes freely, mysteriously, from spigots and faucets, some unspoken instinct makes people guard it, take care, recycling dishwater onto thirsty heirloom roses that have flourished for over fifty years.

This is the One-Hundred Year Drought, people say with awe in their voices, an unspoken hint that it might not end, the kind that comes every hundred years. Hadn't the Anasazi, those ancient people much more adapted to this desert, people with no faucets, no spigots, hadn't they suffered 30 years of this, until finally the last of them fled?

Enough of Stock Tank. I want to go find the weird beaked figures on the map, near Johnny's ranch.

I climb back up the hill to where old Willy sits with door still hanging open, beckoning me to get back in and go somewhere cooler. We drive on until we come to an old weathered wooden sign with hand-painted letters in faded white, "Taylor Ranch, 2 miles."

Turning onto the sandy ranch road, I soon spot a grove of cottonwoods, and we stop at a little shady spot in the trees at the edge of a stream. This must be Willow Creek, aptly named, for its far side is edged with a heavy stand of coyote willows. These waters come from elsewhere, some place the drought hasn't yet discovered.

I look around while Buddy takes a dip in the cool water, which appears to be only a foot or so deep. It's pooled deeper under big cottonwoods, massive gnarled trees with big heavy drooping limbs, one giant bent into a U-shape, short trunk now kissing the ground that nurtured it.

The water undoubtedly comes from the mountain range far in the distance that's home to Coffeepot Peak. I can barely make out distant turrets and ridges through the haze.

A cowtrail wanders out through the thick willows and sumac, and Buddy tells me there are indeed cattle nearby, his ears pointed forward and his eyes with that wily look that cowdogs have when near stock. At a bellow in the distance, Buddy gets a wild grin on his face, but stays obediently at my side.

This has to be the place—the Taylor map reads, "Cross creek at first cottonwood grove." But how does one get across the creek and then through the willows? The creek banks here are too steep to cross in a vehicle, and those banks also hold deep eddies and pools. Walking along the creek, I soon discover an old plank bridge, timbers covered with rusted-out tin nailed down to protect the wood.

I walk out onto the planking, but it sways too much for my taste, and I know Willy wouldn't have the courage to cross it. Where, then? I continue down the creek and find that it soon widens out, the banks becoming negotiable, and I see where an old road crosses at a natural crossing, the water only six inches or so deep.

I get Willy, and we drive down the bank of the wide stream, dip into its rocky bottom, spin out, and speed back up, leaving narrow tire marks on the banks. For a moment I thought I could feel quicksand in the creek, a patch where there wasn't any rocks. It would be hard for Willy to lie down and roll if we got stuck, standard advice for anyone caught in quicksand.

Now on the other side, the faint road breaks through the willow thicket and parallels the wash, and we follow, winding around for a slow quarter mile. Another half mile away, I can see where the stream closes in, clutched tight by canyon walls. Pulling out the map, an arrow points into the narrows with the words, "Go through here."

The two-track ends at a turn-around where the wash emerges from buff-white Navajo sandstone walls. "This'll do," I tell Bud, parking Willy and taking out the food box. "This will be a great camp, lots of water. Let's call it Dandy Camp. We can base out of here and explore this whole area at our leisure, then go swimming in this stream, right here in the desert. Let's have a little lunch, then go see what we can find, little Buckaroo."

Buddy wags his tail, looking back as if wondering if the cattle will fare OK without him. I take shelter from the sun in the shade under a juniper, which must be a good idea, as a small single-leaf ash has done the same thing, growing steady and green, the only deciduous species of tree in this redrock desert.

An old fire ring speaks of late night fires under a desert sky, a sky filled with wood sparks floating until they look like they'll touch stars deep in the heavens. In the cold ashes is a brown glass bottle, flattened like a piece of mica, melted by heat. Must've been a pinion fire, pinion wood burns hot, burns in degrees Redrock instead of Fahrenheit or Celsius. Another ancient juniper stands near the firepit, half-dead, part of its branches hacked off for firewood.

Buddy Blue dips again in Willow Creek, shakes, rolls in the sand, scratches a hole in the sandy shade next to me, turns around several times, then lies down and starts licking his paws. A small dust devil comes along and, seeing Buddy, shakes the tree, asking if it too can rest a while, but changes its mind and moves on.

Rommel's Desert Rats in the Sahara discovered that covering your body with clothing like an Arab Bedouin keeps the sweat on your skin, cooling you off. Often such clothing was black. Ravens also wear black, their feathers absorbing heat, creating a circulatory effect that causes the blood to cool.

Finally, I get my pack ready: canteen, flashlight, matches, extra food, camera, notebook, everything we'll need for a long afternoon. I take off my boots, tie the shoestrings together and hang them around my neck, as we'll have to wade through the narrows. As we walk to the creek, I turn and look back to see Willy's windshield shining in the sun, calling us back, fearful of being left, fear of abandonment. "We'll be back by dark," I say. Buddy turns to see who I'm talking to.

The water comes up to my knees, getting my jeans wet. It's cool and refreshing, and I use a thick willow stick for balance. We soon pass through the narrows.

And now, suddenly, a different world—a land of pinkish-red fins and domes and hidden gardens, and the further I walk up the creek, the deeper and wilder this world becomes.

Willow Creek gurgles, happy to be here, free. The sound of captive water is different from that of wild water, for water flowing through an irrigation ditch is very different from free-flowing water. One can sleep to the sweet sound of a stream, its roiling loud bubbling and splashing, but channel that same flow through a concrete ditch between concrete walls and the sound will torture you through the night. It resonates differently, has a regularity to it that never changes.

I take the map from my pocket: "Big fin with double cedar tree in pocket on top about 1/2 mile after narrows—bear right and follow big wash to tiger wall, weird beaked figures around corner."

The weather's perfect, cool, sky the color of Charlie's blue eyes, cottonwood bark the color of his hair. All is quiet, and as I walk, I recall another time, a time with Charlie, over in the canyons near Radium, where the deepest blue sky butted up to gold canyon rims. We were hiking up canyon under a slight breeze, surrounded by dull golden-red sandstone with charcoal bands here and there. It was autumn.

Four ravens circled high above the canyon, riding thermals and playing, their wings folded back, making throaty calls as they flew, wings out, wings in. Charlie called them "Corvus Quatro."

"What the hell does Corvus Quatro care about the Cold War?" Charlie asked. One of his buddies, Hubert, had just got out of military prison and come home to Radium a few days before. First thing Charlie and Hub did was go to the 66 Club and get drunk, where, according to Charlie, Hub had entertained everyone with top-secret stories about the Yucca Flat Test Site over in Nevada.

In June of 1957, Hub had been part of a squad that sat in a five-foot-deep trench near a big test shot, awaiting an Atomic Bomb test called Shot Diablo, a seventeen-kiloton bomb perched atop an illuminated 500-foot tower. The shot had misfired, so the troops got to try it again later, this time with a seventy-four-kiloton device called Shot Hood that didn't misfire, the squad hiding in a trench only four-thousand yards from the thousand-foot tower. Shot Hood was six times the size of Little Boy, the Hiroshima bomb.

Hub had planned to be a lifer in the Marines, but after the test he decided instead to go AWOL. Part of the trench had collapsed on him and several others during the blast, and he nearly suffocated. He had his gas mask ripped off by his buddies as they rescued him.

"I breathed in all the radioactive dust coming off that ungodly dust storm," he told Charlie after he got out of the Marine brig. "And I don't care what they told us, that we were heroes, doing this to save the world from the godless Communists, we were nothing but a bunch of damned guinea pigs, and we knew it. Grown men, crying like babies in that trench. We were sitting with our heads on our knees, eyes closed, covered with our hands, down in the trench, and we could still see the blast. Then they told us over a loudspeaker to stand up and watch the fireball, and you wanna talk about something godless, whoever created that monster was evil incarnate. We found out later the main reason they'd put us out there was to see if troops would panic when they were that close to the Bomb. They exposed us to all that, lied and told us it was perfectly safe, just to see if we'd panic."

Corvus Quatro winged overhead, dipped and floated, spun, played. I remembered a quote from the British writer Arthur Koestler about the Atomic Bomb: "Hitherto man had to live with the idea of death as an individual; from now onward mankind will have to live with the idea of its death as a species."

"Hub still in jail?" I asked.

"Prob-ly," Charlie answered, slowly. Hub had got in a fight with a WWII veteran that night at the 66 Club and ended up in the county jail. He'd just got out of the Marine brig, he hadn't even been home to see his parents yet.

High above where Charlie and I rested, high in the canyon's western rim, was an abandoned doghole mine, maybe uranium or vanadium, maybe copper. A huge rock, once part of the rim, now fallen into the wash, held a white arrow someone had painted that pointed up to the mine as if to say, "Behold, the works of man."

The last few gold leaves clung to the single-leaf ash along the canyon bottom, contrasting with red squawbush, orange grasses, and black varnish across the flat surfaces on the canyon walls.

Charlie's old beat-up guitar was slung easy across his shoulder, riding on his back. When we stopped, he'd swing the guitar around to play. I remember him leaning against a rock next to a small clump of golden rabbitbrush, the notes singing out to canyon walls, high and clear like a harp, sweetly, gaining volume and returning through the clear air in harmonies like the colors in a rainbow.

Then out of nowhere—crash! A big rock fell in the distance, down canyon, and we could hear the sickening bounce as it smashed against a wall, landing with a final thud.

Charlie shook his head, a grin on his face. "Guess somebody's trying to tell me sumthin'." He put the guitar down and pulled a smashed paper sack out of his jacket pocket and proceeded to extricate something gooey from it.

"What's that?" I asked.

"Crispy marshmallow goodie, want some?"

"Where'd you get that? Don't tell me you made it."

"No, Mona gave me a batch the other day."

"Mona! You mean the waitress at the 66 Club? I thought she was mad at you."

"Mona's always mad at me. She loves me."

"Mona? How do you know?"

"She's always mad at me."

Corvus Quatro cawed, and I gazed high above canyon rim, shading my eyes with my hand, squinting into sun. Turning back, I saw Charlie was gone. He soon came out from behind a rock, zipping up his pants.

"Shakin' hands with the poor and unemployed," he said, giving me a grin. "But not unemployable," he winked.

The breeze lifted, and a few faltering cottonwood leaves found their longed-for freedom, drifting high into the blue sky, only to find themselves soon tossed to the ground. But listen! Above, a droning sound echoed through the canyon. Fighter planes! They must be training. The planes couldn't be seen, the arc of sky above the canyon too narrow to contain them.

"Noisy bastards!" Charlie said in disgust. He now picked up his guitar again, and the music of a Hank Williams' song echoed on the jet contrails.

Why don't you love me like you used to do?
Why do you treat me like a worn out shoe?
My hair's still curly and my eyes still blue.
Why don't you love me like you used to do?

"Hey, Chin, did you know that your ancestors can be sealed into the Mormon Church after they're dead, whether they wanna be or not?"

"They wouldn't be called ancestors if they were alive, Charlie," I replied sarcastically.

"No way nobody better try to do that to me after I'm dead."

I asked, "Well, what church do you want to be prayed into?"

"The Church of the Holy Bullshitters," he grinned, then added, pointing to colored bands of minerals on the canyon wall above him, "Look! Ice cream, like orange sherbet, grape agate. I want some of this banded sandstone to carve cars." He picked his guitar back up, walked over under the big wall of the canyon and sang, "Joshua fit the battle of Jericho, Jericho, Jericho..."

A car frame, probably 1930s vintage with its rounded back window, lay askew in the wash, along with a rusted back axle and an old metal bedframe. I wandered over to examine it as Charlie started wailing in a voice that sounded like a little kid's, "And the walls came tumblin' down."

Buddy shakes, getting me wet. I've put my boots back on and left the creek, and we're a half-mile past the narrows when the big fin with the double cedar tree on top comes into view. Here, we're supposed to bear right and follow a wide wash until we come to a tiger wall, a wall streaked with desert varnish.

It's warming up. Way hotter than usual for this time of year, and how could it have been snowing just yesterday? We're now at a much lower altitude here in the canyons, but it seems like it's suddenly unseasonably warm.

We walk on. I think about college, wonder what my friends are doing back in civilization. How could I ever explain my life to them, graduates who are now changing the world with important jobs as attorneys and doctors? It's hard to describe, this freedom, Coralee's sweet wild freedom. But even when the cold wind blows, bites right through you, or when a hot wind saps your strength, here is where I want to be. Forever.

I slip into that mental rhythm that comes when you're alone, a sort of undisciplined Zen-like feeling. Maybe that's the real reason I want to be out here, total irresponsibility, no raison d'être. Buddy Blue and Willy will take care of me.

This pale pink stone with a bit of white against blue sky, this yellow-green of rabbitbrush, it all reflects the pure glory of God. Cloud remnants float in the distance along smooth dark rims.

Quickly, I friction-climb a short forty-degree slab of slickrock that juts into the wash, just to see if I can see out a bit. I make it almost to the top, but there's a bit of loose rock underfoot, and I slide back down into the wash, barely managing to keep my balance, like an out-of-control skier. Life's like walking across tippy rocks, across loose scree—you don't want to stay in one place too long.

Now we reach the tiger wall, yellow sandstone streaked with black stripes of manganese oxide, desert varnish. Holding my breath, I round the corner where the wash has swept sandstone into a sinuous curve. The strange beaked figures should be near, and I feel tension, anticipation. Could I be near Davidson's Bird Panel?

Around the curve, a large shallow alcove hides in the cliffwall, draped with some of the finest and blackest desert varnish I've ever seen. It's so dark that I initially mistake it for a cave, but the alcove is only a foot or two at its deepest, more of a simple indentation in the wall. A perfect place for rock art, the perfect artists' palette.

But there's no rock art, nothing. Not even a scratch. The wall must look like the canyons did before the Anasazi got art. Pristine. But the map had said the strange beaked figures were here, so maybe there's another site nearby. I walk down the wash another quarter mile, scanning the walls. More nothing.

Then, as I turn and start back up the wash, wondering if the map could be wrong, I see them. Indeed, strange beaked figures, and strange isn't really the adjective I would used, I would say weird.

There, standing against the far wall, just around the bend in the wash, three large hoodoos, a trio of thin beaked figures probably ten feet tall, looking like they're ready to walk back up the wash alongside me. First glance startles me, they look so real.

The figures are thin, with duck heads, just like lots of rock art I've seen, but these couldn't have been made by human hand. My presumptions led me to think the map referred to rock art, but here, wind and frost have displayed their own artistic talents and humor. Three blind and stone-deaf duck heads, hoodoos lost forever in this hidden and remote Utah canyon, tall thin spires of rock.

At first I'm disappointed, my quest has loomed so large, but soon I drop into the sand, laughing. Buddy runs up to see what's going on. The absurdity of my hunt has finally hit me, surfacing full-blown from the shallows where it's been lurking for some time. I hear Leland's words again, out at the Radium Queen.

I didn't know there was nuthin' to study about that stuff. What do you do with it once you've found it?

So much anticipation, searching, meticulously photographing and recording everything I see, every scribble on stone. If Charlie were here, he'd say it again:

Who gives a rat's ass about a bunch of old graffiti? Now rocks, that's different, go look for rocks. Rocks can bring you power and wealth.

Reminds me of the sign out at his mine:

> *Tengo Dinero Uranium Mine*
> *Power from the earth*
> *Wealth for the people*
> *All regulations complied with.*

Buddy and I continue on. Cresting the top of a fin, I'm suddenly in a secret garden, a depression filled with a large pinion tree, several ancient thick twisty junipers, and cliffrose in bloom, the sweet scent nearly stifling in its thickness. In the sand lies a stone knife blade, what looks to be a perfect Anasazi piece in a shade of tawny gray, its finely honed thin serrations still able to cut, even though the entire thing bears a fine crust of yellow-white patina. Next to it is an even more perfect atlatl point, though cracked in two.

Now looking across the back of the fin, I see down into a convoluted twisting drainage, distant dark cliffs against white. The last vestiges of snow from the big storm have melted off the north sides of the cliffs, leaving long wet streaks like desert varnish. Light plays through the clouds, across the sandstone whalebacks, leaving an inner glow as it moves, dissipating in the tight deep valleys between the huge rounded sandstone ridges, where bobcats sleep in their dens, waiting for the glove of darkness.

Here there be dragons. Abandon all hope, ye who enter here.

Has this wonderland ever been explored? No sane person would run cattle here, and who else would come out here, except a lunatic sun-struck archaeologist? I wonder if Johnny's ever been out in these depths.

I decide to return to old Willy, tomorrow Buddy and I can come back and spend all day here wandering, and since Willow Creek flows nearby we won't have to worry about water. I feel giddy with the prospect of this new exploration, my search for rock art forgotten for now. Here there be dragons. Abandon all expectations, ye who enter here. Here there indeed be dragons, I will soon discover.

And all those stories of long-lost love,
Written on paper-thin sand,
Holy flashflood has stolen away,
Into Mesozoic land.

6
Oh Be Joyful: The Big Empty

The nights were soft and sweet in Radium, with the scent of lilacs hugging the air in spring. Later, when summer had stripped all the purple and white blooms with its heat, the scent of sagebrush on the outskirts of town floated through the night air after an evening's rain.

Radium was the center of the universe, yet I somehow instinctively knew, even as a kid, that the world held more.

Standing on the outskirts of town on a summer night, looking up into the deep sky, stars radiated from the black depths, sparkling like a million points of light on a piece of mica held against the sun. Stars that make you feel tiny, isolated, insignificant, alone. Not like in the city, where the night sky is just a dream. And out there, on the edge of that little town, there was no escape.

Here, on the edge of eternity, you made your own escape. You might try to stay inside, but the night would draw you out, no matter how hard you tried to forget it. Then you had to do something, once you were out there, something to try to make sense of it all, so you sometimes walked around town, up one side of the street, down the other, huge mulberry trees neatly lining the Mormon streets built wide so two spans of oxen pulling a wagon could turn around.

And sometimes you could hear the tiny high-pitched cry of bats as they flitted crazily on translucent wings after insects, and when they weren't out and it was really, really quiet, sometimes you could hear the soft padding of deep sadness in the night.

Sometimes you could glimpse someone else's life as you walked by the big houses, and you'd try to imagine what it was like to live in the white house with the big gables and the wide window that framed a piano and a leather sofa opposite green-flowered chairs.

For a brief moment you'd glimpse a tall thin man walking through the room, carrying a cup in one hand and a book in the other. What was his life like, was he happy? Did he have a wife and kids? Maybe he worked at the local bank, or maybe he was a teacher. In any case, he seemed unaware of the night sky hanging there, just above his roof, hanging with its message of insignificance, blissfully unaware that his life will be too short, no matter how long he lives, that there are no answers to the questions that plague those who watch the night sky, questions about God and love and why.

Sometimes, in the thick of summer night, I would slip out my bedroom window, after my mom was asleep, pause beneath the ominous shadow of the cliff behind the house, then head out, swift, sure, down the road, across the quiet highway, on into the darkness of the huge cottonwood stands near the river.

These same old trees had silently watched the last of the Utes as they forlornly, defiantly, rode their ponies to their new reservation, leaving their traditional home, trees with trunks huge and corrugated, heavy with inward water, trees that I loved in the daylight but that spooked me in the dark.

I'd skirt the big cottonwood stands, senses alive with what might be a cougar tracking me, a quiet snapping of tiny twig. Then on to the railroad tracks that led the length of the valley and to what seemed to be safety, those rails that led my steps without chance of getting lost. The metal shone in the moonlight, stretching onward forever, following the path of the lost Utes westward.

Walking a single rail, arms out for balance, occasional nighthawk gliding above me, I found my way to the edge of downtown Radium, such that it was. There I left the rail and walked the sidewalk in front of stores eerily silent, secretive, holding their treasures hidden from night, perhaps now tended by ghosts who floated around, dusting the glass bowls, the bolts of colorful cloth, the tiny painted calico cats with "Made in Japan" painted on their bases. I hated the emptiness of the manmade by night, would almost rather take my chances in the cottonwood groves.

At the edge of town, near the old stone armory, across from the bowling alley, sat the Rock Garden, Charlie's rock shop, tiny, the last business before the town just seemed to fade away into tumbleweeds and nothingness, a gully blocking the way of progress. And there next to the gully, surrounded by a thick screen of tall palm grass, sat Charlie's old Airstream trailer, its silvery metal skin shimmering in the starlight. Charlie had no electricity, so he read by candlelight. More often than not I would see him sitting on the step of the little trailer, his tan felt cowboy hat all I could make out, and I'd hear a soft guitar strum that sometimes would even sound like music.

The first time I walked to Charlie's by night I felt strange, a bit like those spooks I imagined in the shops, and I didn't let on I was there. I just stood in the shadows for a long time, watching the faint shadow that was Charlie, listening to his sweet guitar in the dark. I felt melancholy, alone, standing in the shadows, on the edge of some black chasm with no name, no meaning, no reason, outcast, lost.

Charlie's self-containment drew me like a moth to a flame, made my own sense of loss even more profound. And I would stand there, transfixed by the soft music, feeling sad and happy all at once.

I didn't realize it, but I was transfixed by Charlie's strong sense of who he was, by what I thought was his strength, direction. I would stand in the shadows, drawn by all this, thinking it was Charlie who drew me, mistaking all this for some kind of attraction to him—and eventually, perhaps mistaking this for love.

After a while, Charlie would go inside, and I could tell he'd gone to bed. Standing in the shadows, alone, I felt like I was even more on the edge of nothingness and would flee, running back down the streets where the ghosts tended the stores, then on back down the railroad tracks, skirting the trees, and finally back to the window that led into my bedroom, all the while wanting to cry out, to cry, to somehow run from the pain, the isolation, the emptiness within.

Sometimes I just wanted to be Charlie, to live in the little Airstream, to have my days defined by the rock shop, my evenings defined by playing the guitar and then going to bed. His simplicity of purpose was appealing.

I tried to stay away, but I soon found myself making the journey nightly, and when I'd try to stay home I felt confined, claustrophobic, restless.

One night I stumbled and fell, cutting my knee. I could feel blood—warm, sticky, running down inside my pant leg where my jeans now had a gaping hole. I was near Charlie's when it happened, I could hear his guitar.

I called out, "Charlie, you there? It's Chinle."

"What the hell! Chinle?"

"Yeah, Charlie, hey, I need help, I cut my leg."

"What the hell you doing out here in the middle of the night. Can't you see it's dark?"

Now at the trailer, I reached out and touched his shoulder. He took my hand, leading me inside, where he got a flashlight and examined my leg.

"Holy cow, gal, you've got a cut, it's bleeding like a sunuvagun. What the hell..."

I replied, "Couldn't sleep, wanted to get outta the house, decided to just walk around, that's all, just something to do. I tripped on a rock and just went down, dunno why."

"Dunno why? For God's sake, I can tell you why, girl, it's dark, that's why. I'm amazed you got this far without killing yourself. Don't you know it's not safe alone in the dark? You're nuts!"

"Just shutup, Charlie, just shutup. I'm a free person, and I can come and go whenever and wherever I damn well please. Now would you please just give me a wet cloth or something before I bleed to death?"

"OK, OK, here, hold this sock on it as tight as you can. I don't think it's too serious. Must sting like hell, huh?" Charlie put his arm around my shoulders. "Does your mom know you're out running around at night like a wild coyote?"

"No."

"Good thing. I'm gonna have to drive you home. Can you walk a block or two so if I drop you off so we don't wake her up? I sure don't want to get myself in trouble."

"It's already stopped bleeding, I'll walk home."

"No, Chin, you shouldn't do that. Look, let me make you a cup of hot chocolate, then I'm going to drive you home."

Charlie struck a match, lighting the little gas burner on his propane stove, setting a pan of water to boil. He then lit a candle, his hair and eyebrows brushed copper with red light from the flame.

"I usually have a cup myself before I go to bed. You know, old Indian alarm clock, makes you get up early and pee, keeps me from sleepin' in. Now tell me why you walked clear across town in the dark to come see me."

"I told you, I couldn't sleep and I wanted to go for a walk, so I just ended up here, no reason much at all."

"OK, OK, but you shouldn't be out at night, too damn dangerous. You might get noticed by the wrong person."

"Nobody out this time of night, and I'm not stupid, Charlie, I sure don't walk down the main road."

"How did you get here?"

"I came down the railroad tracks."

"How can you see in the dark?"

"I can't."

"Chinle, Chinle, Chinle, you're nuts. Why do you want to run around at night?"

Charlie hands me a cup of hot chocolate, then sits down beside me on the trailer's little naugahide built-in couch. It's cozy, warm, and I don't ever want to go home.

"I want to live like you do, Charlie."

"Chin, you don't know what you're saying. Trade a nice house with running water, a shower, lights, room to turn around, for this little pile of junk?"

"No, it's freedom, Charlie, You can just get up in the morning and go someplace new anytime you want. Freedom."

"Well, all that sounds swell, but I think I'd rather have running water, and I get tired of going outside to piss in the bushes. What's up, Chin, what's bothering you, to come over here this late?"

"I can't explain it, Charlie, I just feel restless."

"It's 'cause you're about out of school, Chin, then you can do whatever you want. You can run away and be free. What are you going to do then, go to college?"

"I can't, Charlie, I don't have the money."

"Maybe you can get some kind of help. You know, I went with help from the company my dad worked for, Mobile. They helped out a number of their employee's kids, me especially, since my dad was killed on the job. You can figure it out if you want to go bad enough. What would you study?"

"Archaeology."

"No kidding? I figured maybe geology."

"No, archaeology."

"Sounds good, Chin. But let me warn you, college is the opposite of being free."

"Yeah, but it leads to being able to take care of yourself, which is freedom, isn't it?"

"I guess, but you can darn well take care of yourself already, don't need no schoolin'. Which reminds me, I've been meanin' to ask you if you're gonna keep workin' for me through the summer."

"Sure, I guess." Now I feel warmth, happiness, the throb in my knee forgotten.

"Good, I was hoping you would, kiddo. You're a darn good worker, and I like having you around. You're smart, you know, but don't let it go to your head." He laughs, lightly smacking me on the shoulder.

Candlelight flickers on the blonde-wood walls of the tiny trailer, wraps around the large piece of fool's gold on Charlie's tiny side table, reflects back onto itself.

"Look, Chin, I know you're out runnin' around at night because you're unhappy. You need some friends, kids with your own interests."

"Well, when you meet someone who likes wandering out in the rocks, send them my way, Charlie. Most of my friends just want to get married or get jobs. And I'm not a kid anymore, I'm almost 18."

"Yeah, I know. But that's Radium for you, no concept of the outside world, damn Mormon culture, get married and have a gazillion kids. But you, Chin, you're gonna amount to something someday, damn straight. You need to go to college, you're too smart to stay in Radium. You should go over to Colorado, it's a lot more open over there, you know, you don't have to be a damned Saint or even a part-time Saint. Look, I'm gonna contact some of my college buddies and see if they have any ideas about how to get you some school money."

"When you went to college, Charlie, what did you want to be? A rock shop owner?"

"No, hell no, I sure as hell didn't study my ass off to run a cheesy rock shop. I have a degree in petroleum geology and I'm gonna get back into it one of these days. I worked right outta school for Mobile down in Oklahoma, that was part of the education agreement, but I kept gettin' into it with the high-up muckity mucks, and I got myself fired. I got a big mouth, so they said."

"How long you been out of college?"

"Only just two years is all. You may think I'm an old geezer, but I'm only 24, Chin, just six years older than you, though not much wiser, but at least I ain't out wanderin' around in the dark tryin' to get eaten by a cougar. Did you know there's been one sighted down at the Jungle for several days in a row now? That's that thicket right at the edge of the railroad tracks, right where that stand of cottonwoods is."

"I know the Jungle, we played there a lot when I was a kid. I'm more scared of being in town, Charlie. Those old stores feel weird when I walk by them. At least cougars are alive."

"Yeah, I hate Radium at night, I won't even go to the rock shop. It's a spooky place, don't ask me why."

"Too much history, too many ghosts."

"Damn straight. Too much civilization. Too many dead radium miners. Look, Chin, I'm with you. If I could figure out a way to make a livin', and it wouldn't even have to be much of one, I'd be out in the wilds. I'm like you, I just want to wander around and look at rocks. I'm thinkin' of closin' down the store and headin' out lookin' for uranium, maybe at the end of the summer. Big money there, and I think I know a better method for prospecting than what most of the bums are usin'."

I feel a mixture of chill and excitement, chill that Charlie could leave, excitement at the leaving, the freedom. "What would you do?" I ask.

"I'd prospect by geology, I got a damn degree I need to put to use somehow, all that crap clutterin' up my brain. Everyone else is prospecting by Geiger counter and scintillator and voodoo. All they're gettin' is blisters and sunstroke and snake bites. Not me. I know all about strikes, and I ain't talkin' about strike-it-rich strikes, I'm talkin' about geological strikes. You know, a strike fault, where the strike's parallel to the rock strata, where uranium collects. But hey, kiddo, we need to get you home. How's your knee doin'?"

We sit in silence for a moment, then I hobble out of the trailer and Charlie helps me into his old Scout, drives through town, and stops a block from my house. I get out, and he leans out the window.

"Hey Chin, go straight home now, OK? And tell you what, I really enjoyed our talkin', and hows about us gettin' together this weekend? I'll pick you up about eight Saturday morning if you want to go out lookin' for rocks with me. We'll make a day of it. I need to find some Moki marbles for the shop. Make sure your mom says it's OK. Bring a lunch and a water jug. See you then, and no more night rambling, alright? I'll have to change your name to Ramblin' Rose."

I stand, listening to Charlie's old Scout rolling down the street until it fades into the sound of mulberry leaves rustling in the breeze. A new feeling sweeps over me like moonlight as I walk the rest of the way home. I crawl in the window and soon fall into a restless sleep, dreaming of mountain lions as yellow as carnotite, tawny like yellowcake shining in radioactive sunlight, cougars that fade into cottonwood groves as Charlie holds me tight.

Howdy!

Damn! Is that you again, Yellowjacket? Wow! You look great in that cowboy hat. Where're your spurs, Cowboy Coyote?

Don't get sarcastic, Little Rabbit, or I'll have you for dinner.

The desert sky is immense, hung low with a million distant stars. I long for high mountains, for graceful aspen, delicate snow, happy creeks following their love of gravity.

Go away, Yellowjacket. I want to be alone.

You loved Charlie, Little Rabbit, but he betrayed you. Love is a gift. Take it back. Give it to me instead, I deserve it!

I can't take it back. It was unconditional.

He betrayed that gift. You cannot trust him again.

Yellowjacket, what will become of me?

Silly Rabbit! You will flourish, you will find an even deeper love, that love that you hold within yourself, God's love! You will find that you cannot betray yourself, Little Rabbit.

I miss him, Yellowjacket. He was my heart, my friend.

Little Silly Rabbit! He was nothing more than a foil! He reflected back your essence. You were partly in love with what he made you see in yourself! Charlie took your strength, you helped define him. Take it back! Give it to yourself now! You need it. He will go on, he doesn't realize what he's lost, but someday, Little Rabbit, he will mourn it, just as you do.

I stand high on a ridge, held to earth only by tufted tundra. Low clouds part, and I'm surrounded by ragged sky and ragged cliffs, cliffs protecting earth, a barrier to black space. I see a hint of stars in the zenith.

Coyote, how could he be so cold, just turn it all off, turn away?

Little Rabbit, it doesn't matter. He's Charlie, he doesn't stand on the edge of eternity like you do. You see time and miracles where he only sees wealth and power. You projected into him your own depth. It was never there, Little Rabbit. And now it's time to take it back.

Yellowjacket, once, long ago, I was hiking alone in the mountains, up a winding trail in a narrow valley with aspen on one side and a stream on the other. It was called Bear Gulch. I felt so protected, so happy. I walk softly, Coyote, and as I came around a bend in the trail I startled a coyote. Was it you?

No, no, Silly Rabbit, that was Tawny Vagabond Coyote, my sister. She's very hard to surprise, though, you must have been very quiet indeed. Few walk so quietly as to startle coyotes. Few treasure the earth's reality as you do. It's a Gift.

Charlie has it. He loves beauty.

No, Silly Rabbit, Charlie sees beauty, but he doesn't have the Gift. He sees it, but it doesn't surround him, it doesn't permeate into his very essence like it does you. You must understand that you read the old writings for a reason. It's now time to move along, Little Dogie, forget Charlie, and follow your Gift.

As I was out walking one morning for pleasure,
I spied a cowpuncher out riding alone.
His hat was thrown back and his spurs were a jinglin',
And as he approached he was singing this song:
Yippie ki yi yay, get along lil dogie,
It's your misfortune and none of my own.
Yippie ki yi yay, git along lil dogie,
You know Colorado will be your new home.

At forest's edge, aspen bark turns pink in fading sun. A cool wind blows, filled with wild mountain distance. But now, mountains turn brown, quaking green aspen leaves turn brown, desert returns. I gaze long into the glowing embers of stars, mirrors of Yellowjacket's deep eyes. Once again, I see his sister, jumping as I silently come up behind her and reach out to catch her bushy yellow tail, quickly disappearing into thick mountain mahogany. Someday, in spring, I will return to see the delicate yellow mountain mahogany in bloom.

Buddy Blue and I are back at Dandy Camp. It's late evening, and the rocks have melted from pink back into a more mundane salmon, Buddy listening as coyotes yip in the distance. I wonder if he can understand what they're saying. Are they dancing around some coyote campfire, drinking yucca mescal, throwing sticks in the air and catching them between their sharp teeth? Nearby, Willow Creek dances, happy, chattering, laughing, talking in a tongue known only to water.

Night falls, hawkmoth wings whir as they pollinate the yucca. The creek's chatter is louder. I strain to listen, strain to make sense, but it's the language, the syntax, the lexicon of water, understood only by water. I may glimpse that world by studying smooth river rocks, sandbars, eddies, but it will always be a foreign tongue.

If I could learn the syntax, the phonemes, the lexicon of Ute, Antonio's language, perhaps I could communicate with the Ute universe—but can I really without actually living in that universe, without dancing the Bear Dance, without drumming? I may understand the idea of riding the Ute war pony, but not until I ride in battle hearing Ute war cries do I understand fully.

And when I look to the night sky, I sometimes think I hear angels singing in their own mysterious tongue. What did the ancient Anasazi hear?

The coyotes have gone to bed, or more likely are out hunting rabbits and mice. Buddy has snoozed off, curled up in the cool sand. He wakes long enough to scratch himself, then falls back into his dream, leaving a pattern of dognail marks in the sand, a pattern that locks his movement in time.

I lean back and become absorbed by starlight. The more time I spend in the canyons, the more difficult it becomes to categorize things, and the universe becomes more and more complex, like language. The more lightning I see, the more nuances it has, the more colors, forms, shapes, as well as types of thunder. But eventually there comes to me a gestalt of lightning—how lightning fits in with the winds, the rain, how it lights up the world at night, how it interplays with danger, survival, wildfire. This gestalt becomes, through time, a kindred awareness of the natural world, and I'm no longer just an observer, I now understand the more atomic levels of lightning—as much as I ever dare to, anyway.

I try to learn the language of my senses, to touch my tongue-tip to the rocks to know if they're salty or full of sulphur. I hope that by the end of my journey I'll be able to sense a storm just over the horizon, smell distant water. Then, my fears will diminish, and I will walkabout, free.

But there will come a time when I must abandon all I know to journey into places I don't know, to do what I most fear. Until I have done this, I'll remain incomplete. It's the journey of a lifetime. I will pine and yearn and fail without it.

I must go down the river to those rose cliffs.

But first, Buddy Blue and I will begin our search for dragons, tomorrow.

Walking alone,
Under slickrock sky,
Raven calling,
Black wings fly,
Pungent sweet smell of pinion pine.
All the potholes are empty now,
Dry upon dry.
Will it ever end,
This long goodbye,
To sweet rain?

Last night is but a memory, and now Buddy and I have wandered far from old Willy, leaving behind the big fins of creamy white Navajo Formation and entering the Morrison Formation, dinosaur land.

Charlie and I spent lots of time in the Morrison, in its blues, greens, grays, looking for dinosaur bone to sell in the Rock Garden. I know I won't find any rock art here, as even the Indians avoided the dino graveyards, for here there be dragons.

I had another dream last night, a dream of Charlie. We were together again, and he was taking me out to a new place in Radium for dinner, a very exclusive place, he told me. We entered an anteroom where we had to fill out forms to be admitted. I'd never heard of such a thing, an application to eat in a restaurant?

I handed my forms to a tall fellow dressed in tie and black suit, hair cut short. Charlie laughed, couldn't stop laughing, and I realized I'd just applied for admission to the Mormon Church—we were in the anteroom of the Mormon stakehouse, their somewhat cryptic term for their local churches.

I smile, thinking of the play on words, just like the old crow jokes Gramps used to tell me, jokes so bad you groaned instead of laughing, jokes that made you laugh because they were so bad.

Buddy comes around, wanting to play, and I throw him a small piece of dinosaur bone, which he picks up and spits out, giving me a look of treachery. I study the cobbles and sand beneath my feet, the microcosms of color melting into the plantless austerity of the Morrison, land of extremes—extreme heat, extreme cold, extreme quiet, extreme solitude.

Turning and walking down the wash, the going gets easier, sand still damp from the last big storm. It's already getting hotter than a sunuvagun. Such are the vagaries of desert weather, as well as the starkness of the Morrison, where plants are only shimmering reflections.

Buddy Blue and I left Willow Creek behind earlier—it turned and went another direction, independent, following its own way. We're now at the mercy of a canteen, so we'll have to return to the creek before long.

My eyes catch a piece of color—carnelian agate. The washes often reveal what's high in the cliffs above, erosion carrying it downward. No petrified wood or dino bone here, just lots of agate. Agate and peace, sweet peace.

And something else, something hard to define, to articulate, a form of purity, the purity that comes from fire, the fire of Cougar Sun. The sense of peace that envelopes this place comes from nothingness, from lifelessness. Now a piece of white agate catches my eye. Picking it up, I see spots of blood-red color through its snowy opaqueness.

Pigeon-blood agate. Prized by collectors and jewelry makers—a translucent glaze of white, spotted with drops of ruby.

I lift my eyes and behold an entire field of pigeon-blood agate, shimmering ice laced with fresh splotches of blood in desert heat—and now, standing in the middle of all that agate is a coyote, its pure white coat dappled with red spots.

"You could be rich," it yips gleefully, then jumps into the air, twists, and disappears into a shimmering heatwave.

I walk on, Buddy close at my heels, the rising heat taking away his desire to explore for rabbits and lizards, or maybe he just knows there aren't any around.

Coming to a large bowl of mudstone, an old lakebed, I walk out onto it, sinking to my boot-tops in powder. Coyote tracks! I walk next to them, then I walk on top of them, turn and look behind me, taking immense satisfaction in obliterating them, happy with the deep tracks I'm leaving, even though the winds will soon come and take them away.

Now finding a perfectly smooth round piece of yellow agate, I finger it as I wander, a touchstone. I prefer its simplicity to the pigeon-blood. Simplicity is purity.

The smooth agate reminds me of Charlie, and I can hear his voice now, shouting from across a white stretch of ancient Morrison playa, "Liths! Gotta have liths or there ain't no bone, Chin." Now he's next to me with a handful of green clay that crumbles from his opened hand.

"See this atomic green clay? Get it wet and it sticks in your hands, slicker than bald tires on ice. Let's take some in the Scout. If we wanna get stuck we can put it under the wheels. It's bentonite, full of volcanic ash."

"Charlie, it's starting to sprinkle. Maybe we better get outta here," I reply.

He ignores me, picks up another gastrolith, a dinosaur gizzard stone, hands it to me.

"Lots of liths here in the Morrison. I've found them in piles, it looked like the dino disintegrated and left the pile of liths from its gizzard. This is one of the reasons paleontologists think dinos are related to birds, and some dinos like sauropods didn't have much by way of teeth, so they think they used gizzard stones to supplement their chewing. Did you ever notice that chickens don't have teeth? Anyway, don't you wonder how I got this lith so smooth?" he asks.

"If it's a lith, it was that way when you found it," I answer.

"It's not really a lith. I got it that way by worryin', carrying it in my pocket as a worrying stone. I worry all the time, you know. I worry about you, Chin," he grins.

We wander some more, until finally Charlie comes over and says, "Look at this one, it's a conglomerate." The stone looks like someone stuck pebbles of all colors together, yet it's improbably smooth.

I ask, "How do you know it's a lith and not just polished smooth by a river?"

"Cuz we're high up in the Morrison and this is dino land. Look at it closely—see how the little pockets aren't polished? The rivers and washes have sand that polishes the entire rock, even the little nooks and crannies. Liths don't have smooth little pockets 'cause they ground on each other in the dinosaur's gizzard and they were about all the same size."

He tosses the lith into a nearby wash, then bends down, takes a handful of the green clay beneath us. "Take a pinch of this dirt, Chin, try to mold it into a little ball, the more it sticks, the more clay is in it. When you're out in this country and you see blue clay, it has magnesium or copper. Pour a little water from your canteen on it—see how slimy it is? It's pure clay. You could make a pot out of it. Ever find any Indian pots made out of this stuff?"

Now, suddenly, like that pigeon-blood coyote, Charlie's gone, and I realize I'm fatigued from the heat. I sit down on the cobbled sand to rest, turn my back to the sun. Far in the distance rise ragged cliffs, like immense books in some giant's bookshelf, books with buff-gray spines—the Bookcliffs.

Suddenly, a sense of revulsion takes me. I long for mint-green aspen trees and soft breezes. Now the heat catches me up and eases me into a drowsiness, into sleep, sun high and distant, as if belonging to another planet.

I reach down, pick up a stick, write my name in the sand—Chinle.

Suddenly, from nowhere, foam, water saturated with wet red sand, waves drench the wash, taking my name away, removing it from the land. I hear a voice that sounds like Gramps, "You're not sleeping, Chinle, you're not dreaming. Get up, you need water, get back to Willy, get out of the sun."

I wake suddenly, headachy, hot sun drenching me like a wave of water. There's not a cloud in the sky, everything seems faded by the heat, horizon disappearing into a gray smoky haze. Buddy is lying in the shade of a nearby rock, panting.

"Time to get back, Bud, past time," I say, getting up. I take the canteen off my shoulder, drink long and deep, hold the cool metal against my forehead. Buddy is at my feet, tail drooping, and I give him a drink from the little tin cup I wear clipped to my belt. He drinks it all, wants more, so I refill the cup.

"We gotta get back, little Buddy Blue, let's get back to the creek and old Willy. We need shade, cool water, a stream, ice, watermelon, ice cream, popsicles, orange Knee High pop, a mountain glacier, you name it, anything cold." We head back up the ancient lakebed, back in the direction we came.

Walking slowly now, heat waves shimmering, I pause for a moment. The warmth envelopes me, and once again I'm back in Radium, college break, trying once again, always trying, trying.

Charlie looks as charming as ever, his smile pressed against the pillow. He's a charmer, handsome looks combined with a never-ending sense of sardonic humor. Everyone thinks he's mad, obsessed with striking it rich. But Charlie isn't the only mad U-boomer—guys like Joe and Sparky over at Temple Mountain—dogholers, mad dogs scratching holes into the ground, trying to dig up long-ago buried bones, dino bones filled with carnotite. Pure madness, the same madness that's engulfed Radium.

I can see Charlie's profile on the pillow next to me. He's sleeping on his back, lightly snoring, curls spilling onto his forehead, hair standing straight up where his head pushes against the pillow. An old worn-out bamboo curtain lends an exotic air to the room without really performing much function. Charlie's profile is backlit by the half-moon's light. Moon will soon set behind the rim, leaving millions of innocent stars stranded in the black night.

I reach out and touch Charlie where his white t-shirt sleeve encases the taut muscles of his sun-tanned arm. He moves in his sleep, his breath gently touching my face with a sweet musky odor.

"Where are you, Charlie?" I ask softly.

He turns onto his side and puts his arm around my shoulders, still sleeping. The light sweet smell of sweat draws me near him, and I finally feel myself drifting off to sleep, snuggled down between the blanket and his warmth. I savor his sweetness, the sanctuary of Charlie.

Morning sunlight glares through the window on the opposite wall, into my face, waking me. Charlie's gone. Across the bed, where Charlie slept, lies a Navajo blanket. I study it, it's a First Phase Chief's blanket with elegant white, red, and indigo stripes. Perfect, very old, and very rare. The kind the Navajo women wove many years ago for Ute, Pawnee, and Sioux chieftains. Its perfection and rich colors take my breath away.

Getting up, I find the note on the kitchen counter, by the coffee percolator, drops of black coffee spilled across the top:

Chin, gotta get back out while the weather's good. Take this old Navajo blanket, I bought it from a hard-luck character on Highway 666, the Highway of the Beast, on my way to Monticello.
Good luck next semester, kiddo. Charlie

Slip away, fly away, back onto that long highway, back to college, purpose, self, freedom.

Gramps once said that idolatry is when you put something between you and God, even if it's a person.

False sanctuaries.

My mouth is dry, and it's hard to swallow. I try to breathe through my nose, but can't while walking. It's now so hot that shade has lost its meaning. Sweat drips into my eyes, where no-see-ums cloud. I hear an owl calling in the distance and think vaguely that owls are supposed to call only in the dusk and darkness, not mid-day. To the Navajo, the owl is a harbinger of trouble, at least so says Antonio.

The path is now steep, with tiny loose rocks on the slickrock, like ballbearings. I touch my canteen, make sure the top is on tight so if I fall it won't ooze out and drain what little water I have left.

But now, a gift from God, a reprieve for a few moments as clouds float in front of the sun, passing too quickly. We're now back in the slickrock Navajo fins and whalebacks, and cloud shadow falls on the cliff wall in the canyon below, increasing the depth, and I can smell the depletion of my own salts from my body. To a yogi, the only self-directed way to die that's not considered suicide is to not eat, to starve oneself. Dying of thirst in the desert might be a much quicker, but possibly more difficult, way to go.

Distant rims and rocks take their turns in the shade as the clouds float on. Behind me, high and far away, a squall sets down on the flanks of Coffeepot Peak, bathing it in a haze of coolness, a concept so foreign it's unimaginable in this heat.

I'm totally on my own, there's no help out here, just me and Buddy. It's so totally still—then, suddenly a bottlefly, gone as quickly as my brain can register it, gone as quickly as a desired breeze, gone as quickly as Charlie.

The sand's too hot to touch. I don't know how Buddy can walk, his pads must be tough. Now the bottlefly is back, like a memory of lost love. Clouds bubble up behind distant Coffeepot Peak like the foam in a bathtub. It's better to have the water in you than in the canteen, so I finally drink the last, the metal still cool to the touch, all but a cupful for Buddy, who quickly laps it up.

I can feel my mind getting hazy, hard keeping to one thought. I wonder why some places have blackbrush thicker than others—maybe due to patterns of water flow. Now I see a dry falls, a pourover, rocks parted by water, where slickrock fin tilts into a deep chasm, drops into night, and I somehow know there's an arch down there, maybe from something I saw on Johnny's map.

To my right is a huge fin cradled by a deep crevasse, dropping into the canyon and that hidden unnamed arch. Coyote tracks push deep into the sand, crossed occasionally by newer packrat and lizard tracks, frozen in time, protected from wind by the high fins.

I stand, contemplating the slope's severity into where the arch hides—40 degrees, maybe 50. Loose rock is strewn on smooth slickrock, coils of red on tan like an old-fashioned swirl cake. Silence can be maddening or solace, depending on your state of mind. I've kept just enough water to wet my tongue.

I smell a faint odor like cat urine—yellow cat, mountain lion? Must be really fresh. Now I climb a steep rubble hill, painfully aware of my worn boot-soles, and on top, back to slickrock, the wonderful pleasure of walking on a smooth surface. Cold water calls me, waiting in Willow Creek, back at old Willy. I'll die for want of water, the ravens will be sorry when they realize their snackwagon's gone.

No gnats or no-see-ums here, maybe they all dried up and blew away. Now we drop back into the wash, and I sit for a moment on the bank where it's been eroded by flashfloods. We leave the sand for slickrock again, as the sand's too deep, too hard to walk in.

Sweat bathes my forehead, dripping into my eyes. I have a strong urge to sleep, it's too hot, am I being followed? I hear a swoosh sound right behind me, realize it's my pantlegs rubbing together, wet from sweat. Can't stop, feel grief for Charlie and me, hear voices in the distance, realize it's that fly, must get my life on track somehow, can't grieve forever, sun behind cloud, move while can, can one move through time? It's creepy, feel like throwing up, too hot, must get back to Willy, snow melting on mountains, even they look hot. Stick people watching me climbing, skinwalkers, hot air, lungs burning, weird bird figures lurking behind me. Funny how hot it can get out here, one degree at a time.

I know fins so well, how they lie, the language of fins, in the distance a big storm looks like aurora borealis, curtains of rain, verga, lit up with pinks, maroons, full of lightning. Wish it would come here, slickrock is very grippy except when wet, feel alone, even with Buddy here, he's following at my heels now, tail tucked, slowly, panting, I'm irresponsible having a dog out here in this heat, should've carried more water, not used to two of us, too early to be this hot.

Rock covered with lichen patterns, light green, gray, tan, black, plus larger growths, black on edges. No more pain, am done with it, salt headache, dripping wet shirt, sun so hot, everything's dreamy, quiet. I long for comfort, will die out here, miles from any spring, from the creek, from Willy.

The cold open arms of the endless desert embrace me, chill with uncertainty. I will die young.

I drop down between two huge fins, into the shade, and Buddy and I sit and rest. He digs into the deep sand, down where it's cool, lies down, panting. I try digging in the sand for water with a stick, but no luck. We'll die here, this is a good place to die, far from people grieving for my life, a life so short, so soon over, like that dustdevil.

It's not too bad down here, away from the angry hot wind that gets down in the lungs, making you want to cough it back up. In the far distance, mountains are now covered in clouds, and a few stray wisps of cloud blow in, covering the sun. The wind cools, but only a few degrees, bringing with it a sudden ominousness. Fins merge far in the distance, a wonderland bathed in golden light, then in shadow.

We have to get back to Willy, Buddy Blue needs water, what are we doing out here? Now I hear that fly again, no, this is different, it's getting louder, I'm hallucinating, and now a plane, yellow with double props, flies over, low, tilts as if to get a look, acts for a moment as if it would circle, then flies on. The wind picks back up as clouds move on, smoothing my tracks like a compulsive maid with a broom. A raven glides high in the sky like a tiny black arrow. None of these things have any significance as I continue walking arm's length between fins, where leaves and detritus form perfect lines.

The slot canyon narrows, is blocked, we'll have to climb up and over or turn back. I can now hear the wind but not feel it. Raw beauty, lonely, timeless, infinite, wind carrying a sense of other times in this same place, ancient people wandering through these same fins, no civilization to buffer, to suffer from.

All of a sudden I want to be at Coralee's, or at Callie's. Will anyone miss me? I feel small, unimportant, will I ever find the Bird Panel? Is this just some meager attempt towards some significance that doesn't exist? But look! Here, a perfect mano, used to grind corn and seeds, just lying on the slickrock, just like I once found back when life was good with Charlie.

Wind dies down, sun comes back out, and a huge orange-red rock shaped like a teapot is bathed in golden light against the dark distant blue mountains. Look, a set of tracks, human, not very old, headed out in one direction and not returning. Was someone lost? Was that why the plane?

Now I realize the tracks are mine. Buddy and I are going in circles, just like life. Each person is born in a time that will shift, our early days will be very different from when we're old, the world will be very different. And we wonder, we who are alive in this moment of time, what the future will be, will others understand our moment of time? Will it seem long-ago, dusty and melancholy? Yet it's not, the wilderness is beautiful and solitary, our time will have been much like theirs.

Two fins, one to my left, the other to my right, a small garden between holds a happy pinion tree, a large stand of yucca, and a desert holly, Fremont mahonia. A packrat nest, a morass of sticks, tucks into a large solution cavity behind the pinion, a refuge from winged predators. Such nests hold treasures of time long gone, seeds, bones, even tiny Indian beads.

The fin to my left is pinkish-red, but the other is a light green from lichen growing on its shady side, the northeast. I carefully choose my path, the fin to my left drops into a deep wash laced with deep empty potholes. I'll go up the big fin with the lichen and come out on a path that will take me high—first to the stars, then to old Willy, where he waits for us by the water, the stream of life. Where is Buddy Blue? He's gone—no, he's in the shade of that cedar tree over there. Callie will be sorry she arranged for me to have him, it'll break her heart if he dies out here.

The fin is huge, dropping thirty feet or so into the garden, steep. I choose my path up an undulation, a small crease in the rock, and begin climbing. At first, my momentum takes me easily upwards, then I suddenly begin to slide back, catch myself, stand in place, leaning inwards, hands against the smooth surface, nothing to grasp onto. I'm slowly sliding downward, and I realize that the lichen is slick, the plants so tiny that they blend with the surface of the rock.

Now Buddy is by me, and I catch his tail, looking for another hold, feet still slowly sliding, as he pulls me upwards. The sinews in his legs stand out.

We continue, each foothold tenuous, sliding, and I wonder how it will feel when I land, if anyone will find me if I break a leg. Unlikely. Not alive, anyway. I think of a hunter who went missing in the Waterpocket Fold for 30 years before his skeleton was found. Now we're nearing the crest of the fin, only another 10 feet or so, and it's steeper, my boots fail to grip the ice-like slickness, and I fall to my hands and knees, losing my hold on Buddy, and he bolts upwards without my weight holding him back. I'm now on all fours like a child, crawling, afraid I'll keep sliding backwards, downwards. Finally, I stop sliding and stretch out flat, finally on top, hugging the rock, Buddy panting at my side.

My knees are bleeding where the rough surface has torn through my jeans, like when I fell that night at Charlie's. I look back down, I misjudged the height, it's at least 40 feet. Like most fins, it tapers downwards ahead of me, down into a red sand dune, down to where gravity says I should stay, down to the path that will take me to Willy.

Suddenly, thunder behind, to the east, and I turn and look into a huge black cloud draped with mammatus, so heavy with water it hangs like folds in curtains. Lightning flashes, followed by fear, and I quickly head down the fin into a wide wash, where the sandstone wall blocks the view of the cloud. I can't see the lightning, but I again hear thunder, close.

The clouds are speaking in tongues, their words polished like pigeon-blood agate. Rays from the near-setting sun shimmer on millions of drops of water, but I can't feel any rain, the storm's right next to me, but doesn't touch me.

In a moment, all too soon, sun has broken from a ribbon of dark clouds far to the west, light splashing across the red and pink sandstone all around, lending a pinkish cast to the air. The huge black cloud hangs motionless.

Suddenly, a gift from God, a rainbow spanning the blackness. In the clouds is written "Oh-Be-Joyful," written in spectrum across the sky, and beauty once again surrounds me, moves through me, into my senses, I'm filled with beauty, I walk in beauty, dance along the Beautyway.

Another rainbow appears, a mirror-image of the first, a double rainbow, filling the sky. The land around me, beneath me, glows pinks and reds and yellows with radiant sunrays. Oh-Be-Joyful. I can now die, for I've gazed upon perfection. Now I, too, can speak in tongues, can speak the language of thunder, of rainbow. Oh-Be-Joyful.

The double rainbow hangs in the sky forever, and finally, sun's rays tilt and all gradually melts into the silent black cloud.

Buddy Blue is gone.

Now fear finds me for the first time. I can fear for him but not for myself, is he lost? I call out and whistle until he suddenly reappears, grinning, muzzle wet, body soaked and dripping with water.

Water. Precious water. Willow Creek, somewhere nearby. He leads me there, like a shepherd leads a lost sheep, saying nary a word about his superior senses.

We both drink, lie in the cool water, drink more, laugh, splash, until sun is nearly down. Soon we're back to Dandy Camp, where old Willy has nearly melted into the hot sand, radiator dry.

Horseshoe tracks. A sun-dried note lies on the front seat, held by a branch of crinkled deep-pink Wood's rose blossoms.

Chin,
Rhoda Knight and Rhoda Krosite
Drove to Marble
In a black obsidian Cadillac
With ivory white-walled tires.
But what the heck
Did Rhoda Light do?
Come on by the ranch sometime.
Love?? JR

Rhodenite, rhodachrosite, marble, obsidian, ivory, rhodolite. Johnny must also dream of rocks.

Chin,

Where are all these places I keep hearing you are? Where is Landing Strip? I really need to meet you sometime in the halfway near-future. This has to be one of the most confusing (still confused) relationships (if it still even is) that I've ever had. I don't know anyone who has fictionalized so much of their life to where neither I nor they can differentiate Reality from Myth. Stock Tank?

I don't understand why you won't come see me. Or I could fly out anywhere you wanted. I have something for you that I wanna give you soon.

I'm outta here in a bit.

Charlie

chinle of the wind

yeah, run wild. that's the way of the wind. save the stables for the latter end of the trip.

fine bit of whitman there. ever hear of a guy named grandfather? lives down near ignacio. i never met him but heard stories. he claims to have actually met whitman.

is your poem a chant, meant to be sung to a rattle or drum? give it a tune and let's learn to chant it in the desert when we're there.

we know each other not by sight, but by what we write. indeed.

we need to write poems for each and every place we hold dear. that's the bardic duty for those of us gifted with language skills, to speak for place.

so, your turn. give us a poem for a place you've spent a lifetime in, even if only a wormhole lifetime in the fabric of time. start with the arroyo. and then i'll follow with one of my own. we could do a whole book of those places, eh?

you start a piece, and let me fool around with it. then we switch. i start and you fiddle. could be tricky. i know how proprietary and touchy we writers are. but it would be neat to model a collaboration in writing. don't know anyone else doing that. someday i'll sit at the great peace meadow listening to your peruvian flute. hope we get to meet soon. i feel i know you, but i have no real idea, do i?

love you,
artful

Dear Chinle,

I been in the desert for a quick but refreshing trip to the Escalante country. Went up the Escalante, over to Peek-a-Boo and Spooky, then up Death Hollow. Too tired to write more about the trip. Keep me posted though on any you want to invite me on, I didn't get my desert batteries recharged nearly enough. Went to the S. Ute Bear Dance two weeks ago. I wondered where you were when I was over your way. Take care and keep in touch, hope you're having fun.

Love and keep on living,
Bill

Dear Chinle,

I just realized I hadn't answered your postcard and here it is 9 a.m., with rain pouring down outside my window. I need to get busy and try once more to sell my cat limerick book.

Now that I am free of the Institute, I am thinking of all sorts of wonderful things we could do, most of which require money. When you are working and earning money, you have no time or energy to spend it! Ironic, isn't it? But if you came to Boulder, you could write my biography and still have lots of time to do interesting things with me. Money would be no object, Chinle my dear cousin.

Is your old jeep running still? It probably works best as a lawn decoration. Mamba the Mercedes is doing fine, purring along for now. He has been my one extravagance in an otherwise subsistence level life. I don't think I could go back to a car like my old Bentley.

As for my new relationship, I don't think I should say much, only that I am happier than I have ever been, even though he's married. There is no possibility of anything other than what it is now, but that is so much more than I have ever had so I'm not too worried. I keep looking for someone to share my life with, but not with great hopes of finding that person, certainly not here in Boulder.

Winston (AKA the Fat One, named after Mr. Churchill) is doing great and sends greetings to all. Silly cat insisted on going out in the dark and rain this morning.

My mom, your Aunt Donna, is coming for her birthday later this month. She is the most amazing woman. At 83 she is walking everywhere, flying here and there, and having a great time in California. Did I tell you she came in second in a 5K walking race in Leisure World this spring? Well must go. I love this rain.

Love to you,
Sarah

Dear Chinle,

Good to hear from you. The world's passing me by but that's OK. Tracks in the mud around my trailer, circled three or four times, not a cat. Big tracks with a pad, six toes. Reminds me of a petroglyph in Clover Canyon, a track just like that next to a square face with horns. I love this stinking desert, but I sure hate it. Maybe you should come out here and take a look, sounds like you need a break, if you're covering that much territory.

Fellow came thru yest. wanting good gem-quality dino bone. Told him he was looking at Jim Bone, but he didn't get it. From some Denver museum, said he'd heard about red bone out here. Prob. confusing it with red wood. Pointed him to the Brushy Basin Morrison across the valley. Last I saw he was wandering with the lizards. One time me and Rog were west of GR driving along that old river road, he saw something hanging out of the roadcut, the size of a tree trunk. Swore it was dino femur. Got a sample and boy was he excited. Gonna get rich charging scientists to come dig there, the Roger Bone Dino

Dig. Looked up Ed Wilson, geologist, petrified wood, he said. Rog laughed all the way home. Reminded me of that time you guys rigged the radio and broke in on the newscast, said Rog was wanted for poaching deer, did he ever crack up. Hasn't been sane since. Don't worry, he doesn't suffer from insanity, he enjoys every minute of it. Stop in. Bring me some Black Jack gum and decent coffee.

Gem Bone, I mean Jim Bone

Chin,

I overslept this morning, it's almost 8! I've been getting up before dawn lately...did I mention I have a rough time sleeping? My doctor pal keeps giving me these little white pills that knock me on my ass, but with no side effects the next morning.

I've decided that it would be a mistake to just meet you here in town. I think we should have some rendezvous out in the middle of nowhere. With maps and everything. You know...June 16, high noon, on the top of Mollie's Nipple or something. Somewhere in the Big Empty? Please advise.

OK...Gotta go.

Chas.

7
Pissant: Piceance Creek

I guess that it's about five in the morning, looking towards the east where a dim arc of light is barely awakening. To the west, Orion and the Pleiades still rule the sky, while to the east, Venus is bright, but not as bright as Jupiter. Now, gradually, Orion's belt fades, leaving only a couple of stars that will also soon be gone.

Something woke me, made me sit straight up, but what? It's quiet, and Buddy would be alert if something were amiss, but he's snoring, dreaming of lizard-chasing.

I relax, probably nothing, a coyote, maybe. I cozy back down into my bag.

And now I remember the dream I was having. Buddy and Willy and I were driving into the night, Buddy sleeping on the old Chief's blanket spread out next to me, all three of us flying through the desert air. I was listening to the radio, to a station clear and pure, like the air around me.

A beautiful cadence of Spanish guitar, lyrical and moody, spoke of the Beautyway, wordless, a direct translation. When the song ended, the DJ announced, "That was Franklin Morrison, playing his Alhambra guitar. He's so good I bet you thought he was playing an expensive Martin, didn't you?"

As I wake, the amorphous skyline slowly becomes more defined, taking on the shapes of tooth, pyramid, cliff. Low to the west, one lone star twinkles, then drops below bluff before fading sun can obliterate it. All is gray, but rising sun turns grays to bluish shadow, then to pale pinks and golds.

I turn over in my sleeping bag, unintentionally waking Buddy from his sleep deep in the bag at my feet. It amazes me he can breathe down in there, and so much for watch-dogging it. He crawls up, pokes his head out, looks at me, then turns over and snuggles under my arm. I smile, wishing I had a cup of coffee like when Charlie would bring it to me.

I sigh. It was one of life's great luxuries. He'd smile through blue eyes and wild curly hair, say something like, "You interested, gal? Think your system can handle it? You want some…" He would pause, grinning, standing there in nothing but his low-slung jeans, "...coyote coffee? It's pretty potent stuff." He'd hand me the cup as I'd sit up in my bag, barely awake, as he'd laugh that laugh only Charlie Dundee could laugh.

Now I feel lazy, civilization far behind, here at the edge of the Caineville Reef, land of moonscape and ancient petrified oyster beds. I feel reluctant to get up and start the day, a day in which Buddy and I will head for the high country, try to escape the heat for a while.

The memory of Willow Creek is still fresh, and now I know this is what woke me—that elemental fear I felt there on the fins when I thought we were dying. The deepest fear of all desert rats is the fear of dying from thirst. Ironically, more people die in the desert from flash-floods than from dehydration.

Maybe I'll just move up into the mountains and be a poet, I muse, someday when my life is more mellow and the river runs slow, when I'm ready for Whitman's stables. I'll have a little house by a little mountain stream I'll call Laughing Creek, near a big mountain palisade I'll call Writer's Block. I'll have columbine and wild daisies and dusty-blue camp robbers that chatter and strut like my beloved coal-black desert ravens.

But loving the mountains is a love akin to loving a wild cougar. There's something about that immense geology, those vertical cliffs and knife edges, something that catches your breath with a deep elemental fear that goes far beyond a mere fear of death—a dread of more basic things, things like separation from the earth, separation from comfort, from love, from God, from molecular structure. You can wander aimlessly in the desert, but you'd better watch your step in the mountains.

Time to get up, the desert heat will soon be out in full force, carried here by the cedar gnats and no-see-ums. For some reason, gnats and mosquitoes never bother me much, don't bite me, body chemistry, maybe. Charlie always claimed they singled him out, mercilessly tortured him, followed him around.

"It's the same damn barbarian blood-sucking horde," he'd say in frustration, slapping at the cloud around his head, "They get on you and follow you clear across the desert. Can't outrun 'em, can't hide."

"Ever read any Thomas Wolfe?" I asked, ignoring his diatribe.

"Maybe, can't recall for sure, probably not, he write about gnats?"

"He says we're all lost in America, immense and brooding skies hang over us, and we have no escape, or something like that."

"Very uplifting. What does that have to do with gnats, or with anything, for that matter? Sounds like he was the one kinda lost. He needs to come on out here and get really lost, then he'd appreciate what he was talking about. But as for us, if you know where you are, then so do I, by default, and vice versa, so we'll never be lost. But say, Chin, Where the hell do you find these guys?"

Right now, lounging here in my sleeping bag, I'm smack in the heart of America, right in the heart of the desert, exactly where I want to be. I may not know exactly where I am, but I'm not lost.

Our lives are really just one long day, broken up by nights and some sleep here and there. In the distance, rubble hills of Morrison push against wild jagged points of sandstone, dark maws of canyons. Far in the distance stands the Aquarius Plateau, its gentle slopes dark with forest.

Early morning is my favorite time of day, although Charlie would say, "Yeah, 'cause you're sleeping." But there's nothing like a desert dawn.

Next to me is a piece of red-white agate that looks like a butterfly wing. Not far away is a huge rock with a crack clear through the middle, shattered where it fell from nearby cliff and landed on the hardpan, who knows how long ago?

Now the nearby badland cliffs gradually turn soft red with the hope of dawn, of sun on its way to grace us for the day. Who knows what it sees each night in the Orient? In Chinese script, crises is two characters: danger and opportunity. Will today bring one, both, neither?

Looking towards the long tilted ramps of the Moroni Slopes, there's an ethereal pink glow behind as sun rises, a glow which suddenly turns orange. It's gonna get hot.

I remember being with Charlie once long ago, not far from here, camped in a place that stank of minerals, of sulphur and arsenic. The minerals in this country's water will make you sick (providing you can find water, that is).

A nearby uranium claim read, Ajax 14 West End Center. I'd found another marker that read, Ajax 15 West End Center, then another, Ajax 16 Northwest. Core samples littered the ground. Erosional solution cavities dotted the cliffs—packrat hotels.

It was late fall, and I'd been wandering, collecting tiny round pebbles of orange sugilite that I placed in an old purple bottle I'd found. Dark charcoal clouds were coming in from the west, pushing the blue sky east. We'd camped next to a huge house-sized chunk of Dakota caprock tilted on a mound of red-and-white-striped Brushy Basin, a member of the Morrison Formation.

It was dawn, and the uplands behind us were still dark and mysterious, wearing their cloaks of trees. On the rocky ledge to the north, ravens hopped around on the jutting caprock, doing their morning sundance to keep warm.

Charlie was over behind the Scout, taking a spit bath in the frigid morning air, howling and yelling from the cold water. Rocks turned gold as the obtuse light hit yet more desert. Like now, we were camped on hardpan, hard deadpan, dead hardpan, flat, crusted, no vegetation.

We'd decided to try to beat the storm and go visit some unnamed canyon in the northern part of the Waterpocket Fold, a good distance away. Charlie had been there a couple of years ago and wanted to go back. He'd found some devil's toenails, tiny fossilized clams of some sort that actually did look like curved and twisted toenails.

When we finally got there, it was mid-day and a good breeze danced in the cottonwoods by a spring. Cattails dreamt in deep water in the clefts of long rock ramps, and everything felt uncertain, winter coming. The longer you stay out in this country, the more you enter the Dreamtime, and winter can be the ultimate Dreamtime.

We hiked up to a rise, finding an old abandoned stone house. Across the wash, a doghole mine was hollowed into the yellow cliffs.

Charlie fanned himself with his hat and complained, "More gnats! I hate it when the little bastards fly in your mouth." Turning to me, he added, "Coyote scat everywhere on this green dirt, who ever heard of green dirt? Utah sure is an odd place. But hey, look at all them potential sandstone cars layin' around. I could really do some car carvin' here." Charlie had learned to carve sandstone from a Navajo named Pat Begay, and his specialty was little sandstone cars. He sold them in the Rock Garden, little boys loved them.

"Chin, this may look like desolate country, all these grays and browns, hardly any vegetation but stickers and cactus and as far as you can see it butts up to wild-looking cliffs and buttes and uplifts and monoclines and anticlines—but wait till you see some of its treasures!"

He continued, "Not including these damn gnats, they're biters. Look at them close, little sharp sticker noses. See how some of them are black and some have red bodies? The red ones are full of blood," he grimaced, "Mine."

Later, we returned to our hardpan camp and made dinner, Charlie taking out a can of Sego Milk and murmuring "canned cow" with reverence while pouring it into his black coffee, where it instantly formed a floating scum on the surface. He chanted, "Out here, there ain't much to eat, just bunnies and beans, but never nuthin' sweet. Sometimes sourdough biscuits, and old yeller cheese, but when things get hard-up, it's bark from cedar trees. I made that up, not bad, huh?"

I smiled, amazed at how adept he was at entertaining himself, like a little kid sometimes.

"Chin, you remember Sonny Van Tassel, you went to school with him?"

"Yeah, what about him?"

"He works for Radium Garage. Did you know they call him Earl now? He was really Earl Van Tassel, Jr., all those years. Yep, they called him Sonny till his dad died, then they called him Earl."

"Sounds like the lyrics to a song, Charlie."

"Chin?"

"Yeah?"

"Our lives are hard to live, you know that?"

"Maybe it's all in how you look at it."

"Yeah, maybe you're right, it's attitude. For example, if you was snowbound in some line camp and all you had to eat was applesauce, you'd be damn glad if you had a spatula. Would make you downright happy. Better than having to stick your tongue down in there."

Charlie laughed at himself. He always laughed at himself.

He asked, "What're you readin'?"

"It's a story about two old crows. The first old crow comes bouncin' down the road in an old jeep. The second old crow's sittin' by the side of the road and says, 'Looks like you got a flat tire.'

The first old crow, he says, 'Nah.'

The second old crow says, 'Whattya mean, nah?'

The first old crow says, 'I been ridin' around and the other three swolled up on me.'"

"Real funny, Chin."

I added, "Listen to this, 'A simplicity of faith and confidence in a natural law of supply, a profound belief that there is always abundance for those willing to work creatively. Dollars may disappear but the law of supply is always there to be used.'"

"Incomplete sentence. So what's the book?"

"It's about the history of the oil business. It's called 'The Greatest Gamblers.'"

"They're gonna put me in a book like that someday, you know."

"Oh?"

"Yep, I'm gonna start a research institute and get famous. The Heisenberg Research Institute."

I laughed.

"Chin?"

"Yeah?"

"Why would you want to continue to live in a state of superstition?"

"What do you mean?"

"I mean, why would anyone want to live in Utah with a bunch of ignorant Mormons? They're superstitious. Utah is a Mormon state. Deseret. The Right Place and beehives and industry and all that socialist crap. You know, that's supposedly what Brigham Young said when they crested the Wasatch and saw the Great Salt Lake Valley, 'This is the right place.' He sent out settlement parties to strategic places all over the region and started towns, tryin' to keep out those damn Gentiles, the freethinkers. They hate creative independent thinkers like me and you. They're hard on women, wantin' them to breed like rabbits to populate the earth. You're gonna get sick of Utah some day and leave, mark my words. While you're here, you should wear a cross—Mormons don't want anything to do with the cross, they say it's too depressing. Wear a cross and they'll know you're a Gentile and they'll leave you alone, if you're lucky."

"Geez, Charlie, I don't know. I grew up here, part of Radium is Mormon, they're OK. Sounds to me like you're a bit prejudiced."

"You never tried to start a business. My rock shop would make lots more money if I was Mormon. It's a cult."

"It's pretty much against my religion to generalize people, Charlie. I could say desert rats are a cult, if I knew what a cult was. Just what exactly is it?"

"Well, a cult's a screwed-up religion where they claim to have supernatural experiences above and beyond everybody else, and as a desert rat, the only significant religious experience I've ever had out here was when I drank some of that gyp water at the Poison Strip, and then I have to admit I had quite a few significant experiences. I even saw God himself out there unabashedly wandering around, admiring his own creation, talking to himself, 'Boy, I sure outdid myself on this Sego lily, didn't I? And hows abouts that big cliff over there?' Stuff like that."

"Well," I laughed, "What kind of tracks did he leave?"

Charlie guffawed, picked up the coffee pan, dumped the remainder into the fire, then threw the pan over his shoulder, where it landed in a clump of Datura, moonflower.

"Just fling it, that's what I'm gonna do with all this crap. You didn't want more coffee, did ya? Talk about a religious experience, stuff's evil as hell." He stops, adds, "And I still think Mormons are crazy, the ones who know what they believe and still believe it anyway, at least. But hey, let's go on over to Pissant country, I'm 'bout outta bugs, the kids sure like 'em, sell like crazy."

Soon Charlie's old Scout sang gladly along on flat highway, heading east. Like a faraway never-changing backdrop in some Western movie, the Bookcliffs loomed over us with razor edge, never changing their abrupt countenance, speaking silently of a distance through time incomprehensible by humans. Time and ancient memories, memories fossilized deep in long-hardened sandy beaches and swamps.

We crossed the state line into Colorado, although Charlie always called it the border.

"Ain't in the U.S. when you're in Utah, Chin," he'd say. "It's a world unto itself, run by the Moron Church, excuse me, the Mammon Church."

Ahead, in the distance, slept Grand Junction, the town where the Colorado River swirls the Gunnison River into its slow muddy embrace, coveting the Gunnison's dowry of ancient muds from the Uncompahgre Uplift, a dowry containing tiny flecks of silver and gold from the airy San Juans in the paper-thin south.

A sign appeared, Douglas Pass. A sharp left turn, then another straight shot road, disappearing into the steep cliffs of Bookcliff shale. Nothing changed but direction, an almost imperceptible rising of road, then cliffs suddenly overhead, and the Scout was suddenly climbing hard, surrounded by wildness and Douglas fir.

We stopped at the top of the pass, radiator steaming and solar rays blazing through high cumulus clouds, nowhere else to go on earth but down. Behind, the valley spread far below, thick gray haze bespeaking humans and irrigation and smoke. Still far ahead, Piceance Basin, a thin blue haze bespeaking distance and precious molecules of water suspended over dry canyons.

Charlie and I got out of the Scout, took an airy break, Utah far in the distant haze. On either side of us, thick steep road cuts delineated the pass, cuts made by the strong metal of a government grader oblivious to the delicate fossils turned and smashed by its blade.

Hearing a chinking noise, I looked up, and there, on the cut some twenty feet above us, barely holding onto the extruding shale layers with one hand and carefully chipping with a small rock hammer in the other hand, a man hung precariously, his clothes disheveled and dusty. Parked near the road was an old blue Ford pickup, just as disheveled and dusty and precarious looking.

"Having any luck?" I asked.

"What's luck?" He answered down.

"Well, having any skill, then? Find anything?"

"What would you expect to find here?"

"I dunno, maybe fossils."

"What kind of fossils?" He asked through dirt.

"Hmmm...dragonflies, leaves, spiders, twigs, mosquitoes, maybe an ant or two..."

"I've never found a dragonfly here. But I did find the only fossilized tadpole ever discovered, right here. It's in the Chicago Museum of Natural History. Has my name on the placard."

"What exactly is your name?"

"Brett Rose Petroleum Geologist. And yours?"

"Chinle Miller Rock Art Hunter."

"Rock Art Hunter? What kind of rock art do you hunt?"

"Human. Seen any around?"

He laughed. "Could be. Just start lookin'."

Charlie and I said goodbye to Brett, then headed on, down the other side of the pass, to our destination, a different world of fossilized shales, Piceance Basin. There, long mound-like hills of brown and yellow shale dipped and melted into lower blue shales of Green River Formation, jagged badland hoodoos. A pale-blue sky reflected on washes flowing between the hills.

The late winter afternoon glowed gold like river beaches, like the silt bars on the muddy San Juan River. A sign read "Dept. of Interior Oil Shale Reserve." Oblivious to the concepts of departments, interiors, oil shale, and reserves, swallows rested on the cliffs.

Hills disappeared into green hayfields, nourished by Piceance Creek. The long narrow valley was home to several cattle ranches, houses built from the golden native stone. Piceance Basin, Pee-ance, Pee-ant, Pissant—or so Charlie called it.

A pair of golden eagles turned, circled in a dance choreographed by hunger, eyes searching the ground below for movement, bold birds certain of their lordship over all on the ground, over fuzzy-gray cottontail kingdoms.

The hills ran east-west, traversed by the valley, which ran north-south. Occasional winds whipped through on their way to high mountain ridges, but the clouds continued to run west, defying the winds on their course to desert safety. The temperature vacillated between cold and chilly, depending on the wind.

Cattle flowed through the fields like a river, meandering along on oxbows and S-curves, following the path of hay spread by the ranchers from their horse-drawn hay wagons. Once in a while one or two steers wandered far from the current of hay to get a drink at the stream that mirrored hay's winding path.

Charlie and I, hunting, there in Pissant Basin, hunting bugs. Carefully holding the pale blue shale, I could see many layers of lake shoreline, each holding its own secrets. Carefully, standing the shale on edge, I placed chisel, striking tenuously with rock hammer, the tink tink of splitting, then the hesitant pulling apart of ancient layers. Only then was the secret revealed.

Here, look! A mayfly that once whirred through the ancient dawn, red wings glowing in oblique sunwaves, above long-forgotten shorelines of the immense ancient Sundance Sea, sandy beaches now hardened into thin paper layers of white and pale yellow shales. Long ago were these sandy beaches formed, these marshy swamplands. Dense clouds of strange delicate insects with phosphorescent wings once flew here among large wide-leaved trees, now molded by time into dark-gray shale.

Bug hunting, Charlie and I searching through the layers of time. Balanced as high on the shale cliff as we dared, beneath precarious layers of jutting sandstone, we mined bugs, hunted bugs, armed with rock picks and chisels. We quarried pieces of shale like gold miners, gently chipping through layer after layer, peeling apart the positive and negative plates, striking paydirt when we found spiders with long delicate banded legs, bees with compound eyes, and finely-resolved insects we could not identify.

We gave them names, each moniker selected as carefully as any entomologist would name a new species. Gooney Bug—hundreds of compound eyes, wings too short to possibly hold up the thick stout thorax. Ghost Bug—faded but with perfect resolution, white on yellow shale, an anomaly in a world where charcoal prevails. Raccoon Bug—big black eyes on a small pointy face.

Reveling in our discoveries, we knew we were seeing a world never seen before, as great an adventure as any mountain climber conquering unknown heights. We were obsessed, spending hours without looking up, without talking, barely breathing, covered with dirt and dust from eons ago. We were happy.

Two sun dogs lay on each side of the sun, but looking closely, I could see they were really part of a circle around the sun, ice crystals in the air, portent of a storm. A herringbone pattern in the clouds went the opposite direction of streaks in the cliffs.

I looked down from my perch along cliffline, where Charlie's deep blue eyes reflected ancient time.

"Jurassic," I claimed.

"No, try again," his eyes twinkled. "Ancient ferns."

"Eocene!"

"Of course."

"Ancient history."

"Well, yeah, if you're a bug, otherwise it's prehistory."

Charlie had studied the eons, had passed through layers of time like a ghost filters through solid doors. Deep time had no meaning to him, it was all the same, whether it was time metamorphized, heavily weighted, pressed into near-liquid oil in layers of shale. Time transformed by time.

His sweet blue eyes drew me closer to his time, the now, until my time melted with his.

"You know, Chin, sometimes your dreams just don't come true." Charlie flicked the end of his cigarette into the rocks as we took a break. He was disappointed, he'd hoped to find a fossilized dragonfly, never found before, to our knowledge.

"You'll start a fire, this sage is awful dry."

"Hell, be good to burn the damn stuff up."

November wind blew cold, steady, made the golden seed-laden tops of rabbitbrush bend, as if to lay the seeds gently on the ground instead of whirling them into sky, as would a September wind. Pissant Basin—snow barren, although a few inches of frosted crystals hid here and there in shadow-sheltered places. Gray-white clouds hung motionless as the wind touched the ground, leaving the sky calm and quiet. Here, wind seemed to carry lonesome around with it, too many miles here of lonesome, lonesome squared.

Tink tink, Charlie continued chipping at the shale, the sound changing tenor with different thickness of rock. Suddenly, he cussed as wind brought down a small slide near him.

"We need to give up on bug-huntin'," he pronounced. "We got enough, let's go. Maybe we should go over to Winter Camp and find some logs."

"Logs?" I asked.

"Yeah, radioactive logs. You know, Chin, the kind that'll fry you if you put them in your fireplace, petrified, full of carnotite, worth over $1,000 each."

"Like that yellow one you had behind the shop? What do they do with em?"

"They refine them. Turn them into bombs that'll fry lots of people at once, not just you."

"But they're beautiful! That one had delicate yellows and purples. How can they turn something with such beauty into bombs?"

"They get paid to do it, just like we get paid to find 'em and send 'em to them. That's what prospecting is all about."

We stored the fossils carefully, wrapping them in newspaper. The back of Charlie's Scout full, tires low from the weight, we drove carefully back to Radium, where he'd sell them in the Rock Garden. We were rich in bugs, in fossilized insects. Our wealth seemed endless, timeless.

Tiny golden leaves danced in my hand, were taken by the jealous wind.

Dear Chinle,

I got your card and felt guilty. Your letter about the falcons had so many interesting details that I felt I couldn't respond right away, but now I've missed you!

I read with delight your joke about the two old crows, though I can't say I understood it. Is this an example of the kind of humor you mentioned the locals enjoying? Perhaps I'm just not sophisticated enough to understand the higher levels of satire therein.

My sale in Loveland was terrible. I actually lost money and a whole day. You are right in thinking I should get my stuff into a gallery, but I am finding myself quite timid about that. I am afraid to approach store owners! Don't ask me why. I don't know. I need an agent. If you came here, you could be my agent, people take to you naturally. I can't understand why you're so solitary. Please don't take that as a criticism, I'm a bit envious. It's interesting how family members can be so different, isn't it?

Terry's friend Dick is planning to sell his house in Radium. It's a trailer house in town with a big fenced yard. Not a dream house by any means, but I thought I'd ask if you had any interest. It wouldn't be expensive and would give you a base in the area. You could stay here with me for free and apply your salary to the payment and perhaps return to the desert someday, but then with a true home. My dear cousin, everyone should have a home.

Today we've had a light rain after days of lovely weather and it is beautiful. It is still coming down, very small, tiny drops.

I will be in the Big Apple soon. I can't wait, actually. NY is very clean and safe and beautiful. There are two big exhibits I am excited about: Monet and Modern Masterpieces from a museum in Paris.

And so dear cousin, write to me when you can, we must still take that desert trip together. Winston says hi! Terry has yet to take down the Christmas tree after all these months, and Winston has been busy attacking the red cardinal ornaments—his favorite Christmas tradition. Many have died and many have bald spots where he has chewed their heads. For him this is the true spirit of Christmas.

Love,
Sarah

Dear Chinle,

Remember my Uncle Joe, the Episcopal priest down on the Rez? He's the one who built the church that got burned down by a Navajo medicine man who later joined the new church. Was thinking of him 'cause I just got back from Blanding, stopped at White's Kitchen, and a trucker, an Anglo guy, came in and was pretty shook. Said he was coming across White Mesa, looked out the window and saw a big wolf-like thing running alongside his rig, yellow eyes. When he lost speed on the hills, it would try to get in his cab, left claw marks on the door. That guy was white as a sheet. I saw the claw marks for myself. That thing was a skinwalker, though a bit far afield. I know a White Mesa Ute who saw one once out there, ran it off. Skinwalkers are Navajo, not Ute. What scares the Ute are stick people. Be careful out there. Just 'cause you're a scientist don't mean these things aren't real. Did you ever notice how close Chinle is to the word Chinde, Navajo word for bad spirit? What does Chinle mean, anyway? Hell, I don't know nuthin'. Absolutely nuthin'.

Jim Bone

Chin,

What in hell ever became of you?

Chas.

8
Adam: Coffeepot Peak

"Say, would you mind if I camp here? This is, well, how do I put it without sounding like an ass, this is my camp spot, and I really had my heart set on staying here tonight."

Buddy wags his tail, but I'm speechless. I suspect this dark-haired man who just pulled up in a little white sedan is serious, but he has to be kidding. We're in the middle of thousands of acres of national forest, with places to camp everywhere you look. He and I are the only people for miles around, as far as I can tell.

He continues, gingerly patting Buddy's head, "What a nice dog, he won't bite me, will he? Let me introduce myself. I'm Adam Stocks, and I live in Radium. You know where that is? I own the newspaper there, the Radium Ray. I know it's a strange request, but we're dealing with tradition here, and there's actually a nice spot over by those rocks where the skeeters aren't so bad 'cause it's sunnier. I'll help you move, though it looks like you really haven't set up camp yet."

I can't seem to collect myself to say anything. I'd been sitting on a log next to old Willy, playing my Peruvian flute, Buddy snoozing in the pine needles next to me, but now I feel like I have a part in a surrealistic play and forgot my lines.

Adam begins to look embarrassed. He adds, "I bet you think I'm nuts, don't you, wanting this spot out here where there are a million places to camp. But you see, this is where my old girlfriend and I camped the last time we were together, and it's got lots of sentimental value to me. Oh hell, I didn't want to go into all that, but I really can see you're wondering what kind of a kook I am, to drive in here like this and ask you to move. I'm sorry." Adam extends his hand.

I stand up and shake his hand. "It's OK. You can have this spot. It's no big deal to me, just sort of trying to figure it all out." I smile a half-smile, Buddy seems fine, is still wagging his tail, so I'll trust his judgment.

"Thanks for being so understanding. I'm sorry. It just really means a lot. Can I help you move anything?"

Now Adam's beginning to remind me of an apologetic boy, not a hardened newspaper publisher who deals with mayhem, murder, and corruption on a daily basis. But wait, we're talking about Radium, so he probably deals with who grew the largest zucchini and who just got married in the Salt Lake Temple.

"No, no, it's OK," I answer. "All I have to do is get in old Willy here and drive over there. No problem." I get in the jeep, trying to smile, start up, wave lamely, toy with the idea of leaving entirely, but decide to try the spot Adam suggested. Buddy jumps in through the passenger window, giving me a "don't forget me" look of disgust. It's almost dark, I'm tired, and I want to be close to the trailhead for an early start up the mountain in the morning. Adam seems pretty benign.

I angle the back of the jeep into the camp spot. Buddy jumps back out the window, and I proceed to make dinner, peanut butter sandwiches, one for me, one for Buddy Blue. The fire danger from the drought is just too high to cook anything here in the tall timber. I watch from the shadows as Adam sets up camp—his attempts to erect a small pup tent become comical after several tries. The poles keep slipping out, causing the tent to collapse.

I yell over to him, "Tie the damn thing to the tree limbs. I have some rope you can borrow."

Adam looks embarrassed, walks over, takes the rope, politely thanks me, and quickly has the tent up. He's now collecting wood for a fire.

I yell over to him, "Hey, I don't think it's a good idea to start a fire here in this dry timber. We'd never get outta here."

Adam comes back over, looking even more embarrassed. "You're absolutely right," he offers humbly. "I can't believe I even considered it. I just did a three-part series for the paper about how severe the drought's getting to be. Pretty stupid of me."

I assess him, as he scuffs the ground with the toe of his boot. He's not very tall, maybe 5 foot 9, only an inch or so taller than me, horn-rimmed glasses, intelligent eyes, dark straight hair, olive skin, and a boyish face that's handsome in its own way. Sort of Welsh looking. All in all, a pleasant-looking fellow, maybe in his mid-thirties.

Adam asks, "Just what the heck does one eat if you can't cook? All I brought was hamburger, beans, and buns."

"Well," I hold up my jar of peanut butter, "You can have some of this with cold beans on the buns. A person can survive for 72 hours on just one simple jar of peanut butter. You can give Buddy the hamburger." I hand Adam the jar. He smiles and disappears into his tent, rattling around in there.

I start playing my flute again. Seems like no matter what color I start with, it always turns into the blues.

"What's that song you're playing?" Adam yells from inside his tent. "Sounds like the blues."

"It's supposed to be 'Tall Timber,'" I yell back.

"You mean that cowboy song by the Sons of the Pioneers?" Adam yells.

"Yeah," I answer, trying to remember the lyrics, something like "Timber, timber, timber, timber," not too complicated, each word sung by a different singer at a different pitch, ending in a deep falling bass.

"Say, I never did get your name," Adam sticks his head out of the tent.

"Chinle Miller," I yell.

"You're Chinle?" Adam pulls himself out of the pup tent and walks over to old Willy.

"So I've been told," I answer dryly.

He has a package of hamburger patties for Buddy, making an instant friend of the little dog.

Adam continues, "I wondered about the DESRAT painted on the back of your jeep. I know a friend of yours."

"Who's that?"

"Charlie Dundee. You know, the Uranium King over in Radium."

"You know Charlie?" I feel my heart sink. Seems like everyone I meet knows Charlie, especially since I'm trying to forget knowing Charlie.

"I've done many stories about him for the paper."

"But how do you know he's my friend?" I ask.

"Charlie told me you were his childhood sweetheart. You have a memorable name, part Navajo, part white."

"Childhood sweetheart? I may have been pretty young, but he wasn't a kid, he was out of college."

"How much older is he?"

"Six years. We didn't actually start hanging around together till my last year of high school. I was almost 18. He hired me to work after school in his rock shop. He was 24, not exactly a child."

"Well, you have to understand that Charlie's still a child, always will be, no matter what his chronological age. He and I play poker together, and he's definitely a child when he loses. I've won the Tengo Dinero twice and his house three times. Good thing for him I don't collect, he'd really have a temper tantrum. I sometimes go to his big parties up on the hill. Charlie loves to party. He's mentioned you many times. Told me about your archaeology project. I should do a story on you, out here wandering around. Not many women, or men for that matter, get to live like that."

"Not much of a story."

"Well, just what do you do, exactly?"

"Mostly just wander around."

"Sounds good to me," Adam laughs. "I'm serious about doing a story. Why are you up here in the mountains looking for petroglyphs? I thought they were mostly down in the canyons."

"They mostly are. I'm on a personal research project this time."

"Mind if I ask?"

"I guess not, but you'll probably think I'm nuts."

"Well, you'll be in good company."

"I'm wanting to climb this big peak and see if I can hear it hum."

"You're right, I think you're nuts. Do you have some scientific basis for this research?"

"No, just that when I'm out in the desert, I can sometimes hear a distant hum, like a big B-52 airplane way far away, over the horizon. It's always in the key of A, I can match it on my flute. Look, I'm not the only nut out here, 'cause I've talked to other people who can hear it. A friend knows a guy from over in the San Juan Mountains who climbs the big peaks a lot, and he says he can hear it up high, so that's why I'm here."

Adam lets out a low whistle. "And I was worried about you thinking I was loony, no offense, just kidding. I've heard a lot of interesting things as a newspaperman, and I've learned not to discount them until I investigate. I've had lots of surprises, things I thought couldn't possibly be true, but were."

"Like what?"

"Oh, lots of things, but one example is the time old Cleo Hunt over in Catalpa Town called me and said that trilobites weren't really extinct, and he could prove it. I was pretty skeptical, but it turned out he'd discovered a modern descendent of the darn things. It was verified by scientists and all, but he took a lot of flak for it initially. I've learned in this business to believe everything until proven otherwise. The Radium Ray has won lots of awards, excuse my bragging."

"I've met Cleo, he's the one who gave me Buddy Blue. You mean there's more to write about in Radium than who drove to Catalpa Town to visit relatives, that sort of thing?"

"Man, you wouldn't believe that town. It has it all, especially since the big U-boom. The town tripled in size overnight, you know. We had tents on every square inch of space, new trailer parks sprung up in cow pastures, and every night Main Street was lined with prospectors sleeping in their vehicles. If you wanted to make a phone call, you had to wait sometimes six or eight hours. Some people would drive over to Grand Junction to make a call, as it was faster than waiting in line. Imagine driving 120 miles one-way to make a call. Charlie would fly friends over there in his plane to make phone calls. One guy placed a call to his home in Salt Lake, got tired of waiting, drove the six hours up there, and when he got home his phone rang, it was the call finally coming through. It was truly crazy. Talk about stories! It's settled down some since then, the boom's startin' to run outta room, but there's still lots of good tales. Between you and me, though, I'm sick of it. This was a forgotten corner of earth before all this and I miss that."

"So Charlie has a plane?"

"Has several. He's the one who built the airport. Wanted it for business and also wanted people to be able to fly in for his parties. You wouldn't believe the celebrities that have been to little Radium. I myself have met a number, but I try not to advertise their visits in the paper, as it makes some people resentful, some of who are my advertisers. You know, lots of people out there lost everything looking for yellowcake. Charlie has quite a reputation in Radium. He knows how to spend his money."

"Is he married?"

"No, he's too busy to get married. What people don't realize is that Charlie still works very hard. He's down in that mine every day, managing it, and that's a hard hard job. And very dangerous. I wouldn't do it for anything. Some of us feel that Charlie deserves all that money. And he's smart, too, he looked for uranium where everyone said it couldn't be found. He knows his geology."

"That he does," I answer, thinking of the Charlie I knew long ago, selling Moki marbles in the Rock Garden. But all this talk about him makes me want to go back down to the desert and disappear up some side canyon. I change the subject. "Have you ever heard the desert hum?"

"No, I can't say I have. What tune does it hum? Just kidding. What do you think it is?"

"I've talked to a lot of people about this and heard lots of opinions—the earth's rotation, magnetic forces, maybe even the sound of the atoms in the universe or in our own heads, who knows. I'm a trained scientist, Adam, but all I can say is that I've heard it many times and have virtually no explanation. There have been times it's nearly driven me crazy, it's so noticeable and persistent. I've even heard it inside houses, but only in desert towns, I've never heard it anywhere but the desert. That's why I wanted to come up here."

"So what will it prove if you hear it up here?" Adam asks.

"I dunno, I guess it won't solve the mystery, maybe just add to the puzzle. Other places have it besides the desert, though. There's the Taos

Hum and the Yellowstone Whispers, for example, and people in Great Britain hear it, too. I have a friend who's into Eastern stuff, you know, like yogis and all that, and she says that yogis can hear it when they're in deep meditation. She says it's the sound of the universe vibrating. Anyway, all I know is I hear this hum in the desert and it drives me nuts sometimes, and I'd like to figure it out, though I doubt if I will. Have you lived in Radium long?"

"Since I started the paper, about six years ago."

"You must've come about when I took off for college. I was born and raised there. Left just when the big boom hit. But you've never heard the hum?"

"No, but I've seen the green flash," Adam answers proudly.

"No kidding?" I ask. "I've never seen that. I've heard of it, though. What causes it?"

"It's a chromatic aberration."

"Kind of like the desert hum, huh, which is maybe an aural aberration."

Adam continues, "I was on Mt. Garfield, over by Grand Junction. Just as the sun went down, it turned a glowing green, only for a split second. It has something to do with the bending of light. It's the same thing that causes stars to twinkle."

"I thought that was caused by the atmosphere being thick."

"Exactly, and all those molecules bend the light. I guess the green flash does the same thing, but just at the instant the sun sets, and is in the green frequency."

"Whatever that means," I reply.

"Yeah, I sure ain't no scientist, that's for sure, maybe it's wavelength," Adam responds. "I guess it's mostly seen from high places, the tops of mesas and places where you have a big horizon, like on the ocean. And I once saw it right up there, on top of Coffeepot Peak," Adam adds, nodding toward the peak above us. "I was with Deana, she was my girlfriend, but she turned just as it flashed and didn't see it. It was our last time together."

Now Adam quickly changes the subject. "Say, do you know that new song by Johnny Horton? 'Lost Highway.' I think it's by Hank Williams originally."

"No, haven't heard it yet," I reply.

"It goes like this," Adam starts singing, his voice a surprisingly rich tenor, bending notes like the atmosphere bends light.

I'm a rollin' stone
All alone and lost,
For a life of sin
I have paid the cost,
When I walk by
All the people say,
He's just another guy
On the lost highway.

He stops, then adds, "I don't know why I felt compelled to sing it just now, I like it, it sort of fits me, I guess. Maybe it's all these big rocks around here, you know, rollin' stones, ha ha. But anyway, I think I'll call it a night. Thanks for being so understanding about my camp spot. You gonna climb Coffeepot Peak tomorrow, huh? Maybe I'll see you on the trail. Thanks for the peanut butter. Never suspected it would go so well with pork and beans on bread. Food sure tastes better when you're hungry and camping out."

Adam turns and walks to his tent. He gives me a quiet nod, then I hear the raspy sound of the tent's zipper, and soon crickets fill the night.

I sit for a while and play my flute softly, thinking about a cowpuncher who could be singing by the campfire at this very moment, Johnny Taylor.

When it's nighttime,
And crickets are callin',
And the coyotes,
Are makin' a wail,
I dream, by a smoldering fire,
Along the Navajo Trail.

The last sunrays disappear, a slight breeze stirs the air, aspen leaves rustle, and faraway in the new night a coyote yip yip yips, forgetting the words to the song.

Buddy's ears perk up, listening. I unroll my sleeping bag on the pine needles, crawl in, and he crawls in too, snuggling down at my feet. I fall asleep, wondering once again how he can breathe way down in there.

Buddy Blue wakes me early, panting and burrowing his way out of my sleeping bag. I toss and turn, trying to go back to sleep, then remember where I am—in the tall timber at Coffeepot Peak, looking for the desert hum, or rather, listening for the desert hum, or maybe now it's the mountain hum.

I hear Buddy scuffling around and pull myself out of my bag, wondering if maybe he's having it out with a porcupine, a very real possibility up here.

Buddy emerges from Adam's little tent, where he's been scratching around for more hamburger, which he probably dreamed about all night. I walk over to see if he's caused any damage. Adam is obviously already up and gone, his tent door unzipped and hanging wide open.

No damage done. I zip the flap, then slip out of my longjohns into my jeans and shirt and wander over to a nearby small rivulet and wash up. After Buddy and I share a quick breakfast of more peanut butter sandwiches (he compliments the chef by burying his), I pack still more for lunch, fill a canteen from my waterbag, and we head up a trail by a hand-carved sign that says "Coffeepot Peak Summit 3 Miles." Beneath that, someone has carved "Billy Eagle" next to a thick rough-carved thunder bolt. I wonder if Billy Eagle is a sharp-beaked resident of the upper peak or maybe one of Antonio's Indian friends or perhaps both.

Buddy and I start up the rocky trail, which crosses the small stream, then quickly narrows and soon switchbacks up the steep mountainside. No gentle alpine meadows here, just immediate altitude gain.

Huge pine trees canopy our walk, light filtering onto deeply grooved bark. Buddy walks at my heels, ignoring the little kamikaze chipmunks that pop from nowhere right under his nose then run for cover at breakneck speed, little striped tails curved perkily above their backs.

The map puts the altitude gain from camp to peak at 2800 feet, a stiff climb, but especially so if you're not used to the elevation. Coffeepot Peak tops out at 11,371, making it the highest summit in the region.

Maybe I'll hear the hum on top, although it's actually more of an excuse to get out of the desert heat and enjoy the mountain cool. I've been homesick for the mountains with their cobalts, lavenders, and purples, so different from the reds, cinnamons, and ambers of my beloved desert—but I know I'd get homesick for the desert the first snowstorm up here.

"Love's like that, sort of fickle," I say to Buddy. He handily shoves his head under my hand so I'll pet him, grinning like a fool.

We slowly climb on and on, up and up, half expecting to come upon Adam around each switchback. The trail narrows, and at times it's so steep I can nearly reach out and touch the tops of trees I've recently passed below. I watch where I place my feet, as one misstep would put me scrambling, and even though my fall would probably be broken by a tree, it would still be filled with regret.

After about a mile, I figure we've climbed a good 1,000 feet, every step steep and rocky. Now the trail comes out on a high bench, where it turns on the flank of the mountain, then swings around for an approach from the back.

I stop and sit on a rock, looking out on the desert below, far away, a panoply of vermilion, each shade belying a ridge or rocky outcropping. The horizon melts into blue-gray mists at the edge of the earth, its curvature apparent from this height. It makes me feel heady—any hum I hear will likely be the sound of my own vertigo. To the north, behind Coffeepot's nearest neighbor, Arrow Peak, I see the amorphous shapes of dark thunderheads ominously starting to form.

Looking upwards, I note that the upper shoulder of Coffeepot Peak is cloaked in scree, layers of loose rock. I drink from my canteen, offer some to Buddy, continue on.

I think of similar places over in Colorado, in the San Juan Mountains, where alpine ruggedness warns you to never climb alone. One misstep and you're at peace forever, floating into the thin air of white horizons, avalanche chutes, cirques and kettles, immense headwalls that reek of sheer verticality and granite forces.

But every climber I know sometimes climbs alone. The mountains draw you and you go, whether you have companions or not. That's just how the big peaks are—gentle tundra bluebells surrounded by haughty and stark gray amphitheaters, sudden lightening, rock glaciers, wind-blown avalanches.

Now, high above timberline, Buddy and I are embraced by hard blue granite and soft gray-green tundra. Pale delicate elfstars and brief summer sun dance in a pas de deux, lovers soon to be parted by winter's fierceness.

Suddenly, sky fills with fluid motion and raucous voice—a western mountain bluejay lands on a boulder ahead of us.

It casually preens its powder-blue feathers under dusty dark cloak and royal crest. Too casually.

Are you called Chinle?

I study it, smile, answer, *Only by those who know my name. Who are you to ask?*

Feathers ruffle, annoyance. *Coyote Yellowjacket sent me.*

Who's Coyote Yellowjacket? I ask.

More annoyance. *Actually, I'm Coyote Yellowjacket. You called me.*

No, I didn't. You don't belong up here. It's too high for coyotes. They freeze their long noses, noses always where they don't belong.

You want to talk.

About what?

Love. You were thinking about love. These little elfstar flowers reminded you of lovers.

Lovers? What's love? I forgot it existed.

Feathers ruffle again.

No you didn't.

OK, Little Coyote-Jay, I'll humor you. Do you believe in love?

Of course, Little Rabbit, everyone believes in love.

Well, then, who do you love?

Coyotes love rabbits.

Little Coyote-Jay, what's so wrong with wanting to be loved?

Everyone wants to be loved, Little Rabbit.

What does love mean?

Love means anything you want it to mean. Quite often love means justifying your own life through someone else.

Little Coyote-Jay, you're a cynic. Why is love so hard to come by?

Perhaps what you want isn't really love. Perhaps you want someone to lay their soul down for you, Little Rabbit. Perhaps what you want is a bit more than love.

No, Little Coyote-Jay, I think I just want to be loved, to enrich someone else's life.

You are loved by many, Little Rabbit.

No, it's not like that, it's more than that.

Give it up, Little Rabbit, give it up. It's an elusive search. And perhaps the price is too high for you to pay.

Quakies far below shake in breeze born on high snowfield, breeze laden with roar of distant thundering of water tumbling unexpectedly over high rockfall. With a flash of blue, Coyote-Jay is gone, like delicate thin snowcrystal in spring sun.

Far away, hundreds of miles below, out in the sea of desert, a Mussentuchit coyote squints in sun at a distant horizon of white peaks, then howls with poignant longing for cool shade filled with columbine and rocky waters.

Still climbing upwards, scree now predominates, small flat rocks slip and shift and settle beneath my feet. I head straight towards the top, each step carefully chosen for stability. More than once I feel the rocks begin to slide beneath me. Scree doesn't usually slide very far, but it's so steep that any downward movement is unsettling, a haunt of potential avalanche. Buddy climbs slow, light, waits patiently, and I envy the stability of four legs as I try to move quickly.

Finally we crest the ridge and I think we're near the top, only to see another ridge high above. Such is the nature of mountains—engaged in the now, focused, you look up to find you're not where you thought you were. Kind of like life.

The air is cool and thin, and I have to stop often to catch my breath. I recall the time Charlie and I were trying to climb Mt. Sneffels over in the San Juans in Colorado. It was a tough climb, steep and dangerous. Finally, jubilant that we'd made the summit at last, we turned to see the real peak a good 2,000 feet above us, on the far side of a chasm. We named the subpeak we'd climbed Disappointment Peak. We found out later it was actually called Kismet—fate, destiny.

That same day I heard a hum, a very loud hum, but it wasn't the same hum I'm hoping for today. It was the hum of electrical energy filling the air, trying to consolidate in the form of lightning. My arm made a crackling noise as I pointed upwards, and I turned to see Charlie's hair standing on end. We both dove off the summit, sliding downwards through scree.

We were a mere 100 feet below the top when lightning hit where we'd just been. The force knocked us both from our feet. Charlie swore he saw the ground-shock flash beneath the rubber soles of my boots.

Finally, after what seems like forever, scree becomes final summit block, boulders so large each has to be climbed, each an entity unto itself, an exercise in Zen patience, each making way for the next. Buddy scrambles easily up, and sometimes he helps me, letting me hold his scruffy tail to help stabilize myself as I pull my way upward.

Now, finally, we're on top, a half-acre or so of tundra scattered with boulders and barely enough air to breathe. Suddenly, I hear a sharp whistle of warning—a tiny pika scrambles for cover, having just noticed invaders. How these little hamster-like rodents can survive up here is a mystery. They spend half their lives gathering grass and the other half eating it, hiding from winter. My friend Jack says he once climbed the Grand Teton to find a coyote enjoying the view, but maybe it was really hunting pikas.

I look around. Still no sign of Adam, maybe he's hiking that lost highway he was singing about last night. An old tin can is wedged into a crack in a boulder, and the words "Summit Ledger/Coffeepot Peak" are written on it in black marker. I open it and pull out a small notebook.

> *Roger Miller 6-7-61 Isn't this Arrow Peak? How do you climb the wrong damn peak?*
>
> *Yeller Cat and Cactus Rat 6-21-61 Be kind to the animals cuz yer one too*

I shake my head, can't believe those two desert rats were up here. I wonder if Roger's any relation to me, then add my name to the list, using the stub of pencil in the can.

Chinle & Buddy Blue 7-10-61 Climbing the Beautyway

I add a penny to a pile on the boulder near the register, then turn to take in the views.

Everywhere, all around me, beauty. Each direction I look I can see forever. To the north, Arrow Peak, to the south, Sunlight Peak and a number of lower subpeaks, all part of this long massive ridge. The San Juan Mountains stand far to the east, summits draped with gray scree-scarves melting into deep blue cloaks of timber. Summer sun has long ago melted what little snow fell there last winter. I wonder what the pikas drink when the snowfields dry up. Maybe all they need is in the stems of the tundra grasses.

I sit for a while, wondering what Johnny and Coralee and Joe are doing, where they are in that far distance. Buddy suddenly lets out a short bark, the sound trailing off over the edge of the mountain, falling into a thick depth of thin air.

A head pops up from behind a boulder near the very edge of the summit. It's Adam.

"Over here, y'all!" He yells. Buddy and I are soon on the edge, me hanging on to Buddy, more for my peace of mind than a comment on his likelihood of falling off. The little dog is generally much smarter than the company he keeps—he'd be back down at camp sleeping in the grass by the little stream if left to his own devices.

Adam smiles. "Have a seat. How was your climb? Did you know that the Chinese say that the tops of mountains are sacred places? I think it's 'cause you're directly over the center of the earth."

I reply, "Adam, you're always directly over the center of the earth, no matter where you are."

He continues to smile and nods, "Want some raisins? Got any more peanut butter?"

I pull out the sandwiches, handing him and Buddy each one. He says, "Thanks. It's nice to be around someone who's always prepared.

Were you a girl scout when you were a kid? Next time you're in Radium I'll buy you lunch. You know, Chinle, I was looking way down there, there's a huge forest down there, I've hiked through it lots of times, way over there in the mountains by Radium, and from here it looks like a tiny little meadow, and I was thinking that this is what the earth must look like to a meteorite, just before it burns up and kaboom is gone."

"Well, that's a perspective I've never really thought about before," I answer.

We sit in silence for a while, munching and pondering.

He finally asks, "Do you think it's possible for a meteorite to start a forest fire?"

"Geez, I dunno," I answer. "Probably, if it strikes the earth. How hot are meteorites?"

"Well, they're darn hot, hotter than H-E-double-hockeysticks when they come through the atmosphere. But when they actually strike, those few that make it to earth, I think they might still be hot enough to start a fire."

"Guess it's possible," I reply, keeping my eye on the dark clouds now rapidly building to the west. I nod my head in that direction, silently, and Adam nods back in affirmation. Fear of lightning needs no words.

He asks, "What's that shining over there behind you? Looks like gold."

"It's a pile of pennies. Tradition has it that if you leave a penny when you come up here, you'll get married soon."

"Wonder why I never noticed it before. Maybe somebody took the pennies instead of leaving one, some rascal. Did you leave a penny?" He asks.

"Yup."

"Do you want to get married?"

"Probably not."

"Well, you'd have a better chance if you'd comb your hair," he grins, then adds, "Just kidding. Then why'd you leave a penny?"

"Hate to break tradition," I smile. We sit in silence for a long time, then Adam smiles and quietly starts singing, his voice subdued but with feeling:

Do you remember,
The good times we had,
Drinkin' all that whiskey,
When things weren't so bad...

He gazes out into the distant haze, says, "Hope you don't mind my singing, I drive people nuts, singing all the time. That blues song reminds me of Deana. I hiked to the top of this peak for the first time with her. She was an administrator at Capitol Reef National Monument. I was working as a gardener in the orchards they have over there, it was before I'd started the newspaper. We had a relationship for four years, broke up, got back together, broke up again. On November 29th we had a huge argument, she walked out my door in tears, and on December first she committed suicide by shooting herself in the head with a park service revolver."

I sit silent, shocked, not knowing what to say. Adam continues.

"Just like that, shot herself in the head. Violent suicides are usually the province of the male, not of sweet, sensitive women. She seemed like she'd lost track of who she was. She started worrying about the future. In retrospect, I think I had something to do with that.

You're on my mind,
Everywhere I go…

She started singing the blues, just like you with that flute, everywhere she went, the blues. The damn blues, of all things. She had a very sweet voice. No more good clean music. Lordy lord, damn, she started cussin'. A nice girl like her, cussin'."

I sit in silence, sensing his need for me to just listen, some kind of purification or closure in the making, maybe. He continues.

"She just had this pain that wouldn't go away, no matter what she did. It's that pain that lurks in all our lives, that deep pain that we all know is waiting there in the shadows, just waiting for the right time for us to show some sign of weakness, then bam, we lose everything. One minute you're fine, then you're in pain.

Goodbye baby,
So long forever now,
Don't really matter,
'Cause you never meant me no good anyhow...

In retrospect, the whole thing made me question Deana's sensitivities, to do that, leave that for other people to deal with, but when you're in that kind of pain, I've realized since that nothing matters. It just doesn't matter.

You know, Chinle, We get caught up in all kinds of things to help us forget how close our mortality really is, but you know, it's always out there, looking at us, over the far distant rims like some giant of the earth. Eternity, our own death, all those regrets, just standing there looking over the horizon. Sometimes at night I see that giant, I can see his eyes, they look like the belt of Orion in the night sky, cold, wintry, distant, and yet too close. That's when the cold winds blow right through me and I feel the terror, the aloneness, that Deana must have felt just before she pulled the trigger.

I found out later, when her friends were taking care of her stuff, that she'd been on medication. She'd been diagnosed with serious depression, and none of us knew. What a private hell she must've been in, and she didn't even tell us. When you first mentioned the desert hum I was a little leary, it kind of reminded me of some of the things she was beginning to see and hear. I've been taking this hike to the top every year, sort of as a memorial to her. It's something I just have to do. I can't explain how all this feels or how it changed my life."

Adam gazes out into the distance. All's quiet except for the sound of the wind. Finally, Adam continues.

"I have a film can buried on the summit here with my notes that I've logged every year—it also contains Deana's first and only message that she left on that first hike. Wish we'd known about the penny legend, maybe we'd got married and everything would've been OK. But actually, the hike up here isn't so dreary and depressing as it used to be. A touch of melancholy of course, but then everything I do is laced with a certain melancholy—that's just me—pitiful old Adam. Should've been a poet."

Adam now stands and buttons his jacket. He shrugs his shoulders, a gesture that seems to absolve him of the whole thing.

"But this time it's different, 'cause this time I'm going to spread her ashes here and try to forget it all. I've had these ashes for seven years, I can't believe it, it seems kind of morbid to me now, so I guess I'm ready to make my peace with it all and move on. And I'm also going to dig up that film can and toss it off the edge.

This is the last time I ever want to stand on this mountain," he says, simply. "I'm a desert rat, I miss the desert, and you know, what I'm not seein' up here are those desert no-see-um's, I even miss getting bit by the little buggers." He smiles, attempting to be light, but the whole mountain feels steeped in regret.

Dark clouds are moving closer, and the wind now begins to pick up in earnest, spraying Adam's face with a shock of his own dark hair, tendrils sticking to his cheeks like fingers of electricity. He slowly takes an urn from his daypack. It's a simple porcelain vase, unembellished, dark brown with the words "Deana McCloud" roughly painted on it in white brush strokes, as if Adam has an entire collection of such urns and has to keep them sorted. The lid is anchored with old tape, yellowed and stiff.

Suddenly, the wind brings a distant scent of flowering rose bushes from far far away in the tidy back yard of a little bungalow in a tree-lined town somewhere to the west, a little Mormon town with wide streets. Buddy wakes, nose to the air.

Adam fumbles a bit, releases the lid, stuffing the tape into his jacket pocket. Solemnly, he turns to the wind and holds the urn to the sky. I step back as far as I can without losing my footing, wondering where the wind will take the ashes.

Beginning a low prayer, Adam reminds me of a monk, quiet, private, intent. But soon his prayer turns into a song, and his voice is like the wind—clear, strong, with promise of sweet rain.

Some distant day you'll have a dream,
Of what your life might have been,
When you walk on that Milky White Way...

Tears fall off Adam's cheeks, are carried upwards by wind into boiling rain clouds above. Soon his tears will fall again, way over on the rich red cliffs near the little town of Torrey, the direction the winds are herding the clouds. A little yearling fishhook cactus will catch Adam's tears in its purple wax blossoms.

"Goodbye lassie, back to the Highlands with you."

Adam suddenly flings not just the ashes, but the entire urn high into the sky. Caught by wind, it tumbles upwards for a moment, and a thin stream of dark ashes erupts from it like a tiny volcano, then blows to the west as the urn falls thousands of feet into open air below us.

Breeze catches ashes, bearing them to the far rims and lakes on the Aquarius Plateau, to the white rocks, to the places in Capitol Reef that Deana loved. The urn falls thousands of feet, then shatters far below onto a large black boulder covered with red and green lichen. Some day, a tiny black ant will find a tiny brown shard and take it home in wonder. But one small piece of urn is caught again by the wind and continues its flight, airborne, tumbled high into thunder and mammatus clouds. It will come down later, far, far away.

Adam finally speaks. "Going, going, gone. You know, Deana was the only person who ever loved me. When she died, I lost my bearings. Now I'm lost in the going, going, gone."

I stand quietly, still saying nothing, finally answer, "Well, Adam, like some things, like haggis, for example, you have to let people have a taste of what you are if you want to be loved."

He looks surprised, studies me.

"Look," I continue, "It takes courage to let somebody know you, the real you. You always risk loss."

Adam answers, "Yeah, I guess so. I start thinking my pain is unique, and I feel that old existential haunting, but I know deep inside I'm human like everyone else. That gives me some small comfort."

"Don't cut yourself short. No expectations."

After a long silence, punctuated by distant thunder, Adam replies, "You're right, Chin, you're right." He smiles, wild hair scratching at his cheek. "But why can't you do the same with Charlie?"

"What's Charlie told you?"

"Charlie and I are sorta friends, as good as you can be with a guy like him. He told me he made a total ass of himself with you. We guys don't usually talk about this stuff, but since I'd cried on his shoulder, he told me about you. I don't understand why you won't give him another chance."

"Adam, I'll tell you the truth, something I don't usually tell even myself. That night on the hill when we broke up I got a little glimpse into the depths of Charlie's soul, and I didn't particularly like what I saw. When Charlie got rich, he decided that money was all he needed to make him happy, and he discounted everything we had. Our relationship, at least from his side, had been based on need, not real love. At least he was honest at the time, and that's exactly what he told me. But me, I still love Charlie, nothing's changed. I'm like little Buddy Blue here, it's an unconditional love."

Adam asks, "So why don't you get back together with him?"

"I can't ever do that. Charlie's bad news for me. He betrayed what we had, and I know he'd do it again, given the right circumstances. We're talking about a deep level of trust here, or lack of it, that is. Charlie's an opportunist. But now he's discovered that money really doesn't buy happiness."

"But you could just not love him so much, just turn it off and not care. Think of the kind of life you could lead on the arm of a good-lookin' guy with all that money."

"It's called integrity, what kind of person would I be if I let myself be reduced to that? And it's kind of hard to just stop caring. I think you understand what I'm talking about."

"Unfortunately, I do."

"Adam, when I was a kid, I found a baby magpie that couldn't fly, it was ready to die. I hand-fed it and it got strong and grew. Then it suddenly died anyway. I was heartbroken. My mom told me that wild things don't live in captivity very well. You and me, Adam, we're kind of like those wild things, don't you think?"

He nods glumly.

"Anyway, Adam, you know how they do this blood-brothers thing in the movies—the white man and the Indian cut themselves so they'll bleed, then rub their wrists together? Let's do that. We have a lot in common. I want you to be my blood-brother."

Adam looks incredulous."Are you serious? How would we get ourselves to bleed?"

"It's no big deal. My cousins and I did it all the time when we were kids. We had lots of blood-brothers, sisters, they were forever, though I've lost track of mine. Here, let me show you."

I take out my pocket knife and quickly poke a tiny hole in the end of my finger.

"Fingers are good,'cause the blood's close to the surface there and it hardly even hurts. OK, your turn."

Adam takes the knife, looks at me incredulously, then slowly, tortuously pokes a small hole in the end of his forefinger.

"Does it hurt?"I ask.

"A little,"he grimaces.

"OK, let's rub our blood together. Here, smear yours against mine. Hurry, it's already drying up."

We hold our fingertips together, Adam grinning like a kid.

"Now, we have to promise to be loyal friends forever. Do you promise?"

"I do."

"Me, too."

Now Adam looks concerned."I'm A-negative, what are you? What if our blood's incompatible and we die?"

"It doesn't matter, what's important is that now we're blood brother and sister. Forever. We now have to stand and salute each other."

"Chinle, you're nuts."

We both face each other and salute. Adam groans.

"What's wrong?"I ask.

"My legs are getting sore,"he answers, slowly lowering himself back onto the rock.

I sit next to him, and he puts his arm around my shoulder. We sit together, watching misty clouds cloak the far distance.

Finally, I say,"We really should get outta here before these clouds drop."

"Yeah, we should. I just find my one-and-only blood sister and we get zapped by lightning. That's life—par for my life, anyway."

We both sit for a moment longer, savoring the wild landscape, black clouds settling in. Finally, I ask, "Can you hear that?"

"Hear what?"

"It's a deep hum, far, far away, from over in the desert."

"That crazy desert hum thing again," he says.

We both sit a while longer. Adam adds, "I figured out what it is, by the way."

I look at him, surprised. "What?"

He answers, quietly, "It's the angels singing softly in the stars shining bright."

Now, suddenly, strands of golden sun break through sullen clouds and spray over the flanks of nearby Sunlight Mountain. After a moment, clouds close again and move swiftly over us, but there's no lightning. A soft rain soon blankets us, forcing us to take our leave of the summit. I notice Adam dropping a penny onto the pile as we go by.

I smile to myself. Adam's forgotten to toss the film can over the edge. Maybe I'll come back someday and read what's in it.

We finally reach camp at dusk, wet, legs sore. Scattered clouds begin to abandon the sunset, soft pinks draining into dull gray. A few stars open above in the clearing night sky as a full moon rises dramatically over the shoulder of Arrow Peak where summit stands tall.

A family has set up camp in the spot next to Adam's tent, and the smell of hotdogs roasting on a campstove drifts up the trail. Buddy immediately makes friends with the kids, and the family invites us to join them. Come to find out, they own the Zion Times-Independent up in Salt Lake, and soon everyone's caught up in newspaper talk.

After a cup of hot chocolate, I politely excuse myself, tired, and wander over to old Willy. Buddy will show up later, snuggling down in my bag, his breath smelling of hot dogs, potato salad, and toasted marshmallows.

And now, as I slip into the Dreamtime, that last solitary windblown piece of Deana's urn finally completes its journey from the top of Coffeepot Peak to the sculpted country far, far below, at last released by the storm. As Adam and his new friends discuss the wonders of offset printing, the fragment of porcelain settles gently onto pink Burr Desert sand, where it will peacefully lie forever, serenely reflecting a perfect moonlit image of the Sea of Tranquility.

Bitter snow, crisp beneath black soul,
Tall gray aspen, silently tolerant of this intrusion,
Shadow rim under moon's graceful curve.
Mortal, not finite, I climb,
Lungs aching, beneath Northern Cross.
Twisted crevasse, wonderfully deep,
I acknowledge you, friendless, with tip of ice axe.
Now I know that only those who have fear,
Can meet courage.
And now, alone, high on summit,
Pulled by wind and serendipity,
Into the dance,
Like light into rainbow.

Dear Chinle,

I think you should definitely try to sell your poems. They are inspired, though you might want to try some of the old iambic pentameter structure just for fun, and you should read some of the old poets like Donne and Spencer to truly understand the art. I don't mean to be a bother, but why don't you come over to my place for a while and take a break? You can fulfill your creative genius and even take some poetry courses here.

While you are writing poetry, I will be overseeing the finishing of the texture on the wall downstairs and then the painting. Don't know if I will be having lunch with Linda. She mentioned it and if she calls I will go. I will definitely tell her that you are now living in a cave outside of Radium or someplace she could never find you. Come to think of it, I could never find you myself, dear cousin.

Well, must go. Will write again soon. Terry and I are actually talking about a trip in a month or so. Hope I have sold my bungalow by then. It's such a nuisance.

With love, Sarah

Radium Ray Newspaper
Another UFO sighting, this time by numerous people in a region stretching from Grand Junction, Colorado to Price, Utah. Even local law enforcement officers saw the object, which appeared to be saucer-shaped and have a band of green and blue lights around its middle. The object skimmed along the front of the Book Cliffs for 100 miles, then shot into the sky, according to eye-witnesses, including Officer McCourt of Wellington. Anyone with photos is encouraged to call the newspaper.

Dear Chinle,
Moved closer to road, feels better than in under those big cliffs. Get more early morning sun, lots of dry sagebrush around the trailer, have to watch the weeners for ticks. Got your postcard. Gonna make a run over to Junction in a few days to get supplies, coffee, sugar, cocoa, canned milk. Bring any or all if you come b4 next week, will pay you back. Did you know Sego above Thompson was named after milk? They liked the name on the can. Meteorite hit three nights ago over by Whipsaw, spent last two days looking for it, worth some money. Last night saw two coyotes watching me, 20 feet away. I invited them to dinner, but they looked insulted, me treating em like dogs, got up and left. Checked out tracks and by God one has six toes. Maybe they think my weeners would be an easy lunch, but I ain't seen a coyote yet that can outdo a badger, and weeners make badgers quake in their sleep.
Hope to hear from you again,
Jim

Godless Gotterdammerung
James Agee,
Time Magazine, Oct. 15, 1945
When they got news of the Atomic Bomb, intelligent men were filled with awe. There has been much talk about how to get the new monster into an unbreakable cage—and few admissions that the real monster is the human race. Nobody knew just how deadly or prolonged the radioactive poisons would be, yet they went ahead and made and used the Bomb. Perhaps only like men among soldiers and scientists, trained to think 'objectively'—i.e., in terms of means, not ends—could such irresponsibility and moral callousness be found. There is something askew in a society in which vast numbers of citizens can

be organized to create a horror like The Bomb without even knowing they are doing it.

It is fair to expect such men to be aware of the consequences of their actions. And they seem to have been so. Yet they all accepted the assignment, because they thought of themselves as specialists, not as complete men. The scientists who refused reacted as whole men. Today the tendency is to think of peoples as responsible and individuals as irresponsible. The reversal of both of these conceptions is the first condition of escaping the present decline to barbarism.

Dear Chinle,

Thank you so much for all your advice. It is fabulous—like having a personal guide to Utah!

We went to a party here in Boulder and the house was beautiful: balconies, lofts, skylights, etc. I now plan to redo my place in an Italian style.

I will study your letter in detail later today and write again. I was starting to worry when I didn't hear from you.

I have been doing some gardening, actually moving sand and rocks here and there. I am totally exhausted today. The bungalow inspection is Monday. O happy day.

Talk to you soon.

Love,

Sarah

9
The Gift: Taylor Ranch

The fire plays a game with shadow and ember, dark and light. Together, merged with fire and shadow, warmth and cold, Johnny and I. His long legs are encased in amber-brown worn chaps that softly reflect the glowing fire, a glow that soaks into his brown felt cowboy hat. A mandolin on the log next to him glows ebony-red from the fire.

He's pensive tonight, but that's how cowboys are supposed to be, caught up in a lonely freedom. I envy him that freedom, that solid destiny of cattle dispersal and gathering, that well-rooted religion of yucca and sagebrush, and his companion of solitude, trusted, always there. He has nothing, everything.

The fire greedily consumes dry wood, hot and steady. Fire has integrity, honesty. It's always fire, nothing more, nothing less. There's a beauty in its simplicity, a terror in its simplicity, in its purification. Purification comes slowly, painfully, like a searing light into your soul, then the beauty surrounding you is revealed.

We're both lost in a past, his memories holding warm-walled canyons and cold bedrolls, mine holding the textures of Charlie's smile. I don't know how long we sit, for pinion logs burn forever.

A distant coyote reminds the world of loneliness. Not far away, another differs in philosophy with a bemused high-pitched round of yapping. Johnny looks up from the fire, seeming a bit surprised that I still exist. I like his green eyes, his friendly open look. This man would never betray me. This man would never love me. He pokes the fire with a stick.

"Ever own a horse, Chin?"

"Yeah, I used to. A whole herd, to be exact."

I think back on corrals built of sticks and pebbles, holding spirited blacks and bays and palominos and buckskins, each with lovingly bestowed names, pedigrees, and matching tack.

"A whole herd! Did you ride a lot?"

"Well, I had to exercise them every day, so I ended up riding about every waking moment."

My dresser drawer was partitioned into stalls, complete with nametags, horse blankets, buckets, bales of hay, the horses themselves, all cut from ranch catalogs. Black Rose. Buck. Desert Shadow. Halima. Stormy. Sharif.

"Every waking moment?"

"Yeah. I had to take each one out at least once a day. Sometimes I'd pony one while I rode another, but they had to be out."

Black Rose was a Mustang, black as night. I'd groom her with soft horsehair brushes, then carefully place a velvet blue saddle blanket on her back, careful to smooth her hair so she wouldn't get saddle sores. Next, black tooled parade saddle, heavy with German silver, then black leather bridle with silver conchas. Her hooves were shined black with shoe polish, and her long black tail touched the ground.

"Any Quarter horses?"

"Just one, named Buck. Had Arabs, a Mustang, an Appaloosa."

"Which was your favorite?"

"I had a soft spot for Shadow. He was an Arab. His granddam was sent to Canada for safekeeping during World War II by King George of England. Her name was Turfa, a very famous mare. She'd been given to King George by King Ibn Saud as a gift."

"Sounds pretty fancy."

"Yeah, but Shadow was all heart. He'd go all day without getting tired. He'd do anything I asked. We rode a lot of trails together. I cried a lot when I lost him. He was a beautiful burnished gray, the color of blue steel."

"What happened?"

"Lightning."

"Too bad."

"Yeah. It broke my heart."

"How old were you?"

"I dunno, about eleven."

"What happened to the others?"

"I gave them all away when I fell in love. I think I was about twelve, and his name was Bobby. He was my best friend's brother."

"You gave them away?"

"Yeah, a girl of twelve doesn't have a heart big enough for horses and a boy, too. Something had to go."

"Who'd you give them to?"

"My little cousin, Christine. She envied me having them, helped me with them, and promised to take them out every day. She was seven. But she didn't do it. That was the end of that. I think they ended up on a shelf, collecting dust."

Johnny looks at me with amusement, grins, shakes his head. His own horse, flesh and blood, snorts in the darkness, hobbles softly clanking.

"Johnny, how long you been cowboyin' around out here?"

"Too damn long. Since I was a baby."

"How old are you?"

"Thirty, last time I counted. How old are you, Chin, since we're askin'?"

"Almost twenty-four."

The fire pops, sending a coal tracing through smoke and into a patch of rice grass outside the fire ring. He reaches out with dusty boot and kicks dirt onto the glowing outcast. Pensive again.

All is silent. I notice a large gray spider with dark gray markings toodling along, and at first I think it's a tiny frog. It's headed straight for the fire, so I pick up a small stick and head it off. Frightened, it backs up on its haunches in defense mode, its face to me, and sits frozen in fear for a long time. Finally, it turns and runs, citizen of a different world, silk thread spilling behind it like a climber's belay.

"So Johnny, why don't you do something besides cowboying?"

"What would I do?"

"You could go prospecting with me for a while. We might strike it rich."

He looks at me through shimmering fire, once again amused.

"Well, you and me could survive on most nothing, but I'm not so sure about my folks, they need my help. Besides, I already got a mine, the Radium Queen. In fact, I'm heading back over there as soon as we get these cows over to Coffeepot."

"We could rustle steers."

"Yeah, we could do that. I know 'em all by name. They're like my kids, they come to me when I call."

As if on cue, a low bellow from the cold distance, beyond the realm of warm firelight. Johnny smiles. I like it. It's honest, unassuming. I wonder if he's ever loved a woman. He looks at me as if he knows what I'm thinking, and I feel suddenly shy. I get up and put a twisted log on the fire.

"You know, Chinle, sometimes I hate this damn ranching business, that's why I learned to fly. I could make it without the ranch, but the ranch can't make it without me, my folks are getting older. But I have an idea. Why don't you come with me to Unaweep in early October and help with the fall roundup? We could use an extra hand, and you sound like quite a horsewoman. My mom and dad will be there, and even Grandma Callie."

I feel flattered, but I also feel fear, a fear for my own direction and independence. It's those sparkling eyes, they remind me of Charlie. Always Charlie.

"Can't. My fortune's out there, waiting," I gesture towards the desert, trying to make light.

I look into the distance, and Johnny's eyes return to the fire. I see a brief moment of disappointment, then resignation.

"Besides, I don't even know where Unaweep is."

"It's over in Colorado, at the end of the Uncompahgre. It's where we run our cattle all summer. It's quite a roundup. About 1,000 head."

"I don't have a horse."

"You could use one of mine. I have a small cavvy, real horses, over in Escalante Canyon. They eat that meadow grass and get fat all summer. Escalante Land and Cattle Company. The Musser Boys' headquarters, my uncles, mom's brothers. I even have an Arab you could use, if you won't tell anybody where you got him. You know how to ride, don't you?"

"Yeah, I actually did have a real horse when I was a kid, a half-mustang named Biscuit, a wild little thing, went trail riding a lot, sometimes even when I didn't want to but she did, she'd just take off. But let me think about it. It means delaying fortune and fame, you know."

Once again, that honest smile. We lapse back into silence, and Johnny picks up his mandolin, strums a few chords, and quietly sings to our mutual love—the fire. His voice is tenor and mellow.

If I could see you just one time,
How it would ease my troubled mind.
If I could hold you one more time,
And then pretend that you're still mine.

It's getting late, fire's burning down and it's chilly, but I feel reluctant to let go of this internal warmth, this moment. I think of an old koan:

Doing nothing, sitting quietly,
Spring comes, the grass grows by itself.

I decide that this time I will accept what life offers. I say, quietly, "Well, I thought about it. I'm game. Count me in."

Johnny looks mildly surprised, the crow's feet around his eyes softening. He pulls his legs under him, leather chaps creaking, and I notice he's still wearing spurs. He looks a lot different than when I first met him at the mine. I wonder what he looks like when he's flying—maybe he wears an aviator's leather jacket and scarf, a man of many personas.

Unaweep. Sounds a little sad, but maybe there's a different kind of fortune for me there. Who knows? Something about that name.

Maybe it's really something about those eyes, that honest smile.

"Unaweep this fall, Johnny, but in the meantime, I have to find the Bird Panel for Gramps."

"Promise?"

"Yeah, no matter what, I promise."

He nods just as lightning strikes behind a nearby fin.

"Maybe you'd like to go flyin' with me sometime, just let me know when you do. Storm comin' in from the west, Chin. Looks like it's moving fast."

Just as he speaks, a sudden gust of wind washes across the fire, taking sparks with it and leaving the once-dying flame glowing strong in its wake. Johnny quickly jumps up and kicks sand onto it.

"Aren't many trees around here, but this damn cheat grass could catch," he says. "We really shouldn't even have a fire going out here, it's damn crazy, just wanted some hot dinner for a change."

I get up and help him kick dirt onto the fire. The wind gusts stronger, blowing sand back into my face. The sky lights again with a huge glow of sheet lightning.

"Damn," Johnny shades his eyes against the wind. "Hope this is just a quick front passing through. Sure didn't look like anything was coming in before it got dark."

He quickly grabs his hat as the wind tries to steal it. Another flash, this one an enormous bolt. I can see where it strikes the near horizon, and I count—one-thousand-one, one-thousand-two—stopping at one-thousand-ten—it's only two miles away.

"I'm gonna sit it out in old Willy, Johnny, you're welcome to join me."

"Yeah, might as well. Beats sittin' out under a cedar tree and turnin' into charcoal."

Johnny grabs his bedroll and throws it into Willy just as another blast of wind hits, sideways, now carrying a promise of raindrops filled with sand. I grab the jeep door and push it open against the wind, Buddy jumping in so quickly he tumbles into the back.

We all sit silently in the jeep, watching the lightning, lost in the display of light and power. Suddenly, a corkscrew scratches sideways across the sky, bursting into a half-dozen points of light like a connect-the-dots puzzle which then just as quickly fade. Bead lightning, very rare.

Johnny and I turn and look wide-eyed at each other, and he suddenly puts his arm around my shoulder, pulls me to him, and kisses me before I realize what's happening. It's sweet, and I put my hand on his for a moment—it's warm, comforting.

"I've always had a dream of dancing with a pretty woman in the rain," Johnny smiles, "But it looks like this storm's gonna be yet another dry one. Oh well, maybe next time. Say Chin, I don't know what your dream is, but if it came true, would you still want it?"

"Beats me," I reply. "I'd like to have the chance to find out, though."

"How's your heart these days, if you don't mind me askin'?"

"I dunno," I reply. "Haven't seen it lately. Left it in an arroyo way over on the Swell somewhere, probably never find it again. It's probably washed on down to the Colorado by now, beat up, tangled in rocks and weeds and shredded tree limbs."

Johnny says nothing, but I see him wryly shaking his head. He points to a cloud of distant dust in the twilight, "Man, that's what I call a dust devil!"

"Yeah, they call them willy willies down in Australia."

"Reminds me of Joe's old dog, Duffy. He does that a lot." We laugh.

After a while the storm passes, dry, rainless, and we finally silently tumble away from each other as the wind sways the grass gently in a final promise of tomorrow, be back tomorrow, maybe with sweet rain.

Now I lay in my little pup tent with Buddy at my feet, thinking of Johnny's warm arms around me. I toss and turn, unable to sleep, thinking back to a night long ago, walking in Dry Park, over in Colorado, walking as night struggled with full moon and wind, but a different kind of wind, a wind that followed me from Radium, like a Sons of the Pioneers song.

Listen to the wind,
Wonder what he's sayin',
Seems to be a sadness in the sighin' of the wind.

Prickly cactus warned me to stay on trail as I walked silently and slowly, head turned to the deep sky hung with low stars, high clouds behind. A screech owl circled, calling to its prey. Aloneness, partnered with loneliness.

Wonder where he goes,
Darlin' can you hear me?
Thought I heard you whisper in the sighin' of the wind.

Defiance of fear is called courage. Courage is easy when you have nothing to lose. All I have left is my soul, yet I have no courage. I am alone. We're all alone.

Sets my weary heart a longin', yearnin', dreamin',
Starlight lost its meanin',
Since you went away.

Once again, Charlie's deep eyes, gentle unassuming laughter. A sense of deep loss. The night opened into sunwaves on towering rose cliffs in the far distance. Rose cliffs, downriver.

Now he's turnin' cold,
Wonder if he's lonely,
Can't you hear me callin' in the sighin' of the wind?

So wonderfully alone. Like the juniper tree, like the pinion pine cone, fall to the earth and no one knows. Part of nature. Oblivious to your beauty, uniqueness.

A lone two-point buck passed in the moonlit canyon below, slowly grazing, contented, occasionally gazing about him, young, ostracized from the herd as a potential threat to the leader. Quietly, another young buck came into view. Often such bucks range together. These acknowledged one another, passed, choosing solitude over companionship, at least for now.

Separation. A presage of another separation, death. Is death but a simple passing, a transition? Does it presage life? The huge dead juniper nearby serves as a refuge for many small creatures, perhaps more useful now in death than in life, and perhaps more beautiful. But it will gradually decay, be forgotten. Did it want desperately to make a difference, to leave a legacy? I sigh. We humans are so arrogant. Or is it fear?

Chinle, my friend, if you stay out here in the desert, you will die.
Yellowjacket, my friend, if I don't stay out here in the desert, I will die.
Perhaps, but you'll die young out here. In the game of chess, that's check, my friend.
Maybe, but I will die happy. Checkmate, Yellowjacket, my friend. Now let's get some sleep.

Next morning, after breakfast, Johnny waits by the cold ashy remnants of the campfire, even though I can see his horse is saddled and ready to go. In the nearby pasture, the cattle bawl, snort, ready to get on with their journey.

I can tell Johnny has something on his mind by the way he's thumping his fingers against his jeans. He paces a bit, restless, finally leans against old Willy. I sit quietly on a big juniper log, finishing my coffee, trying to interpret what the cattle are saying. These are purebred Herefords, blue bloods in the world of cattle, purchased to upgrade the Taylor herd.

Finally, Johnny comes over and sits down next to me.

"I have something to give you," he says, reaching into his denim jacket pocket. He pulls out a small white box, places it in my hand.

I know it contains some kind of jewelry. I never wear jewelry. How could Johnny not notice that I never wear jewelry? The box is light and has stamped on it the words Nancy Hanks #2 Mine, Unaweep Canyon. I look up at Johnny.

"It's not from me." He looks nervous.

"Who's it from?" I ask.

"Open it, you'll know."

I open the box. It contains a very simple but elegant silver chain. On the chain is the purist piece of amethyst I've ever seen. Expensive.

Not from Johnny. I hold the amethyst up to the sun. It's dazzling, a hint of rare purple in pure ice.

"Who's it from, Johnny, if you didn't buy it?" I demand. "It's from Unaweep."

"Can't you guess?" He looks solitary, eyes distant.

"No, I don't know anyone rich enough to buy me this. I don't know anyone who'd want to buy me this."

"Sure you do. Charlie."

"Charlie? Why would Charlie buy me this?"

Johnny looks at me, steady, analytic.

"Johnny, Charlie told me he never loved me. He said I was an encumbrance." The stone is ice in my hand.

"Maybe he feels guilty. I was over in Radium while you were gone and told him I'd seen you, and he wanted me to give it to you. Take it. It's the least he could do after giving you so much trouble."

"If I take it, he'll feel that everything's alright. It's not. He keeps sending me postcards like he wants to get back together. Here, give it back to him. Tell him I don't want it. Tell him he's a bastard. I don't accept gifts from bastards."

"Chin, take it. He doesn't want it back. It means nothing to him. He just wants to make himself feel better. I know what he's like, I grubstaked with him, remember? We were partners. Charlie can be a lot of fun, but deep inside, he's a self-centered ass. Keep it."

"I can't. I don't want it."

I close the box and hand it to Johnny. He reluctantly takes it. We're both uncomfortable.

"You should never have agreed to give it to me, Johnny. Charlie knew I wouldn't take it. He knows I never wear jewelry. He's using you."

"No, I think he actually thought you'd accept it. It's his way of apologizing."

"I don't accept that kind of apology, I want words. My forgiveness isn't for sale."

"Chin, let it go. Charlie's not worth your anger, he's not worth any of your emotions, any of your thoughts. Forget him."

"I know, Johnny, but he betrayed me."

"You're still letting him hurt you every day that you don't forget him."

"I can never forget him. I can never forgive him. I gave him my heart, he betrayed me."

Johnny puts his arm around me. It feels comforting, but I don't want to be comforted. The wall is thick, well-built, strong. Charlie built this wall, a true craftsman.

"Chin, Charlie doesn't deserve you. You can never love anyone else until you forget Charlie, you have to do it for yourself, not for Charlie. Chin, you deserve someone who will love you like you loved Charlie."

"I would never betray someone who loved me like that. Besides, how can I forgive him when he's never said he was sorry? Seems to me to forgive somebody for what they've done to you without them being sorry is to just invite more trouble."

"Chin, look, take this gift, pretend it's from me, not Charlie."

Johnny takes the white box once again from the pocket of his faded jacket and slips it back into my hand.

"Here, pretend it's from someone who cares about you. Forget Charlie. This is a gift from me. Take it, put it on. It will protect your heart so it's never broken again. It's one of the nicest gems in Utah. It will help you when times are hard. Take it, think of how the earth burned to create it. It belongs to you, not Charlie. Forget the bastard."

Johnny takes the amethyst from the box and puts it around my neck. It feels timeless and cold, like Charlie. I hold my hand over it until it begins to take my warmth.

Now Charlie fades, warmth pushes out cold, the stone belongs to me, echoes my heartbeat. Somewhere beneath the pain I still love Charlie. I feel tangled, like the roots of a mountain mahogany trying to grow on granite ledge, twisted to find every grain of soil, every drop of water.

Charlie always said such trees have character. Pain builds character, but the strong happy trees have deep roots, thick trunks.

Slim gray eastern mahogany,
Smooth-barked lowlander,
Wandering through mossy paths,

At night, when no one watches.
Happy with abundant water and rich soil.
Unaware,
Of distant, distant mountain mahogany,
Even now in delicate white bloom,
Precariously perched,
High above roiling stream,
Clinging to granite, roots in snow.
A fragile existence,
Yet so much closer,
To those distant mysterious stars.

"Johnny, I think I'm ready to go flying. Do you still wanna go? I think it's time to move along, little dogie."

Johnny looks vaguely surprised, pleased.

"I gotta finish up here, then we can leave, probably another few days, though, still gotta tag and vaccinate and take this bunch up on the upper pasture. Our hired hand is coming today to help. You're welcome to hang around if you want. After we're done, I want to test my scintillator from the air, you can help me."

"Can we take Buddy Blue?"

"Don't see any problem with that. How about meeting me at the Temple landing strip four or five days from now, maybe we better make it a week just to be on the safe side. What is today, anyway? On second thought, I'll meet you at the Temple Junction Café and we'll have breakfast first."

"It's closed," I answer.

"No kidding? OK, let's just meet at the strip around seven, a week from today."

Now Johnny's arms are around me, but the amethyst holds us apart, ever so slightly. Johnny's right, it will protect me well.

He adds, "By the way, Chinle, Charlie named a street in Radium after you, you probably already knew that, didn't you?"

"No, I didn't. Chinle Street?"

"Chinle Way."

"Where is it?"

"It's over in his new section, Dundeeville, where he's building houses for his mining honchos. He's naming the streets after his friends. Also himself. Not just Dundee Street, but Charlie Dundee Street."

"What a narcissist."

"You got that right. He named one after me, too, Taylor Way. And guess what, Chin? Chinle Way and Taylor Way intersect. I'm not making this up, honest. See you Friday."

Dear Chinle,

Where do you get those crazy cards? Sure, I believe in jackalopes. Did you get that card at Harvey's Mercantile in Loa? He has a jackalope on his wall, you can see where he glued the antlers on. You know, jackalopes is a mix between an antelope and jackrabbit, the Utah species is real religious and has lots of babies. Can imitate human voices. The jackalope sings only on dark nights before thunderstorms. I heard one just the other night. Scared the bejeebers outta me and the weeners. Write.

Jim

Dear Chinle,

No matter where you are, I want to come for a visit! I am very nervous about the sale of my bungalow, but things seem to be going smoothly. Two other bits of good news: I finally passed the rental license inspection after spending $800 on improvements. And I found the entrance to the ant nest that has been plaguing my downstairs tenant. In this regard, I am anti-insect rights. As far as I am concerned the Queen must die!!!!!!!!

Also, is there a better place to camp than Antelope Flats? Terry won't camp except in a campground and we both actually just prefer a nice motel. Is there one nearby? I am excited about the trip and the possibility of seeing you even if it's just a brief visit.

I have become quite lazy lately. I hope it's just the weather. I don't put much faith in chiropractors to tell you the truth. I think they can do a lot of harm. But I love massages.

I normally have no back pain ever, so I don't understand where it came from. Though I did weed in the garden for 2 hours without stopping! My gardener George couldn't come so I decided to have all the fun. All better today though.

Winston and I are well. Very well in fact. I do hope we can meet up, my dear cousin.

Love, Sarah

12 Fighting Men Ride Out Blast in Trenches Well in Advance of Main Body of Troops: Explosion Set Off From Tower
Las Vegas, Nev. (AP)
Twenty-two hundred marines crouched in trenches Saturday witnessed the most spectacular atomic blast of the spring series—a shot that flashed blinding white then turned a beautiful rosy orange during an unusually long lingering afterglow.

The predawn test, first to involve marines maneuvering in helicopters, was set off from a 300-foot tower.

After the explosion the ground troops, from Camp Pendleton, Calif., and Camp Lejeune, N.C., scrambled up and advanced in a tactical exercise toward a mock enemy. Their trenches were 4,000 yards from Ground Zero.

Six marines and six soldiers rode out the blast in trenches well in advance of the main body of troops. Authorities would not disclose their distance from the blast. The exercise commander, Brig. Gen. William C. Bullock, said there were no casualties. The brilliant flash was seen in Los Angeles, 250 miles away, as an orange-yellow glow illuminated the entire sky.

The dirty white cloud that shot skyward after the shot bore down on the resort community of Las Vegas, 75 miles from the Atomic Energy Commission's Yucca Flat Proving Ground, at a fast clip. But as it neared the city the wind veered and it appeared the cloud would pass well to the north.

Observers here felt no shock wave and heard no sound from the blast, sixth of the spring tests.

Rabbits were exposed to the blast for the military effects test. Sheep were used to show the marines the effect of the Bomb on living things.

10
Duffy: Temple Mountain

Back at my camp spot near Temple Mountain, sitting on a flat rock, I take out my notes, flipping through several pages until I come to a sketch I made while up on the Swell at Eagle Canyon, near Swasey's cabin. Nearby, Buddy sleeps under a big juniper.

Yesterday, after leaving Johnny, I found some duck-heads rock art, and they're exactly like those I sketched up at Eagle, making me wonder if the artist was one and the same. Why not? The climate was different a thousand years ago, wetter, springs everywhere, making it easier to wander greater distances hunting and gathering. Studies from packrat nests indicate that instead of juniper-pinion scrub forest, this country was once covered with tall Douglas fir trees.

This harsh beautiful land must've looked quite different, wheat-colored cliffs with soft green fir trees everywhere. Hard to imagine, but the contrast of reds, golds, and greens must have been beautiful.

Back to my sketches. Concentrating, looking for similar elements, now it dawns on me that something unusual is going on in the direction of Joe's mine—the squeal of tires spinning out, the gunning of an engine. Buddy gets up, perks up his ears. Now a vehicle is coming fast down the road, squealing tires as it rounds the corners.

Just then I see Duffy, Joe's little scruffy salt-and-pepper terrier, emerging from the wash, climbing the bank, and trotting on up the road back towards the mine. He must've been hunting rock squirrels.

The truck noise gets closer. Panicked, I whistle, yell to Duffy at the top of my lungs, just as a rust-colored pickup rounds the curve.

The pickup barely makes the curve, tipping dangerously towards the wash, skidding as the driver spies the little dog and hits his brakes. I can't make out who it is, other than someone with dark hair. Before I can even pray, I see the front wheels barely miss the little dog, but the back wheels catch him up, hurling him into the wheelwell against the truck, then out onto the road.

The truck slows for a minute, and I hear someone yelling, cussing. Then the driver guns it and skids on down around the next bend.

I quickly put Buddy into the jeep, run to Duffy's side, a sick feeling in my stomach, wishing I could change the events of the last few moments, turn back time, my gut telling me this will end badly.

I gently put my hand on Duffy's silky side—no breathing, no nothing. Just then, I know his soul's released, he's dead.

I sit beside him, in shock for a few moments, feeling only a sense of wasted life, a sense of human arrogance and cruelty.

"This didn't have to be," I say softly.

Now I hear another vehicle, and Joe is standing by me, looking down at the little brindled terrier.

"How did this happen?" Joe asks in a quiet voice, a voice full of disbelief.

"That bastard sumsabitch in that pickup just ran over him."

"What color pickup?"

"Rusty orange."

"Will you be a character witness for me if I go to jail, Chin? I'm going to kill the bastard." Joe gently picks up the little dog. He carries Duffy to a soft sandy spot at the edge of the road.

"I'll bury him in a bit. Let his spirit look around, say goodbye to this damned screwed-up planet. I'm gonna kill O'Riley. Watch over him for me, Chin."

Joe walks away, shoulders held in resolute squareness, over to where one of his workers, Johnson, sits in Frankintruck, an old pickup cab mounted on a 1942 military 6x6 undercarriage. Door slams, engine guns, they're gone down the road, leaving me and Duffy alone.

Well, probably just me, 'cause in all truth, Duffy's gone too, probably chasing bunnies through the pearly gates, at least I hope.

Duffy's body has already begun to stiffen, millions of cells screaming out for the warmth of blood coursing through his veins, crying out for his life, their life.

Gone.

I touch his silken side, then his paws, red sand still sticking to them, his pawprints still fresh in the sand, tracking his exuberance only moments before. Now dead, gone, in a flash. I begin to cry, rocking back and forth on my heels.

"Poor little guy, poor little guy. Godspeed your soul, little guy, Godspeed."

In the distance, I hear shouting, a gunshot, another, then two more in quick succession. An engine revs, and soon I hear the rumble of Frankintruck coming back up the road.

Now Joe's standing by me.

"Let's bury him, Chin," he says, quiet, resolute. He takes his jacket from the truck and wraps it around the little dog, gently placing him in the back.

"Get in," he says. "We'll bury him up by the mine." I run and grab Buddy, and we swing up into the cab.

Johnson pushes down the starter rod on the floorboard with his foot, which pushes the starter gear into the flywheel. He then quickly jerks his foot off the rod before it kicks back. We head up the road, bouncing on Frankintruck's wide bench seat, Buddy in my lap.

The truck slowly climbs the steep hill to the mine. We get out, Joe picking Duffy up out of the bed, still wrapped in the coat. Johnson gets a shovel, and Joe points to a place by a large upright chunk of buff sandstone, still holding the little dog close. The sand is soft, and the digging doesn't take long. Johnson, never saying a word, nods to Joe, then slowly walks back into the depths of the mine, where the faint sound of machinery means Sparky or someone's working.

Now Joe gently lowers Duffy into the little grave, still wrapped in the jacket, body still warm. I'm crying too hard to help him finish the job. Joe shovels the dirt back in, on top of the little body.

"C'mon, Chin, it's OK, he's just a damn dog."

I look up at Joe, he's all blurry. I rub my eyes on my sleeve.

"C'mon, Chin," he holds me close to him. "Just a damn dog," he repeats. Now he's crying also, silently, I feel his chest heave as he tries to stifle it.

He lets me go. I walk over to a bank where clusters of delicate purple scorpionweed bloom and carefully pick several clusters, place them on Duffy's grave.

"Yeah," I reply, "Just a damn dog."

Joe and I stand there a while, eyes wet, looking down at the ground that now holds his best friend, damp sand pressed against soft gray eyes, silky ears, little round belly, once-wagging tail.

I finally ask, "Joe, did you find the bastard that killed him?"

Silence, then, "Yup."

More silence, then finally, he adds, "It was that sumsabitch O'Riley, just like I thought. He'd finally run off the road and we caught up with him. He claimed he didn't see Duffy. He's drunker than a skunk."

"What did you do, Joe?"

"I shot out his sumsabitch tires. I wanted to shoot him too, but Johnson stood between us. O'Riley's gonna have to walk to the highway and hitch a ride, 'cause I told him if he didn't get the hell outta here right now I'd kill him. Same if I ever see him again. The boys know me, know what this damn dog means to me. He'd started walkin' when I left, walkin' real fast. He won't be back, he's a coward. If he does, I'll run him down just like he did little Duffy. The bastard's gonna get himself killed someday."

Joe takes out his pocket knife, carefully feels the sharp blade with his thumb, then walks to the big sandstone rock above Duffy's grave. He begins carving, soft stone easily giving way to the crisp blade edge.

I walk over to a rock and sit down, still crying, Buddy Blue at my side, subdued.

After a while, Joe's back.

"Go look," he says softly, sitting on the truck bumper. I walk over to the grave.

DUFFY BEST DOG EVER
8-7-61

I sob, and now I feel Joe standing behind me. He puts his arm around my shoulder.

I turn, say, "Good job, Joe. When I go, do the same for me, would you?" He's quiet, silently toasts me with his coffee cup, toasts Duffy, eyes wet.

"To Duffy. Best dog ever," he says, eyes filling again. "Best friend ever. He loved me no matter if I was happy, mad, drunked up, sober, he didn't care, as long as I gave him a bite of bread crust dipped in bacon grease. Always licked my fingers, drove me nuts. Never had a friend like him, Chin."

"I know," I reply.

"I mean, you're my friend, Chin, but you have to admit, you wouldn't eat the slop I fed him," Joe tries to smile. "I gotta go to Green River tomorrow for some welding, but the next day, Friday night, we'll have a wake. I took O'Riley's rum. Us and the boys, we'll have a helluva party for Duffy. We'll howl at the moon. Might even chase a few rabbits. Come on up to the camp by dark, Chin. Plan to git good and drunk. Tell me you'll be there."

"Got nowhere better to be, Joe."

"And say, if you see Coralee, tell her what happened, would you?"

"Isn't she in Rangely?" I ask.

"No, she reopened the Temple Café, just last week. She's doing a helluva job. Hop in." Joe revs up Frankintruck, and Buddy and I are soon back to where Willy waits, sleeping in the sun, not even noticing we've been gone.

I sit on Willy's bumper for a while, still feeling like I'm in a dream, trying to erase the vision of rotating truck wheels, Duffy's little body turning with them, over and over. I need to get away from this place that holds the little dog's death.

Bud and I get in, and I push Willy's pushbutton starter. We take off up canyon, turning south off the Temple Mountain road onto an old two-track trail that cuts across the back of the Reef, across the heads of several canyons, deep cleavages that drain the Swell through the fierce upthrust of the Reef, their fading walls cloaking a dark purple distance.

No point obsessing on the pain. I stop at the mouth of the first canyon, gather my pack, fill my canteen from the water bag hanging over Willy's radio antenna, and am soon hiking down the wide wash.

Scanning the walls, I search for rock art, images of the ancient ones. Instead, images of the little dog fill my eyes, are all I can see. Buddy drags along, sensing my mood, desolate.

Canyon walls close in gloom, like the sandy walls of Duffy's grave. To hell with deep canyons. I crave openness, big skies that soar into eternity, not deep quicksand sinking into a morass of obscurity.

To hell with rock art. To hell with the ancient ones. To hell with death, decay. To hell with Charlie, to hell with attachment, the mystics say it's the cause of all pain.

Scanning the rim, I see a dark narrow chute that cuts at an angle through the cliff. Maybe I can get up on top, the odds of scrambling up are better here than further down in the heart of the canyon. I tell Buddy Blue to go back, a command he knows and obeys, though I seldom use it. He has water in a pan in Willy's shade.

I'm soon looking up the steep crevasse, chute hung with shadow. Pressing my back against one side, feet braced against opposite sides, I start jamming my way up, pack and canteen dangling off my shoulder, banging into the rock. The chute is longer and steeper than I'd thought, a trick played by light.

Don't look back down, just continue pushing up, wedged into crack, intimate with sandstone, millions of tiny quartzite particles rubbing and abrading my shirt, millions of people going their way on this planet, yet no one aware if I slip and fall.

Only God knows if you fall to the earth, like the sparrow in the Bible. This chute is absurdly steep, now making me forget everything but my tenuous hold on this planet—focusing only on my survival. Gramps once told me that life is basically a conversation between oneself and God, and right now I'm holding up my end of the conversation quite well.

Eventually I'm on top, where I catch my breath, then turn and look back down, a good 40 or 50 feet at a steep angle. My stomach catches a bit in a knot, but then comes the exhilaration of making a good climb, adrenalin shooting through my veins, through my nerves, straight into my deepest core.

I stand, arms spread out, and shout, "To hell with mortality!" My words vanish, no echoes, absorbed by huge dusty gray cumulus clouds building over the Swell. "To hell with civilization! Open the door and let the wolves in!"

Let the wolves in so they can teach us what it's like to be part of nature again. I build a small cairn so I can find my way back, since everything looks different from above.

The view sweeps on forever. Below and all around me is the San Rafael Reef, that huge syncline of giant shark's teeth that break into huge domes of white Navajo sandstone, domes interwoven with crevices containing potholes so deep they're called tanks.

The San Rafael Reef. So oceanic-sounding, so out of place in this dry lonely desert. Unlike reefs in the Pacific, this dry reef is made of layers of sandstone, some laced with petrified blue and red coral, of mollusk and clam-like marine creatures washed into huge uplifted beaches of a long-dry primal sea. A reef now mineralized and petrified, its water long ago wrung from it by bleached sun.

Far to the north, far beyond the Reef, I can see a hint of the Bookcliffs, buff and gold Green River shale full of fossilized bugs and leaves and black petrified wood and memories, melting into Mancos and eventually into Morrison mudstones and siltstones containing bleached dinosaur bone and smooth gizzard stones.

To the east, far across the deep canyon of Barrier Creek and on past Dripping Spring, nestled between huge red cliffs, lies Radium. Radium, way over there, always way over there, and that's fine with me. I sit on a big rock, taking my lunch from my pack.

Closing my eyes against the light, I think back to another time, maybe three or four years ago, a time with a similar view, a time when Charlie informed me that all this distance bothered him, made him feel damn lonely.

We stood on a point like this, further north, and Charlie had his arm around my shoulders as if to keep me from floating away into the vertigo, that dramatic overwhelming of the senses caused by the intricate interplay of canyons and shadow canyons.

We'd heard of a place called the Black Box and had come looking for it. One of Charlie's friends in Radium, Bobby Hatt, told us about it, and now the three of us were there to explore the canyon, to see something new. And Charlie was right, it was a damn lonely place. But its loneliness appealed to me.

We camped where we could see the faint glow of distant Green River at night, then the next morning we headed out, dusty and half-lost, following roads made by the single passing of another equally lost vehicle long ago. We could barely make out tracks, threaded into deep ruts made by flashfloods.

Detouring around the ruts, we drove slowly, gradually, into the elusive shadows beckoning ahead at the end of a syncline, and we knew we must eventually reach sheer canyon walls. Finally, not even the faint hints of track were left to guide us, and our wheels were blocked by greasewood and rabbitbrush.

Parking Charlie's Scout, we filled our canteens from his water-bag, then filled our stomachs with as much water as we could hold. Who knew how soon we'd dehydrate from desert air and solar heat? We grabbed packs and ropes and began walking, still following that gradual downward course, but now we could see the walls of a side canyon. Bobby pulled out a topo map, confirming that this little canyon, Drowned Hole Draw, led into the Black Box of the San Rafael River.

Angling towards the draw, we found ourselves rapidly dropping, soon scrambling down, down, until we were carefully free-climbing unstable rock. Blue fossils rimmed with white caught our eye, mollusks with crystallized organs that looked like small geodes. A peregrine falcon arced overhead, and wind whistled as the bird dove into canyon proper, just a few hundred yards ahead of us.

We anticipated the Black Box. Some instinct already made us feel the awe of its depth—the falcon didn't slow its flight, the canyon must be deep to accommodate such speed.

Now we could see the bottom of Drowned Hole Draw, only fifty feet below, but hinting of a deeper depth nearby where it fell into the Black Box, which held the dull roar of the San Rafael River.

"It's usually lots quieter. Must be entertaining rainwater," said Bobby.

"I thought you'd never been here before," answered Charlie.

"I haven't, but I grew up on the banks of the San Rafael. I know how it sounds. It flowed right by our ranch. Hell, it flowed right over the ranch when it rained a lot."

"Where was your ranch, Bobby?" I asked.

"Down the other side of Black Dragon Canyon, to the south, where the river frees itself of the canyons. The Hatt Box Ranch. It's still there, what the river's bothered to leave and not erode away. We finally gave up on the place, it flooded every damn spring. Moved to Radium."

Now in the bottom of Drowned Hole Draw, we could see signs of high flashfloods on its closed-in walls. This little feeder canyon was incredibly raw, primitive, rugged, a mere thirty feet wide. Sand ebbed and flowed around rocks like a stream, like a scene in a Japanese garden—sand tended by the Buddha of Water. Here and there, bighorn scat littered the sand.

Rounding a curve, we stood in awe—Drowned Hole Draw ended suddenly, dramatically, in a bottomless pothole of blue-black water. Nothing but a two-foot rim of sandstone separated the pothole from sheer verticality dropping into the dull roar we'd heard earlier. The little canyon just ended, just like that, spilling itself in a kamikaze dive over the high cliffs of the Black Box.

Bobby looked grim. "If we can get down into the main canyon, there's a twenty-mile hike/swim out, assuming the water's passable. We'll come out not too far from Tidwell Draw, where we can meet up with my cousin Jerry, he works in the Big Hole Mine there. He said he'd give us a ride back to the Scout."

Charlie looked just like he had when we stood at the point, grim and damn lonely. But now this loneliness didn't appeal even to me.

Waterstriders, lords of surface tension, skimmed the surface of the pothole, oblivious to the two-foot ledge separating them from oblivion. The deep pothole protected the Box from our eyes, holding us back, adding mystery to rugged terror. Should we proceed?

"Tell you what, let's hike up canyon, take a closer look at Drowned Hole Draw. Might not be back up here for a long time," Charlie said dryly.

What he really meant was, let's delay the Box until we could summon more courage, maybe never.

Turning around and going up canyon, we immediately came upon a series of gentler, shallower potholes. Looking intently for brine shrimp and other seasonal water creatures, we saw only the ubiquitous waterstrider.

We soon came to a ten-foot dry waterfall that blocked further progress up Drowned Hole Draw. We managed to scale the canyon wall and bypass the pourover, but we now saw another pothole, this one even bigger, a huge swimming pool in rock that blocked any hopes of moving onward.

"Well," I offered, "we can climb out here and go back to the Scout, or we can go back and explore the Box."

Bobby's heart was set on the Black Box. Charlie admitted to feeling a bit of sheer terror at the unstable walls. I suggested we go back and take a closer look, so we hiked back down canyon to the edge of the Box.

The ledge between the pothole and the drop off into the Box could only be accessed by crawling above the pothole along a narrow cut in the wall. Carefully, we crawled out on hands and knees and looked over the edge, examining possible routes—easily 600 feet to the river, loose rock everywhere. Bobby accidentally knocked off a small rock, which quickly became a rockslide.

"So much for any Bighorn," I remarked, although we all knew that only an animal with ropes could be on those sheer walls.

We couldn't see the bottom of this canyon, this gouge on the map called Black Box. Its walls were rotten, jagged, the kind of rock that makes climbers religious. It looked as if it were just recently formed, no signs of erosion. Probably limestone. Perhaps its creator was an earthquake. The dull roar below said otherwise, but I liked the drama of my theory.

"Looks like my kind of stuff," Bobby stated matter-of-factly. "Potential death fall, little protection, falling rocks, and high possibility of complete failure. Then you get down and maybe can't even hike out, there may be places where it flows under rocks. I'll go first."

"It's lunch time," Charlie said, "I wanna eat."

Bobby looked at the sun, concurred, deftly hanging his legs over the edge and pulling out a sandwich.

Sitting quietly, we wondered where the falcon went, wondered if we'd make it back out of the dark abyss below us. Through binoculars, the river didn't look too bad, not all that deep, probably wadeable, the roar maybe a trick of the jagged walls and echoes.

We sat in silence. Finally, I said, "Fellows, you can go ahead, and I'll drive around to Tidwell and meet you. That way you'll have more food and water, 'cause I think this little escapade might take longer than planned. Maybe the rest of your lives."

Charlie gave me a look of relief and added, "I'm not goin' neither. It would be sheer stupidity to climb down that wall, and I'm not that dumb. You're not going without us, are you, Bobby?"

Bobby didn't answer, looking disappointed. Then, without further ado, he proceeded to silently start over the edge by himself. We watched in dismay as he free-climbed down, leaving his rope behind.

Charlie tried to call him back, but it was too late—Bobby was already sliding, faster, faster, down a steep black chute, now bouncing off rocks into thin air, now free-falling in a slow circular motion, a motion just like the tires on the rust-colored pickup, and now Charlie has slipped after him, dissipated into the mists of the Black Box below me, falling, falling...

I stand on the edge, dizzy, horrified, calling out:

Charlie! Charlie! Oh my God, Charlie! Coyote!

I'm here, Little Raven, I'm right here. What's wrong?

Coyote!

What's wrong, what's wrong?

Coyote, what can I do?

There's nothing you can do. Sit down before you fall.

But Coyote, I need to help them!

There's nothing you can do. They're gone, both of them. Sit down before you fall.

What's become of them?

Sit down, Little Raven, there you go, slowly, like that, now crawl back over here across that ledge.

Coyote, it hurts, it hurts like when I saw the little dog die.

I know, I know, here you go, come on across and sit here in the soft sand by this pothole, where it's safe.

Coyote, I hurt so much, it hurts so much.

I know, Little Raven, now let's go back to the Scout.

Coyote, I hurt, what can I do? I hurt too much.

You need to get going, Little Raven, you need to get out of this desert. You need to forget the hurt until later. Get going, Little Raven.

I know, Coyote, but I ache, I ache with the uselessness of it all.

Don't be mistaken, you don't hurt anything like those two hurt, or like that little dog hurt, so don't be self-centered. C'mon, let's go.

Coyote, I'm tired of pain, death. I'd rather it was me than them.

You have no choice. It's not your time. They're gone.

Everywhere I look, it's painful. I don't want to look anymore, Coyote.

Remember, Little Raven, you told me when you were old and couldn't see, you just wouldn't look? Well, do that now, just don't look. But remember that your eyes are not the only eyes. There are other ways to see, my friend.

What do you mean?

What if you could see with Duffy's eyes?

I'd see red sand all around me, darkness, death.

No, you might instead see O'Riley out in the desert.

What do you mean?

O'Riley's walking out there, at this very moment. He's falling to the earth and crying his eyes out. First time in his life, Little Raven. And Duffy's there with him, licking his face. Now they're crying together, Little Raven, O'Riley's crying and Duffy's howling. Try to see with his eyes, my friend. Try.

I jolt awake. I've been dreaming. My neck's stiff from leaning on the rock.

I get up, disoriented, then realize where I am. The pain of Duffy's death pours across me like a red flashflood. I'm awake now, the Black Box was a dream, just a dream. I think back—in reality, no one tried to climb into the Black Box, we had all hiked back out and safely driven home, and that was that. Bobby's probably down at the electric company in Radium right now, ready to get off work soon. And I know Charlie's still alive, at least last I heard.

But Duffy's death this morning was no dream. Did O'Riley really see him in the desert, like Yellowjacket said? No, I was dreaming, Coyote Yellowjacket was a dream, too—I can't even get away from the trickster in my dreams. But he was right, I need to get going, get away from this desert, stop having these dreams, talk to someone. But who?

Coralee.

I'll go to the café. Coralee will talk to me.

I sit for a minute, still shaken, then get up and start back, soon finding the cairn I made above the chute, the route back down. But I'm too unnerved after the dream to try the steep straight hold—I can still see Bobby and Charlie tumbling into the depths. For a while, I stand on the edge, looking down to the wash below, trying to work up my courage.

From nowhere there's a buzzing sound in the distance, and soon an airplane is near, flying low.

Someone rim flying, trying to get a scintillator reading, probably AEC boys. A yellow plane with double props buzzes on, then wavers, turns, and flies back, directly overhead, he's spotted me. I want to hide. I hate the damn things, the noise, intrusion.

The plane circles, returns again, flies over, then circles and returns yet again. This time it's so low I hit the ground as it passes over, its wheels feeling like they're right above my head.

I stand, angry, half-wishing it would crash. I change my mind as a downdraft catches the wings and the plane twists a bit. I hold my breath.

The plane recovers, and now I notice something tumbling through the air, a small brown package, which lands near me. It's a paper sack, duct-taped shut, with a note scrawled on the outside:

"Moon me if you're OK."

It's Johnny! I can't believe it. Does he know it's me? What's he doing out here? I open the sack.

"Well, I'll be gotoheck," I whisper to myself. The sack holds two cans of Miller's beer, still cold. It's a wonder they didn't explode on impact. Or worse yet, hit me.

The plane comes back one last time, and I wave, toasting Johnny with a newly-opened can. He waggles the plane's wings, gains altitude, and is quickly gone.

I smile, thinking of the likelihood of standing on this rim and drinking cold beer. But the moment's quickly gone, and I soon begin to worry about getting back down by dark. It dawns on me that I probably ruined any hopes of a rescue, if I am unable to get back down.

Looking again for a place to descend, I eventually find a route where the cliff appears to stair step down somewhat gently. I'll try here, and if it doesn't work, I'll come back up and try the chute.

It's a slow route, and I have to back-climb partway up several times, but I finally reach the wash, sliding down a small eight-foot pourover on my rear-end, sandstone neatly abrading a hole in my jeans.

Now the canyon feels homey, safe, not morose like earlier. Shadows drape the walls, telling the night animals their day is beginning. Evening primrose opens, white blossoms calling the moths to pollinate, pink showing the job's been done.

I'll camp at the head of the canyon, go see Coralee tomorrow. I'll build a big fire, have the canned stroganoff I've been saving for a special occasion, give part to Buddy for being so good, drink the second beer, then look at the Milky Way, picture the Taylor House in Catalpa Town with its big screened porch and rose garden, and I'll sleep deeply, peacefully, no dreams, secure in the knowledge that the stars shine even while I'm asleep.

Next morning, I doze late, dawdle, sitting on a large rock and watching a pair of brown rough-legged hawks riding the canyon's thermals. Throwing my gear into Willy, I notice a spider web only a few feet from where Buddy and I slept, a dreamy net spun with the distinct shiny elegance of the black widow.

I catch a quick movement at the web's edge, up under the rock. The spider, with its icy black legs, is trying to hide. I leave it alone, no need to flip it over to know it has a red hourglass on its thorax. I leave it be in thanks for the same regard during the night.

A thick stand of cottonwoods across the canyon speaks of water, and Buddy's wet belly confirms. I fish my clothes out of one of the jerry cans strapped to Willy's back bumper. The can's filled with small rocks, and water—everything sloshes around as Willy and I go down the road, leaving my clothes as clean as if I'd gone to Millie's Dime-O-Matic. The final touch is to rinse everything in fresh water, which I haul from the spring. I hang the clothes on tree limbs to dry and spend the rest of the day going through my notes, getting organized, being lazy.

Sitting under desert varnish
Wordless poet
Wiggles toes in sand
Patiently waiting.

Sunlight now at an oblique angle and ready to disappear behind the rim, clothes dry, I decide to go on down and see Coralee. I head back to the Temple Mountain road and down towards the café.

I first stop at the Temple Junction Motel to check for mail. No letters. But the manager, irritated, informs me that one, two, three times a call has come in for me. He's a rough-looking hombre named Harry who wears baggy pants that collect under a paunch. I look at the note: Call GR 24-113, collect, urgent. I dial the operator in Green River, who puts the call through. A voice answers, faintly, "Chief's Automotive, Moki Max here."

"Hello, this is Chinle Miller, and I have a note to call this number collect. I'm at Temple Junction."

"Hang on a minute."

Another voice, deeper, "O'Riley."

I say nothing, silence.

He waits a moment, then, "Anybody there?"

"Yeah," I reply.

"Chinle Miller? Look, I talked to someone down there, they said you're a friend of Joe Hughes. That true?"

"Yes."

"Well, you probably know about the dog. I'm calling to say I'm sorry. I was drunked up. Would you pass that along to Joe?"

I don't know how to respond. Finally, "No, I can't do that, Mr. O'Riley."

"Why not?"

"You need to tell him yourself."

Silence, I sense irritation, finally a reply. "He said he'd kill me."

"Well, I can't blame him, I saw the whole thing, and I don't think the loss would be too great. But maybe he'd listen to your apology before he took aim. You'd be that much ahead, at least."

A long pause, then, "Yeah, maybe you're right. I need to tell him. But I don't know where he is."

I don't answer. Another pause, then he asks, "Still up at Temple?"

"Yeah, the Yip Yip, about a mile above where your pickup's still setting, he hasn't moved all that mining equipment in the last day as far as I know," I answer sarcastically.

"Well, I need to get back up there, but I don't have a car."

"Well, just start walkin'. It isn't going to get any easier, but you'll be off on the right foot, at least. Look, O'Riley, say, what the heck's your first name, anyway?"

"James."

"OK, look, James, I'll tell Joe you're coming and at least to let you talk before he starts shooting. That's the best I can do. When do you think you'll get here?"

"I dunno. Wait a minute." I hear muffled talking in the background. "Moki says we need to go first thing in the morning if we're going to get my truck and haul it back."

So, that's the real reason he wants me to go talk to Joe, he's coming up here to get his truck and he's scared, it's not that he's particularly sorry. I feel like telling him to go to hell, but I remember what Coyote said in my dream, "Try to see with Duffy's eyes."

"OK," I answer, "but I don't know if I can get up there before that."

"Well, I'll be there in the morning, so if you can talk to Joe tonight, that would be good."

"We'll see how it works out, no guarantees," I hang up the phone.

"Two bucks for a long-distance call," says Harry, looking at his watch.

"It was collect, but nice try anyway," I reply as he gives me a sheepish grin and fishes a Kool cigarette out of his pocket.

Outside in the dusk, I think about seeing Coralee, but decide I need to get to Joe's before dark, so me and Buddy Blue and Willy head for the Yip Yip Mine.

Winding our way through the dusk, through the canyon to where it opens up, we drive up to the old rock shack. Joe's probably camped up the hill, by the mine portal, where he and the guys usually sleep. It's nearly dark, and I don't trust finding my way up there, so I yell.

"Joe, hey Joe! You up there?" Pause. No lights, no campfire, they're already sacked out. "Hey Joe, anybody home?"

Now I see a flashlight beam, it wobbles, turns my way.

"Who's hollering down there?"

"Joe, it's me, Chinle. Come on down."

"What's up?"

"Just come on down. I need to talk to you."

"I'll kill myself trying to get down this damn cliff in the dark. What's up?"

"O'Riley's coming in the morning."

Now the light wobbles its way down the steep grade, accompanied by plenty of cussing. Finally, the light shines in my eyes, sizing me up, passes over to Willy, sizing him up.

"Dammitall, Chin, a man could get killed slidin' down that hill. Where's O'Riley? I must've just fallen asleep, it's been a long hard day. We hit a vein of what looks to be good high grade stuff." Joe looks unearthly, like a specter, in the backlight of the flashlight beam, and I notice he's wearing only longjohn bottoms and boots.

"Good, good," I answer, what he's saying not really sinking in. "Sorry to bother you, but O'Riley's coming up here first thing tomorrow, and he'd prefer you didn't shoot him."

"That no good sumsabitch..."

"Now just wait, Joe, he wants to apologize. He says he's sorry about Duffy. I talked to him on the phone, he kept leaving messages at the motel for me. Give him a chance, Joe."

"What the hell, Chinle, like he gave Duffy?" Joe replies, angry. "You trying to pacify me so you get all the fun of shooting him? Hell, you're the one who saw the whole thing happen, you're telling me not to kill the bastard?"

"I know, I know, Joe," I answer patiently. "But for some reason, I think he finally did something he's ashamed of. Give him a chance, Joe. I'm willing to. It'll just eat away at you if you can't forgive."

Joe snorts, "Forgive? What the hell, Chin, since when did you start preachin'?"

"C'mon Joe, go on back to bed. I'm gonna camp down the wash a ways. He'll have to come by me before he gets here, so I'll come along, too. Let's just see what he has to say for himself, OK?"

Joe shakes his head. "No promises, but OK, Chin, blessed are the peacemakers and all that BS. If we hadn't just hit it rich I wouldn't be feeling so generous. Did I tell you we hit a big vein, an ancient streambed? Looks to be pure tuballoy."

"What's tuballoy?" I ask.

"What's tuballoy? It's the secret name for uranium they used during the Los Alamos days, everybody still calls it that, and tuballoy is turned into oralloy, enriched uranium, and by God they're gonna call me Hot Rocks Tuballoy Joe. Anyway, I'm gonna buy Coralee a house. Did you see her down at the café? Hell, I might even buy you a house if this thing comes through, you can't camp out in this damn desert the rest of your life. To hell with O'Riley, I got bigger things on my mind. Hell, maybe I'll even buy that bastard a house. OK, Chin, see you in the morning."

Joe stumbles back up the hill while I turn old Willy around and drive back down the road, then set up camp on the edge of the wash.

Soon settled, I toss and turn in my bag, Buddy finally crawling out and sleeping on top of my feet. Maybe Joe hit it rich, after all this time...maybe Coralee's going to finally have something...good thing she didn't go back to Rangely...O'Riley's coming back...maybe I should kill the bastard myself...I really need to go talk to Cleo over in Catalpa Town and see if he knows where some rock art sites are, he knows this country better than anybody...wonder where Johnny is tonight...wonder where Charlie is...hope I don't have any scorpions under my pillow tonight…

Finally, I get up and pull the bottle of Irish Cream from the bottom of my food box, take a swig, and fall fast asleep.

I wake early, under the big pinion tree where I threw my sleeping bag last night on the soft pine needles. It's a windy day, overcast, and I can feel the hint of rain in the mountains.

Looking up, morning light filters through the wide branches that hold huge pine cones. Stiff new growth on the tips of the tree's branches are light yellow, giving the tree the effect of being covered by lit candles.

Laying here, I think of a story Joe Hughes told me last year, after he'd helped me get unstuck, the first time I ever met him. It was a story about why he won't camp by trees. His cousin, Jake Shumway, had his tent melted into the ground when a lightning bolt hit the big juniper it was near.

"Broad daylight," Joe said, "and the clouds were a good mile away. If Jake'd been in that tent, well, goodbye Jake, he would've been blasted clear into where he belongs anyway."

He continued. "Jake was the one they put in prison for grave digging. He was selling these Anasazi pots to rich people back east, makin' his living that way. Everybody knew he was doing it, but hell, a lot of them would've done it themselves if they'd had the time and wherewithal. Jake finally started hiring a pilot, a rim flyer with a little Piper Cub, to scout the remote canyons, lookin' for alcoves, cliff dwellings, that sort of thing. Everything was going real swell for Jake until he conveniently forgot to pay his pilot one time too many.

The pilot told the sheriff what was goin' on. The sheriff didn't give a rat's ass, but when the government brownshirts caught wind of it they decided to make an example of Jake. Seems like Jake underestimated that most basic bond between thieves, the love of money. And now he's in prison up at Poin' de Moun', got six more months."

Looking up through the pine boughs, I think of Jake, wonder what one does all day in prison up at Point of the Mountain near Salt Lake City, then I think about how I used to camp out on our front lawn when I was a kid in Radium, under a big tree like this.

Now fully awake, I stretch and get up, slipping into blue jeans and denim shirt. Just as the hum of a vehicle comes into range, I remember O'Riley's on his way.

A shiny green flatbed truck swings around the curve in the road, a hundred feet or so from my camp. The truck has lettering on the side: Chief's Motor Co., Green River Town, Utah. Willy and Buddy Blue and I are soon following them, eating their dust for breakfast.

By the time I arrive, Joe and Sparky are already down from the mine, face to face with a large man, the three of them squared off. The other man, probably Moki, waits in the flatbed truck. I sense trouble.

O'Riley's dark eyes and hair, square face, Navajo silver belt buckle, all tell me he's at least part Navajo. A glimmer of red in his hair bespeaks a bit of the old country, Ireland. He's holding something under his old tattered cotton jacket—something that's moving.

"Are you Chinle?" He asks, looking annoyed, then adds, "Thought you were Dineh, like me."

I answer, echoing his mood, "You must be O'Riley. Thought you were Scots-Irish, like me."

O'Riley looks at me for a moment, a hint of confusion crossing his face. He ignores me and turns back to Joe, who eyes him warily, waiting for what looks like an inevitable confrontation.

O'Riley opens his coat. "I wanna make peace, like in that show Broken Arrow."

Inside, cradled in his arm, is a little puppy, blue-black speckles on white coat, one eye circled by a black ring. "I call him Bandit, but you call him whatever you want." He hands the little wiggling pup to Joe.

Joe looks surprised, and the lines around his mouth soften. Sparky steps back, tension dissipated.

O'Riley continues, "I came to get my truck. I didn't mean to hit the dog, I was drunk."

Joe says nothing, holding the little pup in his arms, rubbing its little spotted nose with his fingers as it licks him.

O'Riley finally says, "Your dog, the one I hit, he came to me out in the desert, in the dark, I'd been walkin' for a long time. Maybe I was drunk, but he had a light around him. You don't know the Dineh ways, but it's a sign, and I'm leavin' this country for good and goin' back to my grandmother's family near Teec Nos Pos. You can have the blasted burro."

Before Joe can answer, James turns, climbs into the truck, and he and his friend rumble off down the road.

I decide to spend the day near Temple Mountain, since I want to be at the Yip Yip for the wake later tonight. The remnant of an old mining road, left over from the radium boom, climbs the steep hill across from Cleo's drill hole, and I decide to walk up it and see what's there. Buddy chooses to stay behind, chewing on a big bone that Joe gave him up at the mine.

It's a steep climb, but I discover that I'm quickly on top, where it opens out to a broad expanse of slickrock, then tumbles down the other side into the neighboring canyon, Big Wildhorse. I'm back up on the Reef again, only this time at a much lower part, and the going's not nearly as rough as yesterday.

Looking down into Big Wildhorse, I see a huge alcove a few hundred feet over and just below me. I can get to it if I take my time and watch my step. The canyon floor isn't far below, maybe only a hundred feet. To the head of the canyon I can see a small two-track road coming in, and now I see a green pickup parked maybe a quarter-mile away, where the road dead-ends in a small grove of cottonwoods, probably another spring.

Now I'm in the alcove, it's cool, and the half-roof, arched above me, has signs of soot from campfires, but no rock art. I look around for a while, kick some of the sandy floor away looking for artifacts, then lose interest and sit on the edge of the cliff, hanging onto a thick single-leaf oak for safety, watching the canyon below, enjoying the cool breeze. Suddenly I see movement below.

Graceful as a ballet dancer, directly below me, the little yellow-brown coyote rears upright on her hind legs and poises with forelegs in the air, steady and motionless. Then, in a perfect slow-motion parabolic arc, she ripples into a hard-hitting pounce with her front paws, lets out a yelp and stuns her prey, a small black-eyed pinion mouse.

Gathering the little furball into her sharp canines, the coyote shakes her head furiously back and forth to break fragile mouse neck, then tosses the tiny rodent into the air, catching it in a game of exuberance designed to ensure a quick death.

After several tosses she grows bored and swallows the dead mouse whole. She then lies quietly in the warm yellow sand, licking her paws, subdued.

Quietly, I sit high above, watching. Does she know I'm here? Obviously not. From my vantage, I can see more than she can, and now I notice a man hiding in a nearby boxelder thicket, holding a .22 rifle, ready to turn the tables on the yellow-coated hunter.

He now begins to raise the long barrel to his eye, very slowly. He'll take one ear to the Ekker Ranch over by the river and collect his bounty. I won't let him kill her, I've had enough of death, I'll warn the little coyote, sister to Coyote Yellowjacket.

But, unexpectedly, the little songdog stands and turns, facing the man full-on with a direct gaze. He hesitates, rifle barrel drifts downward. Perhaps he doesn't think the little coyote can see him, yet still he hesitates. He hesitates for what seems like an eon.

Coyote waits, dignified as prankster coyote could ever be, enigmatic brown eyes set in tawny yellow coat. Her ears are now cocked, as if listening for the rifle's death report.

Barrel half to his eye, the man watches. A boldness about her speaks of an ancient heritage of freedom in this desert, a sweet sandy independence that perhaps he envies deep inside.

At last lowering the gun, the man stands, now in full view of the coyote, her dark gaze drawing him in.

Casually, she sits on her haunches, curious, unafraid. Finally, the man leans the gun against a rock and likewise sits on his haunches, watching the little songdog. After a while, she yawns, now bored, turns several times in a full circle, scratches at the sand, then lays down, nose nestled in her shaggy tail. She is soon asleep.

Still on his haunches, the man rocks on his heels and begins to sing in a low voice, as if lulling a child to sleep.

Buffalo gals, won't you come out tonight,
Come out tonight, come out tonight,
Coyote gals, won't you come out tonight,
And sing by the light of the moon.

Coyote half-opens her eyes, looks at the man drowsily, then goes back to sleep in the warm desert sun. Finally, he slowly stands and backs quietly away, rifle resting in the crook of his arm.

High above, I watch, hidden. Neither know I'm here. I watch the little coyote sleep while the man slowly walks back to his old beat-up pickup, where he spits in the dirt.

"Damn coyotes," he yells. "Damn gotohell coyotes." He roughly tosses his rifle into the window rack, gets in, and slams the door, his window falling half down from the impact. Flooring the accelerator, sending dirt and rocks flying, he yells at the top of his voice out the window, "Damn coyotes!"

Echoes bounce over and off red cliffs, waking the little yellow desert songdog, who stretches and stands and shakes, ready for a drink at a nearby pothole. She drinks and soon is gone into shadow.

Far away to the south, in the immense and wild Dinétah, the Navajo Nation, the echo's memory finally reaches Coyote Trickster, who carefully cocks one ear, listens for a moment, then grins a sharp toothy grin of self-importance.

It's a look only he, Navajo Deity that he is, could muster.

Now it's night, and I'm back at the Yip Yip Mine, where I park old Willy next to Frankintruck. The two of them can trade lies while I'm gone. Buddy and I walk up the hill to Joe's camp. Moonlight pours over everything, lighting the fire in the distance with men's faces shining around it, lighting everything but the blackness in my soul.

Finally up the steep hill, I can see the mine portal gaping in the cliff, not far from the large sandstone rock next to Duffy's grave. Joe nods his head in recognition as I sit down on a large pinion log near the fire. Buddy goes to Joe, and Joe gently strokes his head.

Hank leans against a nearby juniper, one foot resting on an empty oil can. He touches his hat and smiles at me, then asks, "Joe, I don't mean to be a jackass, but doesn't a wake usually have a body? Where's the body?"

"Shutup, Hank," Sam says, stirring the fire with a long stick, "You're being a jackass."

"We already buried him, Hank," replies Joe, fire burnishing his red hair in the deepening night. O'Riley's little pup squirms in Joe's arms, and he lets it go. It begins playing with Buddy.

"Where's the grave?" Hank asks.

Joe motions, and Hank wanders over to the big stone, Buddy and the pup now at his heels, comes back, wiping his eyes with his shirtsleeve. "Duffy was the best dog ever, Joe, just like it says." Just then he trips over something in the dark, nearly falling.

"Damn it, Joe, I dunno why we can't take out this damn scraggly bush. It's always in the way, damn ugly, too."

"Leave it alone, Hank, I've told you a million times if I've told you once, that's Mr. Cliff Rose. Leave him alone, dammit."

I add,"Cowania mexicana. In spring, the sweet scent drifts forever, Hank. Cliffrose."

"Nice, Chin, nice. I suppose there's some lesson here. You remind me of my dang eighth-grade teacher, always had lessons from nature."

"Did you learn anything?" I ask.

"More than I ever wanted to know. My brain got too full and I had to drop out before it exploded," Hank replies, now back by the fire. "Damn ironic, we're rippin' the hell outta this mountain and he's worried about a stinkin' bush."

Silently, Johnson throws more twigs onto the fire, which devours the new fuel with a roar. Sam backs away a bit, watching the fire burn the end of his stick, then asks,"So what exactly is a wake, Joe?"

"It's an excuse for drinkin', not that we need one," replies Sparky, his back against a large rock, legs stretched out, feet near the fire, now holding the pup in the crook of his arm, Buddy lying next to them both.

"Ain't wakes Catholic? You Catholic, Sparky?" Asks Hank.

"Nope."

"You Catholic, Joe?" Asks Hank.

"Nope, Jack Mormon," replies Joe.

"'Bout as bad," comments Sparky."I used to be Jack Mormon myself, but now I'm so far from that damn church I can't even say Jack. What about you, Chinle?"

"Jack Buddhist," I retort.

Hank snorts, says,"Hell, you're all a bunch of heathens, except when you're prayin' the mine won't cave in. But was Duffy Catholic? I mean, why the hell are we having a wake, if nobody's Catholic?"

Joe answers,"Duffy was Scot's terrier, or at least part of him was, the part that was frugal and buried bones all over the desert."

"Scots ain't Catholic, they's Presbit-arians," says Sparky."Irish is Catholic."

"What if you're Scots-Irish, like Chin here?" Asks Joe.

"You're Catholic-Presbit-arian, which means you get drunk with dignity," Sparky answers, grinning at me.

"I thought we was havin' a wake, not a damn religious inquisition," Sam pipes up, on his way to examine the headstone. He's soon back, flashlight batteries nearly dead, half-tripping over the bush.

"Damn, Joe, that's a helluva gravestone. Hope mine's half that nice. Duffy was the best dog ever, no doubt about it. Let's get started here, Joe. I brought a contribution." He pulls a bottle of whiskey from his jacket pocket, coughing as the breeze floats the smoke his way.

"I got O'Riley's rum out of his pickup," Joe adds, popping the cork and taking a swig. His face screws up. "Rotgut. Damn cheap half-breed."

Soon the bottles begin making the rounds, everyone staring glumly into the fire, no one sure what to say.

Finally, "Duffy sure was a good dog, huh Joe? We all thought the world of 'im," Sam offers.

"He was my best friend," Joe replies.

"I understand, Joe. I'd take a dog over any of the likes of us myself. Dogs just ain't like people, they have brains and are a lot more like-able."

"Cleaner, too. Always lickin' themselves."

"First time I met Duffy he tore into my leg. It was over in Radium, and I was cussin' him, hoppin' around, while he hung onto my pant leg. The Mormon bishop's wife was watchin' the whole thing, laughin' her damn self-righteous ass off."

"Duffy was a good judge of character, even if he was half-blind."

"You know, they say them Scots are good engineers, and I'd have to agree, at least so with Duffy. Always tryin' to fix everything."

"How so?"

"Always tryin' to oil everything up, he'd WD-40 it. At least he'd ask permission first, would stand there and whine, had manners. Then when you'd had enough and told 'im to just can it, he'd do that, whip out the can. Quite a dog."

"Yeah, and that can was always full."

"Then after he'd oiled everything up, done his job, he'd go sit by your bedroll and whine till you'd tell 'im to shut the hell up, then he'd get right in the middle of where you wanted to sleep and wouldn't budge. Would growl at you, too, bite cha if you'd try to make him move so you could go to bed. Drove me crazy, no offense, Joe."

"Yeah, then he'd whine and ask permission to get off. Damndest thing I ever saw. Say, you're sittin' on the rum, Sam."

The bottles make the rounds again as Joe throws more sticks on the fire. The alcohol burns in our mouths, gradually tutoring us in the methods of the wake.

"Duffy used to go by everything and WD-40 it. He'd lift his leg just like that, every time. He figured everything needed fixin', I guess."

"What else do you remember about Duffy, boys?" Joe's eyes glisten in the firelight. "Tell me more."

"He was a helluva dog, Joe, the best. I'll never forget the time he was sleepin' on that rusted-out bed frame in the old stone house. We were outside and all of a sudden we heard the most God-awful howlin'. We went runnin' inside, thought he must be snakebit, but his hind end slipped down in that old frame, he was stuck."

Laughter, silence, firelight flickers. It's now pitch black, and the fire seems like the only light in the world.

"Best coyote-chasin' dog ever."

"Only barked at 'em," someone corrects.

"Well, best lizard chasin' dog in the world. Rock squirrels, too."

Sam starts coughing, takes another sip of rum.

"Joe, how old was Duffy, anyway?" someone asks.

"Dunno, was a stray, but I had 'im 11 years."

"Hell, he was an oldtimer, just like me," Sam muses. "Hope I go that fast."

"Just watch that powder, or you will."

"I used ta have a dawg," Johnson now informs everyone moodily, full-on drunk, speech slurred.

"I didn't know that," Joe says, surprised. "I thought you didn't much like dogs."

"I shore liked that dawg, miss 'im," mourns Johnson, looking sad.

Hank, himself now half-drunk and melancholy and suddenly feeling sorry for Johnson, says, "Tell us about 'im."

"Name uz Bones."

"Bones? That's a helluva name for a dog, Bones."

"Bones. The darndest dog I ever sawr anywhere, 'cept Duffy. That darnt thing, I kept him on a chain, on a snap."

It's the most talking at once that Johnson's ever done, and everyone listens as the firelight dances shadows across his contemplative face.

"Old Bones, he could unsnap that snap, go whenever he wanted, come back, snap it back up. I've never seen anything like it. Man, he just loved ta chase cats. He just chased cats all the time, but he made sure nobody ever saw him takin' off that snap." Johnson falls back into silence.

Hank's brow wrinkles. After a minute, he asks, "How'd you know he'd been gone?"

Johnson answers, belligerently, "Prove he wasn't."

Several of the men groan. Someone's added another bottle of whiskey to the rounds. We all sit in silence.

Now Sparky, staring into the fire, starts softly playing his harmonica to the tune of "Oh Danny Boy." Soon Hank starts singing, his sweet tenor wafting down canyon, where a startled kangaroo rat stops, sits up like a dog on its hind legs, then wiggles whiskers as if smelling the sweet smell of rum drifting on the air.

Oh Duffy boy, the pipes, the pipes are callin',
From glen to glen, and down the mountain side,
Oh Duffy boy, it's you must go and we must stay.

Johnson and Sam are now snuffling a bit, unashamed, and soon everyone joins in the singing. The chorus drifts on to 'Swing Low Sweet Chariot,' then Hank ends with a beautiful ringing solo to 'Amazing Grace':

Amazing grace, how sweet the sound,
That saved a wretch like Duffy.
He once was lost, till Joe he found,
Half-blind, but he could WD.

His singing fades into a mixture of snorts and laughter. Now a guitar appears, and Sam begins strumming, singing to a simple three-chord tune:

Oh, Duffy was a cowdog,
He rode the western range,
Workin' for the Re-Bar Ranch,
Up on the Yeller Cat plains.
Now he and Joe went out one day,
Got caught in a great big storm,
But right nearby was a nice big cave,
To keep 'em good and warm.
That cave had one big problem,
Was home to a big wildcat,
"He'll eat yer mangy coat," Joe said,
But Duffy didn't worry 'bout that.

Suddenly Sam stops, putting the guitar down.

"What the hell, Sam, why'd you stop?" someone asks.

"That's all she wrote," Sam answers.

"Wattya mean, what happened then?"

"I dunno," Sam replies, tipping his hat back.

"That's a helluva way to end a song," someone complains.

Fire nearly out, crescent moon sunk behind the eerie jagged outline of canyon wall topped by juniper trees, the wake begins to wear out.

"Let's go toast Duffy one last toast, over by his headstone," someone suggests, even though the bottles are now empty.

We all manage to stumble over to the marker in the darkness, where we stand for a while in silence until Sparky startles us from our moroseness.

"Here's to Duffy!" he yells, "to Duffy!"

We all join in, "To Duffy!"

The cheers expand. "Here's to Joe, to Bones!"

"Here's to strikin' it rich!"

"Yip Yip or bust!"

"Yip Yip or bust, boys, Yip Yip or bust!"

Our voices echo loud and then echo soft off the cliffs into the deep canyon, reverberating ever so softly, even after Sparky and Hank and Sam stumble off to collapse into their sleeping bags.

Oblivious to all but a pressing need, the normally reticent Johnson WD-40s Mr. Cliff Rose, then collapses near the fire and immediately is snoring softly.

Everything now quiet, Joe and I sit on opposite sides of the fire, watching the embers pop and die along with the occasional flare-up of a drop of pitch. The smell of pinion smoke permeates our clothes, our hair, our future memories. The little pup sleeps snuggled next to Buddy.

Finally, Joe looks up, eyes focusing not on me, but somewhere into the perfect smoke between us. "Helluva wake, huh?"

"Yeah, if you like wakes," I answer dryly, tired, a bit too pensive from the rum.

Joe answers, "Chin, you're too damn sensitive. You take things too hard. Life's always testing our level of commitment to it, don't you know that?"

For a moment I feel betrayed by his criticism. I answer, "So you're saying it's my own fault I feel like this?"

"Look, Chin, this planet's a sumsabitch. What else is there to say about it? The sooner you accept that, the easier it is."

"Sounds like the road to bitterness and apathy to me, Joe."

"No, Chin, no need to be bitter, and apathy's not the answer, either, dammit. Detachment's what you need. Apathy means you don't care. Detachment's a survival mechanism for those who do. And you can always count on something pulling you out of it, just like all this."

"Apathy and detachment both sound the same to me, Joe, like a good way to get outta feeling." I toss a small stick into the fire, it flares up for a moment, lighting Joe's bleary eyes.

"Beats drinkin' too much."

"So what am I supposed to do, Joe, just shut off my feelings?" The rum's making me argumentative.

"O'Riley turned out to be a better man than even he thought he was, just look at this little pup here." Joe slowly strokes the length of the silky little dog from ear to tail. "And whattya mean, supposed to do? Who does the supposin'? Chin, you're askin' Joe Hughes here, the poor bastard who's got uranium in his blood, the poor bastard who despises the rich but who works his ass off tryin' to be like them. Wrong guy to ask, but I suppose you can do your own supposin'. You for sure ain't the type to do what someone else supposes you to do."

Silence. Somehow he's making sense, though he's half-drunk and not making sense.

Smoke's turning direction now, a quiet breeze picks it up from its bed in the embers and drifts it into my eyes. Finally, I ask, softly, "Any regrets, Joe?"

After a moment, Joe answers, "Sure, plenty, like fleas on a dog. I regret my whole damn life, pretty much. But no point in sittin' around cryin' like a baby." He pokes at what's left of the fire with the toe of his boot till the boot starts to smoke.

"Look, Chin, time sure as hell don't stop 'cause you're feelin' bad. But you're a smart woman, you just ain't graduated from the school of hard knocks yet. Probably never will. You'll have all the instructors sittin' around the campfire cryin' with you, tryin' to figure out the meaning of life."

Still feeling defensive, I ask, a bit sarcastically, "Any words of wisdom for me on that, Joe?"

"Alright, you asked. Live life doin' your best given the circumstances, run the race best you can, no point havin' regrets, 'cause if you could go back and do it all over again, you'd do it just the same way as first time around, 'cause you're still you and we poor slobberin' human beans just won't never get it. My advice? Quit tryin' to figure it out and enjoy your time here. This world will go on after we're gone. Just ignore death, it ain't worth a second thought, ain't worth the damn nag it rode in on."

Joe spits into the fire. It sizzles, the alcohol burning. He stares into the embers for a long time, cuddles the sleeping pup close to him, then says again, softly, "Death ain't nothin' but cowshit." He spits again, adds, "Chin, I need to get somethin' off my chest."

"Joe, don't tell me anything you'll regret later."

"Nah, I gotta get this offa my chest, it's killin' me." He stares into the fire, unblinking, until I say softly, "Go ahead, Joe."

"You know I was a pilot in the Army Air Force, don't you?"

"No, Joe, I didn't know that, though I knew you were in the war."

"War's truly hell, Chin, truly hell. I flew a B-29 bomber, was a hell of a pilot, too."

"Bet you could tell a story or two, huh, Joe?" I offer.

"Yeah, I can tell a story or two, but I'd just as soon not. Chinle, while my buddies were precision bombing military targets in Italy and Germany, I was flying the South Pacific, doing pretty much the same thing. Until the spring of 1945, that is, almost the end of the war, then I started flying over Japan."

Now I sit up straight, afraid of what Joe's about to tell me. Hesitantly, I ask, "Joe, did you help bomb Hiroshima or Nagasaki?"

Joe looks at me, surprised, "Hell, no, Chin, that's even worse than what I did do, though not by a helluva lot. No, that wasn't it. You may not remember, you were too young, but Secretary Stimson made a big deal all during the war that the Army flyboys were hitting only strategic military targets in Europe, and I think that's what they were doing, talking to my buddies who flew with the Fifteenth. They had orders to not touch cities like Vienna at all, and to avoid civilian targets. The Brits weren't so honorable, as you may know if you've ever heard of Bomber Harris. He was the head of the Royal Air Force, and he's the one that bombed Dresden, Germany's cultural center."

Joe pauses, continues, "But when it came to the Japs, we changed our policy. Guess they didn't merit the same kind of semi-civilized behavior we gave the Germans, since they didn't look like us or use the same kind of alphabet. Starting in the spring, we flew missions to Japan, and we left our gunners behind."

"What does that mean, Joe?" I ask.

"It means we didn't need gunners to target-in bombs. General LeMay had us get rid of the gunners. We used incendiary bombs, don't need a target, everything's the target. We dropped them from 5,000 feet, and I'll never forget it.

On March 9, 1945, I helped bomb Tokyo. We destroyed over 16 square miles of the city, and the death toll was estimated at 40,000 to 100,000 people. All in all, before we quit, we ended up destroying over 56 square miles of that city, not to mention a bunch of other Japanese cities. Did it fast, too, in a week or so. We just firestormed everything, little kids, women, old people, dogs, cats, parakeets, goldfish, you name it.

That first night over Tokyo, we hit a heavy wind, and it whipped the fires into an inferno. It was like a tidal wave of intense heat and flames that swept across the city. We could see it as we flew out, and believe me, we all loved our country and hated the Japs, but none of us were feelin' like we did on Pacific flights where we hit ships and military targets. I'll never forget it. I sometimes wish I was dead. A couple of my buddies did kill themselves later. I wish now I'd refused to go, let 'em court-marshal me, though they probably would've strung me up."

The night chill seeps in, as the fire begins to die. Joe continues, "I've had nightmares about it for years, I see this old woman who looks like my grandma, though she's Japanese, and she's on fire and screaming." Now Joe puts his head in his hands and begins to silently weep.

I'm speechless. I don't know what to do, to say. I walk over and sit next to him, put my arms around him. He's warm and sweaty, and I just sit there, holding him, as his chest heaves.

Finally, after what seems like a long, long time, Joe sits up, pulls away from me, rubs his eyes with his shirtsleeve, puts his arm around my waist. We both just sit there, staring into the fire, until Joe finally gets up from the rock. He's on his way to bed now, I suppose.

"Joe..."

"Yeah?"

"You're not responsible for following orders. You were doing what any soldier would've done."

"I know, I know, so I like to believe. They call it the Nuremberg Defense, your superiors are responsible, not you. Thanks, Chin, thanks for being so understanding. You're a true friend, but like I said, no sense sittin' around blubbering like a baby. But just don't ever blindly follow someone else's deal, think of me. Make sure you know what you're doing, 'cause you are responsible, I don't care what anyone says, war or no damn war. And if every person, every soldier, would refuse to follow those kind of orders, no matter which side they're on, we wouldn't have any more wars, not like that, anyway. We wouldn't have that damn Bomb."

"What bomb?"

"The Atomic Bomb. If every one of them scientists had refused to work on the thing, like some did, we wouldn't be living under this madness, this Cold War insanity."

"But Germany could've got it first."

"Crap, they weren't even close. Besides, I said everyone, and that includes German scientists, Russians, everyone. Some guys, they took 4-E when they got drafted, conscientious objectors, we called them conchies, and everybody made fun of 'em, even threatened 'em. But it took courage to be a conchie, and some of those guys were even smokejumpers, they weren't yellowbellies. If people would just follow what they know deep inside is right, politics and governments be damned and go to hell. You know, democracy will never be the same, now people are afraid, and that's when they give up their freedom for supposed security."

I say softly, "Yeah, Joe, I know. Fear makes us afraid of the dark, but the night's the only time you can see the beauty of the stars." Now we're both quiet, stars shimmering above.

"Joe," I finally add, not wanting to end the conversation on this black note, "Joe, I have a question for you, before we call it a night."

"Sure."

"What set O'Riley off in the first place? Why was he driving like a lunatic?"

"He was drunk."

"I know, but there was something else, something made him mad."

Joe answers, "He came up here to the mine, hung around for a couple of hours, was drunk when he got here and still drinking cheap rum. You know how those Injuns are, can't hold alcohol a bit. He finally got up the courage to demand that I pay him for Opal. He says I stole her. Wanted $50, which was ridiculous, even if I had."

"Did you?"

"Hell, no, Opal's wild. She don't belong to anybody, kind of like some women I know, no offense. O'Riley said he had her down at the doghole he was working, over on Muddy Creek, and I came over and stole her. Truth is I found her begging handouts over by the motel, so I brought her up here to work for us. Happened more than once."

"Where's Opal now?" I ask.

"God only knows," Joe answers. "Last time I saw her, she was high-tailing it over towards Temple again. She's probably in O'Riley's camp as we speak, or else runnin' with her buddies over at Little Spotted Wolf. She can only take so much of bein' civilized. Johnson, you know him, he's not much of one for words, but he ran O'Riley off with his rifle after O'Riley got all worked up. Damn half-breed thinks everything belongs to the Indians, and as far as I'm concerned, they can have it—all of it—this damn desert, this damn alkali, this damn atomic poison dust, all of it."

"Joe?"

"Huh?"

"How come everybody hates the Indians?"

"Guilt."

Joe stands for a minute, picks up the little sleeping pup, mumbles goodnight, then carefully makes his way, first trying to wake Johnson, then disappearing into his tent.

He reappears with a sleeping bag and wraps it around Johnson, then says, half-grinning, "I forgot we made a strike. The Injuns can have all but the Yip Yip. Goodnight, Chin. You OK to get down the hill?" I nod yes, he pauses, disappears again.

I watch the embers for a while, then kick dirt at the last little sparks. Something upwards catches my eye—a metallic cobalt meteorite skims the sky, pale cliffs reflecting for a moment like blue tinfoil.

Coyote's out there somewhere, playing his tricks. Quietly, I gather Buddy and we fade away off to where old Willy waits. We tumble slowly, very slowly, down the road in the darkness together, down to the camp where restless dreams wait in the shadows, half-hidden in the bushes like yellow songdogs.

Curled down inside my sleeping bag, I toss and turn, dreaming of a little spotted pup running exuberantly in circles around the deep potholes of Mormon Tanks. Suddenly the pup falls in, scratches frantically at the steep sides, panicking, unable to crawl from the deep icy water, black water that turns into a blacker fire.

A dark figure emerges from the shadows, a figure with spun circles for eyes, like those of the shamans on the desert varnish deep in the canyons. The cloaked figure stoops and pulls the little pup safely out, then turns and looks directly at me.

Antonio.

Don't forget the City. It will take courage, but the petroglyphs there are for you.

Now the figure turns away and fades like the phosphorescence of a cobalt-blue meteorite.

Finally, at last, like old welcome friends, I dream of rocks.

Dear Chinle:

Yes, rain, though today the sun came out and the Flatirons were spectacular! I haven't heard from Linda, but I ran into Peggy while shopping yesterday. She looks great and is still married to Gary. It has been a long time. They seem to have a fun life together-trips to France, etc.

It looks like Terry's friend Dick is going back to Utah to settle. He couldn't find any place he liked better. He is an odd duck, I must admit. And I finally sold my bungalow! I am in shock. Of course it is not over until it's over, but I think everything will go through.

Now as soon as that is wrapped up I'd like to offer you a part of my new project, the Black Canyon Golf Course. I really need to do something productive with that land Davis left me in Montrose, it's just sitting there. I have a few ideas. An 18-hole golf course and tennis club. And I worry that the name "Black Canyon" makes it sound like a big hole in the ground, though that's the name of the national monument there. Can you help me come up with something a little more positive? Just let me know how much capital you need for your part. I am ready to write a check.

Terry says no trip until after next week. He told me he is making progress on his very very late taxes: yesterday he actually cleared a space on the dining room table and took some of his papers out of the file cabinet.

Well it's a bit late and Winston and I are both sleepy. Write soon. Chinle, please let me know how you are doing. I don't hear from you often enough to allay my fears of you out in that desolate country all alone.

Love,

Sarah

P.S. I found a book I think you might like, something to read around the campfire. It's called "You, Too, Can make Millions as a Writer," by Harry S. Kursh. I especially like this quote: "The question of whether one wants to live life or write about it must first be answered before proceeding to a career of failure or success." Let me know where to send it.

Early the next morning, I pull into the gravel parking lot of the Temple Junction Café, parking Willy under the newly painted "Home-style Cooking, New Management" sign.

So, Coralee's back, running the place now, I muse, her baby-blue '55 Thunderbird parked in front. I'll get breakfast and say hello.

Pushing the heavy door open, I quickly duck a set of chimes hung from the door jamb, then I sit down in that same cracked burgundy naugahide booth like when I first met Coralee. Like then, I'm the only customer, and DUKE is still carved into the table top, immortal as long as the place is in business.

Finally, kitchen door swings open and the sound of a male voice wafts into the café, "Running Bear, loved Little White Dove, with a love big as the sky..."

Coralee and the smell of potato pancakes are now at my side. "Chinle! Hey, I didn't know anyone was in here, didn't hear the door chimes." She sits down across from me, her curly shoulder-length auburn hair pulled back, a beautiful silver filigree stickpin pushed behind her left ear and a smeary pencil behind the other.

She smiles, looking at me with those direct green eyes. "What the heck you been up to, gal? Haven't seen you for ages! Pretty slick, how I took your advice and made my own job out here, ain't it?" she smiles. "And by the way, thanks for gettin' me and Joe back together." She puts her hand on top of mine on the table.

"I thought you were gonna kill me and him both," I tease, smiling.

"Yeah, I sure can get mad at that guy, but I guess I'll keep him anyway. By the way, you're invited to the wedding, you know." Her eyes twinkle as she holds up her hand, showing me a cheap dimestore rhinestone ring. "Joe says he'll get me a real one when they strike it rich, but I don't care, this one's good enough for me."

"You're getting married! When?"

"Exactly a month from now, 2 p.m. at the Taylor Mansion in Catalpa Town. I can't afford to have any invitations made up, and who'd make them out here I don't know, so I'm just telling everyone."

"The Taylor House?"

"Yeah, you know, the big house on Rosetree. The Taylor family built it way back. Joe's family's been friends of the Taylors for a long time, his grandparents and all that, fellow ranchers. It's a beautiful house, Mrs. Taylor has a big rose garden, that's where the ceremony will be, then we'll have a big potluck afterwards, and Duke's gonna play for the dance, but you don't need to worry about bringing anything, just yourself, no gifts, you've already done enough. I know you don't have nothing to wear, so maybe Sparky's girlfriend Maureen could loan you something, she's about your size, and she could do your hair up real nice, too. But don't worry about it, just be there, OK, Hon? Promise? Come the day before and spend the night with me at Maureen's, her sister Dixie will be there, too. It's the little white house across from the park, we're gonna party."

I smile, squeeze her hand, then pull something from my jacket pocket, lay it on the table.

Coralee catches her breath. "Oh my gotoheck! It's the copper compact Joe gave me! I can't believe it, where'd you find that? You have no idea what that means to me."

"It fell out of your purse in my jeep the day we went up to Temple Mountain. I've kept it till I could see you again," I answer, watching Coralee finger its smoothness, turn it over, read the inscription. "It's a beautiful gift, Coralee, and the poem you wrote is still inside, it's wonderful."

Coralee blushes a bit, then answers, "Gee, Hon, that's just a little thing, I write stuff like that just for me, it's not good enough for anyone else to see."

"I like it, especially the part about sweet wild freedom."

She makes a face, "Well, so much for freedom, getting married, huh? You seen Joe lately?"

"Yeah, I just came from up there, was up there late last night. Did you know about Duffy? We had a wake." I decide not to mention Joe's big strike—if it's real, I'll let him tell her. "Joe told me he's coming down here today, though fair warning, he'll probably have a bit of a hangover."

"Oh, good, good, good," Coralee answers. "I need his help. Say, Chinle, you haven't seen a little black and white spotted pup, a blue merle, with a little black band around one eye, have you?"

"What?" I ask, surprised.

"Yeah, I got it for Joe, I knew about Duffy, I got the pup the next day. Joe stopped here on his way to town and told me all about it, all about how O'Riley hit Duffy, that bas..., well, I shouldn't swear, so I won't say it. But I had to go up to Green River to get groceries, and I saw the pup there, a real cute little bugger, and they let me have him. I was keeping him out in a little pen just right by the back door here while I worked, where I could check on him once in a while, and I went out and he was gone, yesterday morning, first thing. Just like that, flat out gone. No hole under the fence or anything. I know somebody took him. Dammit, I was gettin' really attached to him, too. Called him Patches."

I shake my head in disbelief, then close my eyes and sigh. O'Riley.

"What's up? Have you seen the pup?"

"Yes, I know where the little dog is. He's with Joe, in fact he's probably on his way down here right now. Joe can tell the story."

"With Joe? What? I'm confused."

"The little pup's with Joe, and he's on his way down here, so I'll let him tell you the story, 'cause it's going to take a while. In fact, I think he's got a lot to tell you, so not to worry. But Coralee, I need to talk to you."

"He has the pup? I can't believe it. Will wonders never cease! But talk, Hon, I'm sittin' right here, talk away," she replies.

"I don't mean to be all serious, but I keep having strange, well, it's like I have strange dreams, and sometimes I'm not sure I'm dreaming.

It's starting to be upsetting, and I need to talk to someone about what it might mean."

"Geez, Chin, Hon, what kind of dreams?"

"Well, sometimes it's a dream, and sometimes it's like there's someone there and they're talking to me. Sometimes I kind of think it's just my imagination, but sometimes there's an unsettling feeling."

"Like for example?"

"Well, the other day, after the thing with Duffy, I had a dream, I dreamed about people falling off cliffs. It was terrible. That kind of thing, though usually they're not violent like that. And sometimes, well..."

"Geez, Hon, I don't know what to say, I've had lots of crazy dreams myself, but I always forget them and they go away after a few minutes. It wasn't me falling off the cliff, was it? Or Joe? Are you sure it's not just from sleeping outside all the time under those big cliffs? That would make me uncomfortable and have weird dreams, especially over under those weird ghost figures by Cleo's drill hole."

"No, it's not like that. I guess I just need to talk to somebody."

"Did you ever hear about the Yellow Circle Mine, over by Kane Creek?"

"No."

"It's pretty famous, Hon. You know who Howard Balsley is, don't you?"

"Yeah, he's the uranium guy from way back."

"Right. His mine, the Yellow Circle Mine, was discovered by a guy named Charles Snell, who dreamed about a rock with a big yellow circle on it. Charles was a cowpuncher, and he got Howard to grub-stake him until he could find that rock with the circle. Howard believed in the dream, and sure enough, Charles found the circle. That mine's one of the biggest producers ever, though Howard sold out before they really struck it rich. The rock's over by Howard's house in Radium, he took it home."

"Coralee, sometimes I picture a coyote talking to me. I've never told anyone this, maybe I'm going nuts."

"Well, being alone out there would do that to anybody. But hey, I know who you could talk to, especially if you want to know about coyotes! You ever met Billy Tsossie? He works at one of the mines up Temple, not too far from the Yip Yip. He's a Navajo, they know all about coyotes. He's here at the motel when he's off work, Room 12, a very nice fellow."

The cook, a tall scraggly-looking man in his 40s, comes into the restaurant, singing, "I got stripes, stripes around my shoulder, I got chains, chains around my feet..." He nods to us, grabs a bottle of ketchup, then retreats back into his stronghold.

Coralee's brows knit together, and she says in a low voice, "Muttonhead's checking up to see if I'm around so he can have a drink. He's the kind of guy who thinks since the beer he had for breakfast wasn't bad, he'll have another for dessert. Ha! That's a Johnny Cash song. Well, anyway, Navajo Billy's a real nice guy. But don't forget, you're coming to the wedding, aren't ya, Hon?"

"Of course, I wouldn't miss it for anything. But hey, could I get a grilled-cheese sandwich to go? I hate to run, but I'm going on over to camp at Cleo's drill hole where the petroglyphs are. I'm gonna go flying with Johnny Taylor early tomorrow."

Coralee jumps to her feet. "Oh my gosh, what kind of a waitress am I? You bet, that's a Big Can Do, Hon, won't take long, comin' right up in a jiff. Want some orange juice, too?"

"Sure, thanks."

She asks, "Say, I have a new thing—it's called an Atomic Burger, comes complete with carnotite mustard, gamma-ray ketchup, and radon pickles, along with a big strike of fission fries. It's really good, wanna try it?"

"Sounds great! Make one for Buddy Blue, hold the mustard, ketchup, and pickles. And I'll stick with the grilled cheese for me."

She squeezes my shoulder, then pauses and shakes her head, "I'm tellin' you, gal, stay away from that drill hole, that place is haunted." She stops, reconsiders, "Did you say Johnny Taylor? You didn't tell me you know the Taylors, Hon. Now there's one good-lookin' man, you be careful."

She laughs and quickly opens the swinging kitchen door, the cook's deep voice singing out, "I fell into a burnin' ring of fire, I went down, down, down, and the flames went up higher..."

Coralee calls, "Order up, and don't burn this one, Muttonhead."

She sits back down beside me and gives me a hug, her arm around my shoulder, talking a mile a minute, as usual.

"Chinle, Hon, you're always bringing me good luck, you know that? Even though I agree with what you told me about luck being homemade, how we make it ourselves and all, but when you're around, good things happen to me. I'm so happy to hear Patches is OK, I still can't believe it, and you found my compact, and Joe's on his way, I can't wait to see him. But who the heck is this Buddy Blue fellow?"

Just then, two tired-looking miners come in, caked with red dirt, the first whacking his head on the chimes while the second ducks.

"Dangitall, Coralee, when you gonna git rid of these stupid chimes?" asks the first as Coralee hands them menus. "They's supposed to go outside for the wind to knock around, not inside to knock your brains around."

"Chet, you know it's the only way I know if somebody comes in," Coralee replies. "Besides, you wouldn't even realize you'd been hit in the head if you didn't hear the noise, you're so thick-skulled. They're just little things." She winks at the second guy. "Now whattya want? The usual? You could try the yellowcakes, those are my new kind of pancakes, I use a little yellow cake flour to make them look like carnotite. I also just got in a fresh supply of chocolate squirrel ice cream." She takes her order book from her shirt pocket and pulls the pencil from behind her ear.

The second man corrects, "You mean chocolate swirl."

Chet asks, "Is it real ice cream or that dang sherbert stuff that ain't fit for a hog?"

"It's not sher-bert, it's sher-bet," corrects the second man.

Chet ignores him, studying the menu. "Gimme the regular. Same for Bert here, too, since I'm payin' off a bet."

"Do you mean Bert's regular, or yours, Chet?" asks Coralee.

"Mine," Bert answers, then adds, "You got us all spoiled fast with your good cookin', Coralee. I know all about bad cookin' from my ex-wife, Louise."

Coralee pats Bert's shoulder, then disappears into the kitchen. Now Chet gets up and goes outside, ducking the chimes. He soon returns with a screwdriver, removes the chimes from the doorjamb, screws them onto the door itself, testing his work by slamming the door.

Coralee reappears, carrying a paper sack with my order in one hand, a clear bottle of something green in the other. She quizzically looks for another customer, then sits down by me again, says, "Hey, listen, Hon, I've been thinking about how you live, and I want to try it out, what say we go out for a few days, take a little vacation. It would do Joe good to come down here and take care of the place for a while, he'd appreciate what I do. Besides, it'll be a good test to see how much he really loves me. Let's call it a last fling before the wedding, we'll go out on our own and do whatever the heck we want. Hey, come outside with me for a minute."

We go out to the front, next to a teeming hill of red ants right by the steps. Coralee opens the top of the bottle, pours a slimy green liquid into the anthill, looking satisfied as the ants begin madly rushing around. Soon most are caught in the sticky liquid.

"We'll take Joe's pickup, that way we can get everything in, your little jeep's too little," she says. "Let's go over in that country north of Radium, I haven't been over there for a long time."

"Sounds great, Coralee, it would be a lotta fun."

Now she looks around, her voice quiets, "Yeah, and I wanna make sure I'm doin' the right thing, gettin' married and all, Hon. You're a woman who keeps her own counsel, you'll be good for me, I know I'll come back knowin' one way or the other." She kicks dirt over the now mostly silent anthill.

I grimace, "OK, I'll be back after we go flying tomorrow, we can make plans then. But Coralee, after Joe comes down from the mine, I think you'll know pretty much what you want to do, at least that's my guess. What is that stuff, anyway?"

"I normally don't mind ants, Hon," she replies guiltily, "but these guys are vicious, they're coming into the café." She holds the bottle up. "It's dishwashing soap. Works good. Called Joy. Ironic, huh?"

Now she's back inside, and I'm gone, me and Buddy Blue and Willy on our way to camp at Cleo's drill hole, haunted or not. As we pull out, I notice a low-slung red station wagon parked in front of Room 12 of the hotel, so I stop. Buddy waits in the jeep, happily munching his Atomic Burger.

"Billy, my name's Chinle. You got a minute? I was talking to Coralee over at the café, and she said I should talk to you."

"Yeah, sure, Coralee, she's a very nice woman. What do you need to talk to me about, Chinle? Is that your real name?"

"Yeah, but it's just a nickname. Do you have a minute?"

"Sure, I just got down from the mine, I'm done for the day, but I have to tell you, I'm tired and hungry, I just worked a straight 16 hours, I need to get over to the café. Man, workin' for wages is pure slavery."

"Wait, I just got a sandwich and fries, they're still hot. You can eat this while we're talking. I won't keep you but a minute."

"This your dinner?"

"Nah, I'm not even hungry. Billy, I won't keep you, I mean, I hope you'll hear me out and not think I'm nuts, but I need to talk to someone who knows the Old Ways, the ways of your people."

Billy laughs a bit nervously, takes the paper sack, examines the contents, sits on his bed, wipes his hands on his dirty pants, and starts eating. "I dunno, I'm not a medicine man, maybe you need to talk to my uncle, John Holliday, he's a medicine man down in Monument Valley."

"No, don't worry, I don't want to know anything sacred or things I shouldn't know. Look, I'll get right to the point. Your people believe in Coyote Trickster, he's one of the Navajo deities, isn't he?"

"Yes, he's a deity, but not a very nice one. What do you want to know about him? I don't know that much about him, and to tell you the truth, I don't want to."

"I know, I know," I reply. "I'm not sure how to ask this, but what would you think if someone came to you and said that there's a coyote that comes to them and advises them, talks to them?"

"Talk to Coyote? That's very bad. To my people, Coyote is the Trickster, he's someone to definitely be avoided. We would never want to talk to him, never, he's not to be trusted. You're that archaeologist I hear about, aren't you? You're not going to write any of this down, are you?"

I sit down on Billy's dresser, glum. "Yeah, I'm an archaeologist, I study rock art, and I really need your help. Say, you know a Ute guy named Antonio, works up north, lives in Cisco?"

"No."

"Billy, do the Navajo hate coyotes? What would you do?"

"Oh, we don't hate coyotes or anything like that, but we feel like you leave us alone, we leave you alone, but stay away from our livestock. We don't hunt them unless they're messing around with our stock. But to have a coyote come to you, follow you, sit with you, pay any kind of attention to you is bad luck, bad bad bad luck. You be careful out there, you don't want any coyotes around, Coyote is the Trickster."

"But Billy, I'm not Navajo, I'm white. So would this apply to me, do you think?"

"I dunno, that's what we believe. But if you're not Navajo, and you don't believe Coyote's bad, maybe Coyote's not bad for you. Same thing with owls, we believe the owl brings messages, tells us something's going to happen. You shouldn't ignore an owl. My nephew and niece were out one day and an owl came to them, flew down in front of them, screeching, but they didn't think to tell anyone about it. A couple of days later their brother was killed in a car accident. The owl was trying to tell them something was going to happen, to take precautions. They were young, they didn't yet understand the Old Ways."

"How would one get Coyote to leave them alone, let's say Coyote was coming to them and talking to them, giving them advice and stuff like that. What would a Navajo do?"

"Whoo, I dunno, I think they'd hightail it right to a medicine man, have a protection prayer, then a Beautyway Ceremony. They'd be pretty nervous, I know I would." He looks around, adds, "Let me tell you something, a little story from my cousin, Jim Lee, who works over in Radium. Maybe you know him?"

"No."

"Jim works for Les Robertson, they're the ones building houses for Charlie Dundee, the fellow who struck it rich with that big uranium mine over there. He's building a bunch of housing for his workers, and he named one of the places Coyote Run. My cousin tells me that it's a bad place, it has bad bad energies, especially the last two houses over there on the cul de sac. All kinds of bad things have happened there, when they were building it, everything went bad.

Jim says he got sick when he worked over there, and he was in one of those houses working late at night, he's a plumber. Twice now he's seen dark shadows, tall, very tall shadows, and one had glowing eyes. He was outta there, I can tell you that. His legs ache when he's over there, and I think there's a burial there or something like that, something very bad. What do you expect with a name like Coyote Run? Coyote's the Trickster."

I pause for a while, then ask, "What exactly is the Beautyway?"

"The Beautyway is a ceremony you have done when things aren't going well for you. Hózhó kind of means on the side of beauty or harmony, blessedness. Hózhó nashaadoo is to walk in the Beautyway, it means you're walking in the right way, the good way, the way you should be, in harmony. It's hard to describe. But the Beautyway ceremony is to restore the Hózhó, the harmony that has been upset by violations of the natural order, like mining."

He continues, "Let me give you an example of harmony. One time I was up on the mountain, hunting for deer, when I noticed a big black bear coming my way, I was laying down in the tall grass, kind of hiding, waiting for deer. The bear just kept coming, I'd move my hands a bit, that kind of thing, to let him know I was there. He came within 20 feet of me, just wondering what I was, just stood and looked at me, then he turned and walked away. I wasn't afraid, the bears are our grandmothers and grandfathers. But a friend of mine, a non-Navajo, he saw it all from the hill above where he was waiting for his deer, and he asked me why I didn't do something. 'What would I do?' I asked. He said, 'Man, I would've shot over his head to tell him to go away or something.' I said, 'That's my grandfather, why would I be afraid of my grandfather?' My friend doesn't understand, he doesn't know the harmony, the Beautyway.

Let me give you another example, an opposite, and that's all this mining we're doing up here, we shouldn't be doing it, and Leetso, the yellow monster, is again raising his ugly head. In one of our origin stories, our people were emerging from the Third World into the Fourth and present world and were given their choice between two yellow powders. One was yellow dust from the rocks, the other was corn pollen. The Dineh chose the pollen and the gods were very happy. Then the gods warned the people to leave the yellow dust in the ground, as it was evil. Now, I do not know if Hózhó, harmony and beauty, will be restored and Leetso defeated.

Chinle, these mines don't feel good to me. The Hózhóni is a balance between people and nature, and mining is a disruption to that, it's disrespectful to the earth. These mines are bad. My people will suffer for our part in this. But some places feel good, they have a good energy. Out by Willow Creek, west of Catalpa Town, is like that, I really enjoy going out there and wandering around. But up above, in the big fins above there, it has a bad energy and I don't like it."

He continues, "But as for Coyote talking to someone, I don't know if it's you or somebody you know, just be really careful. Not too long ago, my buddy and I were down on the Rez, down south of Bluff, just riding around on our horses, when we came upon an Anasazi village, towers and all, up in the cliffs. You could tell it had never been touched, no tracks around. It was amazing. We could still see the handprints in the clay in the walls. Anyway, as we turned to go, my buddy saw a coyote, and it wasn't 10 minutes later his horse threw him and broke his leg."

Billy crinkles the sack and tosses it into the trash can at my feet. "But I gotta go on over to the café and finish up eatin', like I said, I'm pretty hungry. Come on back sometime—I don't usually talk like this, aren't too many whites interested in our ways, most of them are just prejudiced against us and wish our ways would go away. See ya around."

I ponder Billy's words as I head for Cleo's drill hole. Once there, I look up at the ghost-like rock art figures, sullen and quiet, and decide that tonight I will refuse to dream.

Early the next morning Buddy and I head for the airstrip down by the café, Willy pretty much driving himself down that sandy road while I ponder the ongoing half-dreams I had of coyotes howling all night.

Dear Chinle,

Went over to Lone Cone country and camped on the flanks of the Uncompahgre. Watched the moon rise over the alpenglow on the Juanies and the sun set behind the Sallies all at the same time. Tried to figure out if I really do exist or if I'm just a figment. Couldn't figure anything out except the fishing, caught some nice trout. Weeners love camping in a tent, they all sleep in my bag. I crawled out, too crowded. Heading out to meet up with dino bone people. Stay in touch.

Jim Bone

Dear Chinle,

Cheer up! You could limit your time to 20 hours a week, that is the equivalent of $41,600 per year!!!! This is fantastic money. In fact, I only earn that amount when the stock market blossoms.

Meetings, however, are a different matter. I hate meetings. You would not have to go to meetings. I would make all the decisions, freeing you to be creative.

Probably we are both already unemployable. I haven't even been doing any gardening lately. And, my dear cousin, what was that mention you made of a fellow named Yellowjacket? What an odd name. I hope you are cautious with the people you meet out there.

This week I received Derek's photo. He looks older than mid-50s and he is somewhat bald, but I like his looks. And his note, as usual, was great fun. I am becoming more and more interested.

Here in Boulder, it is truly beautiful these days. The sun has reappeared, the whole valley is intensely green, flowers everywhere. Yesterday morning for the first time, I hiked to the top of the 1st Flatiron. There is a little path between the 1st and 2nd Flatiron, which is spectacular. At the top and around the back of the 1st, there is an incredible view of the 3rd Flatiron. Except for the occasional cries of the technical climbers and the frequent cries of ravens, I was all alone. When I descended and reached Chautauqua, a Rocky Mountain News reporter took my photo and name. I may be in the paper: "44 Year Old Boulderite Scales 1st Flatiron!"

My Winston is on a reduced caloric diet. No more moist breakfasts. He doesn't like it, but he is beginning to get back his svelte, kittenish looks.

Will let you know our travel plans—soon, I hope.

Love to you,

Sarah

P.S. Really, I did the math. If you get $400 for 20 hours, that works out to $20 per hour. If you had a full time job at $20 and worked the regulation 2080 hours per year, it is $41.6K per year! I see though that you are not into the regulation 2080 hours. My dear Chinle! I can't understand why not. I say this as I sit in my living room in shorts and roll over to the fridge in my spiffy new task chair to grab some grapes and pop them into my mouth. I myself am totally committed to the work ethic, the corporate way of life. Especially for those workers in the companies which are included in my stock portfolio. They should work 3000 hours per year for the same pay!

Dear Chinle,

Thanks for the card, glad to know you're still out there and continuing your search, which I know will be rewarded. Maybe not by fame and fortune, but by secret canyons and hanging gardens. I'm still a bit jealous, I guess, although the domestic life is pretty good (Millie's looking over my shoulder, so I had to write that - ha). Actually, it's true, and will get better, the baby's due soon.

We had a great weekend over in Dominguez Canyon, right at our back door practically. I found an entire panel of nothing but bear paw glyphs. About 30 of them. Must be bear country—maybe the bears learned how to do glyphs from the natives. Or maybe it was the other way around.

I've been meaning to write and tell you about a fellow out in the Mussentuchit country over your way, he should still be out there, I met him at a conference in Bluff where he had some fab photos of rock art. Go find him, if you can, name's Colt Freeman.

Love and keep on living,

Bill

Dear Chinle,

We are leaving for Radium Thursday. Can we meet up somewhere? I hope so. Let me know. Please call me collect.

Love,

Sarah

11
Hidden Splendor: Muddy Creek

"It's a perfect day for flying," I state the obvious. Johnny nods his head, and I can see he's checking the instruments, so I turn my gaze back to that perfect sky. Last thing you want to do is distract the pilot when he's checking out the plane.

Johnny has a look about him that speaks competence, common sense, a look that, like crowsfeet, comes with doing—no theorizing here. He turns to me and nods, says, "Everything seems to work. Let's go flyin'."

"How many hours you have in the air, Johnny?" I ask.

"Oh, about 2,000 logged, but actually lots more than that. Soloed when I was 16. Pretty much all canyon flyin', landing in places most people don't even know exist."

I grin, "Let's go flyin'."

Now the little Cessna 195 purrs as Johnny pulls out the throttle, bit by bit, slow and steady, like you'd pull a stick of dynamite out of a wooden box. Buddy sits in the back, looking out the tiny window. We're off the ground quickly, way before the dirt runway runs out, and it all has the feel of something that's been done 2,000 times before, smooth as vanilla pudding, something you could do in your sleep, pulling back the throttle like that, smooth, slow, and steady.

Now we're banking to the left, still smooth, flying over Chute and Crack canyons, and now, quickly, we're over Ding Dang Dome, then Muddy Creek, and then we circle north towards the San Rafael River. "It's not called the San Ra-fay-el," an oldtimer once corrected me as we stood looking into the muddy waters of that quicksand-infested slow-moving river, "but San Ra-fel. Say it like that and they won't know you're from someplace else, you can leave 'em guessin'." Always good to keep folks guessin', I guess.

I turn and watch Buddy, sitting in the back seat, at first kind of hunkered down, but now seemingly enjoying himself, nose to the air coming in from my side window.

"That's Hank's Bottom to the right way over there on the San Rafel River," Johnny yells over the air noise, banking the little plane so I can see. "That's where my family weathered out the Great Depression, down in a little rock house by the river. They didn't get to town too often." He smiles with understatement as we study the tiny winding trail off a bank of cliffs down to the riverside, miles and miles wonderfully from nowhere. "The Hank was Hank Taylor, my uncle."

I'd stake my life that Johnny knows the canyon country of Utah like no other person on earth. He learned to fly from Levi Wells, one of the pioneers of canyon flying in southeast Utah, flying that's akin to Alaska's bush flying, flying where you'd dang well better know what you're doing or you won't be limping home to tell about it.

Johnny told me earlier that Levi's first airplane ride was in the navy, where you could sign up on a board and fly with the next guy out for practice, and you got whoever was available, you'd check out a flight suit and just go. Levi got a Navy dive bomber, and they practiced dive bombing over and over his first time up in an airplane.

"Back when I was a kid," Johnny now muses, "there wasn't much by way of roads, and the only way you could get around, especially when it rained and got muddy, was to fly. Now that uranium mining's a big thing, I sometimes fly miners and supplies around."

"Can you fly in to the Radium Queen?" I ask.

"We haven't been workin' up there very long, but that's on my list, bulldoze a strip up there. Sure would make things a lot easier. Hey,

I about forgot. What the heck were you doing up on that big cliff the other day?"

"Thanks for the beer," I laugh. "Moon you, my ass."

He grins. We've now turned back to the south and swung out over the Flattops, and I can see the sinuous declivity of Barrier Canyon to the southeast, home of the Holy Ghost and other great Barrier rock art figures. Now, to our right, is the mirage-outline of the San Rafael Swell banked in its fortress by the jagged Reef. Johnny turns, and we're soon near the long serrated knife-like face, and the sun strikes the huge monocline, turning the white Navajo sandstone buttery yellow.

The little plane drones on, we're flying south, towards Catalpa Town, and I casually remark to Johnny that I've always wanted to see the Hidden Splendor Mine, Vernon Pick's mine, once second only to the Tengo Dinero until it ran out of steam. Johnny doesn't say anything, and I'm not sure he hears me over the air noise, but he banks the plane towards a complex of spiderweb-like canyons. Now I see Muddy Creek below again, barely a trickle, even with a recent rain. Johnny tells me Levi Wells once did an emergency landing right there, in the creek.

Johnny's still silent, and we're soon entering the face of the Reef, dropping into a deep canyon. I hold my breath as we twist and turn, following the narrow course of Muddy Creek, now losing altitude until our wingtips nearly touch each side of the canyon, or so it seems. I grin, not sure what to think, but by now I know I'd fly anywhere with Johnny Taylor.

Down, down, like slow-pouring buttermilk, and I see a series of pourovers coming down the canyon wall, where frost and water have dripped and etched sand particles away, gradually molding a perfect place for waterpockets, each now filled with a jewel of reflecting sun on water from the recent rain.

Muddy Creek turns again, and now I can almost reach out and touch junipers and desert holly that jut out from the canyon walls. Another twist and we're nearly down in the creek, when suddenly I see a tattered red windsock and what maybe just might be an old road. Without to-do we're on the ground, and how Johnny can land this little plane so smooth on this little dirt strip grown with weeds is a mystery.

You'd better know right where that strip lies, too, 'cause you sure as H-E-double-hockeysticks can't see it till you're right on it.

"That's just a little taste of canyon flying," Johnny grins, turning the plane around.

We get out, and Buddy leaps out behind us and immediately starts sniffing around. Johnny stretches, turns, gazing up at the red ramparts above us that hold the Hidden Splendor Mine. "I like to land in these places and get out of the plane, feel what it's like out here. Nothing like it anywhere."

Several doghole mines form dark cavities in the rusty sandstone above us—the holes look abandoned. When the longhairs at Los Alamos invented the Bomb, it began the mad uranium scramble that changed the San Rafael forever. Einstein later said that had he known where his theories would take humankind, he'd have become a watchmaker. Einstein also remarked that he didn't know how the third world war would be fought, but he knew the fourth would be waged with sticks and stones.

Wisps of white clouds dance slowly across a turquoise-blue sky. I kick at something, a piece of weathered wood, pick it up and turn it over. Hercules Powder. Just like over in the wash by Temple, the same Hercules responsible for the doghole mines above me in the cliff bands.

I stand silent for a long time, soaking it all in. There's something about the vertical bluffs and twisting canyons out here that makes you want to forget civilization.

"Just leave me out here, Johnny," I say.

"I could do that," he replies, grinning. "Should've brought a picnic," he adds. "Say, Chin, you know the story of this mine?"

"Kind of," I answer, "It was found by Vernon Pick, who sold it and got rich, then the ore ran out."

"Well," Johnny says, "You probably know that as a service to prospectors, the AEC boys make anomaly maps over in Grand Junction. Anomaly refers to radiation readings, places where the radioactivity is higher than normal. They use Geiger counters on the ground or scintillaters from rim-flying airplanes, like the one I want to test out today."

"Anyway, it's common knowledge that these maps often become public knowledge after becoming private knowledge. Everyone knew this was the case with Vernon Pick and his nine million-dollar Delta Mine, which was renamed the Hidden Splendor after it was bought out by the big boy, Floyd Odlum and his Atlas Corporation."

He continues, "Two of the AEC boys in the deal were investigated by the FBI, supposedly, anyway. Both quit the AEC and went to work for Pick."

Buddy is taking off after something and I call him back. I look up again to what's left of the mine workings, tailings, rusty equipment. Here mad-dog miners scratched holes into the ground, digging up ancient sticks, logs yellow with carnotite, not like the Tengo Dinero, whose ore was black with pitchblende, uranium oxide, that purest of uranium-bearing minerals.

"When did he find the mine, Johnny?"

"Oh, it's been almost 10 years or so ago, I think 1952. Nobody knows where Pick went, but first California, then maybe Canada. The mine hasn't been closed very long."

"You know," he continues, "There've been a number of mines located by rim flying, and I think Pick's was one of them. The stories he told about finding it on the ground just don't hold up."

"What do you do exactly when you're rim flying? Fly close to the rims with a scintillator?" I ask.

He laughs, "Yup, pretty much. Problem with rim flying is you have to get out there really early, before dawn, because you fly really close to the ground. You only have a few minutes you can fly that low, 'cause as soon as the desert starts to heat up, you start getting tricky thermals."

"Just how low do you fly?"

"A good pilot can skim 20 feet or so next to a rim or above the ground. Used to be if you went beyond about 50, you wouldn't pick up that tell-tale ping, but the new equipment's getting better. That new scintillator I wanna test today supposedly can go to 1500 feet."

"What do you do when you find something?"

"Well, you try to figure out where you are so you can either go back on foot, or you try to land nearby and go stake it right then and there. You have to be careful, 'cause there's pretty much always somebody out there who can see you, and if you circle around much, it'll be staked by the time you get there."

"Crazy."

"You said it."

"So, after you stake it out, what happens then?"

"What then? You mean mining, all the insanity? Well, here's what happens, typically. First, you stake a claim, then you can hopefully borrow or lease a cat and bulldoze in a road. You gotta get a drill in there, probably also borrowed, so you can sink a bore hole, or maybe a bunch of holes.

Drilling's a pain, you have to light the gasoline tank to fire the motor, then you hear a whirring sound, and that's the drill revolving, then all of a sudden it grinds, and the bit screws itself into solid rock. You have to have a diamond point in order to chew through all the hardened detritus. So you're there, that old drill's whirring, and chips of rock and dust are spewing out from the deflector all over the place as the bit burrows on down.

As you're going along, you pull up cores, which are pretty much foot-long cylinders of sandstone, and you lay them on the ground in order of their occurrence so can tell how deep your strike is, providing your prayers come true and you find anything. You check out the cores for traces of uranium, which is usually a bright yellow ore. But if you're real, real lucky—and don't worry, you won't be—you may get cores that are a dirty gray, sort of like coal, and that's pitchblende, pure uranium. You've struck it rich, as they say.

But the odds are better that the drill breaks, your pump breaks, and your drill bits wear out. You're poorer than ever, so you manage to wrangle some credit at the hardware store and keep on goin'. But if you do find some ore, the battle's just started.

First, you gotta get investors, and before you can do that, you have to block out the claim and estimate the tonnage for the ore body from your core samples.

So, finally you convince some suckers to back you so you can open the mine. To actually do that, you have to hire help, drill through layers of rock, blast holes with explosives, muck out the debris with shovels, timber the sides so it don't cave in, and as the gap widens and deepens foot by foot, and the tailings pile grows, you eventually get down to the depth of the original discovery, and when you get there, you pray like hell you've got something. If you don't, you cry and cuss, and if you do, you jump and holler.

And if you get enough money, and your mine gets pretty big, you'll have mucking machines, slushers, shovel loaders, and ore cars. You'll need jackhammers, compressors, shovels and wheelbarrows, and a truck or two or three to take the ore to the nearest mill or AEC buying station, which is sometimes hundreds of miles away.

And while you're doin' all this, you're poisoning yourself with atomic dust, so you're pretty likely to end up like the old radium miners—dead, that is."

He continues, "Why go through all this torture? The reason is that you know deep inside you're gonna strike it rich, and you know even deeper inside that workin' for wages is to be avoided like hell.

And that's uranium mining, Chin. And the end result of all this is the Bomb, so we can blow ourselves and the whole world into smithereens." He pauses, studying the cliffs, then asks, "Ready to go? Got Bud?"

We take off, scooting along that sandy two-track towards dark cliffs that cradle the far edge of the brushy runway. The climbing sun turns cliffs deep red—they're bounded by rubble, rocks climbing each other, scrambling to get out first.

Now we're quickly back in the air, and Johnny's going to show me what he calls a river slot. First, he banks the plane over Hondu Arch, more of a big hole in the cliffs than a true arch, then we're suddenly on another planet, for what I'm seeing below me is like nothing on earth. Johnny nods at the huge crack that's opened beneath us—it's the Chute of Muddy Creek, an infamous slot canyon that stretches for over 15 miles, twisting its way through a nearly underground world filled with flashflood debris 20 feet above the creek. We circle for a while, but it never looks real.

We slip back towards the Reef, and suddenly those chalky white ramps of Temple Mountain thrust skyward beneath us, and a small sidetrack forks off and crosses the wash, winding to the flanks of the mountain, stopping immediately under a small hole, a doghole. Johnny waggles the wings at two figures on the ground, probably Joe and Sparky. A tiny speck next to them with four legs confirms it is them and Patches. We fly on.

Quickly, we're back at the little dirt strip by Temple Junction Café, where we land and get out of the little plane, taking a moment to recover our land legs. Far to the west, probably right over the Hidden Splendor, hangs a gilded cloud, suspended by cool air. A few clouds float further north, peach and gold, hanging in the direction of Temple Mountain.

"I'll be back tomorrow, Johnny," I laugh, giving him a big hug. "We'll let tomorrow's warm air currents take us wherever they want to go."

He laughs. "A glider would be fun, wouldn't it? Problem is, not too many places you'd want to try to land one in this country. Oh shoots, I completely forgot to try out my new scintillator. Tell you what, Chin, let's go back up again soon, heck, we could fly over Radium, even over to Colorado, if you want."

Buddy looks a bit disoriented, lays down by my feet.

"Johnny?" I ask.

"Yeah?"

"You ever flown into the Mussentuchit?"

"Nope, musn't touch it."

"No, I'm serious, is there any way you could get me in there?"

"I doubt it. I can ask Levi if he knows of anything that would serve as a strip, he's probably been in that country, but it's just one big sandbox."

"OK, ask him. Let's go, I need to find somebody out there."

"There ain't nobody in the Mussentuchit, take my word for it, unless they're lost."

"Just ask, OK?"

"You bet, Hon."

Dear Chinle,

I don't understand why you're not interested in working on the golf course project, especially since you could have one of the condos and it's SO close to where you are. The real estate market there is as hot as it is in Boulder. Good if you are selling, horrid if you are buying. Let me know. You've got to get a home soon. After traveling out there, I'm even more perplexed, how can you live in an old jeep? Whatever do you do when you need a nice soothing hot bath with Dead Sea salt crystals?

Love,

Sarah

Hi Chin,

Welcome back if you're back...you sure move around. Same old shit here. FUBAR, Fouled-Up-Beyond-All-Recognition.

Charlie

Dear Chinle,

The guy from the Denver museum is back, brought a whole pack of people with him. Am guiding them around, spent last week out and they're coming back later when it cools off. Have me a full-time job then. Six of them, all scientists, one an anarchy-ologist like you, says he knows you, name's Lischka, from the university in Boulder. Spent most of our time south of GR where Rog found his big dig (ha).

Found some nice bone, some with crystals inside, and I found a small rock cliff with something strange inlaid in it, looked like a giant chicken wing. I know it's bone, but they can't believe it. They said nobody had ever found a dino wing before, and pterodactyls weren't in this country. How the heck do they know? If it turns out to be something, they were gonna name it after me, but I told them to name it after Roger. The Rogerbonedactyl from the Roger Bone Dino Quarry. There's no time like the past. Ain't life strange? Come up when you get a chance.

Jim

12
Randy: Temple Junction

Something's happening in front of the motel as I pull up to the Temple Junction Café. Coralee's standing on the front steps, along with the cook she calls Muttonhead.

"Chinle, we're about to have a big shootout," she says matter-of-factly. "We'd probably better all get inside. Maybe we should call the sheriff, though it'll all be over by the time Hugh gets here from Catalpa Town."

"What's going on?" I ask.

"One of the boys just dumped a load of tailings in front of the motel. God only knows why, and Harry's about ready to kill him. They're having an OK Corral standoff right now. Let's go inside before we get shot."

I leave Bud in the jeep and head over to the motel, against Coralee's protestations, where a truckload of tailings sits right in front of Room 12. Billy Tsosie's nowhere to be seen, and Harry's arguing with a man next to a dump truck, undoubtedly the culprit. The man is yelling back.

"If you didn't give these damn redskins a place to sleep, they'd go back where they belong, that's why, you sumsabitch. A bunch of us are sleepin' up the road in damn army tents while you give these worthless Injuns soft beds."

I know this man, he's from Radium. I went to high school with him.

"I'm gonna call the law on you if you don't clean that mess up right now," Harry threatens. His face is beet red, and he looks like he's about to have a heart attack.

"Call away, they'll give me a medal."

"My God, Randy," I interject, "What're you smokin' to dump radioactive tailings all over?"

He groans, "Chinle! What the hell you doing here? You stay outta this."

Harry, looking like he's ready to start shooting, says, "I'm going to give you one last warning, you bastard, start cleaning this mess up now."

"Harry, let me talk to him," I entreat.

Randy mutters, "I'm done talkin', made my statement, it's right there on the ground, says it all." He steps up onto the running board and swings into his old Diamond T dump truck. Harry disappears into the motel. I grab onto the handle of the door, jump up onto the running board, hang on.

"Leggo, I'm headin' out," he warns.

"No, you lose your mind? They'll send you to jail if you don't simmer down. You got your wife and kids to think about. I don't know what's going on, but I know this isn't the way to deal with it."

Randy tips the steel dumpbox back down with a crash, then guns the engine and starts to pull out. I hang on.

"Leggo, dammit, get the hell off my truck."

"No. And if you don't stop, you'll have me on your prison record, too. Just stop and let's talk for a minute, then you can do whatever you want."

Now Coralee's next to the truck, yelling at Randy, "Stop the truck, you're gonna kill her! Stop the truck!"

Randy is now on the main road and beginning to accelerate. Harry emerges from the motel, rifle in hand. I wonder if he'll shoot with me hanging here. He puts the rifle to his shoulder.

"Randy, for God's sake, stop! Harry's got a gun pointed at us! If I jump, he'll shoot you."

Finally, the truck slowly rolls to a stop. I see Harry start our way, but Coralee stops him.

"Thanks, Randy. Scoot over."

I push my way into the narrow cab, shoving Randy over to the passenger side. The smell of alcohol permeates everything.

"You know, Randy, you and I go way back. He had a rifle pointed right at your head."

Randy replies, "Sumsabitch dogdamned Jewboy."

"This is kinda like that time you ended up in jail right outta high school, isn't it? If I remember right, you were pretty sorry about that one."

"Don't preach to me, dogdammit. Those dogdamned Injuns are sleepin' in luxury while we're on the hard ground, freezin' our asses off. It ain't right. Harry's a sumsabitch."

"Look, it's his business, and this is America, home of the brave. That means Indians, the Braves. He can house them if he wants, it's called free enterprise."

"It's called reverse prejudice."

"Maybe they got there first. They sure got everywhere else first."

"Naw, he charges them more and they're too stupid to even know it. He has two rate sheets, the bastard."

"Maybe you should offer him what he charges the Indians, and he'd give you a room."

"I wouldn't stay in that bedbug-infested hole if it was free."

"Then just what the hell you trying to prove?"

"I just want him to know he's a sumsabitch, that's all."

"Well, that sumsabitch is going to get your ass thrown in the calaboose. You need to decide if you want to go back to the mine and sleep on the ground or spend a few months in jail, either way, you're gonna have to clean that mess up. If I were you, I'd start on it right now. We can get Joe's loader down here and have it done quick."

"I ain't done nothin' wrong, and I ain't gonna admit it."

"Don't admit nuthin', just clean it up."

"It's just a pile of dirt, only a few yards, Harry can have them Injuns scoop it into the ditch."

"No, it's not just a pile of dirt, it's radioactive dirt. It's poisonous."

"That stuff ain't gonna hurt nobody. I'll push it into the ditch myself."

"No, dammit, you have to move it."

"What's the problem? We have tailings all over the damn place. No time to be all fussy, we're talking national security. In fact, now that I think about it, I gotta get back to the mine, that next Bomb's waitin' for me to dig some hotrock. Could make the difference between war and peace. Get out, I gotta get the hell outta here."

"Hugh knows where you work, Randy, he'll find you, throw you in jail, muy pronto."

"Damn." Randy's quiet for a moment, then, "We go way back, don't we, Chin?"

"Yeah, c'mon. I'll drive up, get back in practice, haven't driven an outfit like this for a while."

I yell out the window, "We're comin' back with a loader. Tell Hugh not to bother. We'll be back." Coralee grins, gives me a thumbs up. Harry looks relieved.

Tension broken, Randy laughs, "Chin, I know you can drive a dump 'cause I remember you drivin' the one we sorta accidentally put over the cliff that time when the highway was gonna cut right through my grandpa's place. Man, them was the good old days, wasn't they?"

"Yeah, before you fellas started rippin' the hell outta everything. No offense, but I'm sort of torqued that you'd dump radioactive tailings all over, Randy."

"Well, what the hell got under your saddleblanket? What's the problem? If it wasn't for atoms, we'd all be dead."

I reach over to the gearshift and shift up. The truck slowly lumbers up the hill towards the Yip Yip. I answer, "The problem is we're destroying everything."

"Shift back down again. Double-clutch it or you'll rake the gears. Can't afford a new transmission."

I slip into neutral, accelerate, take my foot off the accelerator for a few seconds and shift down. The acceleration makes the transmission's input gears turn at the same rate as the output gears.

Johnny continues our argument, "Give me a bloody break, Chin, humans ain't that powerful, to destroy everything."

Now I rake Johnny instead of the gears. "Tailings are toxic. Eighty-five percent of the radioactivity in the ore remains behind in that crushed rock. The half-life is 80,000 years. That means in 80,000 years there will be half as much radioactivity in these tailings as there is today. We don't have any records of human existence going back that far. That's this stuff you dumped in front of the motel, Randy."

I continue, "And these tailings are blown by the wind, washed by the rain into the water. We tear up everything, leave toxic glowing piles everywhere, kill everything we see. When will we learn we're part of the earth, too?"

"Don't be so damn self-righteous. You're exaggerating it. Sure there's a little damage, but if we don't get fuel for the Bomb, we'll have communists running over everything, and so much for the freedom you love in your little jeep, huh?"

"Don't be condescending, buster, or I'll whack you right between the ears like I did when we took that raft down the river."

"You mean that wasn't an accident?"

"Listen, we should leave the uranium in the ground, O'Riley's right, we're poisoning ourselves."

"The AEC says there's nothing to worry about, it's safe. If I didn't know you better, I'd swear you were on the other side. Too much schoolin'."

"Which other side is that?"

"Which other side? C'mon, you know, the Redskis."

"When you guys are done, won't be nuthin' left for the Redskis to want. Dig it up, tear it up, shoot it up, whatever."

"Shoot it up? Shoot what up?"

"Everything. Rock art. Cougars, rabbits, birds, coyotes."

"You been watchin' too much Bambi."

"Why didn't you shoot that little coyote that turned and watched you?"

"What coyote is that?"

"You know what I'm talking about, the coyote over at Big Wild-horse."

"How in hellsbells do you know about that damn coyote?"

"I was on the cliff above you. You started singing to it."

"Well I'll be gotohell. I musta been drunk, don't remember a thing." He pauses, adds, "Aw, c'mon, Chin, this is gettin' ridiculous. No need to argue when I'm always right, right? Now I'm remembering how we always did this in high school, you always tryin' to convince me of somethin' or other. You damn Scots-Irish are a bullheaded bunch. And why the hell you think you can spy on me like that I'll never know."

We stop at the bottom of the steep hill up to the Yip Yip. Randy can walk up and get the loader. He seems to have sobered up.

"OK, but remember, it has to be dark before you can see the stars."

"What the hell, Chin, what the hell is that supposed to mean? And what the hell you pickin' on me for? I thought we was friends, buds. Right? Right?"

"You can hope to God I never tell Jenny about this. Bring Sparky along, he can drive the dump. You can go get those tailings, take 'em back to the mine, restock it."

"Oh, that's real funny. Don't you tell my wife, she gives me enough hell already. I'll owe you one, Chin, as usual. Tell 'em I'm right behind you. I'll get that crap out of Harry's yard, right now, faster than you can say sickum. Nice to see you again, gal, come over for dinner sometime."

"A real pleasure," I reply with sarcasm.

"Hey, I got the idea from Johnny Taylor, he did the same thing once," Randy entreats.

"Yeah, but it was an accident," I reply.

"Dammitall, must be nice to know everything."

"I'll wait and follow you."

Dear Chinle,

You're an archaeologist, tell me what you think. Was over on Cedar Mesa, went to see Kev Murphy, you remember him, he's the guy your horse bucked off when we was kids. We went up there to look for arrowheads. Was just walking along, enjoying the scenery, when all of a sudden out of nowheres I felt like crying, had the strangest feeling that something bad had happened right there. When I walked on, everything was normal again. Strange. Anasazi country. Some bad stuff going on back then, maybe even cannibalism. Weatherill found some bad stuff in Cave 7, though nobody knows exactly where it was, but somewhere near there. Hard to believe when you're out in that beautiful country. Take care, wherever you are. Jim

Dear Chinle,

I wish so much I could have seen you. We passed through Radium Friday and bought gas, and I looked for you. It was HOT!!! I don't think I could live there.

We had a wonderful trip: Arches, Wild Horse Point, Natural Bridges, and more: Bryce, Capitol Reef, Zion (saw collared lizard). It was good for the soul.

Your work sounds fascinating, but don't you ever get tired of that heat and sand? After the trip, I now understand why Grandfather called you Chinle: a complex and multi-colored rock formation. This is a good name for a complex and multi-faceted person! (Picked this up from a brochure at Capitol Reef.) Of course we visited your favorite places! We studied your letter and followed all instructions to the letter. I told Jan and Jim you were a world famous expert on Utah and that we'd be fools not to take your advice.

Perhaps we can get together when I get back from Europe? Unless of course Derek sweeps me off my feet and I never come back. My car's air conditioning is working now. It is splendid.

This is a very hurried note, but I wanted to let you know that you were present in my thoughts during the entire trip. Maybe I can help you with a project when I come over there. Now it's back to work. I have a million things that must get done no later than yesterday!!!

Love to you,
Sarah

chinle
lost in the maze, now that's an enviable fate. i love being lost.
because everything i find on the way is milagro! chance not predicament.
keep losing it,
art

13
Vacation in Heaven: Not the Road to Radium

"Geez, think we have enough stuff?" I ask Joe. He crams my sleeping bag into an empty bucket wedged between shovels, water jugs, rock hammers, and assorted tire chains, an amorphous mass in the back of his old pickup.

"We'll see," Joe answers, scruffy red hair drifting into his eyes. "I sure don't like the thought of you gals gettin' out wherever you're goin' and havin' problems. You stay up in that cool country on the mesa." He rubs Patches' head, says, "I sure hope you think of me trying to run a damn café while you two are out there having fun. Especially knowing there's all that uranium waiting up there at the Yip Yip."

"Joe, Hon, you're going to look just fine in an apron, don't you worry about a thing," Coralee laughs, "And there's nothing to it," she winks at me. "Muttonhead does all the cookin', so all you have to do is take orders, and if you're gonna marry me, you need to learn that for sure."

He groans, and she gives him a long kiss goodbye, pats his rear. "We'll be back in three wonderful days. And the boys will take care of the mine just fine. It's assaying at .30 uranium content, did you know that, Chin? Charlie's assayed at .34, and he's a millionaire!"

Coralee and I are soon on our way out towards the country north of Radium, rambling at a top speed of 55, the old truck rattling like its tires are ready to fall off. The dogs are in the middle between us, Buddy Blue grinning while Patches tries to lick his face.

A big shiny metallic tour bus with tinted windows and the words "Peoples Choice" whizzes past, and we can feel the eyes of gray-haired tourists dressed in cotton pants and low-cut alligator shoes, hair slicked back. Somehow the bus leaves a longing in its wake, or so we imagine, the shuffled herded retirees envying our scruffy raggedy adventure. So we imagine.

Fortunately, there's a road exactly where we want to go, and we're soon on a narrow backroad with a sign saying "Not the Road to Radium," a memorial to a preacher's wife who thought it was, promptly got stuck, and spent three days wandering in the wilderness singing hymns to herself, shivering and shoeless.

She got lucky. It snowed right after they found her, roared with a horizontal fierceness right out of hell itself, dropping the temperature to 10 degrees above zero. But that was much later in the year, I note to myself, looking at the horizon for traces of oncoming storm. Nothing, just a blue so blue it makes you think it's the only color there ever could be, blue.

We soon pass another sign: "Road Impassable When Wet," then a corral—a rustic landmark out in these big open overgrazed flats—and now the road changes character, ruts and narrows, and drops down a long easy hill into a wide canyon, itself corralled by huge rough cliffs. The road splits, and Coralee, who's driving like a bat out of hell, truck bouncing and shaking and rattling along, asks, "Which way is still not the road to Radium?"

She takes the lesser road traveled, and we jolt along for a mile or two, passing several old rusted-out heaps that must have been radium-haul trucks in their better days. We soon come to what's left of someone's dreams, a gaping hole vaguely framed by dilapidated timbers in the yellow earth—rusty cans, a rusted old barrel shot full of holes, and the faint odor of rotten eggs.

"The Cash-In Mine," says Coralee. She loves maps, studies them endlessly back home, she informs me, but forgets to bring them. She remembers names, but not locations, so she just wings it. I know there's a Cash-In over by La Sal, but it's a distant sixty or more miles away.

We take another fork, this one leading into an obvious dead-end up against the big crumbly sandstone cliffs. Coralee's sightseeing, swerving, making me nervous.

"Watch out!" I yell.

"What, what?" she asks with concern, hitting the brakes.

"Coralee, didn't you see that sign back there?"

"What sign?"

"The one that says, 'No rock hounding while driving.'"

She laughs, guns it, then hits the brakes again as the road ends.

"Joe's gonna buy me a brand new Dodge convertible for our wedding, one with a push button transmission, so he says, anyway. Won't that be somethin'?"

I jump out and lock in the hubs, she puts the pickup into compound, and we crawl up another quarter-mile, stopping under a big juniper tree dripping with blueberries.

Coralee comments, "Did you know junipers can change sex when they need to for survival, Hon? Roy told me that. Remember Roy? Rangely Roy?" Her voice trails off in the rockfall as Buddy and I scramble up the rubbly cliff base. I can see something sticking out of the cliffs and pull my way up higher.

"Coralee, big logs up here!" I shout down.

Coralee reaches into the back of the truck, grabs a rock hammer, and she and Patches scramble up after us.

Sticking out of the cliffs about 10 feet above us are several reddish-brown petrified logs, some several feet in diameter. Coralee hoists herself up, grabbing onto the logs, slips back down. "Crystals!"

I pull myself up long enough to get a glimpse of a hollowed-out interior full of blue-white dazzle and sparkle. "Crystals," I whisper with incredulity.

"The Parade of Logs," Coralee pronounces.

I'm quiet for a moment, thinking of dense palm forests and swamps and giant dragonflies and theropods and sauropods and immense pterodactyls. "Think of what a museum would pay for that," smiles Coralee, giving me a knowing look.

"Coralee," I explain, "You'd feel bad, taking something like that. Stealing it from me, Coralee, 'cause this is public land," I tease. "Besides, it's bad luck."

"We could get Randy drunk, he could do it, and he wouldn't feel anything till he sobered up, probably not even then. You're not gonna help me, are you?" she asks with mock petulance.

Scrambling back up to the top of the cliff, she yells back down, "There's an old road up here. We could drive here and winch 'em out."

"You don't have a cable that long," I yell back. "And you'd ruin the logs."

She disappears over the top for a while, then scrambles back down, loose pieces of rimrock flowing with her down the steep slope, streams of shale clattering around her boots.

We head on down the road, Coralee grousing that we're not winching the bejeebers out of those delicate crystal-filled logs, but she soon forgets and starts talking about some midnight encounter over in some canyon a few years back with what she thought was a flying scorpion but what turned out to be a grasshopper. She then begins to sing.

So many are taking vacations,
To the mountains, the lakes, or the seas,
To rest from their cares and their worries,
What a wonderful time that must be.
But it seems not my lot to be like them,
I must toil through the heat and the cold.
Bringing lost ones in to the Savior,
Bringing loved ones in to the fold.
When I take my vacation in Heaven,
What a wonderful time that will be.

She laughs, changes tunes.

Summertime, and the livin' is easy,
Fish are jumpin' and the cotton is high,
One of these days, you're gonna rise up singin',
Spread your wings, and take to the sky.

I soon forget to listen, enjoying the motion and the sprays of yellow rabbitbrush and creamy buckwheat in bloom and the feel of early autumn in the desert with nowhere in particular to go and plenty of time to get there. Buddy now sleeps with his head in my lap, Patches curled up next to him

Suddenly, the road's half-gone, it's too late to stop, and we're flying across a thin bridge of dirt over a washed-out culvert. Across, we stop and get out to examine our near-fate.

Gingerly, we look down into the gaping holes where the road was supposed to be, dark holes big enough to swallow a car, vacuosities that frame the thin bridge of dirt we just passed over. We climb down into the wash beneath and study the large culvert, old and battered and tangled, barely holding up a small part of the road.

"Must've been a big rain," Coralee observes. She walks around a bit, studying the road like an engineer, then picks up a big rock and heaves it onto what's left of the road. The edge crumbles, clods of compacted dirt falling into the wash below.

In short time, Coralee's completely destroyed what remains of the old two-track. She then busies herself dragging rocks around the gaping hole, building a barricade of sorts. She backtracks and writes *DANGER* in the road with a stick, a warning bound to blow away with evening's breeze.

"Don't want anyone to drive into this, Hon," she says. "Might be tricky to get back out."

"Coralee," I ask, "How are *we* gonna get back out? Do we have a map?" I ask uselessly, lamely pointing on down the old road in the direction we're now committed to going.

She ignores my question. "This is Little Egypt," she says with no further explanation. I know there's a Little Egypt in the badlands down by Hanksville, but it's a distant hundred or more miles away. She adds, "Isn't this country something, Hon?"

We continue driving, working our way in the direction of the Colorado River, its presence hinted by immense tilted red sed-beds and distant flows of golden cottonwoods and salt cedar lit by slanting evening sunrays.

Finally, we stop and make camp next to the rutted road, dragging out a morass of sleeping bags, pans, a single-burner Coleman stove, and warm beer. Buddy growls a low growl, then promptly jumps back into the truck. Patches is at Coralee's feet, looking a bit anxious.

"That coyote's tame," pronounces Coralee as yellow eyes watch us from the top of the road bank opposite where we sit.

"It just doesn't think we can see it," I argue.

"Naw, coyotes are smart. Watch."

Coralee takes a piece of bread and scuds it in the coyote's direction. The coyote watches the bread hit the dirt, then trots over and quickly gulps it down.

"That's an Arches coyote. It's been hanging out over at the campgrounds." Coralee motions towards distant red buttes and fins that mark the boundaries of the monument.

She throws the coyote another piece of bread, then another. And another.

"What the hay, Coralee, you're feeding him all our food!"

"He's hungry, Hon—was hungry, I should say."

"Now all we have left is peanut butter and jam."

"Might as well give him that too. Humans can survive 30 days without food, and you and me could probably do 40, no offense. Besides, I have what Joe calls maggots in the truck. And more bread."

Coralee pulls out a pan and dumps in water and a box of ramen noodles, lights the stove, and leans back against the road cut. The ramen sputters and boils, then melts itself into a rubbery mass which tastes a bit like flavored socks.

"These aren't maggots, Coralee, they're weevils," I inform her. "Rice is maggots."

"You mind washing this pan, Hon?" Coralee asks. "Since I cooked."

"Sure, later."

Coralee throws the pan over her shoulder. "I can't tell you how much fun I'm having, Hon," she declares, lighting an Old Gold cigarette. "By the way, I've been thinkin' about you and Charlie, and you gave me some good advice, so I'm going to return the favor. You go ahead and forget that guy, he's bad news, I don't care if he's rich. Then you just go ahead and do what you want, not what you should. We women waste too much time doin' what other people think we should. And you know, Hon, the way to do anything is to go ahead and do it, and you just go ahead and do that, Hon, whatever you want to do."

"Thanks, Coralee, you're right, I know you're right," I smile.

"You just gotta treat men right, Hon, take my advice, and that Johnny Taylor's a good man. By the way, he's a good friend of Joe's and stops in the café once in a while. Like with me and Joe, well, Joe knows I'm the driver of the bus, and if I ain't on board, he knows that bus ain't goin' nowhere. That's how you do it, Hon."

I laugh, and Patches nuzzles my hand. We sit in silence and watch as the sunset burns on the distant horizon in a million shades of vermilion. Now Coralee disappears into the bushes. I soon hear yelling.

"Jelp!" she shouts. "Rattler! Buzzer!"

I run across a barren flat to where she's jumping around, then quickly walk down the small wash she's pointing towards, carefully scanning for movement in the twilight. I soon spot the snake, hiding under a twisted sagebrush trunk.

"Coralee, c'mere!" I yell. "It's not a rattler."

She's soon there, gingerly looking at the frightened form under the gray branch. "What is it?" she asks.

"It's a Mesa Verde night snake," I answer.

"No way. You're making that up," she replies. "Is it poison?"

"Actually, it is, but it has to chew on you for a long time to get the venom to come out, which is basically impossible. It's more like a bee sting." The little snake tries to melt into the brush as we walk off.

Big desert stars come out, hanging so bright and low it feels like you could reach up and touch them, burn the tips of your fingers. Orion peeks over the horizon, cold winds of winter slung in his massive belt. I pull out my flute, play an Indian-sounding tune.

"Coralee," I say, kicked back, bare feet warming at the hot sagebrush campfire, "Have you ever heard a humming noise when you're out like this?"

"Hon, I'm not out like this nearly as much as I'd like to be, but yes, I have heard a humming, but it was up in the high country, bees, hummingbirds, is that what you're talking about?"

I sigh. "Coralee, I want you to leave me here."

"Are you saying you don't wanna go back?"

"Exactly. I tried to get Johnny to leave me out at Hidden Splendor, but he just laughed."

"What will you do out here?"

"As little as possible."

"What about food and water?"

"You can come back with provisions in 40 days, just before I'm ready to die. I'll be wandering around, singing hymns. I'm serious, just leave me here," I reiterate.

"With great pleasure, Hon," she replies.

"Coralee," I say.

"What, Chin, Hon?"

"Coralee, impermanence is a curse."

"Look, Hon, you've got to stop thinking all the time. Besides, how do you know impermanence isn't a blessing?"

"I just worry that I won't have enough time to see and do everything, Coralee. That's what I like about the desert, there's mysteries everywhere. But there's not enough time to explore it all."

"Just do your best," she advises, "and die knowing you tried."

"Coralee, listen to this, it's pretty serious stuff. Two old crows were sitting in a cedar tree, and the first old crow says to the second, 'I'm sure proud of you, you old desert rat.'

The second old crow, he says, 'What? Whad'ya say?'

The first old crow, he repeats, 'I said, I'm proud of you!'

The second old crow, he looks at the first old crow, disgusted, and says, 'You old rat, I'm tired of you, too.'"

"Geez Louise, Chin, that's seriously bad."

"Cleo told me it."

"Figures."

Before long we're both fast asleep, Buddy and Patches all cozy on a blanket in the cab of the truck. At first I don't dream of anything, then I slip into dreams of big black clouds laced with lightning, of winds that tangle my hair into Orion's wintry belt, of moonlight-yellow coyotes running for shelter under big rock overhangs. A crash of thunder wakes me.

"Coralee, get up, we gotta get outta here!" A bolt of lightning punctuates my words. I see Coralee on her feet, sleeping bag trailing behind her like a huge lizard's tail.

We frantically throw our gear into the truck and jump in, barefoot. "If it rains we'll be stuck in here forever," Coralee sounds almost joyful at the thought, starting the engine. "We got the dogs?" She guns on out, heading in that unknown direction, truck lights shining on a pan abandoned upside down in the dirt.

"This country's bentonite," I say. "Clay mixed with ancient volcanic ash, very slippery when wet." Then I wonder out loud to myself, "Where does this road go, if it doesn't go to Radium?" Same old question. More lightning, pounding earthshaking thunder. The storm's on us in spades. Same old no-answer.

"Let's sing hymns," Coralee suggests, our gear bouncing and clattering, gas cans banging against the tailgate of the truck.

"When I take my vacation in Heaven..." I warm up, just as big splatters of rain begin, splotching the dirty windshield and making it hard to see.

I ask, "What time do you suppose it is?" just as a bolt of lightning sears through the sky directly ahead of us, corkscrewing and twisting on itself, briefly lighting the road ahead.

"Jeez! Did you see that? Wow! It can't be long till dawn," Coralee replies. As quickly as it started, the rain stops, barely dampening the road. We drive on in the dark.

"Coralee," I think out loud, "Coralee, I'm getting old."

"Oh, that's silly, Hon. Just how old are you?" she asks.

"Twenty-four, but it's one less day out here in the desert for me, one less day here in Heaven."

"Yeah, I have that problem, too," she says quietly. "And I'm about to get married, Hon, which means all the fun will soon be over. All we're gonna do for a honeymoon is spend a night at the Pillow Talk Motel in Catalpa Town, ain't that a hoot? Then back to work. But we'll have a real honeymoon when the mine starts payin', which is gonna be really soon, Hon. Do you always have a good time like this when you go out? We should be over on the highway soon, let's go on over to the Silver Grill in Thompson and get breakfast."

Dawn breaks as we ease onto the highway. A big truck with the word *BULLDOG* on its side roars past, and I catch a glimpse of a gray-haired man partly slumped over the wheel, looking tired, rolling on over to Grand Junction to gas up, then on over the highlands to Denver, not knowing how close he came to the Cash-In Mine, Little Egypt, and the Parade of Logs.

"Whatya wanna do after breakfast, Coralee?" I ask.

She doesn't answer, just nods in the direction where the big cloud of rising sun lights up an expanse of fins and whalebacks and water-filled potholes set like diamonds in white platinum rock.

Dear Chinle,

I cannot tell you how sad I am to know that you do not wish to be involved in my plans. It seems so odd to me that I could provide you with stable employment, a home, and good friends (and perhaps you would even meet someone and get married!), and you would still prefer not. I hope you haven't misread anything into my letters, I only wish you the best because you are my dear friend and cousin. And I do so worry about you. Our families have been close for so many years it's just natural, plus you're so much younger.

Since we missed you on our trip, I have decided that I will take you up on your offer to join you for a week in the desert (when I get back from Europe), no frills, no motels, just living like you do. I have my fears and hesitations, but I must see why you won't come to Boulder for myself. I'm anxious to help you on one of your expeditions—should I buy anything special besides pith helmet, laced boots, rock hammer, and jodhpurs? Will rattlesnakes be a problem? Chinle, you know I'm absolutely terrified of snakes.

I will meet you at the airport in Radium. I'll have Sam fly me in and then he'll stay in Radium in case I need to leave earlier than planned.

I'm so looking forward to seeing you again, but I must admit to being a bit fearful. Ah, but que sera, sera, my friend. See you then, dear cousin, dear heart. Please advise me of the best time to come.

Your loving cousin,

Sarah

Dear Chinle,

Been thinking about what you wrote about owls. One time I was up on Cedar Mesa getting firewood, close to Cigarette Springs, decided to go down and cool off, startled a great horned owl where it had been sleeping in that alcove by the spring. I felt bad, it flew right over my head with its great wings,

I told it I was sorry. I learned Navajo as a kid, and the words came out in Navajo. A few months later I was out exploring near Amasa Back and over-estimated daylight, was getting dark and the only way back was down that narrow trail along a thousand-foot rim, too cold to spend the night, starting to shiver, a big owl landed in the tree ahead, I went over to it, it flew to a rock, I followed it, this went on for a couple of hours, and I could tell I was gradually making my way down the rim with the owl guiding me. At the bottom, that big owl flew right over my head to say goodbye. I thanked it in Navajo. Nobody believes that story. Decide for yourself (as you always do). Weeners having a big brawl, better go break it up.

Jim

14
The Letter: Catalpa Wetlands

Sweet nights, but the days before Charlie finally left became more and more bittersweet, Charlie moody and often tense, sometimes playing his guitar by the fire, sometimes playing the harmonica. The more time I spent with Charlie the more a deep underground current in him seemed to come to the surface, like a magma flow not quite breaking through, laccolithic, yet other times boiling and bubbling and erupting with fire, brilliant reds streaked with saffron yellow, fascinating and yet unsettling to watch.

Time with Charlie was never dull, and even when we were both silent there was the question of how did Charlie feel—moody, angry at something someone said or did recently that he'd been brooding on—or the opposite, gentle and loving and full of his own unique humor, a humor that could always make me laugh. Pick of the draw. I felt that he was becoming more unhappy with each day, then I began to wonder if he'd always been like this, but had just hidden it when we'd first got together.

Charlie was good at distracting. Good at making me forget my problems, as well as my own elusive dreams. Forget your dreams, forget everything but Charlie's blue eyes, his curly thick sandy hair, his charm, his charisma. Fall into his world, tumble like a dinosaur gizzard stone in a flashflood, your own unanswerable questions forgotten.

Forget for a while that you're standing on the edge of eternity. Forget you're alone, that we're all alone. With Charlie the universe fades into the background, just me and Charlie. Nothing else exists, nothing else is important, nothing else needs to ever be.

Fall into those blue eyes and all will be well forever, for I love you.

Now camped in the wetlands near Catalpa Town, one of the few places that stays cool under the still-hot sun of early autumn, I spend days exploring in the nearby wilds, retreating here to escape from the heat. Old Willy sleeps next to the tent that's a necessity here in mosquito land, and Johnny and I sit in his pickup and talk, having just returned from a picnic at his Grandma Callie's. Buddy naps between us, full of leftover roast beef, dreaming of Callie's golden dog, Hannah.

We talk of family, of the Radium Queen, of rock art, and finally, for the first time since he gave me the amethyst, of Charlie.

"Did Charlie ever ask you to marry him, Chin, not that it's any of my business."

"Yeah, Johnny, he did. But it was always a someday kind of thing. Why would he want to marry me when he already had me?"

"You mean, he thought he had you, Chin. He got a little presumptuous."

"Well, I don't know, it sure felt like we had each other. It went on for a long time. We spent every possible minute together."

"Then you left for college?"

"No, I should've gone to college right after I graduated high school, but I didn't have any money. Plus all I wanted was to be with Charlie, we had some good times, Johnny. But the beginning of the end was when he went off by himself prospecting. I think he knew I was starting to want more independence from him, I was beginning to be disturbed by his constant moodiness, but it didn't mean I wasn't still in love with him. Going off alone was his way of protecting himself from commitment. He struck it rich, and he ended it in what I consider to be a pretty chickenshit way."

"See, it was just me and my mom at home, and she was always busy, trying to make a living, keep everything together. My dad was killed in an accident when I was little, just like Charlie's, another unhappy bond between us. After I started college, Mom met a guy who had a ranch over by Ridgway, in Colorado, she remarried and moved over there. My mom's a wonderful person."

"What did she think of Charlie?"

"At first she thought it was great, 'cause I got a job in his rock shop, that's how I met him. I was a senior in high school, and it kept me busy and I could make a little spending money. Then I worked for him full-time in the summer. But then later, when our relationship became more obvious, she wasn't real pleased with me hanging out all the time with him. She was worried about him taking advantage of me—which he did, but not like she was worried about."

"What dya mean?"

"He took advantage of me because I loved him."

"Look, it's none of my business, but..."

"No, the way he took advantage of me was by using me to feed his ego, his insecurities."

"He had to be proud to be with you, Chin, I'm sure. You're a very smart and pretty woman."

"Thanks, Johnny, though I sometimes doubt that. He liked the way I laughed at his silly jokes, and he liked the way I loved him so much. It validated him, everything he did. He's really an insecure person."

"He later told me you were hardheaded and stubborn, Chin, and that's why everything fell apart."

"No doubt, he told everybody that, he told himself that, he even told me that, and maybe I am, but he mostly said that after I quit letting him control me."

"You don't seem like someone who could be easily controlled."

"Well, looks can be deceiving. Charlie initially liked the fact that I thought for myself. He liked my independence. It was very attractive to him. But he was so damn insecure that he couldn't stand me to be free, so he gradually started to try to control everything I did. I thought it was his way of showing he loved me, to advise me how I should do things, but that turned into demands. I sensed deep inside something was wrong, I got to where I was unhappy with him and unhappy without him. It's the old case of seeing what you want to see. He used me until he found something bigger and better and more secure, at least in his mind."

"Uranium riches."

"Actually, Johnny, it's power. The money just buys the power. Charlie was just practicing on me, practicing for the big time."

"Practicing power?"

"Yeah, power comes in many forms. It's much more subtle than most people realize. It's not some big guy sitting up there telling everyone what to do, it's gained in subtle ways, through the manipulation of others. It makes insecure people feel secure to know they can get other people to do what they want, it reduces their fears. And then there's the person who finds nice compassionate people who won't tell them to go to hell like they should but will instead put up with them. Haven't you noticed that jerks don't hang out with kindred souls? They're usually with nice people."

"Yeah, there's some truth to that. So why aren't you crazy about me?"

"I am crazy about you, but you're not a jerk—or are you saying I am?"

"No, no way, Chin, just kidding about myself. So you're crazy about me, but just as a friend?"

"Yeah, and that's a damn compliment. I'll never be with a man I can't be best friends with, too. You know, Johnny, I wish Charlie and I had been better friends, we might have made it work out."

"You're kidding yourself, Chin."

"Probably."

"You see, Chin, Charlie's a narcissist. The world exists for Charlie. I know the guy pretty damn well, he lived with me for four years in college, don't forget. Insecure people use you to build themselves up, and they may even think they love you, but it's dependent on what you do for them. It's conditional. When their need for you is gone, whoosh, so's their so-called love."

"Chin, my sister Annie's a nurse over at the Beehive House, and she talks about an old guy who comes to visit his wife every day. His wife's lost it, doesn't have a clue who he is, but every day he comes to her room and sits and talks with her and hugs her and brushes her hair and all that. You know, Chin, that's unconditional love, and everyone deserves that kind of love. For better or worse, in sickness and health.

People like Charlie don't even know what that kind of love is. It's a tragedy."

"You're right, Johnny. I just wish I'd known you before I met him. You could've warned me off."

"Wouldn't have done any good."

"Why not?"

"Cause you were working something out with him."

"How so?"

"I dunno."

"Well, me neither. I've got to figure it out so I can quit obsessing on him and move on with my life. It's been nearly a year now."

"I know, Chin, I know."

"Johnny, what was I working out with Charlie?"

"You can't mistake pity for love, Chin. How did he make you feel?"

"Hurt, sad, alone, just like I feel when I think of him now, I guess."

"A cowboy ain't happy without lonesome, Chin. Maybe Charlie made you feel like you did when you were growing up or something. We go for what we're comfortable with, even if it's not good for us."

"Jeez. You're saying we can be comfortable when we're in pain?"

"I dunno. It's just a theory. In fact, this is the first time I've ever even talked about this kind of stuff with anyone."

"Well, I do know one thing, right now I don't ever want to feel that way again. I just want to be happy, to dance in the mystery of life. But I wish I could go back before I met Charlie and try it all again. Go back, go back, go back…"

"You'd do the same damn thing, Chin, if that's what you needed to work out. Maybe that's why you're not interested in me, 'cause I'm a nice guy, I come from a good respectable stable family, I don't make you feel that comfortable pain, so you don't obsess on me. Think about it, Chin."

"I dunno, Johnny, that seems kind of harsh, and actually I do like being with you. But maybe it's true, maybe that's how I forget fixing-up myself instead."

"You could fix me up and I could get you in a fix." Johnny grins mischievously. "Just kidding, sort of."

I laugh,"Shoots, I can't even fix myself up. Anyway, I'll quit beating a dead horse, but in some ways I think that maybe I just couldn't be myself in the shadow of Charlie, he was just too strong of a personality. He was so insecure that he had to always control me, and I let him, to a certain point. I dunno. Maybe he wasn't insecure at all, maybe I misread him, maybe he used that perception to manipulate me.

Sometimes I suspect he feels entitled, the opposite of insecure. I know he made the stakes awful high, anytime I'd disagree with him he'd get mad and threaten to leave, sometimes he did leave. I should've told him, adios, you bastard. And I got sick of trying to convince him that the world really isn't such a bad place, that people really are generally good at heart."

"Yeah," Johnny replies, "Charlie's hypercritical of everybody. I learned that living with him, poor bastard. He's turned on me more than once. And he's obsessed with money."

We both sit in silence, both unsure what to say next. Johnny's more comfortable exploring for uranium, me for rock art, than we are exploring the human condition. Finally, I say, "I wrote Charlie a letter after you gave me the amethyst."

"I've noticed you wear it. What did you say?"

"I have it in my Hercules box, wanna hear it?"

"Sure."

I jump out of Johnny's truck, return with letter in hand. Johnny's now sitting on the bumper in the cool of the evening, and I join him.

Dear Charlie,

Why are you so afraid? You, with millions of dollars, afraid of being poor? What irony.

Money doesn't buy love, it buys hate. When people are dependent on you and they know money is your god, they start to hate you. Dependency breeds hatred, not love. Freedom brings love. Your gifts are not freely given nor received. You are trying to buy those things that can't be bought.

Security is within you, between you and God. Fortunes are lost in the blink of an eye. Internal security is never lost. You cannot control the universe, that's trying to be God. It's impossible.

The Buddha said, "I do not accept your gift." That particular gift was anger, he said that to a man who was yelling at him. Like the Buddha, I do not accept your gift either. Your gifts have strings attached. You can't buy people, at least not people with integrity. The people you can buy will abandon you when you need them. Money buys only things, it's a tool. You can hoard it, but it will not save you. It's a loan to you from God, to be used accordingly.

I may live my life in poverty, but there's a difference between being rich and being wealthy, and I'll always be rich. The rich give their money away, the poor hoard it. People are all we have. The Bible says whatever you do for others, you do for God and it comes back to you sevenfold. My riches are around me, no one can ever take away the canyons, the ravens, the cliffrose in bloom.

I realize that by not getting back with you I am giving up a life of what some would call security, I could live in that big house. But the price is too high. It's false security. You're not trustworthy.

Everything I say is like pissing in the wind. I loved you, but you're no longer the guy I knew. Or more likely, I never really knew you. Perhaps you mirrored me, made me think you had the same values and treasured the same things as I did, when you really didn't, and it was all an act.

But now I'm free. I refuse the gift, but thanks anyway. Without love, life is pretty much wasted. Chinle

"So what did he answer?" Johnny asks.

"Nothing. I never gave it to him, that's why it's in my box. And I decided to keep the amethyst to remind me what I shouldn't do in the future. As for getting through to Charlie, like I said, it's like pissing in the wind, like wasting your time making a wish that you know won't come true. I decided that he doesn't have the right to know what I think, he would just find some way to justify his negative response instead of hearing what I'm saying. But it helped me to write it, sort of a catharsis. Who knows, it's just the truth according to Chinle, there may be things about him I don't know."

"There are."

"Like what?"

"Charlie's parents were alcoholics. He says he doesn't remember much about his childhood."

"He never told me that."

"He's ashamed of it."

"Why? It wasn't his fault."

"He told me a story about his mom, this is what he grew up with. She babysat his little cousin once, just a baby, maybe six months old. The baby wasn't used to being away from her parents, and she cried all the time. Charlie was about 10, he said he'd try to go pick up the baby to comfort her, and his mom would tell him to leave her alone, that the baby needed to learn she couldn't always have what she wanted. The baby cried for two weeks, then finally quit, and she also quit eating. Fortunately, her parents came back then. But that was the woman who raised Charlie, so that tells you something."

"What a tragedy. What about his dad?"

"He was more compassionate. According to Charlie, he'd hold them and baby them when they were little. But as soon as they were old enough, he started having unreal expectations."

"Like what?"

"They had a malachite-azurite claim, it was called the Bluebird Claim, and Charlie told me his dad expected them to work it when they were just kids, I mean work hard. It was very high-grade ore. They dug it with shovels and sold it to mineral collectors. They worked 10 hours a day, sometimes more, and usually didn't even know what they were supposed to be doing, their dad would be drinking. They finally lost everything, and then his dad got a job as a mechanic with Mobil, but was killed in an accident. There's more, but what's the point? Charlie's parents gave him gifts he didn't want, like in your letter, but kids don't know how to refuse gifts from their parents. Gifts of inadequacy, fear, lack of compassion."

"Johnny, he never hinted at any of that kind of stuff about his family, and I thought I knew him so well. How sad. But all I can do is resolve it within myself and go on. I can't control him, make him feel what I want him to feel, that's the very thing I'm accusing him of doing to me."

"Are you bitter?"

"No, bitterness is a form of self-poison. But Charlie's sadly lacking in integrity, empathy, courage, all things that are pretty high up on my list. I won't let myself feel like that again, and I won't ever expect anything from anyone. Having expectations is kind of a form of using people, I now realize. Expecting someone to really love you, believing that they do, it too much to expect of anyone."

"Chinle, Chinle, you can be so blind."

"Probably."

"We all deserve to have love, we all should have expectations. High expectations. Don't you think Charlie was trying to prove something?"

"Probably."

"The Charlie I know wanted to make it more than anything else in the world, be successful, prove his value that way."

"Pretty sad."

"It had been ingrained in him since he was a kid, the idea that personal value comes with riches."

"I sure as hell don't have that problem. I never expect to have anything."

"No expectations."

"Well, that's not exactly what I meant, it was regarding other people in general. But yeah, I doubt if I'll ever have anything of value materially either. It seems like you have to take it from other people, and I'm just not interested."

"What about creating something, doing something of value, enriching people's lives? That's not taking it."

"Maybe, I dunno. Right now I just want to leave this desert and start all over somewhere else."

"I thought you loved the desert."

"I do."

"Then why do you want to leave?"

"I feel like it's been taken from me. I have all these associations with being here. I feel like it's tainted and I need to start over somewhere else, make a new life, completely new."

"But it's such a part of who you are, Chin. Me, too. Why would you leave?"

"I can't explain it, Johnny. Sometimes you have to leave things behind to set your soul free. When I'm out in the desert, I have so many associations with Charlie that he feels like an integral part of it. Too many memories. I hear his voice in the wind, the trees."

"What about creating new associations?"

"I've tried. So far it hasn't worked."

"What if you fell in love with someone else out here?"

"That doesn't seem very likely. I mean, why would I want to do that? That would just be repeating the problem, not learning from it."

"Chinle, because like you said in your letter, without love, life ain't worth much."

"You can't just force it, Johnny. You can't just have love at the snap of your fingers."

"Maybe you can if you open your eyes. Are you going to leave?"

"Probably, after I finish this damn rock art project."

"Will you ever come back?"

"Who knows?"

Johnny stands, looking down at me, then reaches out. I take his hand. He pulls me up, next to him, against him. I stand, embracing him, close, too close, our arms around each other, intertwined in the darkness, stars above us cloaked with dark clouds, my feelings cloaked with dark clouds and confusion.

He feels warm, strong, and I sense danger, the kind of danger I swore I would run from. Instead, I stand, holding him close, until we both finally break free like ghosts in the night, filled with longing and melancholy, wondering why we can no longer grasp that which we desire, our dull eyes lit with the dim light of lies we've seen come true.

"See you in the morning, Johnny," I say softly. "Let's go flying again."

"I love you, Chin."

"I know, now I know, and I feel the same way, Johnny, but I'm afraid of it. I just need some time."

"Hell, I have time. Lots of time. But I am mortal." He laughs a wry laugh.

He slips away and I'm alone.

The night swings in like a uranium haul truck after a long day, heavy and hot, and Johnny and I are soon on our separate ways, dust and a thick sense of something unsettled following behind both of us.

Dear Chinle,

I was so happy to hear from you. We will get together. I am in the middle of painting a lion and he just doesn't look quite right. I have been hiking a lot with Jan and Jim and now that they are on vacation, on my own.

It is so beautiful right now in Chautauqua. The long green grass, the flowers, the blue sky. We actually saw a rabbit on the Enchanted Mesa last week. It has been like England here with rain every day, but today is a happy change of pace with warmth and sunshine. Same over there?

Hope all is well.

Love,

Sarah

15
Colt: Mussentuchit Badlands

"I came out here and forgot to go back."

A subtle smile crosses Colt's face, and his green eyes twinkle just a little. Sun-bleached hair streaked with gray sticks out from beneath a straw Panama hat.

"I knew I had to come out here. Some of my old friends probably think I got lost and died out here, and I suppose that in a way, I did. The old me, anyway. But it had to be that way. I even changed my name. It used to be Duncan, but now I'm Colt." Eyes twinkle again.

The Mussentuchit Badlands is a place as wild and remote as it sounds. Colt's green Ford pickup with white camper looks out of place against the deep purple and gray badlands.

Colt and Johnny and I kick back in the shade of his camper with his dogs, Daisy, Moses, and Chompers. After lots of sniffing at Buddy Blue, the whole pack lays down next to us in the shade. A hot breeze blows.

We're in no hurry. Over mugs of warm beer, Colt continues. He's intelligent and well-educated, and, I discover, like most intellectuals, a bit contemplative. "I think too damn much," he says, laughing.

On my friend Bill's advice, I came here to ask Colt about rock art, and on Coralee's advice, about dreams. We talk for a long time, since he's photographed a lot of the Mussentuchit. He shows us rock art pictures, but none strike me as anything particularly different from the stuff I've been seeing further east, near Radium and Catalpa Town.

Finally, Johnny asks Colt how he ended up out here in this most desolate yet beautiful of places.

"This whole thing started with the dreams. I've always worked hard—did everything I was supposed to, went to college, got married, had a family, became a teacher. I was supposed to be happy, sometimes I even thought I was. But then I started having these dreams."

Colt's story makes me think of Howard Balsley and the Yellow Circle Mine.

"The dreams initially had very little significance, I hardly even remembered them. At first, I dreamed about things like I'd be looking at a big aspen tree with some sheepherder's initials carved into it, or maybe at a cliff that was particularly colorful. Or maybe I'd dream about a little mountain stream sparkling in the sun. Nothing of any significance, just dreams about things outdoors. I didn't think anything about them.

I eventually got a camera, the dreams sparked some sort of creative urge that I'd long ago hidden. I even started going to the photography shows around the area and meeting a few photographers.

But then I started dreaming about real places. For example, I dreamed once of a big blue boulder of jade in a streambed, somewhere in Oregon, then later I saw a photograph of what looked exactly like it. The dreams seemed so real, just like I was standing there.

I'd dream of looking out over wild mesas and deep canyons, watching the sunset. Or I'd dream of hiking up to old abandoned copper mines and picking up what are called blueberries, little round pieces of azurite. I eventually met a guy who's a geologist and spends a lot of time in the field and who's also a photographer. We'd talk and he'd tell me about places he'd been, show me photos, tell me how he took them. I was like a little kid who'd just discovered jelly beans or marbles.

Not to get all philosophical, but I think that sometimes we have to change or die—it becomes critical to our very existence. Our subconscious somehow encourages us to find what we need. And I needed wild places, I needed to be creative.

I began to feel like I was living a dual existence—working at my stressful job during the day, wandering these wild free places during the night.

And always the wild places. The dreams began to take over my life, and I wanted to go live in these places, be an artist, using my camera as brush and canvas. Keep in mind that I lived in a college town, which was wild only when the college kids partied. I began to obsess on getting out to the wilderness.

My youngest daughter finally went off to college, and my wife left me, leaving just me and my dogs. I decided to sell my big house, and I used some of the money to buy a pickup and camper and some good photography equipment and headed out. Everybody told me I was making a big mistake. I'd be sorry, especially leaving my security and future retirement. But I had to find these places I'd been dreaming about. I knew they were real."

"Did you ever dream of the Mussentuchit?" I ask.

"No, ironically enough, this is the place I love the most and I never dreamed about anything even remotely like it. Most of the dreams were of big canyons and high lonesome mesas. I just stumbled on the Mussentuchit by accident.

Anyway, I wandered around and began taking pictures. I gradually started selling a few, making a meager living. But I was truly happy for the first time in my life.

By the way, as soon as I sold the house, the dreams stopped. I never dreamt about another canyon or mesa. Sometimes I miss the dreams—they were so peaceful and colorful."

"What do you dream about now?" I ask.

"Well, on bad nights, I dream about teaching college again. Good nights, I dream that I have my photos in a gallery somewhere, a dream that's close to coming true.

But I think now that my dreams were of freedom, and now that I'm free, I don't need to dream about it anymore."

"Maybe one kind of freedom is having no responsibilities," Johnny comments, looking sideways my way.

"Well, that may be true," Colt replies, "One type of freedom is just getting loose from everything. But there's another kind of freedom, the freedom where you know who you really are and where you can live by it."

Colt's eyes twinkle again, ever so subtle. The dogs are sound asleep at his feet.

He adds, "But to this day, I hate houses. First of all, they cost too much. Then you have to keep them working—windows leak, linoleum comes up because of the leaking windows, water heater quits on you in the middle of that shower you're having to take 'cause you had to pull up nasty linoleum. But mostly houses confine you, make your life so you're stuck—have to sleep there at night, always have to go home or somebody will worry, even if it's just your neighbor.

I can't even sleep inside anymore unless it's stormy or too cold, I feel like I'm in a tomb, get claustrophobic. And I miss seeing the stars, the clouds drifting across the moon, all that. I think we'd all be better off living outside. Houses breed all kinds of bad things—bugs, people."

He laughs, stands. "That's enough of that. C'mon inside for a minute, and I'll show you that piece of what looks to be carnotite that I mentioned earlier." Dogs wake up, stretch, look around.

Earlier, clouds layered the sky like translucent washes in a watercolor. Now they've turned to an oil painting with long thick opaque brush strokes, a thin streak of blue sky here and there where the painter's hand was unsteady. The air becomes thick and moist.

And somehow, now, here in the Mussentuchit, I know my time in the desert will soon come to an end, my self-appointed exile is nearly over, and my dreams of rocks will end.

I remember a conversation with Coyote Yellowjacket on an evening's walk over in Colorado at a place where purple sedbed cliffs were banked by narrowleaf cottonwoods, a place bearing the ignominious name of Dry Park:

Little Rabbit, is beauty intrinsic, or does it fade away?

I'm silent.

Coyote Yellowjacket persists.

Someday you'll be old, Little Rabbit. You'll be old and maybe can't see so well.

If I can't see, then I won't have to look at you anymore, will I, Yellowjacket?

But if your beauty fades away, will anyone love you? Coyote asks.

Love isn't predicated on looks and beauty, my friend.

Then why don't you humans love what you think is ugly, like the barren blackbrush flats?

Coyote scratches chin with back leg, nearly falling over.

Little Rabbit, what if you're all alone, ugly alone, and nobody loves you?

I'll always have you to cheer me up.

Don't be sarcastic, Little Rabbit.

Coyote pauses, adds, *You'll have lots of memories, the way you live life.*

Walk in beauty, scraggly coyote.

Clouds now solidify, rain hangs heavy.

The two men come back, and Johnny looks at the sky. "Pap clouds," he says. "We need to get goin'."

"Mammatus, like mammals," I correct.

"Like mammary," he responds. "Only mammals have mammary glands, Chin, paps. Pap clouds."

Far in the distance, the Coffeepot Mountains look like a mirage. High on their mountain slopes, quakies tremble in a cool breeze laden with the mist of snowmelt tumbling over rockfall.

And far below, out in the mirage of Mussentuchit Badlands, Colt's dogs squint in the sun at that distant image of white uplands and long for that cool breeze.

Completely oblivious of rock art, uranium, and their own enviable sweet wild freedom.

Johnny eases the little plane into the air, even though we're buffeted by the oncoming wind. We quickly climb up through the dark clouds, though I worry for a moment that we'll fall out of the air. He doesn't look a bit worried, even when a big bolt of lightning fills the sky, striking a nearby butte. Thunder wraps the plane with sound waves, competing with the air currents. Buddy hunkers down in the back of the plane.

Soon, we're above the storm, sky clear and smooth. Johnny taps my knee, points to his headphones. I put mine on.

"Pretty rough back there, you OK?" he asks.

"Yeah, I'm fine. It was exciting, you're a good pilot."

He grins, hair sticking out around the headphones, then points downward at a beautiful pourover through parted clouds. I nod in acknowledgement, thumbs up.

"You like flyin', Chin?"

"Geez Louise yes," I answer, smiling.

He smiles back, "Wanna fly over Coralee's and give 'em a buzz?"

"You bet."

He banks a bit to the left. The plane drones on. Finally, he says, "Chin, you and that fellow Colt sure have a lot in common, don't you?"

"I dunno. How so?"

"Well, I mean, he likes to live the same way you do, you're peas in a pod, and you're both thinkers. He's a nice-lookin' fellow, too, even though he's older, got a little gray hair."

I turn and look at Johnny. He's conveniently checking out the altimeter, adjusting the flaps just a little.

I laugh. "You think I'd want to hang out with him?"

"Never know, two people with the same philosophy and all. He seems pretty smart, too, likes dogs, has a whole pack of 'em."

"Are you jealous, Johnny? I don't even know the guy."

"Ah, nah, why'd I be jealous when you and me ain't even attached?" He pauses, looks at me. "Why the hell ain't we attached, huh, Chin?"

I laugh, "Well, I dunno, maybe it's your looks that're the problem. That's it, you're just too good-lookin'."

"You're kiddin', aren't you?"

"No. You know you're good-lookin', don't you?"

"Not really, there's lots of good-lookin' fellows around. You think I'm an egotist? I thought women liked good-lookin' men."

"You're not egotistical, Johnny, far from it, you're a very nice guy, in spite—see how it is, I start to add, in spite of your looks. And you're right, women do go for handsome men, money works, too, for some, anyway. But too much good-lookin' can be a problem."

"How so?"

"It can be a threat. Your good-looks could affect how women feel, like you could have any woman you want, and it begins a downward spiral."

"No kidding? Do you feel that way about me, Chin?"

"I haven't really thought about it much, Johnny."

"Sounds to me like you have," he grins. "But we're right for each other in a lot of ways. And if I'm good-lookin', at least you are too, so you wouldn't have to worry about it."

"I dunno, maybe that's a problem, I dunno."

"Well, you shouldn't feel insecure if I'm so good-lookin' that women don't like me, right? You wouldn't ever need to worry about me, right?"

"You know, I don't understand how we always get off on this stuff," I answer. "I hate this stuff. I just hate it. Why does everything have to have a hidden meaning? Why can't simplicity count for anything? Why can't two people be together because they like each other?"

He grins. "You brought it up. I actually don't even never look in the mirror, ain't even got one. No gals out here to notice if you're handsome or not anyway. Besides, I know lots of people who are what I'd call good-lookin', and they don't seem to have any problems like that. My family, we always call people shallow who go for looks. Same for money. You know, Chin, out here, we judge people by who they are, not what they look like or what they have. It's the same for how well they do something, not how much they make doin' it. It's what we call democracy."

"It was just a weird idea I had, I don't know where it came from. Actually, I got somebody I need to set straight on all this."

He looks concerned. "Who's that?"

"Oh, nobody you know, just an old acquaintance from way back. He just planted this idea in my head. He's always trying to make me question everything."

"Somebody around here, I know 'em?"

"No, Johnny, it's not anybody you know. At least, I don't think so."

"Well, maybe you should quit talkin' to him, if he makes you feel like that. It's hard enough makin' a go of bein' positive without that kind of friend."

"Oh, I know, believe me, I know. I'll get around to telling him to buzz off one of these days."

Now we bank over the rotten ramparts of Temple Mountain, and we're soon over the Temple Junction Motel and Café. Johnny flies low, makes a big circle, comes back.

Now I see Coralee and Muttonhead on the front step, waving, as we buzz again. Johnny waggles the wings while I wave, then we turn and ease down onto the airstrip.

Dear Chinle,

The lion I was painting is one of my masks for the garden, a sort of cowardly lion from the Wizard of Oz. He came out very nicely in the end and his new owner will pick him up tomorrow morning.

As for Europe, I am up to lots of things over there, but especially mischief. Derek is an architect who is anxiously waiting to meet me in person. We have corresponded several times. My friend Mimi thought we might make a good couple. He renovates ancient farm buildings, loves cats and France. His letters are charming. We are to meet at a dinner party in the Bistro Van Gogh.

I am also traveling a bit with my brother and perhaps attending a workshop on sculpture in France. And other not so innocent pursuits. Those I cannot mention. Ah, life is good. I think, however, I will need to do something dreadful—go back to work on the golf course development. It is unthinkable without your help, since you are so in tune with the land. Think of what a beautiful course you could design! Perhaps you will reconsider. Hope all is going well.

Your loving cousin,
Sarah

16
The Big Rattle: Catalpa Wetlands

Now, with the ever-blue early autumn sky tinged with heat, any hint of cloud is watched carefully—will it bring prayed-for rain or lightning-born fire? More often than not, neither.

But one day, towards late afternoon, a dry wind scours through the country like a herd of wild horses, here then gone, and soon after, a tip of white cloud can be seen above the salmon cliffs to the north.

Within a few hours it has steamed into that entire quadrant of sky, boiling masses of smoke and water and steam and ash. Armageddon. The canyons are burning, and soon so are the mesas between, burning scrub oak so dry you can crumple the leaves like autumn deadfall.

Fire races on up the slopes of the Books in a fiery rage, crowning now across the tops of 60 foot-tall Doug fir, leaving some trees charred and some untouched, jumping wildly across the sky great distances, leaving islands of green in the wake of an inferno so hot it explodes entire trees, leaving smoke craters where roots had been moments before.

Within two days, the cloud rises to ten, fifteen, twenty thousand feet as an unearthly calm surrounds it for ten, twenty, thirty miles, oxygen pulled into its boiling maw, hot air spewing out, causing birds to fall from the air, dead.

"Holy God, the Books are having a blow-up!"

As the cooler evening comes, the air takes on a distant quality, oppressive, as the huge cloud now falls, blanketing everything for miles. It had stood, ominously, for perhaps 45 minutes before its rounded top had begun to fall, taking on at first a horned-look like a jester's hat, then losing its puffiness and contours, eventually falling into a long horizontal brown haze that turned the sun a burnished red.

In both Green River and Catalpa Town, the smell of smoke brings people outside their houses to look, ashes falling from the blanketed sky.

The wind continues to blow, day after day, some days just a breeze, others full-on 20 or 30 mph gusts. It's a hot dry wind, the kind that saps everything—sucks the moisture from the already dry plants, blows the coarse red sand into cracks under doors, and feeds the fire. Each day the monster grows by another thousand or so acres, first five thousand, then 10, until finally it has burned over 30 thousand acres in the rugged high canyons. The limited firefighting forces from the nearby towns are helpless to stop its march.

And each day Catalpa Town, Green River, even Radium, wakes to the smoke. Some days it's a huge cloud to the north, held at bay if the winds are kind and blow from the south. Other days you know it's all around you when you wake—scratchy throat, headache, smell of burning. On these days, the mountains fall into shadows and the rims retreat into smoky distance.

One day Johnny stops out where I'm camped in the Catalpa Wetlands, where I'm trying to hide from Cougar Sun under big Fremont cottonwoods, Russian olives, and mulberry trees.

"Hope I didn't wake you."

"It's OK." I crawl out of my tent, half-asleep, slapping at a mosquito.

A morning dove coos in the big cottonwood next to my camp, sounding nostalgic.

"Geez, Chin, come in and stay at the house, no sense fightin' mosquitoes. Anyway, I just wanted to say goodbye for a while. I'm gonna go fight that Big Rattle Fire up in the Books."

Over to the east, big blue-black clouds boil up. Still in my longjohns, I fire up the little stove and make coffee in silence, wait for it to simmer while sitting cross-legged on a rock, quiet. Johnny sits on his haunches, leaning against Willy, patting Buddy on the head. Coffee done, I throw in a shot of cold water to settle the grounds, pour two cups, sugar in both, no canned cow 'cause I'm out.

Finally, I stand and hand Johnny a cup and say, "How in hell did you get into this one, John?"

He seems relieved to hear me talk. "Need the money, and they need me. I can drive a D4 Cat and make fire line with the best of 'em. That damn fire's eatin' everything up, we gotta stop it. They're recruiting anyone who can talk and walk at the same time, hell, you don't even have to know how to talk."

I hug my knees up against my chest, the amethyst pressed against my skin under my longjohns top. "Johnny, be careful. Whatever you do, don't let anybody know you can fly, they'll have you doing something too dangerous. Building fire line's bad enough."

"I know, but everybody already knows I can fly. Don't worry, Chin. Hey, does this mean you care or something?" He grins, tousles my hair.

"You know I care, Johnny. I wish I could go up there and help. Hey, is there anything I can do? Who do I talk to?"

Johnny frowns. "Chin, if there was, I wouldn't tell you. I don't want you up there."

"Why not, if it's not something worth worrying about on your behalf, why wouldn't it be OK for me?"

He shakes his head, "It's different."

"Why's that, 'cause I'm a woman?"

"Naw, I dunno, maybe. Look, I just don't want you anywhere near that fire, it's a killer."

"I guess I can just stay here and worry, do nothing. Maybe I can get your grandma to teach me how to knit so I have something safe to do while I'm worrying, though I doubt if she ever learned, she was too busy doing whatever the hell she wanted. On second thought, maybe I should get up there and see if there's any rock art in the fire's path and try to record it before it's destroyed."

"Chinle, Chinle." He sits beside me and puts his arm around my shoulders, hugging me to his side. "Look, dammit, you're a free spirit, you'll figure out who to talk to anyway—Royal Walker's the recruiter here in town, over at the Forest Service building. He'll probably find something you can do, but it won't be exciting, maybe something like making sandwiches for the crews, but it all helps."

He gives me a long hug, stands,"Gotta go. Look, I'll be back soon, they work you seven days, then you get three off. Will you be around?"

"Sure, I'll be around somewhere," I reply, angry, though not really sure why. "But look, you promise to stay out of the sky and I'll promise to stay away from the fireline, OK?"

"Deal."

"I think I'm gonna go over to Radium for a few days, then probably go over to the Dark Angel area for a week or so."

Johnny looks pained,"Geez, Chin, why can't you just stick around for a while? I'd really like to see you when I get off. Go help my grandma, she'd enjoy the company, you could help her get ready for Coralee and Joe's wedding, get outta mosquito land for a while." He stops, frowns,"You should stay away from Dark Angel, it's not that far from the fire. That canyon comes right off the Books. Go back south if you want to get back out for a while."

"I know, but the fire's not even close, Johnny, it's gotta be several big drainages over, from the looks of the smoke. It's one of my last places to go. Even though Davidson's map doesn't show he was over there, I suspect he made a foray or two in that direction, from a few comments he's made in some other monographs."

"You're about done with the project?" Johnny's eyes darken.

"Yep, about as done as I'm gonna get for now. I'm running outta money."

"What about asking Charlie for more? Are you gonna see him? Aren't you gonna keep lookin' for that panel?"

"I'm going to find that panel, Johnny, if it's the last thing I ever do. But I think I'll go over to Colorado for a while after the wedding, write up what I've got so far, submit it as my thesis, then come back later and keep looking. I wanna go see my mom. I need some of that cool mountain air."

"Well, don't take off without saying goodbye, promise?"

"I promise, of course I'll say goodbye."

"Say, I could fly you and Buddy Blue over there, it'd be fun."

"Really?"

"Yeah, you could leave Willy at Grams' place, then I could pick you up when you're ready to come back. And don't forget Unaweep."

"That's a thought, you could meet my mom, you'd love her place over there, red cliffs, just like your ranch, same formation even, Cutler. That's the type locality, where they first defined the Cutler, between Ridgway and Ouray, Cutler Creek."

"Sounds like damn beautiful country, Chin, let's plan on it."

I never do get over to see Royal Walker, not being much of a sandwich chef (just ask Buddy Blue). Instead, I decide to head for Dark Angel, supposedly far from the route that Davidson took on his 1935 exploration of the area.

Willy and Buddy and I go into Catalpa Town, get mail and resupply, then go back and break camp. I want to walk the wetlands before I head out, go down by the creek for one last taste of cool air.

The day's a hot fury, and it's not much cooler in the trees. Tall grasses swish around my knees, thick yellow seedheads ready to drop. I watch a black hornet with a red body buzz through silver Russian olives that share a thicket with tall narrowleaf cottonwoods. Beyond stand the red cliffs that cradle the dugway to the west, the road to Willow Creek and eventually on to Torrey.

On the far horizon, billowing up some 40 miles away, the massive remnants of scrub oak, Doug fir, mule deer, black bear, and God only knows what are now ashes falling from the sky.

Here in the wetlands, half-dead willows stand straight, red-purple, with some growth near the bottom of the stems where the plants started growing, then stopped, realizing there was no water. Everything has a dreamy quality, a thick woody smoky smell, even in the shade, where it's at least a good twenty degrees cooler. Even here, it's so hot it feels like it could explode.

Now I see tracks, tracks Johnny and I left—when were we here last? We'd taken Buddy Blue for a walk and were searching for wild strawberries. The tracks are almost faded beyond recognition, but I know they're ours, there's been no rain to change things, and my bootprints have bird's wings, Redwing Boots. Johnny had commented on how easy it would be to track me.

Our tracks take me back in time, and I can almost see shadows that look like me and Johnny, but it's really just the shade of old twisty cottonwoods. I remember Johnny saying we're timeless, immortal, and that after we die we'll be able to move through time, we can return to each day of our lives and relive it if we want, and this will take some of the sorrow away from losing people and places we love. I thought it was a creative answer to a lot of problems, though I didn't believe it.

Now I realize that I love this place, I'll always come back. I've been craving it, its good memories, cool shade, mellowness.

The air is still, there's no sound except the occasional buzzing of a fly, the solitary honking of a pheasant. Buddy startles a deer, I hear a splash and realize we're at the bank of Pack Saddle Creek. The deer stands in the shallows, looking at us, no more than 20 feet away, a tawny brown doe. I grab Buddy and quickly retreat back into the willows, leaving her in peace, not wanting to deny her refuge from the searing heat in the shade of the wetlands.

We'll go now, it's time to go, maybe our last time to really get out and search for my holy grail, the Bird Panel.

But first, Radium.

Golden desert bullsnake,
Enamored with red slickrock,
Whispering as you slide along.
Your love is synchronous,
Unheedingly infinite.
Seeing my shadow, you pause,
Then, boldsnake, continue on.
My existence, my own lost loves,
Insignificant,
In this vast expanse of shadowrock and sand.

chinle

ice climbing. spectacular light, and such an adrenaline rush. but i prefer a good walk. the whole world comes wafting in on the wave of what comes to you, in the woods.

names. names. there we are again. unless one knows the world conjured up in a name, the magic escapes. all you have is the shell, to toss about for effect.

but then some names by their very nature evoke a world. like sunflower. even if you never meet her. whereas molly leaves little objective correlative in mind. if you know her, her name resonates. but if not...

beowulf, eh? maybe you'll read me a bit of old english. i had a linguistic professor who specialized in the pronunciation of chaucer. he wanted me to go on in linguistics. i was tempted. but i loved poetry. i love to hear the cadence of beowulf read in the old way.

funny you mention the sapir-whorf hypothesis, of course sapir's language was a seminal book in my education. yes, sirius. some say that's one of the star tribes that birthed us. it certainly is a powerful heavenly body.

good. the poetry bug's got you. so nice to write on inspiration (instead of demand or deadline) and to have a finished piece without spending years working on it (like my novelist friends).

oh, i like this one even better (though lost love poems are usually tediously tiresome - this one isn't). i love the snake. lawrence taught me that. and the herpatologist that taught me to hold a ten foot bullsnake without fear. and even seeing a 25 foot anaconda in brazil stretched out to full length in the tourist cabana didn't make me afraid, though reverent and respectful.

lots of big words in this poem, and yet the twist of their saying synchronous with the snake's own motion. i love it. i look forward to hearing you read it to me - for its in the reading that i find the most resonance.

but off with me to the temple city. may you travel safe, and the road bring you back, if not for margaritas this week, then one week soon.

thinking of that snake enamored of rock

artful

Dear Chin,

I've missed you. Even though I guess I don't know you anymore. It is so damn hot here, I think I've really gone to hell. Must be about 110...no kidding. Brutal. Whatever became of you? You vanished. Have you become disillusioned with me? What's up?

Chas.

17
Charlie: Radium

Buddy Blue and me and Willy head out, back up Two-Step Hill on the road that leads from Catalpa Town to Green River, then on to Radium. Night swings in, and we turn onto a little dirt road and set up camp near a stand of tall sagebrush. No traffic out here, probably could've camped in the middle of the road, what's left of it, potholes everywhere.

Tired, Buddy and I have a quick Indian dinner of corn, beans, and tortillas, then crawl into my sleeping bag, the little dog sleeping at my feet, as usual, though too hot to be down inside. I toss and turn—now that I'm heading back to Radium, Antonio's words hang in the air, cryptic, immutable.

Someday, if you look clear enough to see, you will learn your real name out there.

Finally I get up and light my lantern, which I rarely use. Must be an eerie sight to the coyotes, a flickering light out in the middle of this empty Utah desert.

Subdued, the excitement of this project has now faded, is now interwoven with hesitancy, maybe even dread. Perhaps more than rock art awaits me out here. Feeling alone, part of me wants to flee, go to family in Colorado. The Bird Panel seems far away, untouchable.

I turn off the lantern and look up at the night sky into the Milky Way—it has a long black gash, and suddenly, I feel again like I could fall into it, lost. I miss Gramps, I miss Charlie, I miss Johnny, and I hold Buddy Blue close against my heart for comfort until he wiggles free. Against my chest, the amethyst feels hard, cold.

Finally, I fall into a rough jagged sleep, images of an Ancient City weaving in and out of specters of distant rose cliffs.

Damn those cliffs to hell, will they always haunt me?

Dawn wakes me and I dawdle about, watching a buzzard circle above me to take a look at Buddy, who's now out and about, sniffing for lizards. I wonder what the little dog would do if he ever caught anything—probably die of shock.

What does a buzzard know of security? What do the collared lizard, the whipsnake, the kangaroo rat know of security? Go ahead, feel secure, the golden eagle will fix that right fast with its sharp talons and keen eye.

Old Willy and Buddy Blue are my only security now. They'll see me through the end of this adventure.

The morning sun drifts its light across distant flats of yellow rabbitbrush and squirrel grass. Nearby is a little hill dotted with blackbrush. Now the lone buzzard is joined by friends, a congenial bunch, light filtering through wingtips, wheeling and circling on a thermal until they're black dots high in the sky.

Fall is nearly here and the buzzards aren't happy, there won't be much going for them out here in the winter, so they'll migrate to greener pastures. Huge patches of sun-dried desert trumpet stand here and there, their tiny spring saffron blossoms dried on stems of long-forgotten Irish green. Strange plant, tall thin wiry stalks with bulges in the middle—the Indians supposedly used the stems for pipes. The bulges hold some kind of moth pupae, so hopefully the moths hatched out before the Indians lit up.

To the east, the Bookcliffs rise like ship's prows, snaking northwards through smoke to where the Battleship juts out, named by pilot Jim Hurst, who flies out of Green River, supplying uranium miners. Charlie and Johnny both know him.

Like Hurst, I fly solo.

To the west are the La Sal Mountains, shimmering white with snow and distance. All around, nothing but desert—Cisco Desert, Green River Desert, Antelope Desert, Stinking Desert, empty desert, a universe of high cold desert. Way in the distance is the mirage-outline of the San Rafael Swell, banked in its fortress by the jagged Reef. Perhaps it holds the secrets of Davidson's lost Bird Panel. Will I ever know those secrets?

I give Buddy a bowl of beans while I munch a Three Musketeers candy bar in Gramps' honor and watch high mackerel clouds hang motionless in the wide sky, mixing with long horizontal tendrils of brown smoke. I wonder if Johnny's OK way over there, fighting the Big Rattle Fire.

Soon, red ants appear from nowhere, hauling off my candy bar crumbs. They must feel like Charlie did when he cored up that rich black pitchblende over in the Stinking Desert.

I wonder about getting this grant—what was I thinking, wandering out in this big empty desert alone for so long?

Little red ant,
Far from home, purposely
I sit here to escape.
And I like the wild onion
on this hillside.
Did the purple flowers
Call to you too?

"Jump in, kiddo." Buddy jumps onto the passenger seat. Willy's finally all loaded up and ready to go, last night's angst faded like the hollow call of an owl.

As the ravens check out our campsite for leftovers, I pull a well-worn card from my jacket pocket, corners bent, a pencil sketch of a juniper tree on the front. Inside, written in pencil, now faded, is a message:

Dear Chinle,
When you are old,
And cannot see,
Put on your specs,
And think of me.
When times get rough, go into the canyons.
They will heal you.
Happy 15th birthday! Gramps

Now we're finally near Radium, crossing the bridge over the Colorado River. I feel a reluctance, a dread. It's been a long time, what if I run into Charlie? I pull over by the road and get out.

Buddy and I slide down the bank to the river, or what's left of it. The drought is now into year six, and its dry heat clutches at everything, searing into every rock fissure, deep into the sand, even into the deepest roots of the willow thickets along a river now a half-dried shadow of itself. Where once it coursed freely and with spirit, the river now slugs along, freewheeling no more, a mere shadow of itself, showing its secrets to everyone, every sandbar and rock that had previously, in its wilder times, snagged unwary floating logs.

I watch a blue heron on the far shore, then skim a few rocks and think back to when I was a kid, riding rafts in this same cool water, touching the branches of old cottonwoods as I passed.

But now, from nowhere, I feel the hand of nostalgia pulling at me like an undertow in the current, dragging me under, into a dark place inhabited by the unresolved, a love that's over but can never be over. I struggle to the surface and begin to go under again. Someone grabs me by the shoulders, is dragging me to shore. I catch a glimpse of coyote-yellow, quickly gone.

I want to run and be free, to run through the sagebrush, dodging and jumping, free from all entanglements—until I jump one last time and am suddenly soaring, soaring like the redtail hawk, spreading my wings and rising up singing, far away from the despair of the past. Free to live in the now and the eternal, not in the dry and lost and repressing graveyards of what might have been with Charlie.

Don't I look really really nice today?

Dammit! How do I know? I can't even see you.

I'm dressed all in yellow fur, with a tawny leather coat underneath. My white teeth contrast nicely.

You're so extremely vain. It's disgusting.

You're jealous.

How could I be jealous of a coyote? Besides, you're not even real, you're just an illusion. One can't be jealous of something that doesn't exist.

I exist. I exist completely, fully, wonderfully, magnificently.

You think you do, but can you prove it?

Suddenly, silence, profound, complete silence, everything turns black. I feel uneasy, the desert reeks of dread, all warmth gone, no buffers left between my soul and eternity. Queasiness.

I'm back.

Color returns, sound returns, warmth, sun.

Did you miss me?

Coyote pauses long enough to read the answer in my eyes, is gone.

I stand a while, watching the clouds capture the sun and slowly release it. I pick up a large dead cottonwood branch and heave it into the water where it splashes and gladly courses downriver, happy for freedom, new adventure, a new future. Maybe the branch and I will meet again down the river, maybe at those ruby cliffs, if I ever take to the water myself. But for now, I must return to Radium. Back in the little jeep, I slowly drive into town.

"I can't believe my eyes! Hey, Chinle!"

Adam Stocks quickly jumps to his feet, tipping the booth table and nearly spilling his coffee.

The Radium Diner is noisy and crowded, the early morning drawing people to the diner's coffee, eggs, and hashbrowns (hot chow for the radioactive, claims the menu).

I walk over to where Adam's still standing. Someone several booths behind him calls out, "Hey, Stocks, got any good scoops?" Adam grins, replies, "Yup, a big writeup about your Wilma Jean dying her hair blonde, George." George guffaws.

Just then a blonde waitress, Wilma Jean, comes by and whacks Adam on the head with a menu. She sees me and makes a fuss, giving me a hug.

"Chinle! Ohmygosh, I can't believe it's you! Where the gotoheck have you been?"

"Whatever happened to Atomic Hair, Wilma?" I ask.

"Oh, I still have it, I got it going good and then bought the diner here. Gosh, it's good to see you, I wondered what happened to you. Stop by the shop, I'll be over there this afternoon and I'll do your hair for free. My gosh, gal!" She slowly shakes her head, adds, "Take your time, be right back."

Adam slips back down into the booth as I slide into the seat across from him. "Chinle, long time no see. Let me buy you breakfast."

"Nice to see you Adam. Sure, I'll have breakfast, but I don't have any scoops for you," I smile. Adam reaches over and untangles my hair from where it's stuck under my shirt collar. Something about my disorderliness drives everyone nuts.

I balance the menu in front of me on the lemon-yellow formica table. "So, Adam, how's life been treating you?"

"Great, just great. How's the rock art project coming? Actually, now that I think of it, maybe I should do that story while you're in town, maybe make some of these idiots quit shooting up the rocks. Let's talk about it later over dinner, OK? You are staying a while, aren't you? Chin?"

Wilma Jean comes to take our order—eggs and toast for Adam, but I talk her into warming up a big bowl of chili for me, along with some cornbread. Adam shakes his head, grinning.

"So, Adam, have you seen Charlie around lately?" I ask, hoping he'll say no. I'm hoping to avoid a chance encounter.

"Yeah, actually, I saw Charlie on my way over here. He was getting gas across the street. You probably missed seeing him by ten minutes. Actually, he's probably around town today, I would guess, 'cause he usually stays a few days when he comes in from the mine. You should look him up."

"Maybe I'll stop by his house on my way through," I say, sipping hot steamy coffee. I touch the amethyst against my neck.

"Look, Chin, he asks about you practically every time I run into him. I think he's like me, worries about you out in the backcountry all by yourself. Never know when you could get lucky and actually get stranded way out there!" Adam grins, his dark hair sticking to his forehead in the heat of the diner.

Breakfast arrives, and we sit in silence, eating, the din around us in full roar. Behind us, a man brags in a high voice about his new Toyota Land Cruiser.

"It's what's called a Big 6 Powerhouse, 135 horsepower engine, take you anywhere, walk right up the cliffs, 67 percent grades, at least according to the salesman up in Price. Traded my Plymouth in on it."

His booth partner muffles something back, then the proud new owner replies, "Oh yeah, you bet! Nine forward and three reverse gear combinations. She's a dandy, Harry, but my wife was sure mad about it when I called her and told her what I'd done, she wanted a car to haul the kids around in. Shoudda seen her face when I drove up and she saw it was a 4-door Land Cruiser station wagon, real pretty blue, with foam rubber seats, lots of luxury room inside."

"You sound like a car salesman, Buck. Maybe you have a new career ahead of you if the mines ever close down." Buck guffaws.

I think about old Willy with his worn seats, cracked windshield, holes in the floor and radiator, bald tires, then I close my eyes and can see some of the places me and Willy have been together. I'd never dream of trading Willy off, just like that. He's worth his weight in gold even if all he did was sit in the yard, worth his weight just for the memories.

Adam studies me, asks, "Are you going to see Charlie, Chin?"

I answer, "No, I'm here to forget Charlie, if you know what I mean. I'm here to see you, check on my mail, then head on out. I'm on my way to Dark Angel."

"Dark Angel? That place has a reputation, Chin, be careful. But Charlie's history, for real? You're not even going to say hi?"

"Adam, remember that talk we had on the top of Coffeepot? No, Charlie's bad news for me. This is a gut check for me, being here. This is the first time I've been back since Charlie left me, one year ago. But now I can't wait to get outta here, I'm heading out as soon as I can, and that feels good to me."

Adam's eyes fall, "Well, gee, I hope we see each other once in a while, Chin. You know I really value our friendship. After all, you're the only blood-sister I've ever had, even though my sister Dee might beg to differ."

I laugh. "Adam, we'll be in touch, I want you to come to my wedding."

His eyes get big. "What? You're getting married?"

"No, but if I do, I want you there. Remember the penny pile on the mountain, you never know what might happen. Or maybe I'll be coming to yours."

"You got somebody in mind?"

"Not really, though Johnny Taylor would be way up on the list. How about you?"

"Oh hell, Chin, in my dreams maybe. Ain't no gals around here worth having, that will have me, anyway. But Johnny's a great guy, he's a real nice fellow, from what I've heard. You guys dating? What about finishing grad school, Chin, if you don't mind my asking. Will Charlie pay for it?"

"I'm done, Adam. This project is nearly over, then I'm finished with school. Besides, I can get more grant money, at least that's what my advisor says, if I need it. But you know what, amigo? I can now tell you I'm a completely different person than when I hung with Charlie, I've changed a lot, and now I'm a free spirit. Freedom is my new love, I dance and sing in its mystery."

"You know, Chin, you should write poetry or something. Whatever you do, don't write for newspapers, 'cause they'll take all that creativity, chew it up, and spit it out."

After finishing breakfast, Adam offers, "Chin, You can go over to my house if you want to shower and regroup."

He catches my arm under his, opens the door, and leads me out into the morning, blue sky overhead, a few wispy clouds drifting lazily.

We lean against Willy and watch the clouds as Adam scratches Buddy's head through the window.

"Chin, there's something I've been wanting to ask you, ever since we met." His dark eyes look serious.

"Ask away."

"Hows come you don't stay home and cook and stuff, like other women?"

I laugh, "Maybe it's 'cause I'm irresponsible. Actually, it's 'cause I have a choice, Adam, and they don't think they do."

He laughs. "You know Chin, there's been lots of characters come through Radium, and a lot of them stayed, but there's never been a gal like you. C'mon, leave your jeep here for a while, let's go over to my house, you can get cleaned up, fix your hair. I need to pick up some stuff I'm working on."

We all three jump in his little white sedan, head for his house down on East Center.

He parks next to a row of dried-up rose bushes. A magpie, dressed for dinner in a black and white tuxedo, sits on the top wire of the fence by Adam's yard, its large beak open, holding a yellow chunk of something that looks like a piece of carnotite.

Intricate patterns of steam rise and dissipate into the warm air as I try to comprehend the swirling phase change of water into nothingness. It's an absorbing pastime, sitting by Adam's little stove, watching the water boil from the teapot, listening to a recording of classical guitar on Adam's stereo called "Franklin Morrison's Desert Serenades." Buddy snores at my feet.

Adam's gone to his office, telling me I'm welcome to stay as long as I want, but I really just want to get back over to the diner and rescue Willy, who's probably wondering where I've gone, missing me, worrying. As soon as I have a cup of tea and get cleaned up a bit, I'll go get him.

Besides, Buddy Blue is bored, and I want to walk around, revisit Radium, see if I have any mail, and head on over to Dark Angel. Like Colt, being indoors is making me claustrophobic.

Thoughts twist round and round like the spirals of rising steam until I finally turn the burner off and pour a cup of hot black Lipton's tea.

I'll write Adam a note, if only I can find something to write it on, and how in the H-E-double-hockeysticks can a newspaper publisher not have any paper anywhere? Looking in the tiny kitchen, I notice notes and phone numbers scrawled directly onto the wall above the table, so I add my own.

Adam,

Thanks. See you at Joe and Coralee's wedding, come out if you get a chance. I'll be at Stock Tank (see map).

XXXOOO, Chinle

I draw a map next to my note on the wall with a dot marked Stock Tank, next to a couple of tiny cliffs and arches, a miniature steer that looks like a dog with horns, some ravens, and a rough sketch of a jeep with the word DESRAT on the back.

Soon, Buddy and I are glad to be outside again, and I throw a loaf of moldy bread from Adam's refrigerator to the magpie, still sitting on the fence, dreaming of a land of milk and honey, never suspecting those dreams would have immediate substance.

Buddy and I walk down Center Street, first by a house painted deep purple with pale-blue trim and a "Welcome, Stranger and Friend Alike" sign above the door, then by an old tar-paper shack with a woven-wire stock fence that holds a few white and yellow chickens (of great interest to Buddy). Across the street is a red-brick house with a trimmed hedge next to a tiny silver trailer with a fat short chimney.

Along the street, globe willows are starting to gold up with the first hints of autumn. Catalpa trees have long ago lost their white chaotic bloom, their huge broad leaves now looking like dinosaur food. The town has so many catalpas that it sits under a snowy canopy each spring. Radium should've been called Catalpa Town, but that wouldn't work, 'cause then there'd be two of them. I wouldn't know where to avoid Charlie and where to look for Johnny.

The street is wide in true Mormon fashion, wide enough to turn a team and wagon around. Radium was originally settled by Mormons, and their influence is evident in the wide streets and profusion of crabapple, apple, peach, pear, cherry, and apricot trees which grace the town in spring with delicate blooms accompanied by sweet perfumes. And don't forget the mulberry trees, planted when Brigham Young had a wild hair that the Saints would get rich in silk and use mulberry leaves to feed silkworms. What a guy, always scheming and running everyone else around, just like somebody else I know.

It seems like time has come down hard here, its presence hanging all over the place, leaving a tangle of lives and hopes and dreams in dust and diary entries. Some of us rail against time and change and all it does to us, but those who accept it with grace seem to get by a little easier. It seems to be a bit kinder to those who refuse the poisoned drink of nostalgia.

As we walk around Radium, I know that someday I'll return and it will all look different, strange, distant and unfamiliar. Maybe by then I'll wonder what all the fuss was about Charlie.

Now we're on Main Street, and we walk by the Atomic Motel and Uranium Café, their combined neon sign flashing the outline of an atomic mushroom cloud. Next is the Moki Trading Post, across the street from the Arctic Circle drive-in with a big sign on the front advertising"Geiger and Scintillators Counters and Drill Hole Probes For Sale."The town seems relatively quiet, unlike the last time I was here when the U-boom was in full swing.

We're soon at the diner and reunited with Willy, and I fondly slap his hood. A note is stuck under the windshield wiper, scrawled on a brown paper sack with what must have been a dull pencil.

> *Chin - OK where the H R U? Come by the house,*
> *more $$ 4 U 4 new jeep, get rid of this pile of crap.*
> *Smitty's for dinner. Chas.*

I shake my head, climb into old Willy and head for the post office. The gray-haired postmistress goes into the back for a minute, then hands me some letters, Chinle Miller, General Delivery. I sit in old Willy and read.

Dear Chinle,

Including a newspaper article. Strange character came through here today and tried to pry outta me what I knew about dinosaur bones. Said he was a uranium miner but he didn't know the first thing about it. Shady. Made me glad I have a rifle. I know he's heard about Professor Sheets and the big wing. A find like that's worth big money on the black market. The Weeners pretty much ran him off. They're little but fearless. I'm big but scared. Will write again later when I have more time.

Jim

Dear Chinle,

It's been a long time, hasn't it? Jim says you guys write, and enclosed is a letter and some newspaper articles for you from him. He's in the Grand Junction hospital and asked me to be sure you know. My trailer burned down and he barely escaped, he has some smoke inhalation and is a little disoriented but will be OK. His dogs are fine, they're what saved him, I'll let him tell you about it later. Come up and visit and we'll talk about the good old days.

Roger Bone

Grand Valley Times

Thompson's Springs uranium prospector James Bone is in Grand Junction St. Mary's Hospital after his brother Roger Bone's camp trailer burned last night. Bone was in the trailer at the time, but managed to escape with minor burns and some smoke inhalation after his three Dachshunds woke him. Smoke from the fire was visible from town, which resulted in Bone receiving help from local citizens. He's expected to have a quick recovery, and the dogs survived with no harm. Cause of the fire is unknown, and the trailer was a total loss. The fire caught nearby shrubs and is still burning out of control in Thompson Canyon. Several firefighting teams are on location.

Deseret News

Paleontologist Harvey Sheets of the Denver Museum has announced a major discovery in the world of dinosaur fossils. Sheets, along with a team of dinosaur experts and archaeologists from the University of Colorado, has been conducting field research in eastern Utah. The team has found the first real evidence that the flying dinosaur bird, the Pterodactyl, was indeed extant in the Western Hemisphere.

"The few Pterodactyl fossils found have all been in Asia, Mongolia specifically," says Sheets. "Our team found a complete Pterodactyl wing, and even some of the skin has been fossilized. This is a find of major significance."

The location of the fossils is being kept secret and has been dubbed the "Roger Bone Dino Quarry" after the brother of the man who discovered the wing. The team expects to begin digging at the quarry early next spring.

Canyon Country Gazette
Two Navajo men were arrested in Green River for attempted theft of a pickup from Chief's Gas Station. The two men are from Shiprock, New Mexico, and are being detained at the local jail until they can be taken back to Shiprock for trial. These same two men were arrested last year for drunkenness in Radium and were released by the Navajo Court. According to Officer Murphy, they admitted to burning Roger Bone's camp trailer. They claim they were hired by a man who deals illegally in dinosaur bones. Murphy says he has arrested the suspect, who is in custody and being interrogated.

Chinle,

I don't know where the hell you are. It's been a hell of a month. Listen, I need to talk to you.

I really want to move, leave this hellhole. I'm experiencing some weird damn paradigm shift or something. This is big. Ever since my dream where I saw the big rock squirrel named Eddie. Unbelievable dream.

OK. Contact me now.

Chas.

I stick the letters in my old Hercules Powder box in the back of old Willy and head on out to the north end of Radium, to where Charlie's mansion stands on the hill. He once told me that he built it up there so he could stand on his deck and piss on the town.

I get out of Willy at the base of the steep hill and look up at the house far above, at the impossibly perpendicular driveway, at the long pipe that connects with Radium's water system, a system that Charlie paid for. Generous of him, but, just like everything, in his own interest.

Studying the long low-slung house, red brick against maroon rock, big plate-glass windows, I can almost see the reflection of the indoor swimming pool where Charlie holds his infamous parties. Now I see a dark figure in the living room window, it pauses.

And suddenly it's night, one year ago, and I'm leaving soon, back to college. The memory grabs me, won't let go, and I'm standing on the deck far above, looking down to where Willy waits.

Charlie's close to me, leaning against the deck railing. The lights of town lie below us—Charlie's front yard is the twinkling lights of a town. He's so close, I feel his familiar warmth, a comfort born of hours together on rocks, nights together by the glow of pinion fire, dreams together in synchrony, like two brilliantly interlaced comets.

"Charlie, are you happy?"

"No, I hate all this crap. You know it's not really me."

"Then why are you doing this?"

"It's an act. I have to be a big deal now that I support half of Radium. People are funny that way. They create you in an image, you have to live it or they're disappointed."

"Charlie, why not just be yourself? If they knew you, they couldn't help but respect and like you. Besides, what do you care?"

I can make out constellations in the lights of town. Casseopia. Taurus. The Pleiades...the Pleiades opened beneath my feet...lights twinkle in sere desert air.

"What do you know about success? You don't understand."

"Charlie, I know you, I understand you, I love you, the real you, not this uranium king enthroned on this high hill."

I move close to him, wrap my arm in his. I feel a coldness, like Black Rocks on the Colorado River in winter, white ice with glazed black obsidian core. He withdraws. A sudden fear envelops me, a fear of the unknown, an old fear of falling through ice into black water. I turn and look into the lights below. Purple, red, gold, garnet rose neon—garnet rose cliffs—distant rose cliffs, downriver. Charlie continues.

"Damn it! You don't know me at all. All you ever did was hang around and keep me from being successful sooner than I was. If I'd stayed with you, I'd still be running that loser of a rock shop. You were just an encumbrance to me. I never loved you. It was just an illusion, a way to fill up the empty spaces."

I've tripped and am slowly tumbling down a slickrock syncline toward a quicksand abyss. I feel a sharp stab in my heart, as I fall into rock with knife edge, then continue, slowly downward.

"Charlie, I encouraged you to go prospecting, even though I missed you. What about all the fun we had? And what about all the times I helped you, especially when you were down? How can you say you never loved me? You loved me a lot, Charlie, how can you deny something that was so good? Charlie, what's going on? Why are you saying these things?"

"Look, Gal, it's just cold reality. You have to understand it was just a romantic illusion. It was fun, although actually it got pretty boring. What I thought was love was just infatuation. I was infatuated with you, but that's over and I have to get on, without encumbrances. But I don't love you."

Fear turns into terror, I hang on the edge of a high cliff.

"Charlie, how could you be infatuated for several years? Infatuations die quickly. We were in love, not infatuation. You asked me to marry you. How can you destroy something so special? Some people yearn all their lives for what we have. How can you just throw something so special away? How can you deny what's so real? Is there another woman?"

"No. There's no one else. But I never loved you. I liked you, but I never loved you. But don't worry, I promise to pay for the rest of your college, just send me the bills."

He's gone. I stand alone. I want to float away, down into the warmth of the lights, like a simple unfeeling moth. I am betrayed. Undeserved. My only wrong was to love Charlie. I'm falling, falling into oblivion, rose cliffs are gone. I must escape. I feel my way down steep stairs. Somehow, I'm in Willy, I drive endlessly into night, into the cold open arms of the desert.

There is no escape, pain follows me, embraces me, engulfs me, becomes me. I will melt into the desert, become a hoodoo, a dead dried blackbrush. No one will know what became of me. I walk into the night, without direction, without strength. I walk until I no longer know who I am. I am cold, I shiver and fall onto a bed of slickrock. I dream of rocks. Hard Kayenta sedimentation streaked with blood-red siltstone. Green mudstone laced with vanadium and uranium. Always the uranium.

I am the desert now. Desolation will be my companion forever.

Coyote, where are you?

I'm over here.

Coyote, I hurt.

What happened? Did you step in a trap?

I don't know, maybe it was a kind of trap.

What part hurts?

My soul.

Oh. That's a very bad hurt. If your leg were caught in a trap, you could just gnaw it off, but your soul, that's more difficult.

Coyote, help me. I want to die.

No, it's not time yet, Little Cactus. Not yet.

Coyote, it hurts too much. I can't bear it anymore. I want to die.

This pain you have, it's very hot, isn't it?

Yes, it burns through my soul.

That's the worst kind there is. It will kill you if you let it.

I want it to kill me. I want to die.

No, no, not yet. Your time will come, then you may not want it quite so badly. You must put this fire out soon, before it burns too deep. This is the worst kind...it's the kind that kills poets and lovers. It's Charlie, isn't it? You must put this fire out.

I can't, I don't know how. I've lost my bearings. I don't know who I am, where I am.

This fire must be embraced. You must suffocate it. You must embrace this pain fully, completely, only then will it go away.

Embrace it? How?

Little Cactus, hold it to you. Let it sear through your heart until you think you will burn away. Let it consume you, make it burn so hot that it cannot sustain itself. Just when you feel it most, it will suddenly go out, and you will have peace. But you will never be the same. Your soul will be scarred, and it will never forget. Feel this pain fully, for your soul will guard itself carefully and you may never feel life this intensely again.

Frightened Cottontail, huddled beneath large rock, hot wind precedes wall of wildfire. Fur explodes, then silence, slow rain hisses the smoldering embers to silence, all is still.

Quietly, sadly, the holy man walks through ash, displaced, his land stolen. His mullein torch, flame once raised in defiance, now blackened, lowered in sacred mourning. Scorched rabbit fur floats on still-warm wind. He knows this harsh land demands a deep love, deeper than white man can feel. Now he has given his gift, peace, to this land he loves. Charred, no one will want it now, no one will pull living pinion from warm earth with cold chains.

Quietly, he weeps, now he too will die. But suddenly, Cottontail, fur singed, jumps from beneath rock, bounds away. Is life truly eternal? The holy man stands, arms outstretched in homage. The land has accepted his gift. In return, his people, the Utes, will survive.

I cannot cry any more. I have found Coyote Yellowjacket's peace, but the price was too high.

Now I'm back in the present, painful memory fades, and a figure stands in the window above. I know it's Charlie. I salute him, carefully take off the amethyst necklace. I'll leave it in his mailbox. It burns in my hand, just like Charlie once burned in my heart.

I pause, remember Johnny's words.

Take it, think of how the earth burned to create it.
It belongs to you, not Charlie.

I put it back on. I'll keep it, it's part of me now, all that's left of Charlie for me. I turn and get into Willy. I leave Radium, Charlie, my past. Forever.

As we top the hill above town, sun begins to set in maroons and golds, touches the horizon to the west, and I now see a huge pillar of light, a huge golden column standing directly over where Catalpa Town must lie, far in the distance, over river and canyons and domes and fins and cougars and bullsnakes and packrats and doghole mines and even crazy coyotes.

I think of the Children of Israel, and I'm tempted to head towards that pillar, but then I remember those rose sandstone cliffs, constant, pure, unclimbable, those cliffs that call my name without speaking.

Following someone else's dreams doesn't work, I found that out with Charlie. Some gifts really aren't gifts. Letting someone else control your life only defers the day of reckoning, for no one but you can control your destiny.

Now the desert becomes familiar again, warm, home. We roll onward, down that lost highway, me and Buddy Blue and Willy, down the path of the heart.

18
Shadowpeople: Dark Angel

I park Willy near the edge of Dark Angel Canyon. I'll camp here tonight, where I can look up at night's depth or down at canyon's depth, whichever suits me best. An immense western sun hangs low above distant blue mesas, muted with a diffuse light filled with smoke. It won't be long till dark. I turn and look into the shrouded depths below.

Come into the canyons and be healed.

Gramps always said the canyons were places of healing, of happiness, of solace. As I look down, I see a ribbon of creek edged with yellow and green. The unbroken smooth canyon walls have only one break in them, directly below where I'm at, a long sandy ramp.

About a half-mile across the canyon is a curve in the cliffs where dark purple shadows hold their own, even in sunlight. Alcoves. Rock art, maybe.

Without hesitation, I slide down the long dune, sinking, orange sand up to my boot-tops as I glissade downward, Buddy close at my heels. It will be slow and hard coming back up.

Quickly down, now by the little creek, we drink sweet water, cold, pure. Now thirst is gone, but pain seeps in and fills where the thirst was. Pushing through whippy willows turning gold, I find a place where the creek is wide and shallow, where blue-white water ripples around stones, allowing me to cross.

Bushwhacking up the other bank, coming out of the willows onto a low ridge with easy passage, I continue towards the alcoves.

Come into the canyons and be healed.

Now I stand at the edge of a wide bench covered with blackbrush and prickly pear, thirty feet or so above the little perennial stream. The waterway is a tangled morass of boxelder and Fremont cottonwoods, underbrushed with willow, sumac, and wild rose, the creek reflecting hints of sunset oranges and reds from edge of sky. The western side of the canyon is already hidden, but the huge eastern walls glow soft pink, following river in gentle contour, curving, then merging with the other side in dark-shaded distance.

Above me, where the bench touches the bottom of smooth cliff, a large alcove leads into darkness, with another long curved alcove high above this one, unreachable, untouchable. A short distance to the left, a third alcove, more of a cave, forms a deeply notched shadow in the shape of an upside-down V.

I pause, go no nearer. Perhaps they are in there, the old ones, waiting, waiting like they have for thousands of years. But waiting for what, for who? Or are they just simply waiting, that thing they do best?

Come into the canyons and be healed.

The thought comes again, not a voice, but a memory of voice, Gramps' voice, long ago. I spread my arms out, turn towards the shadowy alcoves.

"I've come for healing."

Silence. Nothing.

I stand, waiting, the pain within as dark as any shadow. I'm drawn nearer, right to the alcove's black edge, and now the darkness in the alcove becomes faintly lucid. I stand, trying to see into the emptiness. Buddy retreats back into light, where he waits, quiet, licking his wet paws.

Now I can no longer discern what's shadow in reality or shadow in memory, and I think perhaps I see figures in the darkness, barely there, maybe not there at all. My eyes cloud again—Gramps, my grandmother, my dad, all dead, mere shadows, their bodies once wracked by disease—I see pain in their eyes, pain that lasted far too long before death took them, before death healed them in its own inexplicable mysterious way.

I implore, "I'm here, finally." Pain rises within, burns like cold on hot. I loved Charlie, I loved him with all my heart, unconditionally, like I loved these people, now gone.

And now, quietly, darkness seems to part, and behind these shadow figures I see, perhaps imagine, my ancestors, a long shadowy line stretching far into the depths of the alcove, far, far into the depths of the past.

Slowly, the line fades and is gone, and instead I now see the living, those who share this earth—hunted animals, angry men, crying women, a planet filled with pain, a planet with a groaning that permeates the entire vast universe.

I crumple to my knees, "Please, I need healing, we all need healing."

Silence. Nothing.

I weep, head in hands, fingers against cheekbones.

Come into the canyons and be healed.

So many people loved this land—they left, it stayed. I hear a faint drumming, maybe real, maybe imaginary, perhaps from the past, perhaps not.

Now, something in the corner of my eye makes me look up, up, up, into the bowl of a sky that's beginning to twinkle with tiny stars, with distant galaxies embracing planets that perhaps hold similar mystery canyons.

Then I see what caught my eye—a glint of last sunlight catches wing as a golden eagle circles above, swoops downward, tilts wings burnished with sunray breaking through the last cloud low on the horizon.

But higher, a white harrier with black points, that most beautiful of hawks, circles above the golden eagle, occasionally spiraling, plunging headlong into the bigger bird. The eagle could easily kill the hawk. I puzzle why it doesn't, wonder where the smaller bird gets its courage.

I stand, entranced. Now, eagle breaks away, gone, and the harrier is a mere thirty feet above. I can see its full snow-white plumage, feathers, talons, its eyes piercing through me, scanning the canyon floor, perhaps one last look for dinner before retiring for the night.

I smile, purse my lips and make the sound of the redtail hawk, a long piercing down-whistle. The harrier pauses, answers with a sharp short whistle, then, quickly gaining altitude, disappears over canyon rim. Elated, I feel the aerial freedom of wind-glistened feathers. Shadows part, and now I feel joy to be one of the living.

It's nearly dark now, and a crescent moon peeks over the western rim, trying to grasp the tiny bright sphere of Venus with its claws, unable to tighten its pincers. Shadows melt into shapes of cougar, motionless, and the primal feeling of night welling deep within immense canyon walls takes hold.

Time to move on. A sunset-wind drifts down canyon, taking me with it, quickly now, nimbly across shadowy hints of stones in the creek, up the soft sandy dune that's drifted down from rim, forming an upward path into another world—a world unknown to chasm dwellers such as tiny canyon frog and water strider—a world of vista and distance, my world.

Climbing in the near dark, now finally on top, breathing hard, I make out a glint in the moonlight as I stumble, Buddy at my heels. It's old Willy, good old Willy.

Catching my breath, I lean against the hood and feel safe and secure again, as safe and secure as I've ever felt in any warm cozy house. The warmth of Willy's hood holds contentment.

I laugh softly, suddenly happy.

Come into the canyons and be healed.

Gramps was right.

Is it because I walk in beauty or because I made it out in the nick of time—or is it for no reason at all, this sudden happiness?

Once again,
Stars touch earth,
Tracing night clouds with their brief iridescence.
High above the fading cliffs,
Harrier hawk, circling,
Wings tipped with alpenglow,
Musing on impermanence.

Now wind blows, listen to the wind...

Chinle. Chinleee.

Who's out there?

It's me, Yellowjacket.

Wind stops, silence.

Chinleee. Got a minute?

Only God knows, Coyote.

You're so dramatic, Little Chamisa. I need to tell you something important.

I don't believe anything you tell me, Yellowjacket, but go ahead.

Scientists aren't supposed to see illusions, Little Chamisa. As far as I last heard, archaeologists are still considered scientists, you know.

I don't necessarily believe them, Yellowjacket.

Who, scientists or illusions? Chinle, what are you going to do when your luck runs out?

What luck?

The luck that gets you up the canyon wall in the dark. The luck that always lands you on your feet.

What's the problem?

You need a home.

My home's out here, Yellowjacket, just like you. Do you need a home? Would you trade all this for a cage?

What will you do when you're old, Little Chamisa?

I'll die, Mr. Yellowjacket, just like everyone else does. But I'll die in the arms of my own true love, the desert.

Chinle, Chinle, Little Chamisa, what are we going to do with you...

Morning, I wake to the feel of depth near me, the canyon, even before I turn over in my sleeping bag and see the wall below.

I stretch, get up, and do my usual rituals of coffee sipping and raven watching, feeding Buddy, musing.

Now I slip out of my longjohns and get dressed, mindful of what could be a long day in the canyon, a day of hot sun and warm shadows. I carefully get my pack ready—sandwiches, apple, Three Musketeers, dog biscuits, camera, notepad, flashlight, matches, and a full canteen with tin cup for Buddy Blue. Even though we'll be near potable water, I may want to spend some time on higher benches or up in the cliffs.

Finally, I tie my jacket to my pack—who knows what the weather will bring, and the nights are cool now. Ready to go, I put a note under Willy's wiper blade:

9-18-61 C.M. up canyon

The note's a first for me, I never leave notes, but maybe it's just a heightened awareness of my aloneness out here, or maybe it's the ominous dark smoke cloud to the east, the Books still burning, Johnny way over there. Maybe I'm hoping somebody will come and save me from any spooks I meet down in there, down in a canyon called Dark Angel. But then, if I'm so alone, what good is a note?

I could spend all morning in this kind of circular thinking, but now I'm ready, and I walk to the edge and look down. I hesitate, turn back and add my sleeping bag to my gear, tying it to the bottom of my pack, then add more ubiquitous coffee, a pan, and extra food. Never know when I might decide to spend the night, and I prefer the extra weight to having to walk back out, then back in again. I pause, add my climbing rope, wrapping it around the now-bulging pack. I stick the Chief's blanket under the seat, safe. Someday I'll find out more about Nonabah Denetsosie, Antonio's wife's great-grandmother, its maker.

Below me is the blowsand ramp I ran down last night, and I can still see my tracks gouged into the red sand, Buddy's lighter ones dancing next to mine, like a coyote's. The canyon looks different in morning light, instead of the pinks and reds and deep shadows of evening, the walls are now a salmon-rust color, and everything seems washed out, melted together.

I can now barely make out the alcoves down canyon that looked so intriguing last night, and the walls of the canyon have lost their contours. The little creek looks like a ribbon of mirror, and the greens of the trees and shrubs are now less pronounced in the stark direct light.

Buddy and I are soon down the ramp, sliding our way to the edge of the stream, to the natural stepping-stone bridge. The creek's much lower than last night—most streams are higher in the evenings, sometimes even peaking in the midnight hours, a gauge of the distant snowbanks that feed them. But with this drought, there's not much snow left up in the high country.

I pick up a large willow branch, a perfect walking stick, use it to balance across the rocks, then leave it near the bank for the return crossing. Buddy emerges from the stream and shakes.

Down on my knees, I cup my hands and drink as much as I can hold, an insurance against dehydration that all desert creatures practice as often as possible. My knees damp from the cool grasses by the stream, I now bushwhack my way up and away from the water and onto the long bench and alcoves I visited last night.

I remember what Coyote Yellowjacket said about scientists and illusion. Perhaps coyotes are the greater truth, a truth few recognize.

Careful to stay on rocks and not crush the lichened crusty soil, I stop and admire a cluster of bright-red Indian paintbrush, aptly named, each stalk looking like an artist's brush still tipped with fresh paint. Paintbrush, so pure and lovely, yet parasitic and needing a host plant to cling its roots to—just like some people, I muse. Perhaps we all need to cling to each other to survive.

I look up at a sky so blue it reminds me of Coralee, of our camping trip, and I wonder how she and Joe are doing. Their wedding will be soon. As my eyes rest on canyon rim, the blue becomes darker, more cobalt. Canyon rim is pale where it meets sky, an optical illusion where the eye can't hold two primary colors at once, red and blue, so must choose one.

I think of last night, of how hard I pushed Willy to get to this canyon before dark, bouncing and flying over rocks, risking oil pan and tires, then of my dash down the long sandy ramp into the lengthening shadows in canyon depths, no flashlight, no jacket, and finally standing before the alcoves in the near dark, half-afraid and yet fearless.

And now I stand again in this canyon, Dark Angel, one of the most spectacular and mysterious places on earth, and I think of how this morning, for the first time since that night on the hill above Radium, that night with Charlie a year ago, this morning was the first time I awoke with the searing pain gone.

I turn in a circle, surrounded by canyon walls, covered with cobalt sky, the singing creek nearby, and I realize that this is the Beautyway, all that really matters.

Forever climbing,
I find the place where the waters begin.
Heavy boots, following graceful mule deer,
Along rim, in and out, scented juniper.
At last! Spring, winter melts to river below,
Poignantly.
The water here is sweet and clear.
Your loss flows deep, but,
Our time is not yet.
Coyote scat, black spider on white snow,
This is all that matters.
Magpie echo in tall red cliffs,
This is all that matters.
The water here flows clear and deep.

A path works its way into a thicket of sumac, called lemonade bush for its lemony tasting berries. Now it winds through willows, some kind of animal trail. I can see the high cliffs of canyon above, contoured in smooth ripples, concave, a deep pink laced with black manganese streaks like spilled paint. We're spotted by a Hopi ground squirrel, cousin to the chipmunk, who warns everyone with a rapid kik-kik-kik-kik-kik that falls like the notes of a scale, the mammal equivalent to the canyon wren.

The mouth of the canyon closes, cliffs nearly touching, but the trail goes on. We turn into a small side canyon, a box canyon. Why a trail here, into nowhere? Animals don't go nowhere, they seek food and water. Maybe I'm entering a cougar's stronghold, but no, the path is too well-worn for light-treading cougar paws.

Path soon merges with sandy wash, winding under a pinion tree so large I at first think it's a Douglas fir. Well-watered, happy, it exudes a presence that makes me stop. I touch the thick deeply creased trunk of the tree where it sweeps over the wash, branches holding eons of spring rains. I bow to the tree, then move on, sensing a bemusement, not sure if it's from me or the tree or both.

Ducking, Buddy and I wend our way into the depths of this short canyon, now nearly boxed in by towering smooth sandstone walls.

High above on my left is a huge cave, deep enough that I can't see the back wall from my upward viewpoint. Like a wild animal, I begin to feel uneasy, trapped, no escape, but I continue up the narrow wash, now pushing my way through thick stands of green desert holly, in spring blooming with millions of tiny delicate clusters of yellow flowers, but now covered with red berries.

The end of the canyon looms overhead, a huge grooved fluted vertical wash carved into it, downward, ending in a pourover fifty feet above the canyon floor. This little canyon must drain a lot of slickrock above. No place to be in a gullythumper.

The canyon speaks of water, lush growth everywhere, and now I can smell it. I know I must be near the end of the canyon, beating my way through the dark brush, still following the animal trail.

Suddenly, instinct says stop. The canyon walls are tight now, closed in, blocking the sunlight, and the shadows and thick vegetation make it difficult to see the ground. As I stop, I startle, stumble, catch myself, for immediately at my feet the wash disappears into a deep pool, so deep the bottom is black, a pool that speaks of lake monsters in its depths, dark and deep, carved by millions of years of flashflood waters scouring so hard and with such force that they hit the pool's bottom and push the water upward and out.

I stand, quiet, Buddy Blue at my heels. It's a place of holiness, this grotto, the holiness of water in the desert, the holiness of life, the holiness of survival in the torrid heat. Water, holy water.

And it's a place of fear, water so deep, so ancient, so primal, a place where one could easily lose their life, a place of cougar hideouts, of ambush, instant death. Like life itself, it holds the mysteries of life-giving and life-taking, the mysteries of time long ago, of time now, and of time future.

I stand entranced, spellbound by the dark green pool just inches from my feet, teeming with happy fairy shrimp. Dizzy, I hold onto the branches of a nearby pinion, steadying myself from the depths, from the call of ancient voices.

Finally, I turn and slowly walk back down the wash, imagining behind me heavy waters falling, tumbling down through the notched fluted canyon wall, over the pourover, crashing into the pool, now crashing through bushes and trees at my heels like an angry dire-wolf. The tree next to me speaks of the reality of the image, detritus tangled in branches a good 20 feet above my head.

It's easy, when you're alone in these canyons, for survival instinct to clutch like a catch in your side, making you want to leave, afraid to turn and see who or what is following. Never run if you think a cougar sees you, it kicks in their instinct to attack. Run like hell if it's a flashflood, it attacks regardless.

I hurry on, ducking beneath branches, through thick holly and scrub oak, until I'm back out in the main canyon, where sunrays perfectly light the far wall in shades of salmon pink, in shades of life and radiance. The canyon's shadows, the depths of the pool, haunt me forever, weave in and out of troubled dreams, capture me when I'm least likely to think of them.

If I ever go back, I want Johnny with me, maybe the two of us can stave off the feeling of darkness, fear, foreboding, oppression. It's probably the closest thing the desert has to an ancient cathedral, oppressive in the weight of time, the kind of place where people are buried in the walls, like the Magnusson Cathedral in Orkney, or England's Abbey. But, unlike this desert cathedral, those places reek of human transgression and fear of death. Here, death comes the natural way, not from the hands of some human oppressor. Perhaps Yeats was right, death is but a human invention.

Now up canyon, I find a cheerful place to camp, a little meadow of grasses with boxelder trees for shade, next to the creek, not far from a large shallow alcove painted and etched with rock art, nestled in a big stand of desert holly. Our camp will be watched over by mountain sheep, deer, spirals and circles, red-ochre snakes, strange warriors with shields, and ghost-like figures with antennae. Tomorrow I'll study them—tonight they can study us.

Near camp is a fire-ring, an ancient circle of stones, nearly buried. Next to it, partially covered with sand, is a beautiful Anasazi black-on-white mug with delicate birds circling the rim. I finger it gently, place it on a nearby rock shelf where it won't get broken, near a honeycomb of eroded holes, a rat hotel. They can marvel at its beauty while they munch on pinion nuts, the cup a centerpiece for their table.

I take out my flute while dinner, corn and beans, warms on my little stove and play an old Scottish folktune from my childhood. Words come to memory, sweet and gentle.

Ah, the summertime is comin',
And the leaves are sweetly turnin',
And the wild mountain thyme,
Blooms across the purple heather,
Will you go, Laddie, go?

I know somehow my journey is near its end. I think back on all the places I've searched, my explorations for petroglyphs and pictographs, always seeking more than the obvious, more than the hidden. Ever since I was a kid, when the desert varnish glistened with full moon, the rock art has drawn me, the mysterious canyons.

Sometimes I can almost see the figures come alive—deer shaking their huge racks, fearlessly stomping their front feet at hunters' eternally drawn bows, bighorn sheep bowing their heads and turning to run, and the always-present spirals spinning until I get dizzy. I always joked with Gramps that I could read their secret meanings.

"What if it's a prophecy?" he asked, "What if the day comes when you truly can?" I always smiled at the audacity of the thought.

If my true love will not go,
I will surely find another,
To pull wild mountain thyme,
All across the purple heather,
Will you go, Laddie, go?

Buddy lays at the foot of my sleeping bag, and finally I fall asleep, imagining voices whispering through serrated holly leaves in ancient languages, Na-Dené and Uto-Aztecan, languages woven of words I can't understand, swirling through the night like wild horses swimming deep velvety rivers.

Now it's morning, and four vermilion ghost figures stand above me, empty circle-eyes glowing in the dim light of early dawn, sun shining directly on the rock art. Above them, higher on the cliff face, floats another apparition, cloaked in orange, looking straight through me. They seem to be expecting something.

I answer their stares, "Good morning, sha bik'e'eshchi."

No answer.

Full sun hesitates to enter the dark canyon, but canyon finally coaxes it to come visit, just for the day. Dark shadows turn into juniper trees, and four-wing saltbush gently changes from charcoal to silver-yellow.

Sunlight crosses the eastern canyon rim and the shadows evaporate like mist. A sleepy black vulture circles to see if I'm still alive, then continues on, disappointed. Though all other birds flock, vultures often pack together, like wolves, and I wonder if this one is part of the pack I saw earlier.

I give Buddy Blue his breakfast of Roly Poly dog biscuits and start a pan of cowboy coffee—black water, as the Zuni call it. My little campstove sparks happily, glad to be awake. Too much coffee lately, I need to start drinking Mormon tea, Brigham tea, one of the few drinks sanctioned by the Mormon leader. It's everywhere out here, and it's free—the only problem is, it tastes like I would imagine dirty socks would taste.

The pictograph figures are as tall as I am, perhaps taller. They're not far away, painted onto the canyon wall, their feet buried in the same soft detritus I've been sleeping on, canyon duff and dried holly leaves.

Barrier style, they're painted with red ochre and white gypsum, maybe as long as 5,000 years ago, maybe at the end of the Archaic period, a time about which we know little. One of the many great mysteries of this wild country.

I wonder what it's like to be anchored, to stay in one place. Maybe these fellows would prefer to leave, or maybe they like this sheltered spot. One ghost has a large bullet hole above his left eye, exposing the tawny rock underneath, his right eye a white circle set in stone, reminding me of an English bulldog.

Coffee now ready, I dump in some powdered milk and sit on my sleeping bag, slowly sipping from the dented tin cup, thinking of the

Navajo woman Nonabah, who wove the blanket Charlie gave me. I wonder who she was, if she knew anything about these tall ghost-like Barrier figures. I can almost see her collecting plants for the blanket's dye. Closing my eyes, I sit for a moment, and I can see bands of color—white, red, and a rare indigo blue. I imagine I smell wet wool.

The rabbitbrush, the g'iiltsoih, had been especially good this year, thought Nonabah, pulling the saffron-colored flower heads from the stems and stuffing them into the gunny sack tied to her silver concha belt. The early and constant spring rains had resulted in autumn blooms like no one had seen for at least ten years or more. She also broke off small twigs from the bushes, stuffing them in with the flowers, careful to go from bush to bush to minimize any damage.

The deer, the birds, they all ate from the rabbitbrush in the winter, and she softly thanked them for sharing with her, speaking gently in her Navajo tongue. She would soon boil the flowers and twigs in her big black iron pot back at the hogan, add some alum for a binder, and then add the yarn she'd so carefully carded. The light yellow color would be perfect for the trade blanket she would soon begin for a Ute chief, a man of stature, who would wrap it around his waist and then over one shoulder. The last one she made had no yellow, only red, white, and blue, but it was special, made for her daughter's future husband, whoever he might be, but surely a chieftan. Nona began to sing.

Sha Bik'e'eshchi.
High above the stars are singing,
Singing, shining bright.
Down here below the sun is singing,
Singing, shining bright.
All the desert rocks are singing,
Singing, burning bright.
Sha Bik'e'eshchi.
We dwell in the village of desert rock,
We sleep surrounded by desert rock,
Again now we dream of desert rock.
And when, in our sleep,

We speak in the old tongue,
The word for rock,
Rock awakens and sighs,
Feeling our warmth next to its cold,
Happy to hear its name spoken,
In the old way.
Sha Bik'e'eshchi,
The sun is written upon it.

Nona. Indigenous people are like indigenous plants—they live best where they've originally grown and adapted. We were all indigenous at one time, but like the tamarisk, we've wandered far, found our way into foreign regions where we soak up the water, push everything else out, dry up the springs. Removed from our homelands and love affair with our own lands, our cocoons may never open to release us, we may never see our own colored wings.

Some crave those landscapes that speak of survival—green with water, trees, shelter. But others seek places that seem to assure disaster, even death, to the uninitiated eye—the fierce high mountains, the God-forsaken desert—for these landscapes speak of an even deeper need, that need for freedom.

These harsh landscapes have been home to indigenous peoples who learned the secrets for survival here. The Paiute Indians, often spoken of as the poorest of the Colorado Plateau groups, still worked very little for their survival—two to three hours a day hunting and gathering. They spent the rest of their time singing, exploring, cooking, storytelling, laughing.

And part of their survival revolved around small family groups helping each other. But we're alone, all alone, we whites, we've abandoned our families, each other, to the vagaries of life. All alone. You shut off the part of your mind that tells you you're alone, it's too frightening. But when you accept that you're alone, you live your life differently, you live on the edge, you live life more true to yourself, not doing what others want so they won't leave you—alone. Our aloneness follows us like ravens wanting a handout, like camp robbers in the mountains, always hungry.

Now I sketch and photograph the ghost figures. They're powerful, simple, no arms or legs, squarish heads, with faded vermilion shrouds. To my left stands another figure, alone, an unsociable devilish apparition with horns.

His chalky eyes gape like the others, but this imposing specter also has a mouth. A bit disconcerting, this horned-figure reminds me of the Fremont devil I saw when I first met Johnny, high in the San Rafael Swell to the west. Did this one somehow get left behind?

Some archaeologists think these figures represent shamans, holy men. I remember once talking with Bill and another archaeologist friend, Denny Erickson, after a rock art seminar. Denny told us these figures were made by Vikings.

"I refer you to the horned helmets," he smiled authoritatively, then added, "This means that all that country out there belongs to me 'cause my Viking ancestors discovered it."

Bill replied with a snort, "You can have it, Denny, my friend. The more of that damn desert you own, the poorer you are."

Higher on the burnished rock cliff, in a deeper, fresher red is written: Smith Vincet, Aug. 14, 1881. I already knew from the bullet hole that I wasn't the first to visit here, and now I have proof. What was Smith doing in Dark Angel? Was he a cowboy, an explorer, a trapper, a Mormon settler—lost, left behind like the horned figure?

Sun pushes wide orange blades of light onto the cliffs across the narrow canyon, and now I see more shrouded figures across the creek on a golden-red wall.

Looking back at the figures above, I realize they're not looking at me at all, but at these other phantoms. Maybe it's a contest to see who blinks first, a contest thousands of years ongoing.

I again cross the perennial creek that drains the canyon, rabbitbrush and holly intertwined with sagebrush scratching along my jeans. I want to check out the other tribe across from the devil and his buddies.

This canyon is a good provider—waters must run high here to nourish such thick stands of vegetation. Some of the trunks on the sagebrush are over a foot thick.

On this side of the canyon, the walls are somewhat lower, maybe only 100 feet high. Huge concentric rings and massive squares mark where the sandstone has spalled off, tumbling onto the lower gray shales into huge piles of rubble.

The people who made these rock drawings balanced on that rubble, stretching to reach their canvas. Above me floats an entire wall of Barrier ghost figures, possibly as perfect as the day they were made. I count a total of 19—they range from two to eight feet tall.

Torsos covered with simple patterns, vertical white lines or stippling, these ghost people sport an assortment of antennae and earrings. Hollowed eyes stare from ancient faces.

An old Ute leader, one of the last pictograph makers of his people, told me that the color red is sacred to the Utes. His name was Hand-in-Sun. His signature was a red hand above a burning sun. He painted with the red dye used to mark sheep.

I lean against a long squarish block of sandstone, visually tracing the outline where it fell from the wall above. These late-Archaic people were hunters and gatherers, sheltering in alcoves near springs. Nomads, professional wanderers, wandering for a living. Was Davidson ever here, did he see these same figures?

My neck is getting stiff, and the blood flowing through my veins makes me self-conscious in front of all this still-life. I look back to where Buddy is nosing around in the brush across the creek.

Why did the Barrier people choose this canyon for their gallery? Does it eventually cut on through to the hunting grounds where the Bookcliffs level out, that land of ancient Ponderosa pine and pure springs?

Whatever the reason, they chose well. The purple and black patina is perfect, and cliff walls curve and flow like the graceful walls of a holy cathedral.

This rock art of the Barrier people is beautiful in a terrible way, and I know Gramp's lost treasure is here.

"Ruins," I say, simply, standing on the edge of the cliff, hanging onto a small cliffrose. I study all that this simple word captures, a brief synopsis of many lives long ago—Anasazi ruins.

Before me, on the ledge, not much is left but rubble—yellow-red rocks, stacked, not so neatly. No artisan made this, but rather the hand of swift necessity. It's a shelter created for protection while observing the canyon, perhaps. But look! Across the canyon's spur, tucked neatly, vertically into the horizontal crevasse of canyon wall, a small granary is hidden. All this to protect a granary. Protect it from what?

A hot wind blows and blows. Far down canyon, sheer vertical walls lean inward. Up here, I can almost see over the rim, far to the distance—the very tip of Coffeepot—small, like a miniature pyramid, from here but a hint of mountain, not even there unless you already know of its presence. It's like a ghost—you see it only when you believe in it, like the ghosts of this cliff dwelling.

The cliff dwelling—or perhaps fortification is a better word—barely clings to the sheer sandstone. Two very tiny windows peer out of a square cone of plastered rock, and the old roof has collapsed, leaving the wooden vigas splintered and sticking upward like the oars of a sinking boat.

Earlier, below this fortification, I found six perfect spear points partially buried beneath the rubble of cliff-erosion. Each was six inches long, made of deep tan flint with variegated fingers of cream, perfectly fluted, edges serrated with the care and skill of a craftsman with no concept of deadlines. Bits of leather still wrapped the shafts, perfectly preserved by the sere and dry desert air. I looked, photographed, then replaced the cache, let it be, let it dream in sleep.

Now the wind dies, the quiet becomes quieter, the still becomes ominous, and suddenly a brisk wind comes flinging itself through canyon and cedar, exulting in its freedom, cajoling dry red sand into sharing its dance, a dance brief and intense. Wind just as suddenly is gone, leaving behind the poignancy of autumn.

Up here, I can see down canyon for a long ways until walls finally turn. A blue heron rises in the distance, where stream is pooled by beaver dam. I turn back and scan the walls near me, and I see what appears to be a break in the cliff, tucked above a protruding ledge that would hide it from eyes on the canyon floor.

At first I guess it to be an alcove, then I realize that something's not right, it's not dark enough. A large slab of sandstone has fallen to the canyon floor, probably what formed the break in the first place, and a person might just barely be able to friction-climb up there, if they were very careful. Somehow I imagine I can see a small tower at the break.

I look back down from the edge of the fortification, down to safety, physical and perhaps spiritual, Buddy wagging his tail, watching me. I'm up high, it's a view I'm not used to, like a hawk's upper territory. I look again at the cliff structure guarding secrets in no danger of ever being stolen. Then I see it, barely scratched into the stone, nearly thirty years of wind and frost taking their toll: A.D. 1935.

So, my hunch was right, Albert Davidson did come back later, and he came here, into Dark Angel. I feel a thrill, knowing he was here at this very place where I'm standing, and I also feel a chill, knowing I may be close to his lost Ghost City. Or was the A.D. part of the date?

I make my way back down the cliff, vow to quit climbing, it's irresponsible. If I fell, I could only blame myself if I died, but what about Buddy? I give him a Roly Poly biscuit to sooth my conscience.

Far far away, the sacred Ute Mountain watches over all, as the canyon gods dance their own slow ponderous dance of millions of geologic years with steps no mortal can ever see.

After a short break and a short-lived resolution to quit climbing, I decide to see what the break in the cliff is about and start up the large slab of sandstone that leads to it. Standing on the balls of my feet, I search for a depression in the rock, then press my toes inward and drop my heels, feeling the tension in my calves. Looking up, I search the slab for tiny undulations or protrusions, my keys to progress. Instinct says to hug the rock, but instead I push my body out and away, getting better downward pressure, keeping my feet from skating off.

Buddy sits obediently below, watching, keeping guard over our camp. My pack is snugged to my back, carrying only my camera, notebook, canteen, and an apple. Oh yes, and my rope, I'd almost forgotten my rope.

With hands out in front and elbows dropped, my fingers search for dime edges to hang onto as the slab gets steeper and steeper. I can rappel back down, I think, making for an easy retreat, as long as there's something to anchor the rope to.

Finally, just when it gets so steep I think I'll have to go back down, a rather tenuous and unpleasant proposition, I reach the top, crawling onto a small ledge. Next to me are the remnants indeed of a tower.

I look down the opposite side from where I sit, through a break in the cliff, and amazingly, below me lies a large basin, perhaps a quarter-mile or more across, a perfect sandstone bowl with no other entry than the one I'm at, a geologic anomaly. A perfectly defensible place, one person could stand in the tower and protect the entire thing.

Built a thousand or more years ago, the small tower still stands with a strong presence, an unlikely setting at this break in canyon, but guarding what? The basin appears empty, there's nothing there, no rock structures. The tower is only a shadow of its former self, maybe five feet tall, rubble of stacked stones fallen around its base.

And now I can feel something pulling at me, like the pulling I feel of green places when desert seems overwhelming. I hear Coyote's voice.

We'll see how it goes when you're all alone out in some dark canyon with one of those spooky Barrier ghosts.

I look down into the basin, beneath me is nothing but some scrab-bly rock, yellow and veined with thoughts of geologic time. I turn and look back at Dark Angel Canyon, where it twists and meanders on its way, mindless of its own depths, mindless of the myriad human lifetimes it took to be carved. The sunlight catches its rims like a child at play, reflecting off billions of intricately edged drops of quartzite, all cemented together by time into sandstone, now being gradually torn apart by water and the frost cycle.

The ledge I'm on is perhaps thirty feet above the bottom of the bowl. I tie my rope to a large rock and begin to rappel down, down into the mysterious basin, wrapping the rope around my body and playing it out slowly. I can quickly and easily climb back up using a foot prus-sic, wrapping the rope around my foot a few times.

It's getting late, but it won't take long to take a look, climb out, and soon I'm quickly standing at the edge of the large basin, where light dims from tilted rim, and the air suddenly seems stuffy.

Then I know.

It's the City. Antonio's Ancient City. Davidson's Ghost City.

I stand speechless. The rope dangles next to me along the steep cliff, the slow crawl up the slick slab seems like an eternity ago, another world, another existence.

It's dusk, and I look down into a dream.

The City. Now I'm in the dream, a dream of vertigo, infinity, evanescent music, diffused lights. I see shadow movement, figures floating through the dream, a flicker of light from fire of black obsidian, fire of white marble, fire of red blood.

The City. Time floats through firelight, layers and layers like terraced faults in ragged badlands, one layer heavy, oppressive, another layer like clear air in sere desert.

Davidson's been here, but apparently he didn't stay long. Antonio's been here. I wonder what he learned here, in this sacred place, this place of his people. But he's a Ute Mountain Ute, these are the Ancient Ones, the Anasazi. His people came long after the Anasazi were but illusions in canyon dusk. No, these were not Antonio's people.

A great drumming begins. I see a shadow stand now, and it becomes tall, elongated, as it holds something above its head, something long and stick-like. These people are not Anasazi. Can they be Basketmakers? Wetherill thought the Basketmakers were here long before the Ancient Ones, but recent evidence shows they were just earlier Anasazi. But no, these Shadowpeople are older still.

The sky splits, a shooting star, a meteorite lights the universe for a brief moment. Is it burning in my time or theirs? The pale blue light shines briefly on the object held by the shadowman, I can make out a split-willow figurine. Yes, these people preceded even the Basketmakers, much, much older.

Time presses down, the City begins to fade, then returns, as the light from the meteorite is gone. The meteorite was burning in my time. When sun rises each day in my time, the City fades to its own eon, its own time long, long past. The City is but dust.

I stand on the edge of this mythical bowl, watching, as shadows come and go, catching glimpses of ancient faces, ancient rituals, ancient lovers. I see ancient children, now melted by time into tawny shales, salmon and amber petrified dunes, orange uranium oxide used to color china teacups in London. I see many things, I feel many things, but with dawn, everything fades, I remember but little.

I've slept. Sun burns hot, and the rope is the only reminder of my own origins. The bowl is now empty of shadows, filled with dust. Nothing but dust. A fine powdered dust, old dust. I hesitate, begin walking into the bowl. My feet leave deep impressions, the dust is so very fine.

I wonder what's become of Antonio's footprints. Blown by fine wind into another era? How long ago was he here? How did he know where to look? What led him here?

I can hear his voice above the drone of machine spinning through desert night.

Don't forget the City. It will take courage, but the petroglyphs there are for you.

The petroglyphs! I wander to the opposite edge of the bowl. It's immense, even larger when not in shadow and time. I walk slowly along the wall, ever turning inward, yet never closing. There are no petroglyphs here, my friend Antonio. I've come full circle, my dusty footprints now have toes on both ends.

The City. Was it a dream? If so, I shall become a professional dreamer. I shall make dreams for the world, dreams that can surpass the reality of waves singing in ancient seas, of lava molten in volcanic cones, and the infinity of rock and sand.

And still no petroglyphs. Sun is hot, water is gone, I must return. But I must find the petroglyphs. Perhaps they hold my future, perhaps my past.

Day dries on, I must find shade, solar vision blurs. A solitude of tree stands in the very center of the bowl, testament to independence and contrary nature. The center of the bowl is where the shadow held the split-willow figurine above its head. There was no tree then.

I make my way to the small tree. It's an arroyo willow, far from home. A small spring feeds its roots, filling its pale gray-brown bark. Tiny catkins of dried flowers cluster on yellow twigs, and dark green leaves grace slender branches with dignity. White Willow, Arroyo Willow. Are you a descendent of the stick-willow figurine? I pour cool water over my face, then drink. Cupping water in hand, I splash catkins in gratitude.

It's then that I see the rock. It stands along the rim of the bowl, at an oblique angle, visible only when one looks toward sky from bowl's center. I know that rock, have I dreamt of it? It's tall and slender and pale, like Arroyo Willow—White Willow Rock.

Dusk begins. I've been here all night, all day, how can that be? Time has folded. I think of Buddy, waiting. I fear being in the bowl after dark. I'm not superstitious, it was but a dream. But Antonio saw it too, it was no dream. The music is real, I hear it sometimes when I'm deep in remote and untouched canyons. I must go to White Willow Rock.

The bowl is steep here, but I find my way, and soon I stand below the pale rock. It's capped with White Rim Sandstone. It's tall, perhaps forty feet. There are no petroglyphs.

Dusk continues, I begin to hear faint strains of music. I cannot stay. Suddenly, the sun, evasive, horizontal, strikes the rock. Petroglyphs!

Three duck-headed figures stare out at me, a carbon copy of the three hoodoos I found in the canyons over by Willow Creek. Maybe there was more there than what met the eye.

Below the duck-headed figures is carved a neat row of strange bird-headed figures, dancing along, carrying sticks. At the end of the row, an immense ascending moon, then many scratches in stone, like cuneiform. I study, but I cannot read it, it's too ancient.

And now I know, before me, the Bird Panel. Carved into the base of the rock is "Davidson 4-21-35." I smile for Gramps, can taste Musketeers bars, extreme happiness.

A giant snake winds across the huge monolith, split tongue pointing around the corner, trailing, long, around the edge of the pillar. Davidson's sketch!

I step around to the back of the stone. My heart stops.

The entire face is covered with what looks like writing, interlaced with hundreds of figures and symbols, many of which I've seen before, deep in the canyons. I'm frozen for a long time, stunned at what stands before me, until I finally pull my camera from my pack, taking photo after photo until all my rolls of film are gone.

Night grows, the music is stronger. I don't have time to study the rock art, I have to get out. Quickly, I circle bowl's rim, looking for the rope. The Pleiades appear. Darkness comes from nowhere, bearing fear on its back. I trip on the rope, nearly falling. I must leave now, the City will engulf me if I stay another night.

I climb the rope, pause on the ledge by the tower, then rappel down the long slab, quickly, recklessly, until feet touch earth. It's dark, but I'm safe, safe in my own time, safe in my own delusion, my own reality.

I turn and look back up at the rim.

All is hidden.

Somehow I find my nearby camp, where Buddy has been waiting, hungry, desultory. I manage to feed him in the dark, not wanting to use a light, for the darkness feels sheltering.

Stars dance above, and I hear faint distant drumming.

Finally, I sleep, fitfully, restlessly. I dream of willow catkins, of an ascending moon, of petrified dunes. I dream of an ancient language, filled with ancient petroglyphs.

Then, with great peace and for the last time, I dream of rocks.

Yellowjacket, I've failed.

More of your silly nonsense, Little Arroyo?

No, Coyote, I found the City, but I cannot read the petroglyphs there.

Perhaps they weren't meant for you to read. Did you consider that the entire world may not be at your feet?

But Coyote, Antonio said the petroglyphs there were for me. It's important that I read them!

What did you see?

I saw a dark cloud, as if my eyes were very old and losing sight. I could not read them, Yellowjacket. I usually see meaning, but I saw only strange figures.

What kind of figures? Why were they strange?

I saw a neat row of figures, dancing along, carrying sticks.

Why were they strange? Who were they?

They were strange because each figure was like the one before, but a little different. The last was rather magnificent.

Perhaps it was only one figure, but it was changing. What else did you see?

I saw an immense ascending moon.

Coyote smile reveals bright shiny teeth.

Were the figures dancing in the moonlight?

Yes, it did look like that. But why?

Coyote hums, a simple tune, an old tune from childhood.

Yellowjacket, it can't be that. That's silly! Why would Antonio tell me to find that?

Life is simple, Little Arroyo. Life is made for joy and singing and dancing. Perhaps Antonio was telling you that happiness will be yours when you can dance in the moonlight, like Wild Coyote and his many cousins. Dance and sing, Little Arroyo!

Coyote gals won't you come out tonight, come out tonight, come out tonight,

Uranium gals won't you come out tonight, and dance by the light of the moon!

Morning comes late in Dark Angel Canyon, and I wake to Buddy nudging me, whining. I have a headache. Something tells me to dress quickly, Buddy seems eager to be going. Maybe he could hear the faint drumming last night.

Now Buddy is pacing, distressed.

"What's up, Bud?" I ask, becoming more concerned. I cram everything into the pack, realize I've forgotten the rope, go to the slab and pull it down. I feel dark, pensive, my elation at my discovery of yesterday replaced with foreboding.

Buddy whines, nips at my ankles with short bites. "What's up, Buddy? What's the matter?"

Wind turns. Instantly, I know.

Smoke! Coming up canyon. Fast!

We have to get out of the canyon! There's no way we can outrun a fire. I search the canyon walls for passage as the first wisps of gray find us. We can't go up the slab, the City is a death trap, but yes, over there! A long crack that appears to top out. Steep, vertical, maybe a go.

Carrying my rope and pack, I run to where crack meets canyon floor. Here, the canyon walls tilt back and the cliff's not nearly so high, but it's still a long way up, maybe 50 feet, but the crack appears to go all the way. It occurs to me to lie in the stream, but I know it's not deep enough to save us. Maybe the beaver pond down canyon will slow the fire a bit while we climb out.

Carefully, swiftly, I take the rope, rig a harness around Buddy, double check the knots, then tie the end of the rope to my waist. I hastily empty my pack of everything but notes, camera, and canteen, leaving sleeping bag and everything else in a heap. Quickly, hurry now, I snug the pack to my chest so I can chimney up, even though I know there's a danger it may get me in trouble later if the crack narrows. If so, I can always drop it.

Now, nearly in a panic, smoke thickening, I hoist myself into the chimney, my back against the wall, and place my left foot on the wall in front of me, knee high, other foot flat against the back wall. Placing my hands on opposite walls, palms against the rock, I push up with my legs and arms at the same time until I'm fully extended. Buddy springs up, tries to follow. I tell him to stay.

Chinle, what are you going to do when your luck runs out?

Quickly, I now place my back foot on the forward wall about knee high, and my forward foot on the back wall under my rear, while holding myself up with my hands. I move my hands up and push up again. Quick but sure, quick but sure, I can't fall, hurry, time's running out. Chimney, chimney, up, up, rope dangling from waist.

I'll die, just like everyone else does. But I'll die in the arms of my own true love, the desert.

The pack is awkward where it pushes against my chest. I'm having trouble breathing, smoke thickening. I've used this technique before to reach granaries and dwellings high in the cliffs. I pray the crack doesn't widen or narrow too much.

Buddy is staying, the rope isn't pulling. We'll both be in a world of hurt if he decides to run from the fire. And we'll both be in a world of hurt if my rope's too short. Now the chimney begins to tighten, just as I feared, it's tapering. Don't look down, it's too far.

Chinle, my friend, if you stay out here in the desert, you will die.

Both hands in front of me, I crazily push my way up. I know I have to be near the top. Just as the crack begins to narrow even more, there's a small ledge, the perfect foothold, and I stop for a second, pause, legs and arms screaming for oxygen.

Chinle, what are you going to do when your luck runs out?

In a surge of anger, fear, determination, I scramble upwards, thrusting with legs and arms at the same time, and suddenly I can see over the top!

I ain't dead yet, Coyote Yellowbelly!

I scramble up, quickly tie the rope to a nearby tree, use it as a belay and begin to quickly pull Buddy up. He's heavier than I thought he'd be, too many Roly Poly biscuits. With each tug upwards, I wrap the rope around a thick branch so he can't fall if I lose my grip. The rope was barely long enough, we got lucky, Buddy Blue and I.

Lucky again, Yellowjacket, land on my feet.

I can't believe how good Buddy is, he hangs limp, doesn't struggle as I pull him up through thickening smoke, and it occurs to me that maybe he's already dead from smoke inhalation.

But now he's on top, safe, alive, wagging that always wagging tail, and I slip down against the trunk of the juniper, hot, barely able to breathe, a million burning molecules singeing my lungs, heart full of black smoke, arms and legs aching. We're up. We're safe.

I untie Buddy, stand and gaze back down into the canyon. Smoke lifts, acrid tendrils dancing in the hot air rising from below. Now I'm suddenly sick, the kind of sick that comes from smoke inhalation, the kind of sick that comes from realizing that you nearly lost not only your own life, but the life of an innocent, your best friend.

You should stay outta that area, it's not that far from where the fire's at.

Johnny warned us, he knew, he understands the nature of fire, how it moves, how it thinks.

Coiling the rope, I stuff it down into my pack, try to brush some of the ashes off Buddy and assess what to do next. Smoke thickens, mesmerizing—I imagine images of smoky misty twisting coyotes floating through it, then suddenly realize we have to get away from the canyon completely, we'll suffocate, and it could climb up out.

It doesn't take long until we're a half-mile or so from the canyon rim, trudging through a dry sagebrush flat. Looking back, I see smoke boiling from the chasm, and I wonder if the rock art we camped by is safe from the fire. And what about the City, the Bird Panel? Who knows if it's even real, I'll know only after the film's developed. I hug the pack, still against my chest.

We stop for a drink. Collapsed in the meager shade of a tall sagebrush, I watch from the distance as the canyon burns, painful, intense. Charred ashes and smoke, nothing left, nothing. I pull Buddy tight to my chest, all is still, all that remains is the sound of hot ashes hissing as they fall nearby.

Suddenly, I weep for all that once was, for the depth of green, the smell of green after rain, the patches of green moss. Life transposed to death, nothingness. Worse than nothing, small traces of what once was, blackened and acrid.

Buddy licks his paws, surely aware of how close we both came to that final sleep. I can tell the fire has burned on up canyon from us, but it could still climb out, still find us.

But what about Willy? He waits on the rim down canyon, who knows how far, we've walked a long ways in the last several days. Willy has water, food, my priceless rock art notes, and what if the fire found him? We have to get back to Willy.

I try to get my bearings. Sun hot, lungs still burning from smoke, dizzy, I sit for a moment in the scant shade, share water from the canteen with Buddy. He's panting, I try to reassure him.

"It's OK, Bud, we'll make it out. I'm sorry I ever got you into this mess. This makes twice, huh? Looks like I'm never going to learn, huh, Bud? Irresponsible, for sure."

Buddy grins, whines. I pat his head. His whine gets louder, I laugh nervously, it gets even louder, takes on a surreal metallic sound. I startle, jump up. An airplane!

A yellow plane skims over the canyon, high enough over the smoke to avoid downdrafts. It's flying up canyon, but far enough away that they can't possibly see us. I wonder if they've spotted Willy. Could it be Johnny?

Plane flies on, disappears. Now the heat brings oppression, depression, and I know it must be over 100 degrees. We'll never make it. Maybe if I veer back over towards the canyon the plane will see us when it flies back, if it comes this way. Maybe we should just stay in the shade, sparse as it is. My mind rolls on, double clutching, input gears turning the same rate as output gears, a transmission with no reverse.

But look! The plane's back!

"Pray they see us, Buddy," I yell, waving. "Pray to that dog-damned entity that Randy always cusses at."

They see us! Plane waggles its wings, maybe it's Johnny! Plane swoops low, it must be Johnny.

I wave my arms like crazy. The plane continues back down canyon.

Emptiness crashes against itself like the wake of a boat hitting the shore.

"Now what? What's different? What can they do, they can't land in this thick sagebrush. Looks like we're still on our own."

I feel sicker, Buddy looks weary. It's all too much, the heat, smoke, headache, dizziness. I stumble and fall to the hot ground, try to get back up, can't, try again, think of how nice it would be to just rest.

I sleep, hot Cougar Sun blazing deep into my consciousness.

I dream, but not of rocks.

I dream of a Dark Angel come for me, but not in a swing low sweet chariot, but in a shadowy shroud on an Appaloosa horse, spotted black on white, pulling a willow travois.

In the travois rides Buddy Blue, sitting on his haunches, grinning, and now we're going back down into the canyon, me astride the horse behind the black-shrouded figure, protesting, unheard. Buddy Blue turns into a yellow coyote, jumps out, twists and spins and disappears.

Now everything in the canyon is clear, the air is clear, and it's spring, and I know I must see the canyon again, or painful memories will haunt me. I'm alone now, near the alcoves, walking faster than I've ever been able to walk, or maybe I'm flying. I cross the little creek without any feel of water, could I be dead? Suddenly I'm at the larger alcove, and there, growing in the ash, is a bank of pink sweet pea! And appropriately enough, blazing red fireweed. Purple aster and yellow balsamroot. Such color, contrasted against blackened earth! I kneel, awed by the powerful optimism of nature, of life.

And then, as I dream, I understand. Courage and strength come from such fearful charrings. Hounded by the emptiness of eternity, I found Charlie. He was soil, water, sunlight. I flourished, disregarded rumors of lightening.

And suddenly, unannounced, undeserved, wildfire. Bereft.

And although the color has not yet returned, it's not yet spring, not yet spring.

I wake to the smell of smoke, to ashes. It's nearly dark.

Yellowjacket, are you there?

Silence. Blackness bleeds into my heart. I'm alone again, yet again. Where's Coyote Yellowjacket?

Coyote, I need you.

Well, why didn't you say so in the first place? You've never needed me before, you know. You expect me to come running, just like that? I almost forgot about you. Did it ever occur to you to think about me once in a while? What are you doing out here, anyway, all abandoned?

Coyote, I know. I've abandoned myself. I've known it all along. I've known.

Ah, Little Rabbit, here we go again. No wonder you hurt. You can't just go and cut off a part of yourself like that.

I know, Coyote, I know. But it just seems so easy, it's just too easy.

You got all caught up in forgetting yourself, Little Yucca. Now you know better, don't you? You can't love anyone else till you love yourself. If you try, you're just getting more and more lost.

I know, Coyote. But his eyes, those blue eyes, they just pull you in.

What do they pull you into, Little Yucca?

Pull you into forgetting your own problems, your own pain.

Little Yucca, when will you realize that you can't go forward while you're looking backwards?

Coyote, I know. Be kind to me, I need you now.

You have to come to grips with your own fears. I don't understand it. You know you'll never really be alone, not as long as you have me, and you'll always have me, even though you don't seem to care how it makes me feel when you abandon me.

I'm sorry, I need you now, Coyote.

Little Yucca, what you need now is to celebrate your freedom. No more hard times. You have to forget the past, it's over, it can't be changed, the only connection you have to it now is your memory. You can't let it prevent you from becoming what you can become. What's important now is for you to live your life like God meant it to be, to rejoin your own creativity. God is creative, and you were created in God's image, so go and create and be happy.

Will I ever love another man, Coyote?

Of course, if you want to. God will provide the people you need in your life, just like I come back when you need me. It's been a hard time, Little Yucca. Did it ever occur to you that I might have missed you?

I'm sorry, Coyote. I'm terribly sorry.

It's OK, I needed some rest from all your whining and moaning.

I want to surround myself with beauty. Coyote, you know I need the wild places so much. What will I do if I can't be out here in the desert?

There will always be wild places, wherever you go, or you won't go there. Trust yourself, Little Yucca, trust me, trust God, but never forget that your dreams create your path.

I'm going to create new dreams, Coyote, I'm going to walk in Beauty.

Beauty is as beauty does, my friend. Time to rise and shine.

Buddy is whining, licking my face. I have a blinding headache.

I rise through a haze of heat and headache and the smell of crushed sagebrush.

Almost dark, we have to get back to Willy, we're nearly out of water. Slowly, I stand, still a bit dazed, reminded of how I felt that hot day on the fins, of the hot breath of dragons. Gathering myself, I find a landmark in the distance, a jag of cliff to navigate by, and I begin slowly winding my way through sagebrush, keeping the dark maw of canyon to my right as a smoky landmark.

Soon it's night, dark, and Buddy and I continue through shadowbrush. I stumble, falling. Twisted ankle, fall to the ground, into darkness. Too far to go. Tears cloud my eyes.

Yellowjacket, how can I do this thing that seems impossible?

You must do it one step at a time, Little Rabbit, just like you swim the river one stroke at a time, like you climb the cliffs one rock at a time.

Again I stand, stand in a land defined by four seasons, a land stained red by iron blood, a land free from rain shadow, a land created by many magics. Smoke twists around the Bird Panel, the writings are clear, even though desert varnish melts across them. They are very old. I look down, at my feet is a large stick, a thick piece of willow, a walking stick.

Someday, you'll look back to the place you started, Little Yucca, afraid and alone, thinking you could never make it.

The sky turns, the Big Dipper slowly spills out all its stars, and we continue into darkness, occasionally stirring night creatures that skitter away—rabbits, whipsnakes, desert centipedes, scorpions, bullsnakes, maybe even coyotes.

I stop occasionally, make sure Buddy is at my heels, check my direction against the North Star long and out from Dipper's handle, always conscious of the gaping canyon to my right, not wanting to unknowingly step into folds of emptiness.

And each time I stop, take stock of the sky, the emptiness, my bleeding knees, scratched arms, I hear it, all night it's there, I walk into it, through it, a noise like a distant airplane, a large airplane with droning engines—just over the distant horizon.

The desert hum.

Maybe it's old Willy calling to me.

Maybe it's the sound of the Enola Gay, the bomber that carried the first Atomic Bomb.

Maybe it's the sound of Trinity, the sound of Hiroshima, the sound of Nagasaki, all many miles away, over the horizon, sound waves echoing around the earth forever, a warning to all who can hear, will hear, choose to hear, to never forget.

All night we walk, slow, steady, all night, in a dream, a dream threaded with blackness. Now I see Charlie's face, sandy curly hair, blue eyes, captivating smile—it fades into distant, intriguing ruby red cliffs, then blackness.

Again I stumble, nearly fall, but now something's different, there's no sage, no rocks. It's the edge of the road! We've made it to the little dirt two-track I so recklessly steered Willy on days, years ago.

From the looks of the Big Dipper, now nearly downside-up, it must be near dawn. All we have to do now is turn right, stay on the road, and we'll find Willy.

Jupiter in the east so big, dazzling like a jewel, you can see its roundness, yellow, pale dawn behind it, and soon the bluffs far to the west take on dawn's first light, glowing in the palest muted salmons and pinks, with black shadows behind each jutting tooth of cliff.

Dawn. Willy has to be near.

There! Something shiny ahead!

Good old Willy—though lost and abandoned, always faithful, waiting. I hug his cool hood, covered with ashes, lean there a while, set out water and food for Buddy, drink deep myself. The note's gone, wind must've taken it away. I crawl into the front, wad the Chief's blanket into a pillow, Buddy next to me, exhausted, and at last sleep, peace flowing from the rocks.

Yellowjacket, I'm ready.

Ready for what, Little Arroyo?

Ready to be who I'm supposed to be.

What does that mean?

I'm ready to abandon all this study. I take the Sacred, the Mystical, the Wild, I try to quantify it. Endless speculations about a people who must have lived a dream. How can you quantify the past, the sacred?

Oh, you humans are all too good at trying, Little River.

Coyote, I want to live life, not study it. I don't want to just have dreams, I want to live my dreams. I want to live like these old ones, in freedom.

You're being irresponsible.

No, I'm accepting the ultimate responsibility, my friend, responsibility for my own happiness, destiny.

You'll get lost.

I'll stay on the River, Coyote, the Beautyway.

"Chin, wake up, you OK?"

My hair's wet from the trickle of warm water being poured over my head.

"Chin! Wake up!"

I hear Johnny talk to someone, something about heatstroke, smoke inhalation, what to do. I feel arms around me, shaking me.

"I'm OK," I answer as water drips in my eyes, runs down my neck.

Now I see someone else, looks like maybe Leland, and Johnny's pickup sits nearby. Things seem hazy, maybe smoke, maybe my mind, maybe both.

Johnny says, "We saw you yesterday, landed on the road, but you were miles over, we couldn't get to you through all the scrub. We tried to hotwire your jeep, take it out to get you, but no luck. We hiked out a couple of miles towards you, but it was almost dark, so we went back for my truck."

The tense lines in his forehead break as he smiles."Geez, how'd you walk that far in the dark? What the heck, Chin, scaring us like that! Man, do you smell like smoke, your face is all red and smudged. And what's up with your knees, all scuffed up? Holy Moroni."

"I'm OK. Next time, just push the button under the dash, there's no key.You were right about the fire."

Johnny looks at me, steady, green eyes gray.

Then I smile, hug him."Guess what, Johnny. I found it! I found the Bird Panel!"That unknown feeling still embraces me, that feeling of deep peace.

His eyes light up."Doggone, Chin, holy shit, you found it? No way!"

"Yeah, I found it."

"Yeah?" he answers, grinning."Down in the canyon? In Dark Angel?"

"Yeah, Dark Angel. Can you drive Willy back? I'm kind of tired, sick.Thanks for not saying I told you so about the fire."

"We ain't done yet," he grins."And I can't begin to tell you how happy I was when we saw you were OK."

"So tell me again what you saw down there, Chin,"Johnny asks over milkshakes at the Toot 'n Tellum Drive-In at Catalpa Town. Buddy Blue sits in the back of old Willy, slowly licking ice cream from a bowl, savoring every bite.

"Maybe you can see the pictures later,"I answer."I think it's something major, maybe even the Rosetta Stone of rock art. I know Davidson must've thought it was something, the way he wrote about it."

"I've heard of the Rosetta Stone, but what exactly is it?"Johnny asks.

"It was the key to deciphering ancient Egyptian hieroglyphics. It had the same message written in three languages: hieroglyphics, Greek, and the common language of Egypt at that time. If there were such a thing for petroglyphs, it would help decipher the lives of these ancient people."

"Why didn't Davidson record it himself?" Johnny asks.

"I dunno, my theory was that he knew it was significant, and he knew it would take the mystery out of the search, we'd end up knowing less in the long run, but none of that made sense. But now I have a new theory—he just didn't want to fool around there, in the Ghost City, as he called it. He was a scientist, he knew there were things there he could never explain. He wanted outta there, to hell with discovery and being famous, he already was. He was just plain scared, the place unnerved him, who knows what happened."

"Whoeee, you'll have to tell me more about the Ghost City, Chin. But what makes you think it's the Rosetta Stone of rock art?"

"Well, I'm not sure, but I know enough about linguistic analysis to know something was going on there. There were certain regularities of repetition, patterns, that led me to believe it was a translation, lots of symbols, a pattern of what looked like some sort of writing, maybe the first evidence that the Anasazi had a written language, and there was Barrier stuff, Fremont, even some Navajo, too. And part of the panel was in Ute, I know enough to know that, and I could tell that some of the panel was way older than the rest, maybe like an ongoing system for translating as time went on and new people came. But I had to get outta there quick, so the photos will have to tell us more. I'm sending them straight to Professor Van Zandt so nothing happens to them."

"What was the big hurry, the fire?"

"No, I dunno, it was a weird thing, Johnny, I can't even talk about it, maybe sometime late at night around a campfire, it's that kind of thing. That whole canyon's like that. I don't ever want to go back, for sure not alone."

"Yeah, that canyon has a reputation, has had for years."

"Maybe the fire purified it."

"Whatever that means, Chin. By the way, I thought you promised you'd stay away from the fire."

I frown, "Well, you promised you'd stay outta the sky."

He laughs, adds, "I could see where the fire was headed, right across the drainage, up Dark Angel. By the way, they figured out what started it, some prospector's camp trailer burned up and the fire spread, then the winds came and caused a blow-up. There's over 300 guys on it, but it's hung up at the river now, a natural firebreak. By the way, you missed the wedding."

"What wedding?"

"Coralee and Joe's. It was pretty nice. Joe's cousin, Duke Hughes and the Buckaroos, played themselves silly, got all drunked up. Coralee told me later she had a hangover from partying the night before. Not Joe, he was stone cold sober, never seen him so serious. They asked about you."

"Ohmygosh, I forgot."

"Yeah, we noticed. But Chin?"

"What?"

"Just when did you decide to start being responsible and tell people where you went?"

"Whattya mean?"

"That note. When we saw Willy, I landed on the road, your note told us which way to look. Otherwise, who knows where we might've been, that's a big canyon system."

I answer, "Pretty weird, huh? But really, Johnny, what difference did it make? Willy knew where I was all along. He always knows. He takes good care of me, always finds me." I pat the jeep's dashboard.

Johnny shakes his head. "Say, Chin, now that you're done, well, now what? Colorado?"

"I dunno, I guess I'm not quite done, I have one more thing I need to do."

"What's that?"

"Johnny, do you believe in faith?"

"Faith? I dunno, what's faith? What're we talking about here?"

"You know, Coralee and I, when we took our little vacation, our vacation in Heaven, we had some good talks. She says that faith is a law of the universe, like gravity, you can't see it but it's real. It's a connect-the-dots kind of thing, you go from one dot to another, but you never know what the final picture's gonna be until it's all over."

"And?"

"Well, if you have faith, faith in God's love, you will find the path of your heart. She says that a deep love for something is an indicator of what God created you for, and that's what you should be doing. Kind of like an indicator plant."

"OK, but where's this going, Chin?"

"Well, fear is a kind of faith, too, but it's negative faith, faith that something bad's going to happen. Johnny, I want you to have the good kind of faith, faith that I'll be back, no matter what, OK?"

Dark eyes, anger."What the hell, Chin? Now where're you going? Dammitall anyway. Don't forget, you promised you'd meet me in Unaweep."

"I haven't forgotten."

I turn to him, put my arms around him, hold him close. The amethyst burns warm against my chest.

Coyote, I had a vision, a vision while I was asleep in the sage, trying to die.

A vision! How wonderfully quaint! And what a nice time and place to have one!

Coyote, I lived in a house on an escarpment of rose cliffs. It was full of light, green plants, beautiful music, and such happiness! It was full of peace, Coyote!

It was a vision of your future, my friend.

Someone I loved was there, Coyote. But it was different. I wasn't bound to him, held to him. I was truly free, Coyote! And Coyote, there was something else...

Yes, I know, Little Pebble, it was shown to me also.

It was? Have you seen this vision also, Coyote?

Yes, Little Pebble, many times. It's my vision of peace also. You see, Little Pebble, I cannot have peace until you do.

Coyote, why is that?

Little Pebble, don't you understand yet? I'm a part of you, don't you know?

No, Coyote, you're all you. You can't be me too!

Yes, of course I'm me. But I'm also a part of you, my friend. You created me, you see. And as for the rest of the vision, that something else...

Coyote, the house was surrounded by intriguing canyons, pinion forests, mysterious rocks, and, most important, Coyote, freedom. Complete serendipitous freedom. But there, in that house of peace, I was there, Coyote, but someone else was there also.

Who was it, Little Pebble?

I don't know, Coyote. It was someone who truly loved me. The house was filled with peace and love. Who was it, Coyote?

I don't know, Little Pebble. You must find this answer yourself. Perhaps it was Antonio.

No, Coyote, not Antonio. You see, Antonio is like you, he's a part of me, I created him also.

I know, Little Pebble. I've had many long talks with Antonio. I know him well.

Who was this in the escarpment house, Coyote? He makes me think of spring mornings in the mountains, of alpenglow on white peaks and of distant stars. Who is he, Coyote? You must tell me!

Little Pebble, you must find him yourself. Just know that he's there, in your future, and it will come to pass. Be patient. Maybe it's Johnny. Maybe it's you, yourself. Maybe it's the Creator, maybe all of that. Or maybe it's a little coyote pup. But now I will tell you a great secret, a secret I've promised to tell you for a long time.

A secret?

Yes, I will tell you your name, who you truly are.

Coyote, I'm not ready.

You're ready, my friend. And I think you already know, for you helped mold this creature, you and the eternal forces of earth and sky. Your wisdom is a gift, as is reading the old writings.

From who? Who gave it? Who named me?

Your Creator, just as you named me, and just as you named Antonio, and just as you named all those imaginary horses you kept in your dresser drawer as a child.

Coyote, I'm not ready. Don't tell me. I'm not ready.

You're ready, Little Pebble. Who you are is known to the vermilion cliffs and the golden bullsnake and the Sego lily and the little cottontail. The grabens know you, as do the Indian ricegrass and the butterfly milkweed. The canyon mice and the grey-spotted rock-squirrel and the midget rattlesnake and the white-throated swifts know you well. They all love you. They all know you as Uranium Daughter.

Uranium Daughter? Coyote, that's not really a name. It doesn't make sense.

Of course it does. You see, uranium is a highly volatile substance. It's always changing its nature, always becoming something different. Its new form is called a daughter, and each daughter is very different from the parent, the original uranium molecule. The final form, the final daughter, is the strongest, the unchangeable, the most mysterious, yet the most complete.

You began your journey in Radium, at the Rock Garden. Your transformation has been long and very painful, but powerful. Most people never allow themselves to even acknowledge change, yet alone to embrace it, as you have. And you will continue to metamorphize, becoming stronger and continuing to understand yourself and the elusiveness of physical reality until you emerge as the final spiritual being you were meant to be, the final Uranium Daughter.

Stable. Powerful. Unique. Indominatable. Rare. Strong. Elusive. The daughter of joy and pain, sorrow and love, metamorphous and igneous, past and future, rock and star.

And you have now completed that painful ritual you began high on the dark cliffs, but now the ghost has finally been exorcized. This time the crows held their tongues. Do you understand?

Silent for a long time, I feel the amethyst burning, burning, holding my heart in place.

Finally, quietly, I speak.

Yellowjacket, now I understand.

Chin,

You still out there? This is my last letter. I'm heading out for Australia in two lousy weeks...let's talk. Sold the Tengo for a fortune, never coming back to this rathole. Let's talk. Am leaving you the house. Quit claim already filed at courthouse. Sorry about everything.

Chas.

Epilogue
by Adam Stocks

A month after Chinle disappeared, I received a call from Radium Search and Rescue, which had been involved in looking for her, as was Charlie Dundee in his plane until he left for Australia. They'd found Chinle's jeep high on an overlook above the Green River, on the rim of Ten Mile Canyon. Johnny Taylor was later given the vehicle for safe-keeping.

The jeep had Chinle's gear and maps and no signs of foul play. It had been parked under a group of large juniper trees, precluding air searchers from finding it. While there, one of the team members, Auggie Brookings, noticed a tiny splotch of color on the river bank, over a thousand feet directly below.

An investigative team was sent down river from Ruby Ranch by boat, where they discovered that the spot of color was the Chief's blanket that Charlie had given her.

The team, adept at tracking, eventually found Chinle's very precarious course down through a cleft in the cliffs to where she'd placed the Chief's blanket. The tracks then went into the river. Accompanying her tracks were those of Buddy Blue, her beloved little dog. It appeared she'd let him down through a number of rough spots in the cliffs by rope.

Auggie also found a place where a rope had anchored a boat, leaving scratch marks in the sand and scrape marks on a tree. The tracks had been preserved only because of a lack of wind and rain because of the drought.

Where Chinle went is open to speculation. Whose boat she used is also open to speculation, although some think she may have appropriated an old dory once anchored in that area by the Ekker family to cross the river to search for cattle. She had carefully spread the blanket out with large rocks to hold it in place, leaving a note pinned to it, a note she'd carefully wrapped inside the cellophane from a package of red licorice.

The rug, which is supposed to be quite valuable, is in the safekeeping of my daughter in Colorado, in the hopes that someday Chinle will reclaim it, even after these many years. Rumor says it belongs to the famous Hearst collection, but in my mind, it belongs to Chinle. I also still have Chinle's note, a treasured memory for me of her. It reads:

To whoever finds this blanket and note, please give them to Adam Stocks, Radium Ray, Radium, Utah.
Thank you,
Chinle Miller

Adam, I'm going to leave this blanket out on the sandy beach, high enough so the river won't wash it away, anchored with rocks so the wind won't claim it. It might be visible from the air or maybe some boater will find it. It has its own mystery, and now it's yours, providing someone finds it. Perhaps it will see you through some grand adventure, as it has me.

I can see a plane circling in the distance, and I know it's Charlie. How do I know? The amethyst burns against my chest, timeless, cold. Only you could understand the pain I'm talking about, that disquieting bond between you and me.

The boat waits, quietly lapping against the beach with each river wave. Buddy Blue is already in it, waiting, as are Antonio and Mr. Yellowjacket. You've never met them, but they're very close friends. Even while I hesitate, sun's image dances with the water, water flowing down river, flowing to the future. Far in the distance, sunwaves shimmer on towering rose cliffs, radiant.

Rose cliffs, down river. Our dreams show us the path to happiness, amigo. Never forget your heart, never forget to dance by the light of the moon. Never underestimate your own power to transform your life, to metamorphize like a uranium daughter.

My love to you. And, of course, give my love to Charlie, because I sure as hell can't. Tell him he'll always hold a special place in my heart, though. Don't tell Johnny nothing, I'll tell him myself.

Chinle

PS I quit-claimed Charlie's house to you. He gave it to me, and now it's yours. The paperwork's at the recorder's office there in Radium. Enjoy that big pool.

I close my eyes and can see Chinle carefully pinning the note to the blanket, then silently stepping into the boat, finally free. It never surprised me that she didn't return.

That night after they brought me the Chief's blanket and the note, I swear I could hear the desert hum.

Adam Stocks
Slick Rock, Colorado
October 2008

Afterword: That Lost Highway
by Dr. Jan M. Tubbs

The canyons of eastern Utah have long intrigued many, claiming the hearts and souls of adventurers from the time of the mysterious 17th-century explorer Denis Julien (who left nothing but a few inscriptions along the riverways), to modern canyoneers, rafters, hikers—all those who believe that not all who wander are lost.

But some who wander do indeed get lost, and the canyons, always impartial, have never coddled those who come unprepared. And of the many who have found themselves in Utah's canyons, a number have also lost themselves, albeit unintentionally.

In this immense landscape, some simply disappear, as did artist and writer Everett Ruess, who was last seen in the Escalante River wilderness in 1934. Others have followed, never heard of nor seen again.

But some disappear in the process of finding themselves, which is how they wish it to be.

At least, this is what we must conclude in the case of Chinle Miller, born Meg Miller in the little town of Radium, Utah. Chinle was a daughter of the desert, preferring the wildlands to civilization, jealous of her solitude, truly at home only in places that many would consider wild and uninhabitable. Her indomitable spirit craved a landscape that some found fearsome. It was the only place she found freedom.

This, of course, makes sense, given where she was born and raised and her relationship with her grandfather, which played a definitive part in the formation of her character. Chinle's father was killed when she was young, and her grandfather helped raise her and was her hero. Gramps, as she called him, apparently embodied the values that Chinle most emulated, and her friendship with him, the two of them wandering the desert, must have played a strong formative role in her childhood.

We can't help but deduce from her journals that what Chinle cherished in others—strength of character, sensitivity, and a love of the natural world—must have been embodied in her grandfather. These values were surely important to Chinle, and her love for learning about the world around her earned her that nickname, Chinle, a name her grandfather bestowed on her for her love of the Chinle geologic formation, a layer rich in fossils and variegated color.

Ironically, the Chinle Formation is also a layer often rich in uranium deposits. Though fascinated by the history through which she found her life moving, Chinle was also tortured by the knowledge of what her beloved "characters," the uranium miners of the Colorado Plateau, had helped create (the Atomic Bomb) and were helping sustain, that potential bane of civilization (although she cared little for such), and of the natural world (which she cared for immensely). The uranium miners were, in Chinle's view (a view that history has indeed substantiated), desecrating the land that she loved, and worse yet, providing the raw materials that could lead to the possible complete and utter destruction of the world.

It was the early 1960s, a time when the Cold War raged, a time when the Atomic Bomb was referred to with capital letters, a time that underscored the fact that human fear is the most destructive of all emotions, and a time of above-ground atomic tests in Nevada, where test bombs were described by how many times they surpassed those dropped on Hiroshima and Nagasaki.

The AEC, or Atomic Energy Commission, had gone to great lengths to ensure a domestic supply of uranium ore, setting up their headquarters in Grand Junction, Colorado in the 1950s. A uranium boom was the result of the AEC's incentives and lucrative payments for ore, as well as the organization's assistance to miners through such efforts as road building and sending teams of experts to explore and publish maps indicating the most likely spots for a strike. The AEC was an agency of such secrecy that even Congress did not (could not) oversee its activities. Many unsuspecting uranium miners and millworkers would eventually lose their lives to cancers attributable to exposure to workplace radioactivity. Many unsuspecting people downwind of atomic tests (called downwinders) would also die from cancer. Through it all, the AEC would deny culpability.

This U-boom was the closest thing to the Yukon and Klondike booms that the continental United States ever saw, but with one major difference: it was in the state of Utah, a state closely held by the Mormons, who would tolerate few shenanigans. Thus, the U-boom saw little of the dissolution that characterized other rushes—very little gambling, brothels, violence, or alcoholic binges. More than any other boom, it was characterized by pure adventure.

Chinle's life in this setting focused on her love of the plateaus and canyons, on her love of her chosen profession of archaeology, and on fulfilling a grant to study rock art. The year of 1961 revolved for her around the search for the elusive Bird Panel, first mentioned by famous southwest archaeologist Albert Davidson. Her life also revolved around her almost obsessive love of one of the true rascals of her era, the famous and infamous Charlie Dundee, known also as the "Uranium King," who was single-handedly responsible for a great deal of the destruction of the environment near her hometown of Radium through his discovery of one of the greatest-producing uranium mines of all times, the Tengo Dinero.

Dundee had funded Chinle's college studies, and she intended to complete her PhD thesis by finding the Bird Panel and thereby ensuring her place as a top-notch archaeologist. But her primary motive in finding the panel was to honor her grandfather's memory and to also satisfy her endless curiosity. She never wavered in believing that it would provide some clue to the people who created it and the many similar Barrier-style rock art panels scattered throughout the canyons of the region, a people who preceded the Anasazi and Fremont and who are still lost in a mystery many thousands of years old. Her research, now come to light after many years, may soon lift that veil, as well as many others.

The story above is in Chinle's own words and is best told by the one who lived it. Although parts of the story are missing, it's not difficult to piece together the path and times that Chinle walked and lived and wrote about.

A note about her journals is in order. Chinle explored the Colorado Plateau, searching for rock art, an assignment she obtained for herself through a research fellowship to complete her PhD dissertation at the prestigious Plateau University of Grand Junction, Colorado (which has now been absorbed by Mesa College). She very diligently mailed her scientific sketches, photographs, maps, and notes to her university advisor, Professor Van Zandt, for safekeeping. Her little Willy's jeep (which she affectionately personified as "old Willy") had very limited storage, and she always worried about the potential of having these invaluable records of her explorations compromised or lost.

The boxes in which Chinle mailed her research, long in the safekeeping of Professor Van Zandt, have postmarks that track her movement through places in southeastern Utah like Green River, Catalpa Town, Torrey, and Radium. When asked where she lived, Chinle always replied with names like Stock Tank, Radio Tower, and Spring, mythical places that reflected both her nomadic life and a desolation represented by maps that lacked towns and cities and instead held that emptiness of landscape she loved. This emptiness was marked on the maps by simple landmarks like the presence of a spring or stock tank.

In 2007, Professor Van Zandt passed away in Grand Junction, Colorado, and his family, knowing of my own research and publications in the field of Colorado Plateau rock art, approached me with the dilemma of what to do with the numerous boxes containing the records of Chinle's research. She had never completed her dissertation and nothing was known of her whereabouts or even if she was still living. I agreed to take a look at the contents of the boxes.

I was completely overwhelmed with the extensive documentation involved. I immediately solicited the assistance of two archaeologists who are rock art experts, both affiliated with prominent universities.

They were likewise amazed. Chinle had documented numerous panels that have been until even now completely unknown, mysteries locked in the far reaches of canyons unexplored even as late as the beginning of this millennium. Happily, that portion of Chinle's research project is now in safe hands and will be the subject of a forthcoming book tentatively titled "Colorado Plateau Rock Art: Linguistic Evidence May Solve the Mystery." It appears that Chinle was indeed the first to document the Bird Panel other than Davidson's brief mention, which answers many questions and will earn her an honorary PhD before it's all over. It's very possible it will answer for all time not only who the early Archaic, or Barrier, people were, but will without a doubt prove what happened to the mysterious Anasazi and whether or not they had a written language.

Some may criticize Professor Van Zandt for delaying what are sure to become significant findings, but it appears that the professor never gave up on his young student, always hoping and believing she would return, saving her materials for her to do with as she would see fit, hoping she would garner the glory she deserved. We are indebted to him for his patience and careful storage of these treasures.

But back to Chinle the person, the adventurer of the U-boom era, the desert rat. In a separate box, also in Van Zandt's possession, were Chinle's personal journals, accompanied by personal letters from various friends and also from a wealthy cousin who worried endlessly about her, materials Chinle apparently wanted to keep and were eventually thus mailed to Van Zandt by Chinle's friend, Adam Stocks, after her jeep was discovered.

The box that contained her writings is itself of interest, as it's made of wood and has "Hercules Powder" printed on the sides. It appears to be an authentic dynamite powder box, symbolic of the era she wandered in and a most apropos place for her journals to be stored.

Going through these journals was a task that I took upon myself because I felt they provided an invaluable look into another time, as well as into a unique person. Also in the box was a collection of poems penned by Chinle, as well as mysterious conversations with "Coyote Yellowjacket." I have not changed the names of people in her journals, hoping someday someone may provide a clue as to Chinle's whereabouts.

Chinle disappeared in September of 1961. She never contacted Van Zandt again, nor anyone else that we know of. Chinle's only known family was her mother, who lived in Colorado (and who is now deceased), and her cousin Sarah, now deceased and whose daughter now lives in France, and who, as Chinle's closest living relative, has generously granted permission to use the materials that make up this book. Who Chinle went down the river with is a mystery, if anyone, as well as where she went from there.

When Chinle first disappeared, her cousin Sarah posted a large reward for any information leading to her whereabouts, a reward that has yet to be claimed. After posting the reward, and before Chinle's jeep was found, Sarah wrote the following personal letter to Adam Stocks (quoted with permission), a close friend of Chinle's and publisher of the Radium newspaper, the Radium Ray:

Boulder, Colorado
November 8, 1961, 8 a.m.

Dear Mr. Stocks;

Thank you for your kind letter about my dear cousin. As you are aware, Chinle's research dictated that she spend long periods alone in the desert, searching for and cataloging indigenous rock art. This meant that her family (which is myself, as her mother has since passed away) rarely knew where she was, which, quite frankly, drove me to nightly sips of Irish Cream liquor. I can't tell you how distressing it was for me to imagine her all alone camped under some scraggly tree out in the midst of wild animals and vermin such as rattlesnakes and scorpions. And I will profess that the thought of her befriending indigenous people way out there was a bit unsettling. I did all I could to entice her to come home and lead a sensible life. I even offered her a job and free housing.

If, as you said, Chinle is somewhat like Everett Ruess, the young artist who wrote of his experiences before he disappeared, we are still hoping she will reappear, unlike Mr. Ruess. As you have mentioned, Chinle has many friends and few faults, other than her ill-advised (in my opinion) love for solitary and remote places in the desert.

You tell me that a few purported sightings of Chinle's old jeep have been made, all in the desert regions that she frequented. Her little dog, Buddy Blue, her constant companion, is missing with her, I presume. I have hired a private detective, and all attempts he has made to follow up on these sightings have been totally futile (he's continuously getting stuck out there), and he assures me he has coordinated with you, but now I hear you've never met him. And from what you say it appears that there exist a number of 1947 olive green Willy's jeeps in southeastern Utah. Of course, until you informed me of this, I wasn't even aware that Chinle's jeep differs from the others in that hand-painted on the tailgate are the words 'DESRAT.'

My most generous friend, Mr. Stocks, please be aware that I am posting a very substantial reward of $10,000 for any information that leads to finding my dear cousin, and I hope you will be the one to collect, as it appears you have done the most so far. Please keep me apprised of any changes in this situation. I may be in Europe (I've planned an extensive and quite necessary trip touring art galleries), but my housekeeper can always inform you of my whereabouts.

In deep gratitude for your help,

Sarah Miller Cameron, cousin of Chinle Miller (who appears to be lost like Everett Ruess, but minus the donkeys).

Chinle's jeep, old Willy, was found on the rim of Ten Mile Canyon, 1000 feet above the Green River. The little jeep was recovered by Adam Stocks (the now retired former publisher of the Radium Ray newspaper), and the jeep was then given to Johnny Taylor (of nearby Catalpa Town) for safekeeping. Johnny figures heavily in Chinle's journals and surely knows of her whereabouts, if he could only be located (assuming he still lives). I have as yet been unable to locate him. The Taylor family ranch near Catalpa Town was sold some time ago, after the death of Johnny's parents.

Joe, Coralee, and the others mentioned in this book have either all left the area or passed away, though Joe's mine, the Yip Yip, became one of the largest producers in history. All efforts I have made to trace Chinle's whereabouts have been totally unsuccessful. Before Chinle left, she quit-claimed to Adam the house Charlie left her, and Adam eventually sold it, using some of the funds to help pay for his daughter's college education.

Somehow, I know that Chinle is still out there in the wildlands she loves, accompanied by a little dog that could very well be one of Buddy Blue's great-grand pups. Perhaps she and Johnny Taylor married and live in a house set atop the ruby-red cliffs Chinle dreamt of, and old Willy sleeps in the driveway, dreaming of past adventures.

My hope for this latter scenario is great and comes from an old photograph that was sent to me as word got out that I was working on this project. That photo graces the cover of this book, and the handwriting on it is undoubtedly Chinle's, the same graceful flourish that penned her journals, albeit with the patina of time on her penmanship. The lettering on the photo reads, "Me, Bud, and old Willy the day before my wedding."

The wedding she refers to on the photo's inscription speaks to the probability that she and Johnny got married. The letter was postmarked in the small town of Ouray, a town famous for its beautiful ruby-red cliffs of Cutler Formation and also near Ridgway, Colorado, where her mother lived. I visited the town but was unsuccessful in finding anything of relevance. I sincerely hope Chinle is well and happy and approves of this endeavor.

Jan Tubbs, PhD
Grand Junction, Colorado
November, 2008

The following are included to give the reader a sample of Chinle's numerous archaeological journal entries:

May 17, 1961
Nice day but dark clouds coming in from the west. Too warm for late May, maybe mid-90s. Rough two-track along face of the Reef, hope I don't get stuck out here, long walk to GR. Finally got to Moonshine Tanks, very deep potholes (10′), was water source for moonshiners, they mixed boiled coffee with bootleg for color, Joe says, sold for $4/gal. Parked at mouth of canyon, huge alluvial fan you have to climb, wash goes through tight narrows. Found purple bottle fragment (pre-1917), tin cans, old lard bucket. Alluvial fan gives good lookout, bootleggers could see along whole face of Reef. Lithic scatter all over fan, jasper, pigeon-blood agate, white quartzite flakes, non-diagnostic except small delicate corner-notched projectile (Fremont) on ledge above biggest tank, pale-green agate, sketched, saw agate like this in Lisbon V. Rugged little canyon, tough going. Manganese in rocks makes pictures. Didn't go far, tired, maybe pressure change, headachy. Sick of PB sandwiches. Filled radiator and water jugs from tanks, wigglers. Tons of red jasper, gorgeous. My life goes from happy to sad and back in seconds. Clouds ominous, drove (bounced) to Little Spotted Wolf. Old firepit, rubber boot, wild country, saw maybe a bobcat slipping between rocks. Will sleep next to Willy, big moon. Bud is a happy dog.

May 27, 1961
Stormy, big clouds floating, full moon, silver arc behind clouds, lightning to west, late for such. Prob. 90 today, bit windy. Can old silly dinosaurs count peas? Cambrian Ordovician Silurian Devonian Carboniferous Permian. Geology fun, sedimentology boring. Candlestick yucca in bloom, creamy white. Claretcup cactus, deep reds, blooms fading. Must learn scientific names. Sand better after rain, consolidates, easier driving/walking, 6 miles today up down Spotted Wolf C., nothing but three wild burros, Opal's buddies? Big huge bullsnake, pinker than most, maybe adapted because of pink rocks here, can hide better. Cryptanth. Camped where cyn opens up. Reef weird in moonlight, huge escarpment with teeth, huge wave, deep geologic time, lonely, futile. Awareness

a curse. Big fire, hot tea and shortbread Sarah sent. Feel better. Should write her. Seems too far away. Buddy Blue had big cactus in foot, got out with tweezers, he's OK.

July 4, 1961
Explored up at White Rocks, very hot day, could see smoke from Big Rattle Fire. In the canyon, the walls very red from the sunset and smoke. Beautiful salmon pink sunset and reflection on water under boxelder trees. Water very low. Military jets flying too damn low. Found big Fremont blade in the wash where shadow on wall from other wall forms a big cat head. Shadows move fast - the bigger the canyons, the faster the shadows move on the wall. Was dark when I got back to my camp at the wetlands. Went to Callie's picnic, J. and I watched fireworks, very pretty, road by Cedar Lane. Bud loves J., maybe me, too.

"Remember only this one thing," said Badger. "The stories people tell have a way of taking care of them."

—Kenneth Grahame, The Wind in the Willows